ALIBI

ALIBI

JOSEPH KANON

LITTLE, BROWN

LITTLE, BROWN

First published in the United States of America in 2005
by Henry Holt and Company

First published in Great Britain in August 2005 by Little, Brown

A CIP catalogue record for this book
is available from the British Library.

HARDBACK ISBN 0 316 73059 9
C FORMAT ISBN 0 316 73060 2

Typeset in Simoncini Garamond by M Rules
Printed and bound in Great Britain by Clays Ltd, St Ives plc

Little, Brown
An imprint of
Time Warner Book Group UK
Brettenham House
Lancaster Place
London WC2E 7EN

www.twbg.co.uk

For
David and Lizbeth Straus

CHAPTER ONE

AFTER THE WAR, my mother took a house in Venice. She'd gone first to Paris, hoping to pick up the threads of her old life, but Paris had become grim, grumbling about shortages, even her friends worn and evasive. The city was still at war, this time with itself, and everything she'd come back for – the big flat on the Rue du Bac, the cafés, the market on the Raspail, memories all burnished after five years to a rich glow – now seemed pinched and sour, dingy under a permanent cover of grey cloud.

After two weeks she fled south. Venice at least would look the same, and it reminded her of my father, the early years when they idled away afternoons on the Lido and danced at night. In the photographs they were always tanned, sitting on beach chairs in front of striped changing huts, clowning with friends, everyone in kaftans or bulky one-piece woollen bathing suits. Cole Porter had been there, writing patter songs, and since my mother knew Linda, there were a lot of evenings drinking around the piano, that summer when they'd just married. When her train from Paris finally crossed over the lagoon, the sun was so bright on the water that for a few dazzling minutes it actually seemed to be that first summer. Bertie, another figure in the Lido pictures, met her at the station in a motorboat, and as they swung down the Grand Canal, the sun so bright, the palazzos as glorious as ever, the whole improbable city just the same after all these years, she thought she might be happy again.

A week later, with Bertie negotiating in Italian, she leased three floors of a house on the far side of Dorsoduro that once belonged to the Ventimiglia family and was still called Ca' Venti. The current owner, whom she would later refer to, with no evidence, as the marchesa, took clothes, some silver-framed family photographs, and my mother's cheque and moved to the former servants' quarters on the top floor. The rest of the house was sparsely furnished, as if the marchesa had been selling it off piece by piece, but the piano nobile, all damask and chandeliers, had survived intact, and Bertie made a loan of some modern furniture from his palazzo on the Grand Canal to fill a sitting room at the back. The great feature was the light, pouring in from windows that looked out past the Zattere to the Giudecca. There were maids, who came with the house without seeming to live there, a boat moored on the canal, and a dining room with a painted ceiling that Bertie said was scuola di Tiepolo but not Tiepolo himself. The expatriate community had begun to come back, opening shuttered houses and planning parties. Coffee and sugar were hard to get, but wine was cheap and the daily catch still glistened and flopped on the market tables of the pescaria. La Fenice was open. Mimi Mortimer had arrived from New York and was promising to give a ball. Above all, the city was still beautiful, every turn of a corner a painting, the water a soft pastel in the early evening, before the lamps came on. Then the music started at Florian's and the boats rocked gently at the edge of the piazzetta, and it all seemed timeless, lovely, as if the war had never happened.

I learned all this many weeks later in a telephone call she had somehow managed to put through by 'going to the top'. At this time the trunk lines into Germany were reserved to the military, so I imagined that a general, some friend of a friend, had been charmed or browbeaten into lifting a few restrictions. The call, in any case, caused a lot of raised eyebrows in the old I. G. Farben Building outside Frankfurt where I pushed files into one tray or another for USFET while I waited for my separation papers. I had been in Germany since the beginning of the year, first with G-2, then attached to one of the de-Nazification teams separating the wicked from the merely acquiescent. Frankfurt was still a mess, the streets barely passable, filled with DPs and hollow-eyed children with edema bruises. The phone call, with its scratches and delays, seemed to come from another world, so far from the rubble and desperation just outside my window that its news seemed irrelevant. The marchesa was quiet; you hardly knew she was there ('darling, not even a *flush*'). My room had a wonderful view. Her pictures hadn't arrived from New York yet, but Bertie, a treasure and fluent, was looking into it. It was a call that began in what my father used to call her medias res – a plunge into the middle of whatever she was thinking, followed by exasperation when you didn't know what she was talking about. Finally I understood that she had moved to Venice intending to stay, which meant that my home would be there too. The point of the call, in fact, was to say she was expecting me for Christmas.

'I'm still in the army.'

'Well, they give passes, don't they? I mean, it's not as if the war's still on. And I'm sure you could use the break. I've seen the newsreels – it looks just awful there.'

'Yes.' Camps full of corpses, wheeled out in farm carts to mass graves. Feral kids eating out of PX rubbish bins. Women passing bricks hand over hand, digging out. Not what anyone had expected, pushing over the Rhine. GIs rich with a pack of Luckies. What happens after.

'Well, then,' she said. 'Won't it be wonderful? To have Christmas together? It's been years.'

'In a Fascist country,' I said, half teasing.

'It's not the same thing at all. They weren't *Nazis*. Anyway, all that's over. It's lovely here, just like before. I can't wait for you to see the house. Maybe it'll snow. They say it's enchanting in the snow.'

Characteristically, she hung up without giving me her address, so it was to Bertie that I later wrote to say that I'd be spending Christmas in the hospital. After surviving actual combat and the tough early days of the occupation, what got me, embarrassingly, was a rusty nail, a careless step in the debris of a Frankfurt street that caused a puncture wound and required tetanus treatment and a holiday spent with amputees and boys with nervous tics. By the time I finally got to Venice it was February, I was out of the army and the city was huddled against a damp, misty cold.

The piano nobile, as grand and formal as described, was freezing, kept dark but not draftless by long, heavy drapes. The sitting room, warmed by space heaters from Bertie, was comfortable, but the high-ceilinged Tiepolo dining room made meals so chilly and unpleasant that my mother had taken to eating in the kitchen or off a tray, sitting next to the bars of her electric fire. Above us, the marchesa had become so silent that a maid was sent up to check, as if she might be one of those birds that grow still on a winter branch, then suddenly fall over. What would have changed everything was sun, cutting across the Adriatic to seep into all the tile roofs and parquet floors as it often did even in February, but the sky that winter was German: cloudy and grey. In the evenings, near our house, there was no light at all. A fog would come in from the sea, filling the Giudecca channel. Streetlights were spaced far apart to save power, and the calles became dark medieval paths again, designed for people with torches.

I noticed none of this – or rather, it was all so like the grey I was used to that I accepted it as natural, the way things were. The gloomy afternoons were no different from the weather in my head, full of listless shadows, an urge to draw in. Does anyone really come back from the war? The lucky ones just keep going, on to the next fight, unaware that they're breathing different air. The rest of us have to be brought up in stages, like deep-sea divers, to prevent the bends. The boys in the hospital had come back too fast – their faces twitched, their eyes darted at every sound, prey. I slept. The fog that came in at night from the lagoon would fill my head too, a lulling numbness, asking to be wrapped in blankets, left alone. Sometimes there were dreams – really ways of going back, reminders of the nightmare time that was supposed to be over – but mostly the sleep was just fog, opaque and shapeless.

'Just like Swann, *couché de bonne heure,*' my mother would say, but idly, not really worried, for by this time Dr Maglione had come back into her life, so she was spending evenings out, unaware that when she left me with a book I was already halfway up the stairs in my mind, curling up with the fog.

The result was that I was waking early, before first light. It wasn't insomnia – I slept deeply, snug under a warm duvet – but some automatic awareness that the light was about to change, the way plants are said to lift their heads towards the dawn. My bedroom window faced across the channel to the Redentore and I would look out into the darkness, waiting for its lines to start forming, as if Palladio himself were sketching them in again, until finally everything had definition, still murky but real. Then I would put on my heavy wool army coat and leave the house without making a sound, quieter even than the shy marchesa, and begin my walk.

Venice is often said to be a dream, but at that hour, when there is no one out, no sounds but your own steps, it is really so, no longer metaphor – whatever separates the actual paving stones from the alleys in your mind dissolves. The morning mist and the gothic shapes from childhood stories have something to do with this, the rocking slap of boats on the water, tugging at their mooring poles, but mostly it's the emptiness. The campos and largos are deserted, the buoy marker lights in the lagoon undisturbed by wakes, the noisy day, when the visitors fan out into the calles from the Piazzale Roma, still just a single echo. Things appear at that hour the way they do in sleep, gliding unconnected from one to the next, bolted garden door to shadowy church steps to shuttered shop window, no more substantial than fragments of mist.

The walk was always the same. First down along the Zattere, past the lonely vaporetto stations. Just before the Stazione Marittima I would turn into the calle leading to San Sebastiano, Veronese's church, and a bar for stazione workers that was always open by the time I got there, the windows already moist with steam hissing from the coffee machines. The other customers, in blue workers' overalls bulked with sweaters underneath, would nod from their spots at the bar, taking in the army coat, then ignore me, turning back to their coffee and cigarettes, voices kept low, as if someone were still sleeping upstairs. Even at that hour a few were tossing back brandies. The coffee had been cut with something – chicory? acorns? – but was still strong enough to jolt me awake, and standing there with a first cigarette, suddenly alert to everything – the steamed windows, the whiff of scalded milk, isolated words of dialect – it seemed to me that I'd never been asleep at all.

Outside there were a few more people – a boy in a waiter's uniform heading towards one of the hotels, an old woman in a fur coat coaxing a dog to pee, a priest with his hands in his sleeves, staying warm, all the insomniacs and early risers I'd never seen before I became one of them. I supposed that if I headed over to the Rialto I could see the fish stalls being set up and the boats unloading, the early-morning working world, but I preferred the empty dream city. From San Sebastiano it was a straight path, only slightly angled by bridges, to Campo San Barnaba. No produce market yet, just a man hurrying toward the traghetto station, perhaps still not home from the night before. Then right towards the Accademia, following the natural course of the streets the way water runs in canals, looping finally around the museum, then through the back alleys towards Salute, not a soul in sight again, past the great swirling church and out along the fondamenta to the tip. Here, huddled in my coat with my back against the old customs house, I sat for hours looking across the water to the postcard everyone knew – Ruskin's waves of marble, the gilt of San Marco catching the first morning sun, the columned landing stage filling with boat traffic, all the beautiful buildings rising out of the water, out of consciousness, the city's last dream.

I thought at first that my mother would tire of it, the way she tired of everything finally, except the past, but Dr Maglione was an unexpected wrinkle, a piece of future. After my father died there had been a period of melodramatic grief, followed, I assumed, by a series of friendships. But these had happened, if they had happened, offstage. I was away at school, then in the army, then overseas, so what I knew came from letters, and these had been full

6

of other things – volunteer work, openings, her three-week job (unpaid) at the Art of This Century gallery and the inevitable fight with Peggy Guggenheim that followed. Then she had come back to Europe, not really looking for anyone, and suddenly there he was. Not slick or too young or in any way unpleasant – not unlike my father, in fact, grey hair thinning at the temples, quiet, almost reticent. And yet amused by her, the way my father had been, both of them perhaps drawn to a quicksilver quality neither possessed himself. In any case, he was here, making her look brighter, in love with Venice, not even aware the rooms were cold. So I put off going back to New York, unsettled, not sure where any of us was heading.

'He's not a fortune hunter, you know,' Bertie said. 'Besides, if you're after money, why not young money? Much nicer. And you know I adore Grace, but she can be a handful. Anyway, he had doges in his family.'

'That doesn't mean anything.'

'It does if you have them. And he's a real doctor, you know, it's not an honorific. My doctor, in fact, and I'm still here.'

'I thought it was drink.'

He picked up his glass. 'Well, that too. The point is, he's not a gigolo.'

'So you introduced them.'

'No, no. They've known each other for years. Since the old days. When we were all – well, younger than we are now. The parties, my God. I suppose that's part of it. It reminds them. Anyway, you ought to be grateful. You don't want her sitting home alone, do you? Imagine what that would be like. It's the first thing that occurred to me. There she was, all excited on the phone and packing bags, and I thought, what on earth am I going to do with her? In the winter, no less. People think they're going to like it here in the winter – they come for Carnival and wouldn't this be nice? – but they never do. The third night at Harry's, you can see it on their faces. Bored stiff.'

'You're not.'

'It's my home. I know what to expect. The point is, Grace needed a friend and now she has one. She's happy and she's out of your hair. You've got your life to get on with – not to worry about her. What are you planning to do, by the way?'

'I'm not sure yet.'

'Oh, the young. All the time in the world.'

'Right now I'm enjoying Venice, that's all.'

'Are you? Grace says you sleep all day.'

'No, I walk all day. It's the only way to see the city. Then I get tired and sleep at night.'

'Mm, a sort of farmer's life. Up and down with the birds. Are you that bored?' he said, his voice still light, just a hint of concern underneath.

'Not really. I like it. It's like being on leave.'

'From what?'

I shrugged. 'The army. Everything. Just for a while.'

'Don't stay too long, then. You don't want to get addicted.'

I looked at him, caught by the word, as if he knew somehow about the mornings sitting against the Dogana, drifting, the beauty of the place a kind of opiate.

'No. But I want to make sure she's all right. Doges or no.'

'Adam, they have *dinner*. A drink. Chat. Nobody's posted the *banns*. You know what I think? I can say this because I've known you all your life. Before your life. I remember when Grace was pregnant with you.' He lifted his glass, pointing a finger. 'You've got a little too much time on your hands. You're making trouble where there's no trouble to be made – for yourself, really. My advice – I know, who ever listens? – is be happy for your mother and mind your own business. Of course, maybe that's it.'

'What's it?'

'Not enough business of your own.'

I glanced at his thin, almost elfin face, eyes bright and interested behind the half-moon glasses.

'I don't want to be introduced. To anybody. Fix up someone else.'

'I don't fix people up,' he said, almost sniffing at the phrase but enjoying himself. 'What's that, army slang?'

8

'Yes, you do. Those cozy lunch parties and you sitting there watching, like a turtle.'

'A turtle. Listen to him.' He reached to a box on the coffee table for a cigarette, thinking.

'I mean it, Bertie. I can make my own friends.'

'People never do, though, you know. Have you noticed?'

'You seem to do all right.'

He lit the cigarette, looking over the flame with an arched eyebrow. 'Well, I hire them. Oh, don't be vulgar, I don't mean like that.'

But I grinned anyway, thinking of the long line of research assistants, young men known to be in the house but rarely seen, like upstairs maids.

'One would think you were still twelve years old. Ten.'

'Almost,' I said, still grinning. 'Anyway, too young for your black book.'

'Oh, there's bound to be someone. People have sisters, don't they?'

And cousins, as it happened. Or, rather, the cousin's friend, a connection so tenuous that by the time it had been explained we were already introduced.

'He always does that,' I said, as Bertie walked away to join another group. 'He says it gives people something to talk about. It's Claudia, yes?'

She nodded, watching Bertie. It was one of his afternoon drinks parties, too late for tea but early enough to catch the sunset on the Grand Canal outside. Bertie's palazzo was near the Mocenigo on the Sant Angelo side, just before the canal makes its last bend toward the Accademia bridge, and in winter the late-afternoon light on the water was muted, almost a pale pink. What sun was left seemed to have moved inside to the burning fireplaces, making small circles of heat on either side of the room. The crowd was Bertie's usual mix – pale-faced curators from the Accademia, where he was 'attached' without being officially on staff, a few attractive men whom I took to be former research assistants, overdressed expatriates with drinks, and Venetians rich or idle enough not to be at work at five in the afternoon. I had seen her earlier,

9

standing alone by the window, looking out of place and stranded, like someone who'd been promised a drink and then been forgotten. She was fingering her collar button, an unconscious distress signal, then caught my eye and stopped, dropping her hand but not looking away. I started over to rescue her, but Bertie suddenly appeared, moving her back into the crowd, still awkward but at least talking to people. By the time he made his way to me, any shyness was gone, her stare frank and curious.

'What do you usually talk about?' she said, her voice almost flat, as if the effort of speaking English had lowered it, brought it down an octave.

'Anything. Where you learned English, for instance.'

'In London. Before the war. My father wanted me to know English. But of course it's difficult, these past few years. To speak it.'

'It's fine,' I said, looking at her more carefully now. She was the first person I'd met here who had referred to the war at all. She was thin, with dark curly hair and a long neck held erect, a dancer's posture. She had come in office clothes, a grey suit with padded shoulders over a white blouse. Given the cocktail dresses around the room, she should have receded, drab against all that plumage, but instead the suit, with its pointed lapels, gave her a kind of intensity. She held herself with an alert directness, full of purpose, so that everything about her, not just the suit, seemed sharply tailored.

'No, it gets rusty. Rusty, yes?' she said, waiting for me to nod. 'I need practice. That's why I asked to meet you.'

'Really? I thought Bertie—'

'Yes, I asked him. You're surprised?'

'Flattered. I guess. Why me? Practically everyone here speaks English.'

She smiled a little. 'Maybe now it's not so flattering.' She glanced towards the room. 'The others look—'

I turned to follow her glance – maids passing trays, everyone talking loudly through wisps of smoke, laughing as the light faded behind them through the window.

'Frivolous,' I said.

10

She looked surprised, then bit her lip, smiling. 'Yes, but I was going to say old. And you were standing by the fire.'

'So I got elected. What if I'm frivolous too?'

'Signor Howard said you were in the war. So it's different. You were in Germany? In the fighting?'

'At first. Then a kind of cop. Hunting Nazis, for war crimes.'

She stared now, taking this in, interested. 'Then you know. How it was. Not like them,' she said, waving her hand a little to take in the room.

'Maybe they're the lucky ones. Like Venice.'

'Like Venice?'

'You get off the train here, it's hard to believe anything ever happened.'

'Well, from Germany. But even here, you know, wartime – it's not so easy.'

'No, I'm sorry,' I said quickly, imagining the lines, the shortages. 'I just meant, no bombs. You were here?'

'Most of the time.'

'A true Venetian.'

'Not for Venice. My family was from Rome. It was my grandfather who came here.'

'Your grandfather? In America, that would make you a founding family.'

'Founding?'

'Old.'

'Ah. No, but in Rome we were an old family. Since the empire.'

'Which empire?'

She hesitated, not sure what I meant. 'Rome.'

'What, with chariots?'

She smiled. 'Yes.'

'Claudia. A Roman name,' I said, watching her sip from her glass, easier now, even the sharp lapels on the suit somehow softer. 'How do you know Bertie?'

'I don't. He invited everyone from the Accademia. I work there. His friend has a cousin who knew—'

'I heard. I couldn't keep it straight then either. I haven't been yet – the Accademia. Maybe you'll give me a tour. Now that we've broken the ice.'

'There, that's one,' she said quickly, ignoring my question. 'You can help me with that. What does it mean, break the ice? I know, to be friendly, but how does it mean that? Like breaking through ice on a lake? I don't understand it.'

'I never thought about it,' I said. 'I suppose just a general stiffness, when people don't know each other, breaking through that.'

'But not melting the ice – you know, the friendship making things warmer. It's breaking.' She looked down at her drink, genuinely puzzled.

'All right, melted then. But now that it's melted, would you show me around the Accademia?'

'You should have a guide for that. I'm not really an expert on the paintings.'

'I'm not interested in the paintings.'

'Oh,' she said, unexpectedly flustered. She looked away. 'Are you in Venice long?' A party question.

'My mother's living here – for now, anyway. She's one of the frivolous people over there.'

'I didn't mean—'

'No, she is frivolous. It's part of her charm. It's what everybody likes about her.'

'Including you?'

'Sure.'

'A son who loves his mother. Very Italian.'

'You see how respectable. So, how about it? Some lunch hour? I'll help you with your English.'

She looked directly at me. 'Why?'

I stood there for a second, not knowing how to answer. 'Why?' I said finally. 'I don't know. I'm in Venice. I should get to know some Venetians.'

'They're Venetian,' she said, moving her hand towards the others.

'None of them asked to meet me.'

She smiled. 'Don't make too much of that. It was for politeness. And now you want to go out with me?' she said, trying 'go out'. 'You don't know anything about me.'

'I know your people go way back. So that's all right. And you're the first person I've enjoyed talking to since I got here.'

'But it's you who are talking.'

I grinned. 'Okay. You talk.'

'No, I have to go.'

'And leave me with them?' We turned. 'Look, now it's priests.' Bertie was greeting a priest in a flowing scarlet cassock, who extended his hand in a royal gesture, barely moving his head, standing in front of some unseen throne. 'Who's that? Do you know?'

'No.'

'I thought everybody here knew everybody. He must be a monsignor or a cardinal. Something. I wish I knew the difference. You're from Rome – can you tell by the colours?'

'I don't know. I'm a Jew,' she said quietly.

'Oh,' I said, turning back to her.

'Is that a problem?'

'Why should it be a problem?'

'Jews are not so popular. Not in America either, I think.'

'So you don't know,' I said, ignoring it, 'if he's a monsignor.'

'No. Don't you? You're not a Christian?'

'I'm not anything. Not a Catholic, anyway.'

'But not a Jew either.'

'Part. My grandfather.'

'Miller?'

'Muller. Changed. My father was a *mischling*.'

'One grandfather.'

'It was enough in Germany.'

She looked at me, then held out her hand. 'Thank you for the English. I have to go. It's already dark. Do you see Signor Howard?' She glanced around the room.

'He's getting the Church a drink. Come on, no one will miss us.'

'You're leaving?'

'I'm taking you home.'

'No, it's far.'

'Nothing's far in Venice.'

She laughed. 'How well do you know it?'

My mother intercepted us at the door, glass in hand.

'Darling, you're not going. Gianni will be here any . . . He'll be sorry to miss you.'

'Not too much.'

'Of course he will. Don't be silly. The army certainly hasn't done very much for your manners.'

'You say hi for me,' I said, pecking her on the cheek. 'I have to run. This is Miss – I'm sorry, I don't know your last name.'

'Grassini. Claudia Grassini,' she said, nodding to my mother.

'How nice,' my mother said, shaking her hand. 'Finding someone *new* at one of Bertie's parties. You probably think we're the waxworks.'

'We have to run,' I said.

'Perhaps you'd like to join—' my mother started, looking carefully at Claudia, assessing.

'Another time,' Claudia said.

'Of course,' my mother said, a pas de deux. 'Did you say goodbye to Bertie?' she said to me.

'He's in confession.'

She giggled. 'Oh, Bertie and his priests. You have to admit, though, he's the best-dressed person in the room. How did they manage, do you think? During the war. I mean, did they have coupons?'

But by this time we were out the door, walking down the stairs to the hall.

'What was that all about?' I said to Claudia. 'That look between you?'

'She's a mother. She wants to see if I'm all right. You know, like in the market. You feel the fruit.'

I laughed. 'How did you come out?'

'She's not sure. She's a widow?'

'For years.'

'What did he do, your father?'

'Have fun, mostly. Then he got sick.'

'Fun?'

'It was a different world. People did that then – have fun.'

'These people,' she said, lifting her head towards the stairs, then turning to the maid who was holding her coat. 'You don't have to do this. It's a long way. I can meet you at the Accademia if you'd really like that.'

'No, I want to see where a real Venetian lives.'

'A poor one, you mean.'

'Are you?'

'Yes, of course. Who lives like this now?' she said, looking up the staircase to the piano nobile. 'Only foreigners.'

We were alone at the vaporetto station, huddling in the corner against the cold. The fog had come in, blocking out the opposite side of the canal, so dense you felt you could snatch it in handfuls.

'So what do you do here?' she said, hunching her shoulders, hands stuffed in her pockets.

'Walk. See the city. What does anyone do in Venice? Meet people.'

'At Signor Howard's?'

'You disapprove?'

'No, no. It's not for me—' She stopped, then turned away, stamping her feet for warmth. 'Signor Howard helped me, at the Accademia.'

'Bertie likes doing that. Helping people. But you still don't like his friends.'

She looked up at me with a half-smile. 'Do you?'

'Not any more. I'm not sure why. I mean, I've known some of them for years. It's just that everything seems different now.'

'For you. Not for them.'

'No, not for them. It's the same party.'

'I used to see them in the windows, from the canal – all the parties.'

'And now you're inside.'

15

'You think so? Ha, *brava*. The international set. But now it's like you – it's all different. I don't care.'

'I'm glad you went to this one, anyway.'

'Well, for Signor Howard. It was hard to get work when I came back from Fossoli.'

'Where?'

'A camp. Near Modena. Where they put the Jews.'

'There were camps here?'

'You think it was only in Germany? Yes, here. Beautiful Italy. Not so beautiful then.'

'When was this?'

'Forty-four. The first round-ups were in forty-three. At the end. But I went later. It was a holding camp. From there, they shipped people on.'

'To Poland?'

She nodded. 'So you know that. No one here does. No one here talks about it.'

'You?' I said, involuntarily looking down at her sleeve, as if I could see through to the tattooed numbers.

'No, I stayed at Fossoli.'

'So you were lucky,' I said, thinking of the piled-up carts.

'Yes, lucky,' she said, turning to a bright light coming towards us on the water. 'At last. It's so cold.'

The boat, finally visible through the mist, slammed against the dock.

Inside, we found seats towards the back, the windows steamy with condensation, so that it seemed the fog had moved in with us. There were a few other passengers, tired people going home with string bags, teenagers smoking. In the harsh light of the cabin everything seemed public again, the easy intimacy outside some-how part of the dark. The boat moved slowly, following the cone of its headlight, the motors groaning at the reduced speed, too loud for quiet conversation. But in the sudden warmth we were no longer hunched over. When Claudia sat back and crossed her legs, one came out of the coat, an unexpected flash of white, exposed.

'Do you live with your family?' I asked, looking away from her leg.

'No, they're dead. My mother years ago. My father just last year.'

'Oh,' I said, and then there was nothing to say, nothing worth saying over the engine anyway, drawing attention. Instead we sat quietly, suddenly awkward, rocking with the boat, the swaying movement pushing our bodies together so they barely met, then pulled back, like waves. It was a kind of dancing, a permission to touch in public, aware of each other, the warm skin under the coats.

The other passengers sat nodding to their own rhythm, looking up surprised when station lights suddenly appeared, then gathering their packages, unsteady on their feet until the ropes were tied. After San Marco the boat began to empty, until no one else was in the cabin but an old couple who appeared to be asleep. Outside, everything was still suspended in the fog, the lamps on the Riva just pinpricks of light.

'Where do we get off?' I asked, leaning to her ear to say it, so that now there was the smell of her, wool and skin and the faint trace of some perfume she must have put on for Bertie's.

'Soon. I told you it was far.'

'The Lido?' I said, an excuse to stay close to her face.

She smiled, turning to me. 'Not that far. Two more stops,' she said. Then she was silenced by a foghorn off to our right on some invisible ship.

We got off at the public gardens, leaving the old couple to keep drifting out into the lagoon. After a dark stretch bordering the park, the calles took on the usual twists through small deserted campos lit by hooded single bulbs at each corner. This was the tag end of Venice, neglected and out of the way, soundless except for Claudia's heels on the pavement and a few radios chattering behind shuttered windows. The fog was thinner than it had been on the water, so that even with only a few lights we could see the façades of the buildings, plaster peeling from some of them in large patches. Occasionally, overhead, laundry still

17

hung to dry in the damp air, as if someone had simply forgotten to bring it in.

'You see it's not the Danieli,' she said as we walked along a misty canal. 'But still, a water view. That's San Isepo. I'm just there.' She pointed to one of the peeling houses. 'Can you find your way back?'

'Is this where you lived before?'

'No. In Cannaregio. The ghetto. It's a Venetian word, you know that? We all lived there, so it was easy to find us. And after, when I came back from Fossoli, I thought, no, anywhere but there. So I found this – the other end of the city. It's far, but I like it here. At least I can't hear it any more, in my head.'

'Hear what?' I said, looking at her closely. We had stopped by the bridge just before her building.

'Nothing. A figure of speech. When I see the streets there, the ghetto, it reminds me. Of the sirens. Here it's different, it *looks* different, so the memories aren't like that.'

'What sirens?'

'For the air raids.'

'I thought Venice wasn't bombed.'

'No, drills.' She looked away, then back at me. 'You want to know? What it was like? They used the air-raid sirens so nobody would hear. When they rounded us up. So late, all the screaming and the pounding on the doors, anybody would hear it. At the Casa di Riposo – how do you say, old people's home – all the patients, so much noise. So they used the sirens to cover up the noise. So no one would hear.'

'I'm sorry,' I said quietly, embarrassed to have said anything.

'They took all the patients. Even the ones too sick to move.' She turned away. 'Well. Enough of that. Do you have a cigarette?'

I lit it for her, studying her face in the glow of the match. She leaned back against the wall of the bridge.

'So now you know all about me. Where I live, where I work. Now even my memories. I don't go to Harry's. I live here. Not Signor Howard's Venice. Not yours, either.'

'No. Did they take you that night?'

'Later. In the autumn.'

'And then what happened?'

'At Fossoli? You want to know that too? Everything?' She hesitated, then looked directly at me. 'Yes, all right. Look how easy I say that. I told no one. Now some stranger at a rich party, and—' She stopped again. 'Why was I lucky? One of the men who ran the camp raped me. Of course he didn't call it rape. Only I thought that. Every time. So. Is there anything else you want to know?'

I said nothing. She drew on the cigarette, watching me, as if she were expecting me to turn away.

'No?'

'Yes. Why you wanted to meet me.'

She smiled a little. 'That too? All right. I don't know. Maybe I liked the look of you.'

I smiled back, surprised. 'No one's ever said that to me before. Are you always so—' I paused, not finding the word.

'You prefer the old Venice? The masks? The notes? I used to want that. How wonderful to look over your fan at La Fenice. So romantic. But now it's what you say – everything's different. I came back and it's all different. So now I'm like this.'

'My mother came back because she thinks it's all the same.'

She dropped the cigarette and ground it out with her shoe. 'Goodnight,' she said. Then she looked up at me, studying my face. 'Are we going to be lovers, do you think?'

I met her stare. 'Yes.'

'You think so.'

'Don't you?' I reached up my hand, but she stopped it with hers, letting our fingers touch.

'I don't know yet. Maybe. But not the first meeting. I can't do that.'

I leaned closer and lowered my face to hers. A tentative kiss, on the lips, a hint of saltwater; then another, longer this time, our mouths slightly open; then more, taking our time until we were moving over each other, open and excited, and she broke away with a small gasp.

'Can I come in?'

'No, it's too soon. Go home, think who I am. Then, if you still want to, we'll – see each other.'

'Over fans at La Fenice.'

She smiled. 'That's right. Over fans. Do you know how to get back?'

'Walk towards the water.'

I waited while she put the key in the door.

'When will you know?' I said.

She made a teasing face. 'When I know you better.' She made a shooing motion with her hand. 'Just follow the canal – you'll see the gardens.'

On the boat back, I stood at the deck rail. As we moved in and out of the fog, towards the lights, then away again, Venice seemed more than ever dreamlike, something not really there. But once there had been sirens and dogs. Think who I am. Not just another folder on my desk in Frankfurt. More disturbing than that, here, tasting a little of salt. At home, staring out the dark window, for the first time in weeks I didn't sleep.

It took hours for the room to fill up with light, reflecting off the water, then moving along the walls in ripples. I opened the window, listening to the canal sloshing against the house. Too late for sleepwalking but too early for open shops, or anything else. I dressed and headed for the Accademia, but it would be hours before the tall doors opened. I could walk out to the Dogana, my usual morning seat, but all that now seemed to have happened weeks ago, somewhere else. How could anyone just sit, looking? I started up the broad wooden steps of the bridge. Over to Santo Stefano. A coffee and a newspaper. But that was idling. Who could sit? The point was to keep going, now that I had somewhere to go.

The sun held all the way through San Marco and along the Riva, bouncing off the white marble and back against the water. I walked faster. Even the air, after weeks of mist and damp, was sharp and dry, as if it too had cleared its head and decided what to do. And then, like a sudden shift of mood, it was over. The sky began to fill with clouds again, blown back in from the west, and by the time I reached the funfair at the far end of the Riva the shuttered caravans and children's rides were as drab and dismal as they'd been all winter. The brick towers of the Arsenale, glowing like kilns a few minutes before, had turned gloomy.

I crossed the last bridge before the vaporetto stop suddenly feeling foolish, still hours early, the idea of coming here at all like something out of a song lyric, silly in the grey light. The sensible thing would be to catch the next boat back and go to the Accademia at lunch hour. Instead I waited, smoking on a bench near the floating dock, not willing to waste a morning. What time did the staff get to the Accademia? A few people were opening umbrellas. I felt a light drizzle on my face and took shelter inside the vaporetto station. So much for the expansive gesture, sunshine and open arms. Now I was hunched over with a damp collar.

It didn't matter. She came on to the quay and it was just as I imagined it would be – the same direct walk, a glance up from under the umbrella, a sudden stop, and her surprised face, unguarded, absolutely still until something turned over inside, loosening an involuntary smile. She was wearing the same wool coat and sharp-lapeled suit – her only one? – and for a second I saw how she would take it off, just the jacket, nothing else, sliding it back from her arms while she stared straight at me, taking it off for me. Now she hurried into the shelter, folding her umbrella, eyes still wide, disbelieving.

'Have you been here all night?' she said, laughing a little.

I shook my head. 'I get up early.'

'But what are you doing here?'

'I want you to get to know me better.'

Her face softened. 'At this hour?'

'I thought we'd better start. I don't know how much you want to know.'

She said nothing, her eyes still reading my face, pleased.

'I like risotto. Any kind of fish.'

She laughed. 'Do you think I'm going to cook for you?'

21

'Okay. We'll go out.'

'A rich American.'

'I live in Dorsoduro. My room has a view of the Redentore.'

'I'm not going to your room. In your mother's house.'

'Then I'll find something else.'

'I'm not going anywhere, except to work.'

'That's why I'm here. We can talk on the way.'

'To come here like this, at this hour. You must be crazy.'

'Must be. What time do you get off for lunch?'

'You're so sure of this?'

'Yes.'

She looked away. 'Here comes the boat.'

I reached up and moved her chin with my hand. 'I'll tell you anything you want to know.'

Only a few people got on with us, but the boat was already packed with commuters coming from the Lido, reading newspapers or just staring out the windows. We stood away from the rain but wedged near the gangplank gate, pressed against each other.

'Just like the bus,' I said, but of course it wasn't, dipping with the shallow waves, even a morning commute turned into an excursion. The water gave everything in Venice this playful quality. Ambulances were boats, so not quite ambulances. Fire boats and delivery barges and taxis – all the same, yet different, bobbing on the water, somehow looking half made-up. 'We should have a gondola, like the old days.'

'No, they frighten me. So unsteady. I can't swim.'

'In Venice?'

'Nobody swims in Venice. Where, in the canals?' She made a face. 'It's not so unusual. Even gondoliers.' A city people, rooted to pavement. 'Anyway, I never learned. So I don't go in boats. Only these,' she said, waving her hand towards the crowd.

'I'll take you out. I'm good with boats – that's something else to know. You'd be safe.'

'Oh, you have a gondola?'

'Actually, I do. One came with the house. But no gondolier, so it's up on supports. There's a boat, though. We could take that. With life jackets. Go and have a picnic.'

'In this weather.'

'Well, when it's nicer.'

'And you'll be here when it's nicer.' She turned to me. 'You don't have to do this.'

'What?'

'Act like this. Take me on boats. Take me anywhere. Picnics. Like the films. So romantic. It's not like that any more.'

'No?'

'Not for me.'

'What do you want me to talk about, then?'

'What you're thinking. Not this – what?'

'Flirting?'

'Play-acting. It's not serious.'

'No. It's supposed to be part of the fun.'

She looked away, then stepped back to let some passengers get near the rail. We were pulling into Salute. She moved farther away, not wanting to talk with anyone close by, pretending to look at the church. Even in the drizzle, the baroque curves were bright white, like swirls of meringue. When the boat swung out again, she turned to find me looking at her.

'Now what? More picnics?'

'No.'

'Then what?'

'What I'm really thinking?'

She nodded.

'What it would be like. You, taking your clothes off. What you would be like.'

For a moment she said nothing, her look embarrassed, no longer direct.

'I'm sorry. You said no more play-acting. It's what I was think-ing – what it would be like.'

She nodded slightly. 'All right,' she said, and turned to the rail.

Which meant what? Anything. But her back was to me, like a

finger to the lips, and I said nothing. We rode that way, both facing the palazzos. After we tied up at Accademia, I took her arm and we crossed the gangplank. In the open square in front of the old convent, we stood bareheaded, surrounded by umbrellas.

'What time do you get off for lunch?'

'One. Go and look at the pictures.'

'All morning.'

She smiled. 'Some people take days. And now it's the best time – no one's there. You can stand in front of *The House of Levi* as long as you want.'

'A Jewish picture?'

'No, the Last Supper. But Veronese put in a drunk and dwarfs and the pope said it was – what? profane? – so he changed the title.'

'Italian accommodation.'

'Hypocrisy. Well, we had good teachers.' She looked up at me, serious. 'It won't be like that with us, will it? No pretending. Just what it is.'

I nodded. 'So you've decided.'

'When I saw you this morning.'

I leaned forwards. 'Don't go to work.'

'No, one o'clock,' she said, then reached up and put her hand on my chest. 'Get a room.'

I felt a twitch, like a spurt of blood.

'My house is—'

'No. Somewhere no one knows us. Not here. Near the station. One of those places. You can afford that,' she said with a small smile. 'You're a rich American.'

I bent over to kiss her, but she stopped me, pushing against my chest, her eyes playful. 'Later,' she said. 'You can think what it will be like.'

We became lovers that afternoon in one of those hotels off the Lista di Spagna that put up students with backpacks and salesmen from Padua. The vaporetto ride had seemed endless, dripping umbrellas and anxious looks, not talking, the few blocks on foot

24

worse, umbrellas forcing everyone to walk single-file in the narrow calles. In the room, past the sour desk clerk, we were suddenly shy, like the students who usually stayed there, and then she slipped off her jacket with the sliding movement I'd imagined, and hung it in the armoire and turned to me, and I understood that I was to unbutton her blouse. I began fingering it, feeling the warmth underneath, until finally she put her hand over mine, guiding it to each button so that we did it together.

It had been so long since I'd had sex, at least with anyone I'd wanted, that it felt curiously like a first time – tentative and then urgent, wanting to get it right but too hurried to find a rhythm. We hung up all her clothes, an efficiency that became a tease, then a kind of ritual, and when we were naked I started running my hand over her slowly, wanting to touch every part of her, but when I reached down she was already wet and after that we fell on the bed, both in a rush. Without the suit she was round, her skin soft, but her movements were still direct, the way I knew they'd be, never coy, reaching out to pull me into her. Just what it is. Skin on skin, without nuance, first-time sex, so hungry, tongues and sweat and a hurrying you can't stop, over too soon. We lay for a minute, finally not moving, still together, panting. Then she reached up and pushed my hair from my forehead.

'I don't have to go back,' she said.

'No?' I said, feeling myself hard again.

'We have lots of time.'

'I'm sorry I—'

'No, no. Me too. Now we can start.'

And this time it was slower, almost lazy, so that I felt her around me, not plunging in and out, everything slick, but taking the time to feel the moist, hidden skin, the secret part of her.

Afterwards we lay in a tangle, exhausted but not wanting to stop, touching each other.

'What did you tell them, at the Accademia?'

'That I was sick. Everyone is sick in Venice in the winter. My God, listen to that. No wonder.'

The rain had grown stronger, a real downpour now, noisy against the window.

'But it makes it nice in here,' I said, the cheap hotel room suddenly a refuge.

'Yes. And freezing,' she said, pulling a sheet up around her.

'No, let me look at you. I'll keep you warm.'

She moved closer, talking into my shoulder.

'It's the first time since I came back. You forget how peaceful, after.'

The perfect happiness of sex, drowsy and full, something you think happens only to you.

'I feel honoured,' I said, teasing. 'Why me?'

'I told you, I liked your looks.'

'That's right. My looks.'

She raised herself on one elbow. 'And you. Do you like mine?'

I shook my head. 'Your mind.'

She looked at me, puzzled, until I smiled. 'It's an American joke. Don't worry. I like everything. Here. And here.'

She wriggled away from my hand but stayed close. 'Did you have a girl in Germany?'

'No.'

'Why not?'

'I felt sorry for them. You can't, when you feel sorry for somebody.'

'Sorry for Germans?'

'They were hungry. Living in cellars. So they'd do anything – even make you think they liked you. How would you feel?'

'Don't ask me that. I can't feel sorry for Germans.'

'Anyway, I didn't go with anybody,' I said, moving away from it. 'Maybe I was waiting.' I brushed a lock of her hair behind her ear.

'Ha. More romantics.' She was running her fingers across my chest, an idle examination. 'No marks. Were you wounded?'

'No. I pushed paper. Not so dangerous.'

'So you never killed anybody? No Germans?'

'No. Did you?'

'Who would I kill?'

'I don't know. The man at the camp maybe.'

She stopped running her fingers and sat up, turning towards the window.

'He kept me alive. I was grateful to him. Imagine, being grateful to someone like that. Imagine what the others were.'

'What happened to him?'

'He was killed. After the Germans left. Maybe by partisans. It was like that, those first weeks.' She turned to me. 'You don't mind about him?'

'No. Why should I mind?'

'Some men—' She paused. 'I saw his body. Dead. I felt nothing. After all that, nothing. Maybe you get used to it, all the killing. That's the problem. You think you want to kill them all. Where do you stop? The guard who pushed the children on the train? Yes, him. Then why not the ones watching? Why not everybody? And then you're like them.'

'You're not like them.'

She looked up at me. 'Everybody's like them.'

'No, we're not,' I said, putting my hand on her shoulder and pulling her down to the bed, leaning over her. 'Anyway, it's over.'

'Yes.' She reached up, touching my neck. 'I wanted to know. If it would always feel – the way it was with him.'

'Does it?'

She shook her head.

'Good. Let's make sure.'

The afternoon went on like that, stroking each other and then, excited again, grabbing at flesh in a kind of fury, and then dozing off, drugged with sex, hearing the rain in our half-sleep. Even when it was finished we kept touching lightly, not wanting to arouse each other but unable to take our hands away. Once, during a break in the storm, I dressed and ran out for a bottle of wine, half afraid that when I got back she'd be taking her clothes out of the armoire, the mood broken, but she was still there, the sheet pulled up just over her breasts.

'I'm sick, remember? I have to spend the day in bed,' she said while I poured the wine. 'You're soaked.'

'Not for long,' I said, taking my wet clothes off and climbing back in, clinking glasses. 'So, a picnic finally.'

'Oh, on the Lista di Spagna.'

'You should see the water out there. We'll be our own island in a few hours.'

She looked at me over the glass. 'That's nice, to say that.'

We slept finally, lulled by the wine and the steady rain, her back curved into me, and when I woke the sound of running water was coming from the bathroom. There was a thin light under the door. I got up and looked out of the window. Not really late but already dark, as if the water-logged city had simply given up and turned out the lights.

'I don't know if there's enough hot water for two,' she said when I went into the bathroom. 'It was already getting cool. Do you mind? I thought, at your house—'

'That's all right. I'll just watch,' I said, sitting on the edge of the bath. The room was spare, the bathmat just a skinny towel thrown on the cold linoleum. Whatever steam there had been was now gone from the flat mirror over the basin.

'One look, then. I'm getting out,' she said, pulling herself up and posing with her hand on her hip, a kind of burlesque wiggle, then folding her arms across her chest in a shiver. 'Oh, this cold.'

'Here,' I said, wrapping one of the thin towels around her as she stepped out. I held her for a minute, letting the towel blot the water, then began rubbing her dry with another one. 'Come back to bed. It's warm.'

'No, it's late.'

'Have dinner.'

'No, it's time to go home. I have to keep respectable hours. For the neighbours,' she said, slipping on her pants and hooking her bra. 'To be respectable.'

'You're not,' I said, smiling.

She came over and put her hand in my hair. 'I used to be.'

28

I picked up my underwear. 'All right. I'll take you home.'

'No, not tonight.' She looked at me. 'It's better. You stay here.'

'What am I going to do here?'

'You can watch.' She slipped on her skirt, her face sly, as if she knew this covering up would turn erotic, each simple move, even lifting a blouse from its hanger, a secret between us, her body something only we knew, more ours than ever as she hid it from everyone else, piece by piece.

She came over to the bed and looked down. 'And you want to go on the vaporetto?' She leaned down, taking my erection in her hand while she kissed me. 'Sometimes, you know, when it's like this, we want to think it's something else. But it's not, it's just what it is, that's all. It's enough for me, what it is. You understand?' She ran her fingers up the side of my penis, then moved her hand away.

I nodded.

'Thank you,' she said. 'For the day. For the room.'

'Tomorrow?' I said.

She looked at me, then smiled. 'But somewhere nearer. I'll have to go back to work. Not all day, like this.'

'Anything. The Gritti?'

'No, somewhere cheap. With sheets like this.' She gestured towards the rumpled bed. 'So we don't care what we do.'

I got up to follow, grabbing part of the sheet to cover myself, making her giggle.

'Very funny.'

'Well, it is, though. How is that? So serious and then it's funny. You think it's funny for the animals?'

'No, but they don't go home early, either.'

She laughed. 'One o'clock.'

I went over to the window and waited to see her come out below, the wide shoulders of her coat as she moved into a line of umbrellas, people hurrying home from work, none of them turning around to look back, none aware that anything had happened.

CHAPTER TWO

MY MOTHER PICKED that evening, when my head was groggy, still flooded with sex, to put her foot down about dinner with Gianni.

'He's going to think you're avoiding him. I waited until the last possible minute. Where have you been, anyway?'

'Looking at art.'

'Art.'

'I'm not avoiding him. I'm just tired.'

'You're always tired.' She bit her lip. 'Do this for me, would you, sweetie? I don't want to have to make apologies again. It's rude, aside from anything else.'

'Well, I can't go like this,' I said, patting my soaked jacket. Everything crumpled, like the sheets. It occurred to me that I might even smell of it, the whole sweaty afternoon. 'I have to wash.'

My mother sighed. 'All right. Meet us at Harry's. I'll send the taxi back and tell him to wait. You won't even need the traghetto. But darling, quickly, please?'

'All right. Chop-chop. What do you want me to wear?' I said, looking at her, primped, even sporting some of her good jewels.

'We're going to the Monaco, so something decent. You know. *Not* the uniform, please. That wasn't funny at all, at Mimi's. How do you think it makes them feel?'

'It was the only thing I had at the time.'

'Well, not at the Monaco.'

'God forbid.'

She looked at me. 'You're not going to be in a mood, are you?'

'Promise. Actually, I'm in a good mood.'

'I can see. The art, no doubt.' She raised an eyebrow. 'I can smell the wine from here. Go easy at Harry's. As long as you're doing this, you might as well make a good impression. He's nervous about you.'

'Why?'

'Because you're the only family I have. You know what Italians are like about families.'

'What about Aunt Edna?'

She laughed. 'Darling, she's what I use when I want to get *out* of something.'

I looked at her. 'What do you want to get into?'

She turned away, picking up her handbag. 'Nothing. I just want us to have a nice dinner.' She looked back. 'I live here now, you know. Gianni is a good friend. It's not too much to ask.'

'No.'

'You used to be so charming. I suppose it's the war.'

It seemed such an extraordinary thing to say that for a minute I couldn't think how to answer. But she had caught my look.

'You know what I mean. I know – well, I don't know, that's the problem. But you never say, either. And anyway, it's over, that's the main thing. Now look at the time. I'm going to be late.'

'He'll wait.'

She smiled. 'That doesn't make it right.' She gave me a quick kiss on the cheek. 'Don't be long. And no politics.'

'Why? What are his politics?'

'I haven't the faintest idea. I never ask. And I don't want you to, either. It always ends in arguments, no matter what it is. Besides, it's their country – things never make sense to outsiders.'

'All right. No politics. Art?'

'Art.' Her eyes were laughing, full of their old spirit.

31

'Maybe we'll just talk about you,' I said, smiling. 'What could be more interesting?'

'Mm. What could?' she said, throwing me a look, then heading for the stairs. Below us, I could hear the motorboat taxi churning water at the canal steps. 'Good thing I'm going first. I can tell him you're adopted.'

I was ready by the time the taxi returned. It was still raining, and after we rounded the tip of the Dogana and headed across to San Marco even the lights seemed blurry, as if the city were actually underwater. The campanile disappeared somewhere in an upper mist and the piazza itself was deserted, with nothing to fill the empty space but lonely rows of lamps.

Harry's, however, was snug and busy, all polished wood and furs draped over chairs and eager American voices. The bar was hidden behind a line of uniforms, officers on leave. My mother and Gianni were both drinking Prosecco, their second by the look of the half-filled olive dish.

'Ah, at last,' he said, getting up. 'I'm so happy you could come.' A polite smile, genial.

'Sorry to hold you up. Should we just go over?' I gestured to the door and the Monaco just across the calle.

'No, no, there's time. Have a drink.'

A waiter appeared, summoned apparently by thought.

'Well, a martini then,' I said to the waiter, ignoring my mother's glance.

'What is the expression?' Gianni said. 'Out of wet clothes and into a dry martini.' He smiled, pleased with himself.

'Yes,' I said. 'Look, there's Bertie.'

He was at the far end of the room, drinking with a woman in an elaborate hat. Between us was the usual crowd, half of whom had probably been at his party.

'Yes, we saw him earlier,' my mother said. 'Gianni, who's he with?'

'Principessa Montardi.'

'Really a principessa?'

32

'Well, the prince was real. And she married him. Her father was in milk products. Milanese.'

'The things you know.'

'It's a small city. We know each other maybe too well. Ah, here's your drink.'

The martini was strong and I felt the heat of it right away, pleasant, like the warm light of the room. Bertie had waved, the others who vaguely knew us had noticed, and now we could retreat to ourselves. I felt lightheaded, wanting to grin, still thinking about the afternoon. And there'd be tomorrow, another room. Then another. Afternoons of pure pleasure. In Germany there had been an army nurse drunk at a party, and one German girl, who had asked for tinned meat afterwards, both times sad, furtive, closed off, like the country itself now. Here everything was pleasure – sex and buildings glimmering on the water, even Harry's green olives. I realised – was it only the martini? – that I was happy.

'You look like the cat who swallowed the canary,' my mother said. 'What are you thinking about?'

'Just how nice this all is.'

'You're enjoying Venice, then?' Gianni said.

'Yes, very much. Doesn't everybody?'

'Most, yes, I think. Even we do sometimes,' he said.

'Does it bother you, all the visitors?'

'No, it's important for us. How else could we live? Of course you cannot choose your visitors. The Wehrmacht loved us, for their holidays. In the spring all the tables in San Marco, nothing but uniforms. Their city. So that was difficult.'

'Awful,' my mother said automatically.

'You have been in Germany, Grace said?'

I nodded. 'What's left of it.'

'The bombs, you mean?'

'The cities are gone. Flat.'

'So that's how it ended for them. You see how lucky we are. Imagine Venice—' He shuddered. 'How long will you stay?'

'I'm not sure yet.'

'He's been looking at art,' my mother said wryly.

'Yes? Then you will never leave. There is always more art in Venice. Where have you been? The Accademia?'

I nodded. 'No one's there this time of year. You can look at *The House of Levi* for hours and not have to move.'

'Really,' my mother said, surprised.

Dr Maglione smiled in agreement. 'Veronese. Maybe the finest of them. Tintoretto, it's too much sometimes. You must see San Sebastiano, Veronese's church.'

'Yes, off the Zattere. Before the maritime station.'

My mother was now looking at me in real surprise, aware suddenly that my time here was unknown to her, something I did between meals.

'So you know it. I can see you don't need me for a guide,' he said pleasantly. 'Now Grace . . .' He smiled at her.

'He thinks I'm hopeless,' my mother said.

'Hopeless, no.'

'I follow those yellow signs with the arrows and I still have no idea where I am. They always say Per Rialto and I never want to go there.'

'No, especially not there,' Dr Maglione said, laughing.

A look passed between them, so intimate that I went back to my martini, feeling in the way. Even with my skin still flushed with it, I couldn't make the leap from the damp sheets of my own afternoon to whatever time they were remembering. I had not imagined anything beyond friendship, a way to pass the time. And yet there must have been sex, maybe even with sweat and gasps, open mouths. I looked at him, now lighting a cigarette. Thinning grey hair brushed back at the temples, intelligent eyes. But what did she see? He caught my glance, meeting my eyes through the smoke in a question.

'Turned up at last, has he?' Behind me, Bertie had put a hand on my shoulder.

'Hello, Bertie,' I said. 'Where's your princess?'

'In the loo. So I thought I'd say hello. I hate staring at an empty table, don't you?'

'Join us,' Dr Maglione said.

'No, no, she's quick as a bunny usually. I don't know how you do it,' he said to my mother. 'All those layers.'

My mother laughed.

'And where did you get to last night?' Bertie asked me. 'Now you see him, now you don't.'

'I didn't want to interrupt. You were about to go into confession.'

'And so should you, once in a while. I know I don't want to be caught unawares. Between the old stirrup and the ground.' He looked at me. 'You don't have the faintest idea what I'm talking about, do you? Heathen. A fine job you've done, Grace.'

'Still, he went to the Accademia,' Gianni said. 'So maybe that was his church today.'

'Did you?' Bertie said, looking at me, letting the phrase hang in the air.

'Would you join us for dinner?' Gianni said, polite. Or was he already beginning to tire, seeing the evening before us in our odd triangle, idling, talking about Veronese but looking at one another, wary, pretending to be a family?

'*Molto gentile*, but you'd never forgive me. The boredom of her. Old hunting days in the Piedmont. You don't want to hear it, I promise you.'

'What about you?' my mother said, laughing.

'Well, I have to. One of life's little crosses. The husband was a peach, you know. Funny how people find— Oh, look sharp, the Inquisition. Been up to anything?'

I turned to find a thickset man in a natty suit coming towards the table. Neatly trimmed moustache and shiny face, a man who might just have come from the barber's. Gianni stood up, frowning.

'*Dottore*,' the man said to him. Then a stream of Italian, obviously friendly. He put his hand on Bertie's arm. 'And Signor Howard. I'm sorry, don't let me interrupt.'

'No, no. My friend Mrs Miller. Her son Adam. Grace, Inspector Cavallini.'

Cavallini bowed, a stage gesture.

'Inspector?' my mother said. 'Police inspector?'

'Yes. Have you done anything wrong?'

'Do people *tell* you?'

He smiled. 'No, usually I have to catch them.' He nodded and touched my hand half-heartedly, glancing at Dr Maglione.

'And he does. Always,' Bertie said.

'Here? At Harry's?' my mother asked.

'No, here I take Prosecco. Off-duty.' He was enjoying my mother. 'You don't think it would disturb the customers?'

'I think it would make their night.'

He laughed, then said something in Italian to Gianni that I took to be a word of approval, and bowed a leavetaking to the rest of us. 'Signora, a great pleasure. Signor Howard, you are behaving yourself?' He wagged his forefinger teasingly.

'Me? I'm one of the good. As you know. Practically Caesar's wife.'

Cavallini smiled. 'Yes, practically,' he said, and headed for the frosted-glass door.

'Bertie, give,' my mother said, interested. 'How on earth do you know him?'

'I'm a foreign national, you know. We had to report during the war.'

'Report? I thought they locked you up.'

'Irish passport, lovey. Thanks to me dad. So there's that to be said for him anyway. Convenient being a neutral just then.'

'But weren't you both?'

'Not here. Green as a clover. Had to be. Otherwise, you know, I'd have had to leave. My pictures, my house. Then what?'

'Yes, then what?' I said.

He looked at me sharply, then back at my mother. 'Anyway, they couldn't have been nicer. Came to the house, had a drink, and that was it. Never even had to go to the station. Now that it's over, I rather miss it, the little visits.'

'Oh, Bertie, you don't mean it. He's creepy.'

'You don't find him charming?' Bertie said.

'The police?'

Gianni smiled. 'Police are men too. In America maybe it's different.'

'Well, I'll tell you one thing, they're not drinking at Harry's. How can he afford it, aside from anything else?'

'Grace, dear,' Bertie said, 'that is exactly the sort of question one should never ask. Not here.'

'You mean he's—' My mother started, eyes wide, imagining, I suppose, black-market storerooms and goods hidden under raincoats.

'Bertie makes a joke, I think,' Gianni said, calming her. 'It's not so expensive, one drink. Even at Harry's.'

'But imagine a policeman at "21",' my mother said, still toying with it.

'There she is,' Bertie said, spotting the principessa. 'What did I tell you? Less time than it takes to— Fresh lipstick too. She's a wonder. Enjoy your dinner.' He hurried away, intercepting her at their table and helping her with her coat.

'We must go too,' Gianni said. 'Have you finished your drink?' He turned, surprised to find me looking at him.

'How is it that you know him?' I said.

'Inspector Cavallini? Sometimes the police come to the hospital for help. Medical evidence.'

'Really?' my mother said. 'Did you ever solve anything?'

Gianni smiled. 'Not yet. Shall we go?' He leaned over to wrap my mother's fur around her shoulder.

I got up. Dizzy for a second, I pressed against the table for support.

'Are you all right?' he asked, a doctor's voice.

I nodded. 'Just a drink on an empty stomach. I forgot I haven't eaten all day.'

'Too busy looking at art,' my mother said, amusing herself.

The dining room at the Monaco was formal and starchy – waiters in black tie, silver serving trolleys, soft, flattering lights. Gianni made a pleasant fuss ordering us schie and polenta to start, a winter specialty, then took his time with the wine list. I had a cig-arette and looked around the room – a light crowd, off-season, but dressed for an evening out, elegant, as if they, like the quails on the serving cart, had somehow been preserved in aspic. The room was almost as warm as Harry's, immune to fuel shortages. There were arrangements of winter branches, like abstracts of flowers, ice buckets, the smell of perfume. At one point I noticed Gianni smiling at my mother, and I followed his eyes, wanting just for a minute to see what he did and realised that for them the room was somehow erotic. Not cheap hotels and tepid baths, worn sheets and bare skin, nothing that had made my afternoon exciting. For them the furs and perfume and rich food were part of what sex had become. He was looking at money.

'There's something I don't understand,' I said, drawing their attention back to the table. 'Is he an inspector now?'

'Yes, of course.'

'And he has been – I mean, he consulted you on cases. So that means he was working for the Germans.'

'Technically. At the end. We were an occupied country.'

'But he's police. Not a doctor or a waiter or something. Police. Why hasn't he been thrown out?'

'For doing what?'

'Enforcing German laws. And before that—'

'Fascist laws? Yes, you can say it. Well, who knows if he enforced them?' He tasted the wine, the waiter hovering. 'Yes, very nice.' We said nothing as the waiter poured.

'But if he didn't, what makes you think he'll enforce new ones now?'

Gianni smiled. 'Well, it's a question, yes? But you see, you make the problem for yourself. I don't expect him to enforce them – not too many anyway. Just the ones we need to live. The others, we bow, we tip our hat, we ignore. Shall we make a toast? To happier times?'

'Yes,' my mother said, raising her glass.

We clinked glasses – celebrating what?

'You're still troubled by this?' Gianni said, looking at me.

'But if he was a police officer, he must have been a Fascist. I mean, in the party.'

Gianni nodded. 'It was required. But what was in his heart, I don't know. People do things to survive. So we must give them the benefit of the doubt.'

'Innocent until proven guilty,' my mother said lightly.

Gianni smiled. 'Well, innocent, maybe that goes too far.' He looked at me. 'I understand what you mean. But how can I explain it to you? To live under – you know the word tyranny is from the Latin *tyrannus*. So we have known how to live with this for a long time. You bend. Maybe you think we bend too much, but we look at history and it tells us the important thing is to survive.' He opened his hand, gesturing. 'And we did. Now with this good wine. In this beautiful city. All still here, still beautiful. It's the Germans who have gone. We survived them too. For us it's a kind of strength, to bend.' He paused. 'When it's inevitable.'

'Like *The House of Levi*,' I said, thinking to myself.

'What?' my mother said.

'It was *The Last Supper*. He changed the title because the pope didn't like it.'

'The Inquisition didn't like it,' Gianni said. 'More Nazis. Torture. Burnings. Worse, sometimes. Castrating people. You learn how to bend with a history like ours.'

'But that was a question of belief.'

'You think Goebbels didn't believe? Any of them? Right up to the end they believed in something. I don't know what – their own hate, maybe. And when the Inquisition lit the fires under people, what did they believe? To save them. By killing them. Compared to the Church, the Nazis were amateurs. At least the Nazis didn't ask you to think they were right to do it. They didn't care what you thought.' He studied his wine. 'Forgive me, no more speeches. But your painting does it matter what it's called? So long as it's beautiful?'

'No.'

'You see, an Italian answer. And Veronese, you know he was also being a tiny bit naughty. Putting all that in, the dwarfs, the drinking.

A sacred scene. He knew what they would think. But that's Italian too, maybe, to tweak the nose – that's right? tweak? of the Church. You can do that if you bend. The Germans never understood that – they never bend and they destroy themselves. Why?' He shook his head. 'Northern people. Sometimes they are all a mystery.'

'All of us?' my mother said, flirting.

'Oh, you, certainly. A great mystery. But that's because you're a woman. All women are mysteries.' A stage courtliness, the two of them practically winking at each other.

The polenta arrived, covered in tiny brown shrimp from the lagoon.

'Funny about Bertie knowing him,' my mother said. 'He was careful with him, did you notice? I'll bet it wasn't half as easy as he makes out. During the war.'

'No, not for anyone,' Gianni said. 'Of course, Bertie has many friends. I don't think it was dangerous for him.'

'Irish, my foot,' my mother said, laughing to herself. She glanced over at Gianni, her face soft. Not just a dinner companion, someone to take charge of the wine list.

'In Germany, you were a soldier?' Gianni said, keeping the conversation going.

'G-2. Intelligence. We investigated Germans suspected of Nazi activity.'

'Ah, that explains your interest in Cavallini. One investigator to another, eh? You want to compare methods?' He was smiling.

'Ours was mostly pushing paper around.'

He laughed. 'So was his, I think. But it must have been difficult, yes? Surely the real Nazis would lie. So how do you know?'

'We don't always. That's what makes it difficult.'

'Impossible, maybe.'

'Maybe. We still have to try.'

'But why? The war is over.'

'Their crimes aren't.'

'Ah. A passion for justice,' he said, nodding, a paternal indulgence. 'Maybe you'll be a lawyer.'

40

'Maybe.'

'Oh darling, really?' my mother said. 'I haven't wanted to ask. You've seemed – at such loose ends.'

'Don't rush,' Gianni said. 'To be this age, it's wonderful. You don't have to decide anything. Not yet. Not like us, eh?' he said to my mother. 'We have to hurry with everything now.'

'Speak for yourself.'

'Ah, you see,' he said, ostensibly to me, 'how she makes fun of me.' His hand moved slightly towards hers and just grazed it.

I looked away. 'Did you always want to be a doctor?' I asked.

'Well, for me it was different. A family tradition. One of us was for medicine and one for – well, to carry the name. But he died, so it's the end. I have only a daughter.'

'You're married?' I said, not expecting this.

'I was. She died.'

'I'm sorry. Where is your daughter?'

'Bologna. At the university.'

'Medicine?'

He smiled. 'No, an *avvocato*. Another one with a passion for justice. How did it happen?' he said to my mother. 'To have such children?'

'Think of *theirs*.'

'Would you like to see the hospital?' Gianni said to me, not an offhand invitation, an obvious effort to get closer.

'The hospital?'

'For the architectural interest. It was once the Scuola di San Marco. Near Zanipolo. The library has the most beautiful ceiling in all of Venice.'

'Yes, I'd like that,' I said, the only possible answer.

'Even the hospitals,' my mother said, a little dreamy, finding romance in everything now.

'The joke is that you can see San Michele from the wards – the cemetery island. So they say the doctors finish you and the priests at San Lazzaro bless you and the boat outside takes you away.

41

One operation, door to door.' He winked at my mother. 'You see how practical we can be.'

And so it went, through the grilled branzino, the radicchio from Trevisio, the little cups of coffee and the shared plate of biscotti – light, aimless conversation meant to make us easy with one another, a kind of wooing. My mother was happy, enjoying herself, her eyes shiny, catching the light the way her earrings did, in tiny glints. She made jokes, laughed at his, until the table seemed as carefree as one of those afternoons at the Lido. Gianni looked at her with a fondness that surprised and then disconcerted me. And I, who was the object of the wooing, sat wondering why they were bothering. What did it matter what I thought, if they wanted to make eyes at each other and play at being twenty again? What could be nicer? A season in Venice with something to talk about later, over drinks at the Plaza. An old friend, not somebody she'd picked up in a hotel lounge. With a daughter at the university. That respectable. What business was it of mine? The truth was that I didn't want to think about them at all. My mind was else-where, back at the station hotel, in that perfectly hermetic world of sex, where no one else existed. In the warm dining room, with my body loose and tired, all I wanted was my own life.

When we got up to go to the lounge for brandy, I took it as my cue to leave. Gianni would want to sit with my mother in the dim light and look across the water to Salute, letting the evening settle around them. I imagined a kiss tasting of cognac, a last cigarette, low voices – everything the lounge was meant for, what you paid for. But when I suggested going, he insisted I stay for a nightcap. For some reason it took a while to order – everything seemed to have slowed down, even the waiters – and then we drank without saying much. There were only a few other people and a piano near the door, played so softly it seemed the pianist too was logy with food and drink. Gianni fixed a time next week for me to go to the hospital. He sat back with a cigarette, looking contented. Outside the hotel, gondolas with different-coloured tarps bobbed on the tide. I slouched, exhausted. There was nothing to do now but wait it out.

'Such a surprise, darling. A lawyer. So sensible.'

'It's just an idea,' I said, but she waved her hand, brushing it away, and I saw that she hadn't actually been talking to me but to some unseen audience.

I looked over, hearing the abstract, self-amused talk of drink. My mother, like all her friends, had a strong head, but it had been a long evening since the first Prosecco, through Gianni's special bottle of Soave and the Vin Santo at table. Her words were still precise, but everything else about her seemed to have grown a little blurry. Even her lipstick was no longer fresh, faint at the lines. She was nestled into the corner of the settee, her fur draped around her, smiling, in love with the world.

'It's late,' I said. 'We should go.'

'Oh, Adam,' she said, teasing. 'So sensible.'

'If you're tired,' Gianni said to me. 'Don't worry, I will take her home. She's happy here, you see.'

'Maybe too happy,' I said to him, not loud enough for her to hear.

'There is no such thing as too happy,' Gianni said mildly. 'I will see that she gets home.' Firmly, a dismissal. 'Can I call you a taxi?'

'No, that's all right,' I said, getting up. 'Thanks for dinner.'

'Oh, you're going,' my mother said, evidently a new idea to her. She leaned forward to be kissed.

I bent over for a quick peck, and as I stood back I stopped, suddenly dismayed, seeing once again what Gianni must be seeing, not a carefree girl this time but a woman slack with drink, pliable, draped against the couch, her soft white throat tilted up. What he'd waited for all evening, what came after brandy. Did he take a room here, part of the Monaco service? My heart sank a little as I looked at her, a physical drop. When had this happened, this fading into someone else? While I'd been away, not paying attention. And each year she'd become a little more vulnerable, until all it took was a kind word and table manners, someone like Gianni.

I looked at him, half expecting a leer, something predatory, but he was smiling blandly, at ease with himself. What he must be used to, another of the lonely women who floated through Venice, away from home, a little drunk, easy. Without daughters at university and family names. Without anything, except money to buy a little pleasure, an evening out. This one had come with a son – an inconvenience, but now he'd been charmed too, taken care of, and he was leaving. Would they come back to Dorsoduro? Appear at coffee in the morning without even a blush, all of us grown up?

For a second I stood there, trying somehow to put myself between them. It's not what she is, I wanted to say to him – but wasn't it? Isn't it what she wanted too? Who had actually paid for dinner? I couldn't remember there being a bill, the sort of discreet arrangement a lady might make. But how do you protect people? And after all, what was the harm? One of those things. Unless it wasn't. I looked down at her again, wondering what bargain she was making with herself. A fling? But maybe she hadn't even thought about it, just followed an impulse, the way she'd come to a city where she could read menus and street signs but whose real language was unknown to her.

'Darling, you say you're going, then you don't go,' she said, laughing.

I smiled, shaking my head. 'Just thinking.'

'Oh, God.'

I held up my hand. 'All right, I'm off. Don't be too late,' I said, imitating her.

'You don't have to worry,' Gianni said without a hint of guile. 'She's in safe hands.'

The next day I found a hotel near the Rialto with cheap off-season rates and a side view of the canal. The old-fashioned radiator in the room actually produced heat, a luxury that winter, so I took the room for a week, using a chunk of my separation pay. Not what the army had intended, precisely, but in fact the room did finally separate me from the war. Every afternoon we sealed ourselves away behind the fake damask walls, too absorbed in each other to imagine anything outside.

After that first day, we settled into a pattern. At one Claudia

44

would walk over from the Accademia – ten minutes, if she hurried – and we would make love until she had to go back, dressing and leaving me in bed. I think it excited her to leave first, as if the room were in a brothel and she had somehow bought my time. She liked everything about the room – the touristy Murano chandelier, the chipped gold paint on the sideboard – because it seemed to her what such a room should look like, a little tawdry, worn from years of afternoon sex. She never came to my mother's house and didn't want me to go to hers. An affair was set apart from real life, something you did in hotels.

I had never had sex with anyone who responded the way she did, not just with pleasure or curiosity but the way I'd seen children eat in Germany, with a greedy determination to fill themselves up, not sure they would ever eat again. The afternoons were for both of us a kind of daily feast, sampling and tasting. Day after day in our cheap hideaway room, warm with radiator heat, we slid against each other, slick with sweat, until, finally exhausted, we felt the world begin to come back a little. Then she would dress and lean over to kiss me in the damp sheets, not saying goodbye but fixing a time for tomorrow, when we'd begin again. Days of it like this, drunk with sex.

We didn't go out for dinner or have a drink at Harry's or meet each other anywhere but at the hotel. At first she said she had to be careful, she didn't want people at work to know, but after a while I realised the secrecy itself, the sense of being illicit, was erotic to her. When she closed the door to the hotel room, she could do anything, away from everyone, even herself.

Then, after a few days, the afternoons weren't enough. I wanted to know where she went, how she spent her time. Wanted her, in fact, to spend it with me.

'I don't want to go to restaurants. It's nice the way it is.'

'But I want to talk to you. To know you.'

'Who knows me better than you? Do you think I'm like this with everyone?'

'I don't mean that.'

'I know what you mean. I know you a little now too. You like the fans, the masks. Old Venice.'

'What's wrong with that?'

'You know, all the fans, that was to end up here,' she said, patting the bed.

'So maybe we missed something, skipping all that.'

She shook her head. 'No.' She pulled me down to her. 'Do you think we missed something?'

'No.'

'Then it's enough. Here.'

'All I did was ask you to dinner,' I said, kissing her.

'I can eat any time. Wouldn't you rather do this?'

'Yes.'

But a few days later I got a chance to force the issue when my mother came down with a cold and Gianni, now the attending physician, offered me his seats at La Fenice.

'I've never been,' Claudia said, tempted.

'Let's do it right. We'll take a gondola.'

'Ouf. A gondola from San Isepo, with everyone at the window. I'll take the vaporetto.'

'Then you'll come?'

'I always wanted to see it, La Fenice.'

'Do you have something to wear? We can buy you a dress.'

'No, you don't buy me a dress. I'm not—' She turned away. 'I can dress myself. Even for La Fenice.'

I hired the gondola anyway and met her at San Marco, then maneuvered her into the rocking boat for the short trip through the back canals.

'You're extravagant,' she said.

'You have to go this way. Where else can you do it? Pulling up to the opera in a boat?'

'You can also walk,' she said, but smiling as the dark houses glided by, surprised to see a different city from this angle. Under her wool coat she was wearing a long evening dress she said she had made herself, gloves, and rhinestone-studded slippers.

46

'Where'd you get the shoes?'

'Borrowed. A friend keeps them for Carnival every year.'

'Very fancy.'

'Vulgar?' she said, concerned.

I smiled at her. 'No, fancy. Perfect.'

The canals got narrower after we drifted past the hotels and began to circle around to the Fenice water entrance. There was no sound but an occasional snatch of radio and the smack of the steering pole hitting the water. A light mist was rising, just high enough to soften the lights.

'My God, it's beautiful like this,' she said. 'No wonder they come.'

'You've lived here all your life.'

'Not in a gondola. It's different.' She turned to me. 'You make me a tourist.'

We turned a corner into a small lighted basin and one of those scenes that gives Venice its storybook quality – a traffic jam of boats rocking against one another as people stepped up to the pavement, the familiar taxi drop-off made theatrical by the water. After the shadowy canals, the lights here were festive, opening-night bright, catching jewels and white silk scarves.

'You see, it's another city. People like that,' she said. A woman covered in white fur was being handed up to a footman.

'Never mind. They'll all be looking at you. 'Who's that up there in the box?'

'It's a box? Whose?'

'A friend of my mother's.'

'A rich American?'

'No, Venetian. Not rich either. A doctor.'

'My father was a doctor. He didn't have a box at La Fenice.'

'This one had doges in the family.'

'Oo la. A doge's box.'

I smiled at her. 'You don't believe me?'

'You, yes. Maybe not him.'

Then our gondola reached the entrance and I had to help her

out and tip the gondolier, and her attention shifted to the crowd inside. We took the stairs to the second tier and followed the number plates to Gianni's box. Every light in the theatre seemed to be on, making the red-and-gold walls glow, almost burning. We were the first to arrive, so took the seats nearest the rail.

'Who else is coming?' Claudia said.

'I don't know. Maybe he has the whole thing. Here, let me take your coat.'

'A minute,' she said, reaching into the pocket and pulling out a fan, then opening it, her eyes lowered in a mock flirtation over the edge. 'Like this?'

'Where'd you get it?'

'With the shoes. A Carnival costume.'

'Not that, though,' I said, nodding at the brooch on the front of her dress.

'No, my mother's. A friend hid it.'

'Hid it?'

'When I was away.'

She went to the edge of the box and leaned forward, taking in the scene like gulps of air. Below, people were settling in and looking around, nodding to one another, testing their opera glasses, everyone smiling, expectant.

'Look at them, like birds,' she said, her eyes darting around the theatre.

I glanced down – the dresses in fact were as bright as feathers – then over at her. Her dress, a dark blue clinging fabric, gathered at the waist, would have been dull without the pin, but it opened at the neck in a way that drew your eyes upwards, towards the face, flushed and eager, and her hair had been pulled back, exposing her ears, making her look even younger. A different Claudia, girlish and wide-eyed, not the woman in the hotel room. How many others were there?

She caught my stare and pulled up the fan again, giggling, having fun.

'Oh, you brought glasses,' she said as I lifted them out of my pocket. 'Can I see, please?' Suddenly twelve.

I watched her as she scanned the audience.

'There's Rusconi, from the Accademia. My God, what a wife. Two of him. Do you think Signor Howard's here?'

'No idea,' I said, still watching her, face tilted up now as she took in the upper tier.

'Where do they all come from?' she said. 'You always hear it's a small town, but I don't know any of them.'

'Maybe it's small to them. Same people.'

'The musicians are coming,' she said, almost fidgeting now with anticipation.

There was a final rustle of feathers below as the lights dimmed for the overture, then the music started and I moved my chair closer to hers. She was sitting erect, years of table manners and piano lessons, a well-brought-up girl. The back of her neck was pale and thin, and when I reached to touch it with my fingers, she turned with a shy smile, as if in fact we'd been flirting over fans.

The opera was *Così fan tutte*, and since the programme notes were in Italian, beyond my guidebook vocabulary, I just sat back and listened, not even bothering to follow the story. Real fans and full-skirted gowns began to appear on the stage below, as natural there as the gilt-and-red wallpaper. How did they stage tragedies in a room like this? Nothing worse than mistaken identity and harmless jealousy could happen here. When Claudia leaned over to whisper, 'They're pretending to be Albanians,' I almost laughed out loud at the silliness of it, then felt a kind of giddy release. Even Claudia was smiling broadly, almost grinning, maybe the way she used to be all the time, after the piano lessons.

The four lovers were singing an ensemble piece when the door opened behind us. I turned to find a middle-aged woman in a pre-war evening gown, trailed by a white-haired man with a bushy fur-collared coat, like the cartoon plutocrat on Monopoly cards. Everything about her was lacquered – glistening lipstick and nails, dress shiny with bead-work. She looked at us, her eyes moving from surprise to displeasure in a second, obviously put out to find strangers in her box. I got up, gesturing to my front-row seat, but she waved her hand in a kind of dismissal, pretending to be concerned about distracting the people next to us, and took the chair behind.

We spent the rest of Act One speculating about one another – only Claudia in all that rustling and craning of necks seemed to be paying attention to the opera – but it was only when the interval finally came that we could stand and introduce ourselves in the light. Their name was Montanari. I mentioned Gianni and insisted that the woman move to the front row, but she was interested only in Claudia now, literally going over her from head to foot, eyes cold and superior behind the public smile. Then she raised her head, finished, with that peculiar satisfaction of finding someone wanting. Claudia, who had started with a polite nod, moved back a little against the rail, caught by the woman's gaze, her colour suddenly draining away.

'Grassini,' the woman said carefully, repeating Claudia's name as if she were trying to place her, the way her eyes had judged the rhinestone slippers cheap, the dress ordinary, everything somehow wrong.

And for a second I saw it too, not the young skin and high spirits that had made everything seem right before, but someone found out, in the wrong box. There are tiny moments that change the nature of things. I glanced at Signora Montanari, the withering, stupid eyes, and suddenly I wanted to fold up Claudia in some protective cape, safe, so that no one could look at her again. I touched her hand at the rail, asking her to read my face. Never mind about the dress, never mind about any of it. You're not just someone I sleep with.

But Claudia's colour had come back and with it her assurance. 'Yes, Grassini,' she said evenly. 'Perhaps you knew my father, Abramo Grassini?'

The woman blinked. 'Ah. Abramo. No.' She turned to me. 'And you're a friend of Gianni's?' she asked, still assessing.

50

'Yes,' I said easily. 'He's with a patient. I'm sorry about the seat. Will you have a drink with us?'

'No, no, we're meeting some people.' She gathered up her cloak, eager now to leave. 'Please,' she said, evidently offering us the run of the box.

'What was that all about?' I said when she'd left.

'She knows I'm a Jew,' Claudia said.

'Don't be silly. How could she possibly know? She just doesn't want to share the box.'

'No. She knows. Once you see the look, you don't forget it.' She picked up the fan, opened it, and put it against her face. 'Well, so much for this. Let's go.' She reached for her coat.

'Later,' I said. 'Right now we're going downstairs and have some champagne. Then we'll come back and listen to the rest.'

'She doesn't want me here.'

'Well, I do. Would you rather please her?'

She looked up, a small smile. 'One grandfather. It's easy for you. But for me, it's not – comfortable.'

'I'll sit between you. Come on, let's have some champagne.' I held out my hand to her. 'Tell me the rest of the story. Why they're pretending to be Albanians.'

Another smile.

'It's our box,' I said, taking her hand. 'We're not leaving.'

In the end it was the Montanaris who left, midway through the second act, after Fiordiligi sang in the garden by the sea. Signora Montanari had taken the rail seat next to Claudia, and it may be that she finally realised, distressed, how they must appear from below – one young, her pale skin catching the stage lamps, the other expensive and brittle, attractive now only to men on Monopoly cards. Or it may be this was just my idea, the story I made up as Signor Montanari nodded off at my side. But when Fiordiligi finished and Signora Montanari made an apologetic headache motion and slipped out with her surprised husband under the applause, I felt as if we had won something. I moved down to the rail seat.

'We've run them off.'

Claudia shrugged, a wry smile. 'One victory for the Jews.'

But she seemed happier now, relieved, and the music went with her, buoyant, heading into the finale. As things sorted themselves out onstage, something for everyone, it seemed to me that we had got our earlier mood back, frothy again, like the interval champagne.

Outside it was cold and damp, and I put my arm around her as we walked.

'You looked lovely, just sitting there, waiting it out like that.'

'It didn't feel lovely. Bitch. Probably a Fascist too.'

'No, there aren't any, haven't you heard? Same thing in Germany. All disappeared somehow.'

'You think it's funny.'

'No, but I spent months chasing them, so I know what it's like. Anyway, she's gone, so let's have a drink. The Gritti's right up here – they'll be open.'

The street was filled with people coming from La Fenice, wrapped in coats and furs, like the shuttered stores.

'No, it's late.'

'All right, I'll take you home.'

'No,' she said, putting a gloved hand on my chest. 'I'll go. It was wonderful, the opera.' She looked up. 'So, shall we meet tomorrow?'

'I want to go home with you.'

'Why? You can't wait?'

'Not for that.' I stopped. 'It's not that.'

'What?'

I put my hand up to the side of her neck. 'I don't want to skip anything. I want to take you to dinner. Out, like this. I want to spend the night with you. See you sleep, what you look like. Wake up. Make coffee. All of it. Not skip anything.'

'Don't say that,' she said softly, lowering her head. 'I don't want that.'

'Yes, you do. Everybody does.'

She shook her head. 'No. I don't.'

'You mean, not with me.'

She looked up, then turned away. 'It's not enough for you? Just to—'

'What?'

'You know.'

I smiled. Something she couldn't say, not even in the hotel, where anything was possible. A well-brought-up girl.

'Go to bed,' she said, still not saying it. 'It's not enough?'

'No.'

'Ha. Since when? You were happy enough to—'

I brushed back a lock of her hair. 'Things change. I want to be with you. That's all.'

'No, I can't,' she said, moving my hand away. 'I don't want anybody. Oh, what a judge I am. I see you, I think, yes, nice-looking, American. They never stay. They go home. No problems.'

'You want me to leave?'

She looked down, biting her lip. 'No. Oh, it's difficult.'

'Explain it.'

'Explain it. So easy. Some little talk over a drink.' She met my eyes. 'I don't want anything more. It's better for me.'

'How could it be better?'

'It's better. Safer.' She hesitated. 'Sometimes, do you know what I think you see? Another one of your cases, back in Germany. You want to make everything all right again. Maybe that's why you want to be with me. You think you can change what happened. But do you know how it really was? When people think you're going to die, you don't exist for them any more. You disappear, become nothing. That first train, none of them even looked. I thought, this is what it's like, there's nobody else. Then not even you. So you live here,' she said, touching her skin. 'And here.' Her eyes. 'Food, whatever makes you feel alive. Reminds you what it's like. Even pain sometimes. Just to feel it. But not here.' Now her chest. 'Nothing here. You have to stay safe.'

'From what?'

'The others. Everybody. They'll leave you alone if you're playing dead. You think you can get through the rest of it if you do that. But then it's hard coming back – you can't do it all at once. Just seeing things. Eating. Simple things, that's all I can do. Not people.'

'It's not like that any more.'

'Maybe yes, maybe no. Anyway, how do you know? It didn't happen to you.'

'No.'

'To know that everyone wants you dead.'

'Your friend didn't.'

'No, he didn't want me dead. He wanted—' she stopped, then breathed out, almost a snort. 'People. You know what he wanted? He wanted me to like it. It wasn't enough for him, just to do it. He wanted me to like it. To like him. What he could do to me. He wanted to hear it.'

'So you pretended.'

'Well, we can do that. Make sounds. It's what they like. So.' She looked down. 'And then sometimes it would happen. Even with him. I could feel it in me, beginning, and I couldn't stop it. With that pig. I'd feel it anyway – you couldn't take your mind far enough away, it would happen. And he knew. He wanted it like that. At first I was so ashamed, and then – then it was a way of being alive. So I let it happen. Maybe that's worse. Knowing it can happen with anyone. Like animals. So what does it matter who? Does it matter where food comes from? It's all the same.'

'It doesn't feel the same to me.'

'No?'

'No. It's not like with anyone else.'

'Ha, how many—'

'Don't,' I said, stopping her. 'I'm not him.'

'No? You think it's so different? *You* want me to like it too.'

'Yes.'

'All right, I do. I like it with you. So you can be happy. Tell your friends in New York.'

'I'm not him,' I said again, holding her shoulders. 'It's different.'

She looked down. 'But I'm not. I'm the same. I'm the same. In Fossoli.'

'No. What happened to you—'

'It's still happening to me. All those feelings. The hate. At first you want to kill all of them, and you can't even kill one. Not one. And then you know what happens, I think? You start killing yourself. You have to kill someone and there's no one else.'

'Stop,' I said, placing my finger in front of her mouth without touching it.

'Yes, stop,' she said. 'What's the good of all this?' She twisted her mouth. 'Not what you expected, is it? Such talk. A girl you met at a party.

'You're not just a girl at a party.'

'Yes, I am,' she said, pretending to be light, but I was shaking my head. 'No? What happened to her?'

'Signora Montanari looked at her dress.'

She met my eyes, a little startled, then looked down. 'My poor dress. So, what happened then?'

'I knew I was in love with you.'

'Oh,' she said, only a sound, her head bent. 'You don't mean that,' she said quietly. 'You don't even know me.'

'Yes I do. Everything about you. Right then.'

'Oh, all in one look. You're being—'

'I know. All right, not everything. Just enough.'

'What does it mean, to say something like that?'

'What it always means. I want to be with you.' I lifted her head. 'I'll take Italian lessons.'

She smiled weakly, her eyes troubled. 'No. Go to America. Your life is there. Not all this.' She spread her hand. 'But thank you. To say that. The opera, even. I didn't expect—' She leaned and kissed me on the cheek, a flutter of breath. 'It's a good time to stop. While it's all still nice.'

I reached for her, but she put her hand on my chest again.

'No, go.'

'I can't walk away from you.'

'No? All right. Me, then,' she said, her hand trembling. She looked up. 'Don't follow. I'm all right on my own,' she said, then turned and started walking.

'I don't believe you,' I said to her back. 'I don't believe it's all the same for you.' No answer but the click of her heels on the stone. 'Tell me it was the same.'

'Yes, the same,' she said, not turning around, still walking. Then she stopped, her shoulders drooping. A long quiet. 'No,' she said finally.

I stood for a minute, then started moving towards her gently, as if she were a bird that still might be scared off. I stepped around to face her, not saying anything. She looked up, her eyes still uneasy.

'Not the same?' I asked softly.

'No,' she said, the word not much more than a breath.

'Then let's go home,' I said, stepping closer, our faces almost touching.

'You're so sure. How can you be so sure about this?'

'We can get a taxi at the Gritti,' I said, putting my arms around her, feeling her head fall against my shoulder. 'Is that all right, a taxi?'

She nodded, resting against me. 'To the gardens. Not to the house. Signora Bassi, the owner, she lives there too. The noise.'

We were quiet in the taxi, as if Signora Bassi were already listening. The room was plain, up a staircase at the side of the house, overlooking the small misty canal and a back calle full of clotheslines. We stayed quiet in the room, not making love, just holding each other in bed. I did get to see her asleep, hours later, in the predawn when I usually tried to make out the Redentore and wonder how I was going to spend the day. Now in the light from the window all I could make out was the sewing machine and a dressmaker's dummy, her own shape standing straight and purposeful, the way she had at Bertie's party, and in some wonderful way I saw there were two of them now – the public, tailored Claudia at the window and the one only I knew, who'd stepped out of the dummy to crawl into the warmth beside me.

CHAPTER THREE

THE LIBRARY CEILING was as beautiful as Gianni had promised.

'Early sixteenth century,' he said, not a boast, just placing it. 'The carving is the best in Venice, I think. Of course today it's difficult to see.'

The morning had been dismal, and even the long side windows were not much help – the library seemed barely lit. But the ceiling turned the patchy light to its advantage, forcing you to look at it carefully, follow its intricate lines into shadow. Only Venice could have a hospital like this, a converted *scuola grande* whose façade was crowded with trompe l'oeil and marble panels. The entrance hall was a soaring space with pillars, as damp and gloomy as an old church, filled with the ghosts of shivering consumptives, but beyond it the working hospital was bright and up to date with wards and nurses' stations and X-ray rooms, what you'd see anywhere. And now the old medical library, which Gianni had saved for last, a special finale.

'Not as grand as the Sansovino staircase,' he was saying, 'but I think more beautiful. The proportions.'

'It's wonderful. Is it still used?'

'In theory. In practice, no. Now it's – a treasure.'

'Locked away,' I said as he closed the door and we started down the stairs.

'Yes. Otherwise . . .' His voice drifted off in the drafty hall, where families had begun to arrive for visiting hours.

'I feel privileged.'

Gianni accepted this with a nod, then smiled. 'Good. And now, are you hungry?'

'I don't want to take you away from your work.'

'No, no, it's all arranged. A restaurant very near. We can talk.'

About what, I wondered, but Gianni was all smiles and affability, clearly wanting to please.

'Quite a hospital,' I said, looking at the façade again as we came out.

'Well, the *scuola* was suppressed – I can't remember why – and so there was a big public building to use. Not so practical, maybe, for modern times, but in Venice nothing is practical, so you adapt. The facilities are good. And of course it's pleasant, every day to see it.' He pointed to one of the reliefs. 'Saint Mark helping Antinus.'

'Who?'

'A beggar in Alexandria. The series is Saint Mark's life. But I always think if you didn't know, it could be a doctor helping the sick. Appropriate, yes? Who knows? Maybe Lombardo had a presentiment that it would be a hospital.' He smiled. 'Anyway, it's an idea.'

'What happened during the war? I mean, was it a military hospital?'

'No. It was never a war zone here. You know, behind the lines it's a kind of peace. Things keep going. The hospital too. There was always food. In the south, with the fighting, it was different. Terrible shortages. Here at least no one starved, we could manage.' We were crossing a bridge out of the campo, and he indicated the houses on the other side of the canal with their running sores of fallen plaster. 'But no paint, no wood, nothing like that. See there? No repairs, not for years. The city is falling apart. Of course the visitors, for them it's always falling apart, they love the decay. Your mother thinks that. Don't fix it, it's all part of the charm. Well, maybe it's lucky for me she thinks that way. At my age, I'm falling apart too.'

I laughed, the expected response.

'You know we have become good friends,' he said.

I kept walking, not sure how I was meant to answer.

'She has a gift for that, I think. A rare quality. To make people happy. Here we are.'

He turned towards a door. No getting out of it now. But what excuse could I have found?

The restaurant was in the little campo that faced Santa Maria dei Miracoli. In summer there would be tables outside, people writing postcards and looking up at the marble walls. Now it was a poky room with a bar in front and just enough space in back to be intimate without being noisy. Gianni was evidently a regular, known to the waiter.

'You like granchi?' Gianni said to me. 'He says it's the special today.'

'Yes, fine,' I said, toying with my fork, already uncomfortable.

'Wine? I can't, but if you like—'

'No, water's fine.'

For a minute or so we watched the waiter pour the mineral water.

'I'm glad we have the chance,' Gianni said, 'to meet like this.' Leaning forward, opening.

'Yes, thank you,' I said, steering away. 'For the ceiling especially. I never would have seen it otherwise. By the way, I've been meaning to ask – who are the Montanaris?'

His forehead wrinkled for a second, then cleared. 'Ah, in the box. Who are they? They made an impression on you?'

'The other way around. I don't think they approved. They left early.'

Gianni laughed again. 'They always leave early. They come for the interval, to see her friends. The music?' He brushed away the idea with his hand. 'Ah, the crabs,' he said, leaning back for the waiter.

'I just wondered who—' I began, but he'd moved on from the Montanaris, speaking before I could finish.

'I wanted to talk to you,' he said, and then stopped. He sipped some water, hesitant, as if he were putting the words together in his head. 'You know I admire your mother very much.'

I waited.

'Very much,' he said again. 'We have a love for each other. This seems strange to you, maybe. At your age, I remember, it is impossible to think this happens after – what? Thirty? Forty? To have these feelings. But we do. Sometimes even more so. We can't be so careless any more, we know how valuable, to find someone. You're embarrassed, that I'm talking this way to you?'

'It's not that.'

'Yes, embarrassed, I think. It's my English. What I want to say—'

'Look, the point is, you don't have to say anything. If you and my mother . . . It's none of my business.'

'But now, yes. That's what I'm trying to tell you. It is your business now. We want to marry.'

'What?' Blurting it out, as if I hadn't heard properly.

'Yes, to marry. You're surprised?'

'But why?' I said, another involuntary response, not even thinking.

'Why? Because we have a love for each other.'

'Yes, but – I mean, why not just go on as you are?' While it lasts.

'You don't understand my feelings for her. Do you think I have no respect for her position?' Affronted, as if I'd stepped over some cultural divide.

'It hasn't bothered you up to now.'

He raised his eyebrows, then softened. 'That's what you think – I take advantage. You know, we are not children. Maybe it was – a convenience for both. Now it's something else.'

'When was all this decided?'

He shrugged. 'Some days ago now. You don't decide all at once.'

'And she didn't tell me?'

'Don't be angry with her. I wanted to tell you. She was a little

60

nervous, how to say it. And you know, it's traditional,' he said, smiling, 'for the man to approach the family.'

'You're asking for my blessing?'

'I'm asking you to be happy for us. It's important to Grace for you to be happy. It's important to me too.'

This last was a question. He was looking at me, waiting for me to nod, give some assent.

'When is all this supposed to happen?'

'As soon as we can arrange it. While you are still here.'

'And you'll live here?'

'Of course. It's my home. And now yours, whenever you like. I know you'll be in America, but you'll come back sometimes. Where we live there is always a home for you too.'

On her money. The thought, always buried somewhere, now flashed to the surface. Would they stay at Ca' Venti? No, he must have his own, the family house, plaster crumbling, untended these last few years. The daughter with bills in Bologna. Cognacs at the Monaco. All paid for now, taken care of with the scratch of her pen across a cheque. He was smiling at me again, intimate, the same easy charm that must have taken her in. Grey hair, sober suit, not even young – no warning signals at all.

'You don't say anything.'

'I'm just trying to – it's a lot in one gulp. I didn't expect—'

'You know, neither did we. Not at first.'

'It all just seems a little fast. To decide something like this. I mean, it's only been . . .' I let it hang there, waiting for him to finish, but instead he smiled again.

'Only the young have so much time. At our age it's better to hurry. And you know, the wedding, that's your mother's idea, to have it before you go back to America. She wants you to – such an expression – to give her away.'

'The father does that.'

'Well, the family. Why not the son?'

I shrugged.

'Good she'll be pleased.'

61

But it was Gianni who was pleased, smiling broadly, and I realised that in his mind I had somehow consented, given in, and could now be brought into the planning. There would be an engagement party. A friend had offered to perform the ceremony. I picked at my crab and half listened to one detail after another, the whole impossible scheme already worked out, discussed while I'd been somewhere else. Now there was nothing to be said.

And later? I saw the sensible talk with my mother back at Ca' Venti, straining to stay calm, the inevitable hysterics. Bertie would be better – one of his bracing heart-to-hearts. I wondered if he already knew, could get to her before things spun completely out of control and sense became a kind of public embarrassment.

Gianni was ordering espresso, another endless meal, and talking about a trip. But perhaps it was better just to stay in Venice. There were so many details to arrange. To get the house ready for my mother, repairs he wanted to make, a new decorating scheme they'd discussed. It might be better to go away later, a long trip, somewhere new. What they must have talked about over brandies – their new life together.

'Maybe even America,' Gianni was saying. 'It's many years now since I was there. Many changes.'

She'd give a party to introduce him to her friends. The whispered conversations later: Did you see what Grace picked up in Italy? No longer just impulsive, a figure of fun.

'I went all the way across to California. A wonderful country.'

He had put some bills on the saucer and was standing up, smiling at me.

'And now Americans in the family,' he said airily, and as I folded my napkin, trying to smile back, I felt the real implications of his news rush over me, like a prickling of the skin. Not just a folly, not just one of those things. All our lives changed, one way or another.

Outside, the sun was shining just enough to brighten the marble on the church. We started back towards the hospital, Gianni full of more plans. I tried to keep up, an eggshell politeness, but my mind was elsewhere, so distracted that I didn't even look at the group of GIs coming over the bridge, just felt the sudden hand on my shoulder.

'Hey, Adam? I didn't recognise you in your civvies.'

I blinked for a second, taking in the breezy American voice, the sound of my own life coming back.

'Joe. What are you doing here?'

'Seeing the sights. I'm over in Verona, but they let us out once in a while.'

'Still chasing rats?'

'Rat files. Some of Kesselring's boys. They come up for trial next month and they left a paper trail all the way to Verona, so somebody's got to look. You know. But you – what is it, a month now? Two? What the hell are you still doing over here?'

'My mother lives here.'

'Lives here? People live here?'

'For now, anyway,' I said, then stopped, suddenly aware of Gianni at my side. 'Oh, sorry. Joe, this is Dr Maglione. He's . . .' Who was he now, exactly? My mother's fiancé? My new stepfather? Looking at Joe's open GI face, I felt Gianni's foreignness for the first time. Was she prepared for this? Years of not quite getting jokes, living half in translation. '. . . a friend of my mother's,' I said. 'Gianni, Joe Sullivan.'

'Lieutenant,' Gianni said, decoding the bar on his collar and shaking his hand. 'You see, people do live here, a few of us.'

'Sorry. I didn't—'

'Oh, no. Sometimes even I think we're all visitors here. Of course, Verona, it's different. You're enjoying it there?' Now he was charming Joe, second nature.

'Well, enjoying. It beats Germany, anyway.'

'You were friends in the army?'

'G-2. Bloodhound detachment. Sniffing for Nazis. Happy days, huh?' he said to me.

'Every single one. When do you get out?'

'Never. They like my accent. Maybe June, though. Memphis in June, like the song says.' He glanced at the group behind him, too large to introduce. 'Well, I'd better push. Live here. I wish I'd known – cadge a bed next time.'

'You need one tonight?'

'No, that's all right. We got a special deal at the Bauer. Can't get away from the Krauts, huh?' he said, grinning. 'Come have a beer if you can. We're there a few days. Nice meeting you,' he said to Gianni. He jerked his thumb towards the city behind him. 'Quite a place you've got here.'

Gianni didn't react, just watched him go, then started again for the hospital.

'He's a good friend?'

'We worked together.'

'Finding the Nazis. That's who decides?'

'He just finds them. Someone else decides.' I paused. 'He likes to kid around. But he's not as dumb as he sounds.'

'I didn't mean – well, perhaps a little. The world is simple for him.'

'Sometimes it is simple.'

'You think so? I never find it that way. Look at us. We have lunch. Happy news. But for you I think not so simple – a little difficult, even. Who is this man? You worry about your mother. Yes, you do. It's natural. What can I say to make you feel easy? There hasn't been time for us to become friends. Later, I hope. For now, I only ask you to be happy because we are happy.'

'If she's happy, fine.'

'But you are still uneasy,' he said, watching me as we walked.

'I just don't understand the why of it. Why not – be the way you are.'

'And not marry, you mean. Why marry now, so late? Not for children, to make a family. Not for – what? Propriety? We don't have to be respectable, your mother and I. No one cares. Not even you, it seems.' A half-smile. 'So why? I wish I could tell you exactly. Sometimes I think to marry is a kind of insurance.'

'What, for old age? If one of you dies?' Another thing I hadn't considered. What if?

'No, not so pragmatic. I think a way to ensure the love does not go away. To make it feel permanent.'

'Even if it's not?'

'Sometimes, you know, it *is*. Don't you wish this for us?'

I hesitated, embarrassed, but we were coming down the bridge into the campo and Gianni turned to me, not waiting for an answer.

'It's late for us to be a family. You don't need a father, I don't ask that. But your mother must have her son. So you and I, we must try to be friends. Will you do that?'

'Of course. I never said—'

'No, but how you feel, that's something else.'

I looked away. 'How does your daughter feel?'

'Well, that's next. I do the warm-up on you.' He smiled, amused either by the phrase or by the idea that I was the easier of the two. 'She will be suspicious. Who is this woman? What does she want? Like you, but the reverse, the other side. You see, nothing is simple when there are two sides.'

'And there are always two.'

'At least. But all of them smiling at the wedding, eh?' He took my hand. 'Be easy. Everything will be fine. You have my word.'

'I'll hold you to that,' I said pleasantly, meeting his eyes.

He nodded and turned towards the hospital. I started across the square, relieved to get away, but when I was past the equestrian statue I glanced back over my shoulder and saw that he had stopped to look back too. We stood for a minute like that, turning the space between us into a mirror, watching each other.

As it happened, Mimi had come to lunch at Bertie's and was still there when I arrived.

'Adam,' Bertie said. 'You might have let me know. There's not a crumb left.'

'No, I've eaten.'

'How's Grace?' Mimi said, kissing my cheek.

'Flourishing.'

'So they say,' she said, her eyes almost twinkling. 'Have you met him?'

'Yes.'

'You're just dropping in, then?' Bertie said, slightly annoyed.

'Darling, don't be dense,' Mimi said. 'Too late for lunch, too early for a drink. He wants to chat. Which means I'll be in the way, so I'd better be going.' She turned to me. 'Maybe you can talk some sense into him. He's being pigheaded, as usual. Won't help with the ball. Won't even come. Pigheaded.'

'And you're being wicked,' Bertie said, pecking her on the cheek. 'A ball, during Lent.'

'Yes, and they're all dying for a break. Everyone'll come, you'll see.'

'Not everyone.'

'Hm. You and the Holy Father, fasting at home. It's too ridiculous. You know you're dying to come.'

Bertie smiled. 'It's a close-run thing. Very bad of you to tempt.'

'All right, I'm off.' She gathered up her purse and gloves, looking at me. 'So what's he like? I'm dying to know.'

'Who?'

'Who. Dr Kildare.'

'Oh, Gianni. He's too old for you,' I said, kissing her goodbye.

A throaty laugh, flirtatious. 'Bertie, I've been dis*missed*. He must have got that from you. That out-the-door charm. What if I got the monsignor to come? Would that make a difference?'

Bertie was walking her out of the room. 'Not even the pope. It's a matter of principle.'

'Darling, aren't you funny? How would you know?' She turned at the door. 'Don't bother, Elena's there. Adam, talk to him. He just wants coaxing.

When she was gone, Bertie came back to the coffee table and lit a cigarette.

'Two hours and I'm exhausted. I don't know how she does it – she must sleep the rest of the time. Now, what's on *your* mind? Barging in like this. Only happy thoughts, I hope.'

'Very happy. They think so, anyway. They're getting married.'

'Who?'

'My mother and Dr Kildare.'

'You're joking,' he said, putting down the cigarette, not just surprised but shaken.

'That's what I thought when he told me at lunch. But no. Death do us part. Surprised?'

For a minute he said nothing, just stared at the smoke drifting up.

'Marriage,' he said, still taking it in. 'The Magliones, any of those families – you know they don't marry out of—'

'Unless they've got a helluva repair bill to take care of.'

'What are you talking about?'

'Money. We can whisper if it bothers you.'

He glanced up, annoyed.

'Sit down and behave yourself. What's gotten into you?'

'You don't like it either,' I said, sinking on to the couch. 'I can tell just by looking at you.'

'I'm surprised, that's all.' He handed me the cigarette box. 'Here. Now let's take a breath and think a bit. This would come after Mimi – one's head just keeps buzzing. Why marriage?'

'They're in love.'

'Adam.'

'And there's her money.'

'Oh, I don't think so somehow.'

'But do you know? If he were American, I'd know a hundred things about him. All those clues people carry around. But here – how much does he have?'

'No idea. One doesn't, in Italy. I'm not sure why. In France you know right away. Of course, there is the palazzo, you know. He's not on the dole.'

'Which they never sell. Just try to keep up.'

'You've been reading things. Of course they sell. How do you think I got mine?' He watched me light my cigarette. 'That's better. Get some colour back. You can't stay shocked, you know.'

'But you were. Why? Don't you like him?'

'Like him?' he said, uncomfortable. 'He's my doctor. What does like have to do with it?'

'You invite him to your house.'

'He doesn't pee on the carpet, Adam. He's a Maglione. Anyway, we were all young together. Your mother, Gianni, his brother—'

'Cozy.'

He looked over his lunettes. 'Not like that. Grace adored your father. There was never any question of that.' He paused. 'Do you think all the time Gianni—? Hard to imagine him . . .' He drew on the cigarette, back on the Lido again.

'A long time to carry a torch, don't you think?'

'All these years,' he said to himself.

'What else?'

'*What* what else?'

'I don't know. Who he is, what he thinks about things.'

'How would I know? He had a wife who died – of natural causes,' he said with exaggeration, raising his eyebrows. 'He has a daughter, I think, whom I've never seen. An old name. As for what he thinks about things, I haven't the faintest. Why don't you ask him yourself? After all, he's going to be your stepfather, not mine.' He stopped, looking slightly embarrassed, not having meant to become snappish.

'Five minutes ago you were shocked – surprised,' I said quickly, catching his glance. 'Now you're throwing rice.'

'What exactly is it you expect me to do?'

'Talk to her.'

'Talk her out of it, you mean. No. In the first place, people never listen.'

'She'd listen to you.'

'No,' he said, shaking his head. 'I wouldn't even try. She'd never speak to me again. And she'd be right.'

'But it's possible it's the money, isn't it?'

He looked at me, not answering, then lit another cigarette.

'Anything's possible,' he said, then sighed. 'You know, it's possible she's in love with him.'

'Or something.'

'Well, call it whatever you like. I'm not shy. But she's happy. So what does it matter?'

'It will. When she realises.'

'Now I want you to listen to me,' he said. 'Very carefully.' He paused, waiting for me to look at him. 'If you have any sense, you're going to take your – *qualms*, and leave them right here in this room.' He patted the cushion next to him. 'Your mother has been lonely for years. And a grown son off fighting the war isn't much of a substitute – *which* you don't want to be, by the way. She comes here, not even sure why, and now she's in love, or infatuation, or whatever she's in. Happy for the first time in years. It doesn't really matter if he's in love with her or in love with her money. He obviously has *some* regard for her. The family name's important to a Maglione. You don't give it to someone if all you want is a bank loan. He'll give her a life and he'll make her happy, whatever his motivations are. And that's assuming he knows what they are. Do you know yours?'

'I don't want her to get hurt, that's all.'

'Well, very nice, if that's all. It rarely is, in my experience. But never mind. Just pack it up with whatever else is floating around up there,' he said, pointing to my head, 'and put it away. He'll never desert her, you know, not if she's Signora Maglione, and if he – well, everybody goes through a rough patch sooner or later. But you never know. And here's a chance and she's taking it.'

'Even if she breaks her heart doing it.'

'Oh, hearts. They can take a lot of wear and tear. Adam, don't meddle. She wants you to be pleased. Go home and tell her you're thrilled to death.'

I got up, walked over to the windows, and looked out at the loggia where you sat on warm days to watch the boats. A city so beautiful even the Germans agreed not to fight in it. What she'd have every day.

'It might be all right, you know,' Bertie said. 'It really might.'

I walked back to the couch. 'Will you do something for me? Find out what money he has. You can ask around. You know everybody.'

'Not his banker, I don't. And everything else is just gossip. Let's hope for the best, why don't we? Now smile. She'll be watching your face, to see how you're taking it.'

I made a face.

'Well, it's a start.' He giggled to himself. 'Mimi. Goodness, she'll be cross. Now there's a face I'd like to see.' He took off his glasses and rubbed his eyes, then looked at me. 'Adam, I'm right, you know.'

'So am I.'

'And if you are, what's the good of it?'

I said nothing.

'None at all,' he said quietly. 'Not for her.'

'Would you find out about the money anyway?'

'And if he's poor as a church mouse?'

'Then we'll know.'

'Yes, and you'd be right. And still wrong for her.' Bertie sighed. 'What a scourge children are.' He stood up. 'You'd better go. She'll be waiting to hear how lunch went. Smiles all around, right? Happy Families. It's done.'

CHAPTER FOUR

THINGS WENT WRONG with the party from the start. There were no flowers to be found, not even the scraggly winter asters you usually saw in the Rialto market. The weather had cleared and then turned sharply cold, the wind rushing up the Giudecca channel and through the window cracks until even the space heaters felt cool to the touch. One of the power cuts that plagued Italy that season hit in the afternoon, plunging the kitchen into gloom just as Angelina, sneezing with her permanent cold, was trying to arrange the canapés. After I spent an hour rounding up candles, the lights, perversely, sputtered back on, but since there was no guarantee they'd stay on, I spent the whole evening glancing up nervously, Noah waiting for rain.

My mother noticed none of it. Her skin glowed pink, part bath steam, part happiness, while everyone around her turned slowly blue and rubbed their hands by the ineffectual heaters. She looked wonderful – a new dress with a sequinned bolero jacket, hair up, every bit of her in place – and as I watched her move through the room, smiling, pecking cheeks, I thought for a minute that everything had to be all right. How could she be this happy otherwise? Gianni, next to her in a double-breasted grey suit, was smiling too, switching from English to Italian and back again, everybody's friend.

There were Venetians tonight, not just Bertie's set, and I had a glimpse of what my mother's world would be like now – Mimi winking over her martini glass, but also the formally polite white-haired woman holding out her hand for Gianni to kiss, proper as a doge. I wondered how long it could last; the romance of it, and then I looked at my mother's face, beaming, and thought, why not for ever? Wasn't it what everyone wanted? The fairy tale with no glass slipper.

On her bedroom dressing table I had noticed there were now two pictures, me on one side, in front of a jeep in Germany, and Gianni on the other, bareheaded in the cold on the Zattere. One more than before, not competing, not replacing, just one more. Why not be grateful he'd come along to fill the extra space? Why shouldn't we all be happy? Even the party, for all the cold and spotty electricity, was working now. Except that Claudia hadn't arrived.

'No, don't pick me up – I'll come by myself. You'll be busy,' she'd said, but where was she? 'I don't think we should walk in together.' Still reluctant. And now late.

I took another champagne from a passing tray.

'Who are you looking for?' Bertie said.

'Hello, Bertie. I thought you didn't go out during Lent.'

'I'll say my beads later. I couldn't miss this. You should have heard Mimi. Hissing like a puff adder. Oh, these ladies.'

'So she knows?'

'Everybody knows. Grace never kept a secret in her life. But do admit, have you ever seen her looking so well? Not in years.'

'Happy as a bride,' I said, taking a sip of champagne.

He looked over his glasses at me. 'And you, have you been smiling?'

'Non-stop,' I said, nodding. 'Seen the ring?'

'You haven't tried to bite it?'

I laughed. 'No, it's real. Family, apparently. His mother's.'

'Very nice,' Bertie said, then sighed. 'Oh dear. But she does *look* radiant, doesn't she? So where's the harm? Now what? Not speeches.'

There had been a tinkling against glass, the usual rippling *ssh*, people clustering. Gianni stood with my mother, waiting for quiet, then began speaking in Italian, presumably a welcoming toast, received with a few *ahs* and general approval. I just let it roll past me, that indistinct liquid sound of someone else's language, and looked again around the room. Where was she? He paused – were we supposed to applaud? – and then started to repeat the speech in English: thanks to us for being there, the reason no surprise to anyone who'd seen them together, the wonderful, unexpected thing that had come into his life, their double good fortune, of which this speech was an example, in being able to express joy twice, in Italian and English, the honour she had bestowed on him, their hope that all of us would be as happy as they were. All said nicely, charmingly, every note on key. More *ahs*, raised glasses, a public kiss, and, finally, applause.

'Well, it's done,' I said, raising my glass to Bertie. 'Cheers.'

'God bless.' He took a drink.

'Now what?'

'Kiss the bride,' he said, pointing to the group forming around my mother.

'They're not married yet.'

We were starting toward the other end of the room when Claudia came through the door. She looked slightly flushed, as if she'd run up the stairs, and the colour made her pretty, more striking than her muted blue dress intended.

'Hello, there's Claudia,' Bertie said, surprised. 'With whom, I wonder.'

'Me, actually,' I said, suddenly feeling awkward. He turned to me, eyes peering over his glasses, assessing.

'Really,' he said.

'We met at your party. You remember.'

'And now you've become friends.'

'Yes.'

He shook his head. 'What a family. The guests aren't safe with either of you. Next you'll be running off with the help.'

I smiled. 'Not yet. Excuse me,' I said, about to head for the door.

'Adam,' he said, stopping me, voice lower. 'You're not serious about this.'

'Bertie, some other time? She doesn't know anyone in the room.'

'Well, no, she wouldn't, would she?'

'What do you mean by that?'

'Oh, don't snap. I just meant it might not be suitable, bringing her here. What will Grace think?'

'She'll think we're friends.'

Bertie sighed. 'Never mind. It's always talking to a post, isn't it? Just have a care, that's all. You don't want things to get complicated. Rush into things.'

'Tell her,' I said, nodding towards my mother, still hugging people. Bertie followed my gaze.

'Well, Grace.' His face softened with fondness. 'She's not the type, is she, to look behind things? We'll have to keep an eye out for her. She was always like that, you know. Always wanted watching. So one does, somehow.' He turned back to me. 'But I can't take on two.'

Claudia was still near the door, looking tentative. When I finally pushed my way through the crowd, she smiled, relieved, then retreated again when I kissed her.

'Not here,' she said.

'It's all right, no one's looking.'

'But in public.'

'Come meet my mother.'

She touched her hair. 'Where is the ladies' room?'

'You look fine.'

'No, not for that. For the toilet.'

I laughed. 'Sorry. Downstairs. Come on, I'll show you.'

But before we could move out of the room, Mimi came over, martini glass in hand.

'Adam, there you are.' A cheek kiss. 'Are you making a speech too?'

'I'm saving it for the wedding.'

'Thank God for that,' she said, then looked expectantly at Claudia.

They nodded to each other as I introduced them.

'Where has Adam been hiding you? I *hope* he's bringing you to my ball. If he doesn't, I'll ask you myself,' she said to Claudia.

'Thank you,' Claudia said, not sure how to respond.

'Oh, purely selfish. *Try* finding anyone under forty these days. Though I must say,' she said, turning to me, 'Grace looks ten years younger. Ten years. I suppose that's love?' Her voice arched up.

'I suppose.'

'Maybe we should all try it. Except I have. Much good it did me.' She glanced again at Claudia. 'But how long have you—?'

'We met at Signor Howard's,' Claudia said, placing us.

'Bertie, the old cicerone. Lucky he didn't match you up with a priest,' she said to me. 'What can it mean, all the padres? In and out, all day long. What do they talk about?'

'What's new on the Rialto.'

'Just like – chums. Hard to imagine, isn't it? To me they still seem – I don't know, something you see on the bus, not anyone you'd ever meet. Of course, Marian says in Rome it's nothing but. Priests everywhere. But that's Rome. I'm sorry,' she said to Claudia, 'I hope I'm not—'

'No, no.'

'Thank God. I'm forever getting myself into trouble. You say the first thing that comes into your mind and then you see the faces. Not like you, darling. Always so careful.'

'Am I?'

'Grace says you're thrilled. I thought, really? Or is he just being his usual diplomatic self? Our own little nuncio.'

'Why shouldn't I be thrilled?'

'No reason in the world,' she said, a quick return. We looked at each other for a minute.

She turned to Claudia. 'You will come, won't you? To my ball? It's going to be very special, like the ones before the war. Modern dress – I hate period. Carnival's the worst. Those wigs, all itchy and hot. You wonder how they stood it. Oh, here she comes. Clever Grace.' A smile for my mother, making her way towards us.

'Excuse me,' Claudia said. 'A moment.' She slid away from us and darted down the stairs.

'Adam,' Mimi said, her voice low, no longer chirping, 'what's all this?'

'Ladies' room. She'll be back.'

'No, this.' She wagged her finger between me and the spot where Claudia had stood. 'The way she looks at you.'

'Does she?' I said, grinning.

'Don't gloat.' She looked at me and laughed.

Then my mother was there and Claudia was put aside. There was someone she wanted me to meet. Mimi wanted to know about the caviar, which you couldn't get in London now for love or money. Gianni knew a man who got it from Russia somehow. I smiled, thinking about the old Venetian trading routes, evidently still going strong. We had more champagne. My mother was happy. Where was Claudia?

I started down the stairs to check and stopped halfway, spotting her over the rail. There was no one else in the hall, and in the quiet she was standing at the water entrance, brooding, looking across the moldy landing stage to the canal. My mother had had the arched doorway opened and the steps lined with torches, in case anyone wanted to arrive by water, but no one had. Instead the lights flickered on the lonely utility boat we kept there and a jumble of paving stones covered with a tarp, once intended to repair the landing steps but abandoned by the marchesa until some money was found. In the cold, Claudia's breath steamed.

'Get lost?' I said, coming up to her.

'It's like a dungeon. So damp.'

'I know. Even at low tide the steps get covered now. Come on, you'll catch cold.'

'What did she say about me?'

'Mimi? She likes the way you look at me.'

76

'Oh yes? Well, it's the suit.' She reached out, smoothing my lapel.

'Ah,' I said, leaning over to kiss her.

'Wait. They'll see,' she said, glancing into the hall.

I reached over and closed the door. 'Better?'

We kissed for a few minutes, her hand at the back of my neck. Through the door we could hear the party going on, making it all somehow like sneaking kisses in a closet. Then after a while the sounds receded, as if we had left the house, and all we could hear was the slap of water against the landing stairs and our own breathing, loud in our ears, almost panting. The torches sputtered, making shadows.

'We don't have to stay.'

'No, how can we leave? They saw me.'

'We can take the boat.'

'Oh, yes. On the lagoon. In the night.'

'Just follow the channel markers,' I said, still kissing her.

She stopped, pushing me away and breathing deeply, then smiled. 'You're the one who wanted me to come.'

I leaned my face into her neck. 'I don't know what I was thinking. We'll stay here until the torches go. Look what they do to your skin,' I said, taking her chin and tilting her head so that her neck was caught in the light, golden. 'Bertie says you're complicated.'

'No, you,' she said, arching her neck as I kissed it. 'You make it complicated. I was happy in the hotel. Everything was simple. Now look.' She pulled away, smiling. 'We have to see Mama. Am I all right?' she said, touching her face. 'Smeared?'

I took out a handkerchief. 'Here, blot. Then you're perfect.'

'See if there's anyone out there. Think how it looks, coming out of the boat room.'

I laughed but peeked first, then motioned her forward to the stairs.

Either we had become accustomed to the torchlight or the electricity had finally come back at full strength, but the piano nobile seemed brighter than before, the big chandeliers blazing. My mother saw us over Gianni's shoulder and smiled, breaking away from the group.

'Darling, at last. I was wondering where—'

'Claudia, you know my mother. And this is Dr Maglione,' I said, but I saw that she knew him too. Her eyes went suddenly wide in recognition, then closed down, her whole face twisting. She glared at me, accusing, as if I had set a trap, then turned back to Gianni, breathing heavily, someone recovering from being kicked. The moment was one-sided. Gianni, smiling broadly, didn't know who she was.

'How nice you could come,' my mother said, playing hostess, but Claudia ignored her, moving closer to Gianni and speaking Italian, her voice low, her mouth still twisted in a kind of sneer.

Gianni stepped back, as if the words were a physical assault, and answered her in Italian, quick and sharp.

'*Assassino!*' she said, louder, and then '*Assassino!*' almost yelling.

People nearby turned. My mother, pale, looked at me frantically. But Gianni had started to talk again, so fast that the words went by me in a blur.

'You thought we were dead,' Claudia said in English. 'All of us dead. Who would know? But not all. Not all. *Assassino!*' she said again, this time quieter, with contempt.

I looked at her face – someone else, unrecognisable. Now it was Gianni who raised his voice, upset, caught somewhere between scolding and fighting back. The people around us had begun to look uneasy, the foreigners, not understanding, thinking they'd blundered into a scene of volatile Italians, the Italians embarrassed, shocked by what they were hearing. I tried to follow, helpless.

'*Assassino,*' Claudia said again, then, 'Murderer,' and for an odd second, hearing both words, I thought of Gianni's speech, two languages.

Gianni answered, then stepped forward to grab her elbow, clearly intending to take her out of the room. The touch, just a graze, triggered something in her. She wrenched herself away from his hand and reached up to his face, clawing at it, shouting at him again. He grabbed her wrists and pulled her away, leaving scratch marks on his face. I heard a gasp. He held her for a moment like that, hands up in the air, away from his face, letting her body wriggle but holding her hands still, until finally she spat at him and, shocked, he dropped her hands.

No one moved. I saw the spittle gleam on his cheek, the stunned faces around us, Claudia heaving, a hysterical intake of breath. She looked at me, her eyes filling with tears, and then around, aware for the first time of the rest of the room, the appalled guests. Gianni hadn't moved. '*Assassino*,' she whispered one last time. Then she let out a sound, a kind of whimper, and turned to the stairs. She started to run, the darting movement like a signal to everyone else to come back to life, out of the stopped moment, the room noisy all at once with talk.

'What in God's name—?'

'But what were they *saying*?'

My mother was daubing Gianni's face with a handkerchief. 'Adam, I don't understand. Your friend—'

'She's your friend?' Gianni said to me. 'She's a crazy woman.'

'My God, look at you,' my mother said. 'Does it hurt?'

'No, no.'

I looked towards the stairs, but the crowd had swallowed her up, cutting me off.

'It's a Jewish matter,' an Italian said, translating for another guest.

'What Jewish matter? Why Gianni?'

'Her father. It's a confusion.'

'Well, yes, it must be, I suppose.'

But what confusion? I looked at Gianni, now surrounded, then started pushing through the crowd. 'Adam,' I heard my mother say, but I was moving frantically now, down the stairs.

'Claudia!' I shouted, but when I got to the bottom no one was in the hall except one of the maids, standing in front of the makeshift cloakroom with Claudia's coat over her arm. She glanced at me, alarmed, then looked towards the open door. I raced down the hall and grabbed the coat.

Outside, there was no sign of her, just the dark back calles of Dorsoduro. But she wouldn't go to Salute, a dead end. I headed towards the Accademia, trying to pick up the sound of heels, anything, going faster at the corners, where there were little pools of light. At Foscarini I looked left, towards the Zattere. Then I saw a figure in the other direction, running past the Accademia to the vaporetto stop.

'Claudia!' I yelled, but she didn't even turn around, determined simply to get away. I ran towards the lights of the floating dock, the coat flapping in my arms. The boat was loading, almost done, but it was going in the wrong direction, up the canal, not down to San Marco and home. She'd wait for the right one. But she didn't. She looked over her shoulder and ran up the gangplank, the last one on before the crew pulled it back and caught the ropes. I could see her take a seat in the glassed-in section, hunching into herself.

Now what? She'd get off on the other side of the canal and head back. But the next stop was still on this side, not far, just past San Barnaba at Ca' Rezzonico. Impossible to outrun a boat, but the vaporettos were slow and lumbering, even slower in the dark, and this was the part of Venice I knew best, my sleepwalking streets. And what was the alternative? I ran to the end of the campo.

The calles here were fairly direct – no long detours to go around dead ends. I raced across the bridge over the Rio San Trovaso, heading to San Barnaba. No one was out, and my shoes echoed in the empty street, the sound of a chase, desperate, so that when I did pass one old woman she moved to the side, frightened, and I realised that what she saw was a thief running with a stolen coat. My lungs began to hurt a little, gulping in cold air, but it would be only minutes – all the time in the world later to catch my breath. Calle Toletta – shops closed, sealed off with grates. Another bridge, even a few steps now an effort. Finally the open space of San Barnaba, a yellow light slanting out of a bar window.

I swerved right and down the calle to the landing. The boat was already there, motor idling noisily as passengers got off. One of the ropes was tossed back. I was going to miss it again. No, one more passenger, a woman with a string bag, taking her time. I was running so fast now that if they pulled away I might actually hit the water, unable to stop. But here was the gangplank, clanging under my feet. I grabbed at a pole to break my momentum and took a few deep breaths. One of the uniformed boatmen said something to me in Italian, which I assumed meant there's always another boat.

She was huddled at the far end of one of the benches, looking out at the canal, so she didn't see me come into the passenger area, didn't even turn until she felt the coat on her shoulders. She started, then hunched back into herself.

'Go away, she said.

'Don't be silly. You'll freeze.' I sat next to her, draping the coat around her. The boat moved away from the dock. 'What the hell was that?' I said, still breathing heavily. The scene, pushed out of mind during the run, now came back in a blur.

'Go away,' she said again. 'That's who you want me to meet? People like that?'

'Like *what*? Why murderer? Who did he murder?'

'My father. With a nod of his head. "That one." A nod.'

'Gianni?'

'Gianni,' she repeated, drawing it out. 'Yes, Gianni. I saw him do it. *Him*. You didn't know? No, how would you know? You don't know anything, any of you. You come with your money – ah, Venice. Why? To look at pictures. So how would you know? A man like him. That's who your mother meets? A murderer. But that's all over, yes? Let's give a ball, like the old days. Ha. Did I ruin the party? No, have some champagne. Let's just go on like before. Such a nice man. A doctor. Who cares what he did?' All in a rush, snatching at the air for words, trying to keep up with herself.

'Stop it,' I said, taking her by the shoulders. Behind us a few passengers looked up, curious. A lovers' quarrel. A thief with a coat. Nothing was what it was.

She twisted away. 'Leave me alone. Go back to America. Take him. A souvenir of Venice. No one will know him there. Ha. He thought no one would know him here. We're supposed to be dead. And then one comes back. They say that, you know? When you least expect it. A party. And here comes death, pointing the finger. So that's me now. *Brava*. Oh, look at your face. You think I'm crazy. You don't know anything about it. For you it's all nice – kisses, La Fenice, Mama and her nice friend. Maybe it's better not to know. To be so lucky—'

'Stop it,' I said calmly, holding her still.

She shook my hand off and gathered her coat. 'I'm getting off.'

We had rounded the lower bend in the canal and were pulling into San Toma, the Rialto lights up ahead in the distance. I took her hand, holding it down.

'Sit. I want to know.'

'What?'

'What happened. Tell me about the nod.'

She looked at me, slightly puzzled.

'You said with a nod of his head. How?'

'In the hospital.'

'Your father was sick?'

'Yes, sick. Dying. But they didn't want to wait. Why wait for God when you are God? The Jews weren't dying fast enough for them.'

'Who?'

'Who. The Germans, their friends. They searched the hospitals. Sometimes there was an informer. Grini – you've heard of him? No. He used to help the SS. In the nursing home, even. They took them out on stretchers. But not this time. This time there was only your friend. He pointed out my father to them. 'That one,' he said, with the nod. 'Over there.' So the SS took him. You know how he knew? My father told me later. From medical school. They were both at medical school, so he knew him.'

'And you were there?'

She nodded.

'Did he point you out too?'

'No, I did. Myself. My father told them I was a neighbour, to protect me.' She paused. 'Not his daughter. A visitor. Maybe they believed him, I don't know. Maybe I could have walked out, hidden somewhere. But how could I do that? Just leave him? Sick. And they find you. In the end, always.'

'So you went with him.'

She nodded. 'And all for nothing. When we got there, they looked at him – who wants a sick Jew? Let the Germans take care of him. So, another train. And I said – imagine how foolish – I'll go too, someone has to take care of him. And they laughed. Don't worry, you'll go later. At that time the head would send only the hopeless cases. And the children. The Germans wanted everyone, but he kept the workers back. To save them, maybe to bargain later, I don't know. Later everyone went. Unless you were special.' She stopped, then looked up. 'So you see, it was for nothing. They just put him on another train. I always wondered, did he die on the train? He was so sick. He's on the list at Auschwitz, but maybe he was dead when he got there, who knows? Nobody can tell me for sure. Nobody came back, not from that train. No one. That's what *he* thought, none of us would come back. No one would know. But I know.'

We were passing under the high bridge, a dark space between the wavy lights on the water.

'And where do I see him? Meeting Mama. So I ruin her party. Oh, such behaviour. Terrible. And she's with a man like that. My God. She thinks she knows who he is. None of you know. What are you doing here, all of you?'

I said nothing, letting the words drift off, like vented steam. She lowered her head.

'You should go home.'

'No,' I said. 'Not now.'

She looked at me, then turned to the window. 'Oh, and that solves everything.'

'What do you want to solve?'

'Nothing. I don't know. Nobody pays, do they? In a few days, it'll be – gone. Gossip. "Poor man. I heard about that girl. She must have been crazy." And everything goes on. Nobody pays, not those people.'

'Yes, they do. In Germany people are starving. Everybody's paying.'

'You think it's the same? Hunger? No, they won't pay, not the murderers. That's how it is now. Everybody pays but the murderer. And here? Signora Mimi is planning a ball. And the murderer is going to marry a rich American.'

'No, he's not. You think I'd let that happen?'

'Because of this?' She shook her head. 'It won't make any difference. He'll explain. Some story. And she'll believe him. And even if she doesn't believe him, it's better to forget, no? Put it in the past. Easier.'

'You're not being fair.'

'I don't have to be fair. He pointed at my father. At me. You be fair.'

'He didn't point at you.'

'No,' she said quietly, 'I did.' She looked out the window, then back at me. 'So you can feel better when you see him at dinner. He didn't point at me. Just the sick old Jew.'

'I'm not going to see him at dinner,' I said evenly. 'Stop.'

'She'll thank you for that,' Claudia said, and then she did stop, folding back into herself again, staring out the window. We were almost at San Stae.

'We should go back. I'll take you home.'

'No, one more stop.'

'What's there?'

'My old house. I thought I would never go there again, but tonight I want to see it.' She turned to me. 'You want to see Venice? I'll give you a tour. Not the Accademia. This one.'

I said nothing, pulled along by her mood, unsure where she was going now. No one else got off at San Marcuola, so we were alone in the empty square, near a dark silent church and a few streetlamps. She asked for a cigarette.

'You know, my father would never allow it, a woman smoking in the streets. And here, so close.'

We started walking north into Cannaregio, gloomy long canals and workers' houses.

'He would have been ashamed. Imagine. Of this. Think of the rest of it, what it would have done to him.' Talking to the air, to herself.

We passed a shop with Hebrew lettering.

'This is the ghetto?'

'Almost. The edge. In the beginning you had to live on the island, where the campo is. It's easy in Venice to separate people. One island, three bridges. At night they put chains across, to keep everybody in. Except sometimes they let a doctor out, if a Christian was sick. My father used to say, no wonder the Jews liked medicine. It got them out of the ghetto.'

'But that was the Middle Ages.'

'Until Napoleon,' she said, playing tour guide. 'Then you could live anywhere. Of course, most people stayed here, nearby. It was what they were used to. You see the buildings at the end, how high? They ran out of space in the ghetto, so they had to build on top. Nowhere else do you see buildings like this – six stories, seven. So many stairs.'

We turned off the main street into the narrower Calle Farnese, where we were shielded even from moonlight, forced to rely on a corner light and a few slivers coming from the shuttered windows.

'Here,' she said, stopping about a block before the bridge. 'You see up there? Those windows? My aunt lived on the other side. My mother's sister. They used to talk across. Like cats, my father said.'

We stood there for a few minutes, looking at the house and seeing nothing – ordinary windows like all the others, a door flush with the street. Around us, a smell of canal debris and damp plaster. A cat ran past, then disappeared into a shadow. A drab back calle. But Claudia was seeing something else, her eyes fixed on the dark walls as if she were looking through them to the rooms inside, her own past. Family dinners. Homework. Radio. How different could it have been? Then the change – backdoor patients, unofficial. Curfews. Her aunt's window shut tight.

'What happened to her?'

'My mother? She died when I was eight. Oh, my aunt. In the roundup, the first one.'

'With the air-raid sirens.'

She looked at me. 'Yes, with the sirens. You remembered. You can see, in a street like this, how noisy it would be.' An alleyway, every shout an echo. 'Come, see the rest.'

She led me over the bridge on to the island and through a passage so low I had to duck my head. We came out into a larger campo with a well in the centre, an enclosed patch of faint moonlight entirely surrounded by the built-up houses, walled in.

'You see there, those windows, five in a row? That was the synagogue – out of sight, but a visitor could find it by the windows. Five, for the five books.'

I looked up, involuntarily counting the windows, then turned slowly, taking in the whole campo, dingy and peeling, a tree with spiky winter branches, not a hint of warmth anywhere, the coldest place I'd seen in Venice. It seemed utterly deserted, as if everyone had gone away, leaving a few lights on by accident.

'When was the round-up?'

'Oh, dates. All right,' she said, adopting a guide's voice, 'dates. You know Italy surrendered in forty-three? The king surrenders. September. Mussolini, he goes to Salò, and of course the Germans come in. So now, here, it's the occupation. New Jewish laws, much worse. Now we are enemy aliens. My family, here since Rome, now we're aliens. The broadcast was – when? End of November. I remember they came to Jona then for a list. He was head of the community, and the Germans asked him for a list of the Jews living here. Two thousand, I think. Everybody. A good man – my father knew him. What could he do? Yes, tomorrow, he told them, and that night he warned us. Then he killed himself. So he was the first. But now we knew – run, hide if you can. Like rats. You see over there?' She pointed north to a long grey building, prisonlike.

'The nursing home. They couldn't run. Some couldn't even move. So they were easy to arrest. You see, without the list it was harder, they had to take who they could find.'

'Like your aunt.'

'She wouldn't run. You have to imagine. Midnight, the sirens, people screaming, pounding on doors. She couldn't move, the fear was too strong.' She shrugged. 'So they took her. She scared herself to death.'

'But you hid from the Germans?'

'Germans? No, Italians. They used us to do it. Our own. Carabinieri, police, some Fascists. Maybe that's why they waited till it was dark – maybe they didn't want to be seen. Later it was SS. More efficient. With the police, it became a farce. They took everyone to Collegio Foscarini, but there were no facilities, nothing. So people came with food, they would throw food through the windows for the children. Ten days like that. A public embarrassment. So to Casa di Ricovero and they release the sick ones. They didn't understand – no one could be released. So the SS came and arrested them again. A farce. But finally, the train. After that it was mostly SS, with their informers. Grini. He would take them through the hospitals, even the mental hospital. It wasn't enough for them if you were crazy. You had to be dead.'

She folded her arms across her chest, hugging herself, rocking a little.

'You're cold.'

'Of course we didn't know they would go through the hospitals. We thought it was safe there. We were on the Lido then. Hiding, but not hiding. A vacation flat someone found for us, empty, you know. The neighbours pretended no one was there. We still had a little money. How much longer could it go on? It was just a matter of time, if we could wait it out. But then my father became too sick to stay there. He had a friend at the hospital, from the old days. He thought it would be all right. Use another name. Who would look in the critical wards? What for? They were already on their way to San Michele, almost dead.' She lowered her head. 'But they did look.' She stretched out one arm. '*That one.* Dr Maglione. You think I would forget that face? Never. And then tonight, one look and I was back in that ward. But this time, champagne. Everyone smiling. And I thought, he got away with it. They all did. They got away with murder.'

'Not all of them.'

She waved her hand, dismissing this. 'They'll never pay. Who's going to make them pay? You? Me? A scratch on the face. That's my revenge, a scratch. And for that, which one of us, do you think, will no longer be welcome in your mother's house?'

'It's my house too.'

'No, hers. What do you think, we're all going to be friends? If I saw him again, I would do it again. Spit and spit. I can't help it – I don't want to help it. I want to kill him.'

'No, you don't.'

She lowered her head. 'No. Then I would pay. So they always win.' She moved away, glancing up at the tall buildings. 'Look at this place. Who gets an eye for an eye? All dead. It's like a tomb now. I don't even know why I came.'

'To show me.'

'Yes, to show you. What they did.' We stood for a minute looking at the silent campo, peering into the dark passages as if we were waiting for whistles and the stamping of boots to break the stillness. 'You know what he said to me, my father? When they took him for the train? "God will never forgive them." But he was wrong. They'll forgive themselves.'

'Maybe not.'

'Oh, yes. It's one thing you learn in the camp, what they're like. Ask your doctor how he feels. Not even embarrassed. And then one night at a party somebody points a finger. You know what I'd like? To keep pointing – wherever he goes, all his parties, his hospital, just keep pointing at him until everyone knows.' She shrugged. 'Except what difference would it make? It's just what some crazy girl says. And who believes her?' She looked down. 'Who would believe her?'

'I would.'

She turned away, flustered. 'Yes? Why? Maybe she is crazy. Making scenes.'

I put my arm around her. 'Come on, we can't stay here all night.'

She glanced up at the buildings again, stalling. 'Look at it. No one left.'

'Maybe we should leave Venice. Go somewhere else. Rome.'

'Just like that.'

'Yes, why not?'

'And who pays? You?'

'It doesn't matter about the money.'

'And then one day you're gone and it does matter.'

'Why would I go?'

'Everybody goes.'

I held her by the shoulders. 'Not me. Don't you understand that?'

'No. Why? I don't understand why.'

'Why. You think there's a reason? Maybe that morning on the vaporetto. I don't know why. Maybe the way you scratched Gianni's face. I liked that.'

She smiled slightly and leaned her forehead against my chest, muffling her words. 'And that's your choice, someone like that?'

'Mm. Forget about this.' I waved towards the dark buildings.

'I can't.'

I nodded. 'I know. But let it go now, for a while. Come with me.'

She was quiet for a minute, close to me, then nodded.

'But not to Dorsoduro. You understand that? I'll never go there again.'

'Yes, you will. He won't be there.'

'Where have you been all night? I've been worried sick.'

My mother, still in her silk wrapper, was having coffee in the small sitting room, curled up in the club chair next to the electric fire. Her hair was loose, just brushed out, her face pale, with not even the usual morning dusting of powder. An ashtray with a burning cigarette was perched on the arm of the chair, the wisp of smoke rising to mix with the steam from her coffee.

'Although I can guess. Bertie said you've become friends with that girl. Really, Adam. She's obviously a neurotic – hadn't you *noticed*?'

'She's not a neurotic.'

'Well, call it whatever you like. She's obviously something. Have some coffee. What a spectacle. I mean, you like a party to have a little – but not *quite* that much. Gianni's been wonderful about it, but of course it's embarrassing. The worst part is that since she's your friend, he can't help but wonder – well, you know. Which is ridiculous. I said you looked as stunned as anybody. But you might give him a call. You know, talk to him a little. You don't want him to think—'

'Did he tell you why she did it?'

'Apparently she thinks he caused her father's death. Of course doctors have to deal with this all the time. You know, somebody dies in hospital and who's to blame? Anybody will do, really – doctor, nurse, anybody.'

'So he doesn't know who she is?'

'Doesn't have the faintest. She must have seen him at the hospital and – well, you know, when you're in that state.' She looked up. 'Adam, I hope you're putting an end to this. I'm sure the poor thing needs help and it's very sweet of you, but you don't have to be the one to do it. They have people for this. I mean, for all you know she could be deranged. Murdered her father. Really.'

'They were at medical school together.'

'Who?'

'Gianni and her father. He knows who she is.'

She was reaching for her cigarette but stopped, surprised by this. 'And he murdered her father, I suppose,' she said finally, sarcastic.

'No. He handed him over to the SS so they could murder him. They were rounding up Jews in the hospital. Her father was too sick to move. Gianni handed him over. So what does that make him, an accessory? In her eyes it comes to the same thing.'

'That's a terrible thing to say.'

'Especially when it's true.'

'Don't be ridiculous. Gianni wouldn't do such a thing. Is this what she's going around saying?'

'She was there. She saw him.'

'Well, darling, not exactly the most reliable source, considering.'

'Then ask him.'

'Of course I'm not going to ask him. Why would he do such a thing? What possible reason could he have?'

I shrugged. 'Maybe he was an anti-Semite, a collaborator. Maybe he was just a son of a bitch. He handed a sick man over to a death squad. What does it matter why?'

My mother looked at me for a second, then stubbed out her cigarette, taking her time, and gathered herself up out of the chair, balancing the cup over the ashtray.

'Adam, I want you to stop now. I won't have that tone. And I won't have any more of this. Last night was bad enough. You seem to forget it was my party, my evening that got spoiled. I didn't ask for the extra dramatics. So all right, let's put that behind us. Not your fault if she's . . . But now it's over. I won't have you saying these things about Gianni. I won't.'

'Not even if they're true?'

'They're not.'

'How do you know?'

'Because I know him. He's a wonderful man.'

'So was Goebbels, to his children. Before he poisoned them.'

'Is that supposed to be funny? Is it this girl? Have you lost all your sense? Is Gianni supposed to be a Nazi now? Maybe it's not her. Maybe something happened to you in Germany.'

'Yes, I met a lot of people like Gianni. Wonderful. And they didn't think twice about putting people in boxcars.'

'Adam, what is the matter with you?' she said, her voice finally distressed.

91

'The matter is you won't listen.'

'Not to this, I won't. Not any more. I'm going to have my bath.' She put down the cup and started to move away from the table. 'This isn't Germany, you know.'

'Why, because it's beautiful?'

She stopped and turned to face me. 'I don't know why you're doing this. Trying to ruin everything.'

'I'm not trying to ruin anything. I'm trying to help you. You almost married this man.'

She looked at me. 'I am marrying this man.'

'You can't. You can't marry someone like this. Are you that far gone?'

She tried to smile, her eyes moist. 'Yes, I'm that far gone.'

'Have you been listening at all? A man like this—'

'A man like what? Don't you think I know what kind of man he is?'

'No. I don't think you know him at all. You've just rushed into this like you rush into everything else. Except this time it might be harder to get out. Not to mention more expensive.'

'Oh,' she said with a small gasp, deflated. 'What a hateful thing to say.'

'I'm sorry,' I said quickly, seeing her eyes fill, but she waved me away.

'No one can hurt like a child.' She brushed her hair back, rallying. 'Is that what you think? Well, darling, I'm sorry to disappoint you. Or him, for that matter. But really, I'm not Doris Duke. Isn't it too bad? Of course I've told him that. But if you like, I'll tell him again. So he can be absolutely sure what he's getting. All right?'

'I didn't mean—'

'Yes, you did. You're full of meanness today, I'm not sure why. Maybe you don't want me to marry anyone.'

'I just don't want you to marry him. Neither would you, if you'd stop and listen for two minutes.'

'Oh, just him. But the thing is, darling, no one else has asked me.'

'Mother—'

'So we'll do this. I'll tell him again I'm not rich.'

'It's not about the—'

'And if he still wants to go ahead – just on the off chance that he'd like me for myself – will that make you feel better?' She stared at me for a second, then turned to the door. 'Good. Now can I have my bath?'

After she left, I just stood there, not knowing what to do. Follow her and keep arguing? For what? More tears and stubborn indifference, past listening. What Claudia had predicted; the last thing I'd expected.

I picked up the coffee, tepid now and slightly bitter, and finished it, then stood looking at the wall, the light from the water outside moving on it in irregular flashes, out of rhythm, jumpy.

He'd tell her some story. A hysterical response to a hospital death. Who would say otherwise? Were there hospital records? Another name, she'd said. Not even a paper trail. I walked over to the window. On the side table there was a new picture – not the jaunty Zattere one on the dressing table but Gianni in a more formal pose, seated at a desk, with papers in front of him for signing. I picked up the photograph and looked at his eyes, half expecting to find some peering intensity, visible evil. But of course it was only Gianni. How easy had it been for him to point Signor Grassini out? A struggle? Routine? Something he'd done before, in the habit of informing? There wouldn't have been only one.

I looked again at Gianni at his desk. Papers to sign. There was always paper somewhere. Almost without thinking, I slid the picture out of its frame and put it in my pocket. More reliable than memory, sometimes, the paper of a crime.

CHAPTER FIVE

I CAUGHT THE traghetto that crossed the Grand Canal to the
Gritti and then headed towards San Moise. A few days, Joe had
said – maybe he had already gone. But the Bauer still had a
Sullivan registered, and while I was using the house phone to call
him, I spotted him at breakfast in the dining room facing the rio.

'Late start?' I said, going up to the table.

'Late night. You just caught me. Sit, but don't expect too
much.' He rubbed his temples, wishing away the hangover.

'Thanks.' I took a cornetti from the bread basket in front of
him. 'Eat something. It helps.'

'Did I call you or did you call me?'

'I called you. I need a favour.'

'Too late. I go back to Verona at fourteen hundred.'

'That's where I need the favour.'

He raised his eyebrows over the coffee cup.

'Could you run a check on somebody? See what you've got
hiding in the files?'

'Italian?'

I took out the photograph.

'Isn't this the guy from the other day? You always run a check
on your friends?'

'He's not a friend.'

'Bad boy?'

'I think so.'

'What'd he do?'

'Cooperated with the SS rounding up Jews.'

'He wouldn't be the first. They insisted, you know.'

'I don't think it was like that. I think he helped.'

'Adam, for Chrissake, if I had a nickel for everybody who—'

'I know. Frau Schmidt telling on the neighbours. This is something else. He's a doctor. Old family. He had a choice.'

'Army?'

'No. Probably too old. Maybe too smart.'

'So?'

'So, what else? This stuff – it usually doesn't happen just once. You know. It's part of who you are.'

'Fascist?'

'Maybe, but not only that. I mean, what the hell, the mailman probably had a party card. Did he work with the Germans? What did he do? Sort of thing you might turn up in your files.'

'Might.' He looked again at the picture. 'You have a name?'

I took out a pen and started writing. 'He may have used another. That's why the picture – in case somebody might spot him.'

'Somebody like who?'

'Come on, Joe, we worked the same street. You must have somebody just looking at pictures to see what he can see. An old partisan, maybe. Somebody looking to get even.'

Joe took a sip of coffee. 'Is that what you're looking to do?'

I met his gaze over the cup. 'He wants to marry my mother.'

'Jesus, Adam, we're not a fucking reference bureau. If you don't like him—'

'He's a bad guy. I just want to know how bad.'

'Look, let me explain something to you. This isn't Frankfurt. The setup's different here. We're not trying to punish anybody. The Italians are supposed to be the victims, the good guys. We don't keep those kind of files on them. And the Italians, they don't want to know. They settle things privately. It's what they're good at. Since fucking Rome. Some Fascist prick set up a partisan ambush? They don't bother with a trial. They just stick him with a shiv some night and go about their business. You see Mussolini in the dock? Just strung him up at a gas station. They don't want us running trials here. They take care of their own.'

'So what are you doing here then?'

'German trials. The Germans want trials. Or maybe we want them to have them. Anyway, they do. And when the evidence is here, we have to come get it. Kesselring did a lot here before they transferred him back. Just wiped people out. So things get lost in Germany, we find something else here. It doesn't matter where he did it as long as he did it. It's the Germans we're after, not your mother's boyfriend.' He put the picture back on the table.

'So let's see, that means you've got the German army files – what they didn't take. They take much?'

'Some.'

'And you've probably got that cross-referenced with the Salò government files – liaison reports anyway. SS? Nobody kept files like they did, we know that. So what do we have? The army worked with Italians, so there'd be sheets on them there. Secret police reports, for sure. SS would have their own little black book of informers. Somebody like Gianni, they'd probably give him a file all his own, wouldn't they?'

Joe raised his eyes again. 'Yes.'

'In other words, the German files have got practically every-thing we want to know about the Italians, wouldn't you say? Except what they said to each other. And all I want to know is what he said to the Germans. What they had to say about him.'

'An Italian civilian? We're not here for that. They're our friends.'

'Yeah, well, so are the Germans now.'

'We're not supposed to use the files this way.'

'What are you talking about? That's *all* we did.'

'You're not in the army any more. And he's Italian. We're not supposed to—'

'Jesus Christ, Joe, the old man is lying there in a hospital bed and this guy fingers him. In a hospital bed. How much protection is he supposed to have?'

Joe said nothing for a minute, then pocketed the paper and photograph.

'All right. All I'm saying is, this isn't Frankfurt. We may not *have* anything.'

'If you don't, you don't. I'll bet you've got a Herr Kroger.' Our assistant, for whom the files were a series of live wires running from connection to connection, the whole a wonderful bright web in his brain.

'Soriano,' Joe said, nodding. 'Signora. Pretty good, too.'

'Put her on it. She'll know right away if it's worth a little sniffing. I don't want to tie you up with this.'

Joe grinned. 'No, just use my best snoop. You don't change.' He patted the pocket with the photograph. 'You really love this guy, huh? What if I come up dry?'

'There has to be something. A man who'd do that – it's never just once.'

'And you're sure he did?'

'There was an eyewitness.'

'And you're sure—'

'She was the old man's daughter.'

'Oh, she was,' Joe said, looking at me. 'Then she'd know.'

'Yes, she would,' I said, staring back.

Joe sighed and put his napkin on the table. 'Well, this was fun. Just like old times. You have a phone here?'

'On the paper. I'll come to Verona if—'

'No, you don't want to come anywhere near me. It's not Frankfurt, remember? Anyway, I'm not as much fun as I used to be. Can I ask you something? This guy, does he know that you know?'

I looked at him, surprised that this hadn't occurred to me, then nodded. Of course he knew. Claudia would have told me.

'Some fucking wedding,' Joe said.

*

I walked back, taking the wide swing over the Accademia bridge, then sat for a while in the Campo San Ivo. There was a shaft of sun in the square and some bundled-up old people sat on benches with their faces turned to it. At the end of the campo boats swept by on the Grand Canal. Where my mother had come to be happy. So special it seemed not just outside the war but outside time. But that had been another trick of the light, like the hypnotic movement of the water. Nowhere was outside. And now everything here would be Gianni, every detail a daily reminder. Gothic arched windows, flowerpots on terraces, the view from the Monaco lounge. She'd be miserable and, stubbornly, she'd refuse to go. The leaving itself could be easy. My mother had always lived a gypsy life of suitcases and short-term leases. A few days would do it. Bertie could deal with the house. Mimi could make the public excuses. And she'd be out of it. If she'd go.

I saw her face for a second as she'd turned from the door this morning, wounded. By me, every word a kind of betrayal. What would it look like now, knowing I'd asked for his file? But what was the alternative? If he'd lie about the hospital, what else would he lie about? What was the point of finding out later, when she was already trapped, crushed by the disappointment of it? The sooner, the better. She might listen to Bertie. A calm meeting, moving her gently from point to point until she saw. It was just a question of making her see.

I got up and started back to the house. We'd both apologise. We'd tiptoe around it. She'd ask what Claudia had actually said, what she'd seen. We'd talk.

But when I got to the house, she'd already gone out. 'A fitting, for the dress,' Angelina said. 'She left a message.'

I went over to the table and took the paper out of the silver dish. 'Don't forget to call Gianni,' it read, as if nothing had been said at all.

Claudia wasn't at the Accademia, so I walked towards the Rialto and then, on a whim, went to the library and spent a few hours leafing through a bound volume of *Il Gazzettino*. The first roundup had been in December '43, but Claudia hadn't been taken until later – autumn, after a few months hiding on the Lido. I started with July, piecing together bits of Italian until word blocks began to fall into place, the way menus become familiar. Gianni's name never came up. But why would it? Claudia wasn't there either, or Abramo Grassini. Not even the word *Ebreo*. No one had combed through the hospital, looking for victims. No one had been transported. August. Nothing had happened. La Serenissima had survived the occupation doing what it always had – entertaining visitors. The violinists in San Marco would have played waltzes. Not many photographs, only the occasional officer in grey in the background, taking coffee. September. The war was happening somewhere else, troops fighting in the south, only partisan bands in the Veneto. A train derailed near Verona, a munitions depot blown up – cowardly acts designed to thwart the Italian war effort (had the typographer set this with a straight face?), Communist-inspired, probably Milanese. The Communists, in fact, were behind everything, the real threat, more insidious than the advancing Allies or the protective Germans. The monsignor called for peace, an end to criminal acts. But even the partisans were somewhere else, at the other end of the bridge across the lagoon. In Venice, nothing happened.

I started to close the book, letting the pages fall on one another, backwards through the summer, and suddenly there he was, same face, receding hair. I stopped and flipped until I came back to the photograph. Not Gianni, the older brother. Gustavo Paolo Lorenzo, known as Paolo. Dead in the war, Gianni had said, but not exactly in the front lines, according to *Il Gazzettino*. A car accident near Asolo, where he was staying or living – my Italian wasn't nuanced enough to tell. Odd to think of any Venetian in a car, much less dying in one. Is that why Gianni had given him a better end? I looked at the photograph again – Gianni's eyes, spaced wide over the same high nose, a subtly different mouth, the whole look older, not quite as personable. Had they been close? I read through the obituary, looking for some sense of their lives together, but the article was respectful and dull. A long genealogy, a list of charitable associations, but evidently no profession. Only second sons had to think of it. The lucky older brother, who'd lived on what was left. An ordinary, conventional life. The only hint of flair had been a youthful enthusiasm for auto racing – and, the piece did not say but implied, look where that had led. No other passengers in the wreck. Mourned by his many friends and colleagues.

At four Claudia still wasn't back at the Accademia. 'She's not here,' a secretary said in Italian, and when I looked at my watch with a teasing raised eyebrow and said, 'Some lunch,' she said, 'No, she is no longer employed here.'

'Since when?' I said, but she pretended not to understand and shrugged, so I went back out to Calle Pisani and stood for a minute waiting, as if someone were going to come out and explain it to me. Why would she quit? Jobs were hard to get. For a panicked second I wondered if she'd gone to Rome after all, taking off like a startled bird, still surprised at herself. An afternoon train, a note pinned to the dressmaker's dummy. But that wasn't like her. I thought of her that first time at Bertie's party, as straightforward as her suit, and then with Gianni, her hands at his face. No strategic retreats, no notes. She'd be at home, looking out the window at San Isepo. She wouldn't have left. Not alone.

I started for the vaporetto, then stopped and headed back to my mother's to pick up some clothes. I had only a few things at Claudia's, and I wasn't just staying the night any more. Angelina surprised me with a message to call Joe Sullivan. I hadn't expected to hear back for days and I didn't want to take the time to call now – it could take up to an hour just to get through – but since Claudia didn't have a phone, there wasn't much choice. The phone had one of those elaborate receivers you saw in old movies and the sound was usually scratchy, but for once the lines were free.

'You rang a bell with Rosa,' he said.

'Who?'

'Signora Soriano. Herr Kroger.'

'Ah. What kind of bell?'

'She knew the name. Now she's running around trying to put things together. I wish you could see her. Fucking purring. Like a cat with a ball of yarn.'

'Knew his name how?'

'Company he kept. Not that that means anything. Lots of bad company in Italy these last few years. Hard to avoid.'

'And he didn't?'

'No, but it's hard to say. You ever hear of the Villa Raspelli?'

'No.'

'It's a kind of rest home over on Lake Garda. Some banker's house. They made it into a recovery centre for SS brass. Nice. Your man must have made a few house calls there. Rosa remembered the name.'

'He was an SS doctor?'

'Don't run away with yourself. He was a doctor. The patients were SS. How exactly that fits together, I don't know.'

'I can guess. What else has she got?'

'I didn't say she had anything. But if there *is*, she'll find it. Like I say, she's purring. It's a beautiful thing to watch. A few days, okay? She wants to give it to you personally, which means she wants a trip to Venice, but what the hell. If anybody deserves—'

'But why does she *think* there's anything?'

'I don't know. She just said Villa Raspelli and then went down the rabbit hole, the way she does. She finds anything, I'll have her call. This number always good?'

I looked at the phone, the only one I had access to. 'Yes.'

'Meanwhile, don't start packing for Nuremberg, okay? Sit tight.'

'Thanks, Joe. I owe you.'

'Not yet, you don't. I mean, he's a fucking doctor. Who else do you call when you're sick?'

'But they called him, Joe. Not anybody. Him.'

I heard nothing for a minute, just some breathing over the line.

'Why do you think that was?' I said.

Again silence, then a small sigh. 'Maybe he's good at what he does.'

'Uh-huh,' I said, turning my head towards the door, where my mother was standing, cheeks still red from outside. She gave me a tentative smile and crossed the room to the drinks tray.

'He speak Kraut?' Joe was saying.

'I don't know,' I said, distracted.

'That might explain it. Krauts like that, speak the language.'

'And if he doesn't?'

This time he didn't even bother to answer. 'I'll have her call. Soriano, don't forget.'

'I won't. Thanks, Joe.'

'Who's Joe?' my mother said as I hung up, her back to me, fixing a drink. At this distance she seemed small, her shoulders as narrow as a girl's. Who was Joe? An investigator. A rat chaser. Someone who knew about Gianni.

'An army buddy,' I said.

'In Venice? That's nice.'

'In Verona.'

'Still. Want one?' she said, turning. 'I know it's early, but the fitting was hell. Nobody ever says how exhausting it is, just standing. But wait till you see it – so pretty. It's got beads along here,' she said, drawing her hand along an imaginary neckline. 'Oh, but you don't care a bit, do you? Half the time you don't even notice what people have on. What's in the bag?' She nodded to the small satchel I'd packed with clothes. 'Moving out?' Her voice light, her eyes fixed on mine.

'No. Just a change.'

'Ah,' she said. We never talked about the nights away, the unused bed. I was simply 'out late'. 'Did you call Gianni?' Offhand, as if it were an afterthought.

'No.'

'Darling, I wish you would. It would mean so much to him.' She put down the drink and walked towards me. 'Think what it's like for him.'

'What what's like?'

She sighed. 'Well, you, I suppose. I wish I knew why you've taken—'

'Then listen to me. Please. It's important.'

'We've had this conversation, I think, haven't we?'

'Then let's have it again.'

'Adam, I don't care what happened a long time ago—'

'A year, year and a half.'

'I know him now.'

'You think you do. People don't change.'

She looked up at me, her eyes softer. 'You don't, anyway. So stubborn. What a stubborn little boy you were. Always going to set things right. Always so sure. Even in the sandbox.'

'What sandbox? You never took me to a sandbox.'

She smiled. 'Well, how would you know? Anyway, I remember *seeing* you in a sandbox. I suppose some child had taken a toy or something, I don't know. And there you were on your high horse, all three feet of you. Pointing. "It's not fair, it's not fair!" just outraged.'

'Well, it probably wasn't fair,' I said, smiling a little now too.

'Probably,' she said. She reached up and brushed the hair back from my forehead. 'But you're not a little boy any more. And nothing is fair. Nothing in this world. There's only – getting along.'

I took her hand, moving it down from my hair.

'We're not talking about something that happened in a sand-box,' I said. 'People died.'

'Because of him. You think that.'

'Yes.'

She put her hands on my upper arms. 'Then talk to him. Let him explain.'

'Mother—'

'Come to dinner.'

I looked at her, disconcerted. A social occasion, to iron out the wrinkles.

'No,' I said, pulling away, then stopped, caught by the hurt expression in her eyes. 'Anyway, I can't,' I said.

'Yes, I forgot,' she said, nodding to the bag. 'Tomorrow, perhaps.' A hostess taking in a polite excuse.

'No, not tomorrow either.'

'Really, Adam,' she said with a nervous giggle. 'He'll think—'

I looked at her, not saying anything.

'We can't go on this way,' she said. 'It's important. To sit down at a table together.'

'Like a family.'

'Yes, like a family. You know, you're all I have,' she said quietly. Then she turned away, her voice changing, back to Neverland again. 'Well, another day. Goodness, look at the time. I'd better run a bath. You won't be too late tonight, will you, darling?' Ignoring the satchel.

'Not too late,' I said, ignoring it too.

It was dark by the time I got to Claudia's, and she was in fact staring out at San Isepo, just as I'd imagined.

'You'll go blind,' I said, flicking on the light. 'Everything okay?' I put the satchel near the bed.

She said nothing, smoking and staring out the window.

'I went by the Accademia. They said you'd left. Quit.'

'No, dismissed,' she said after another minute's silence. 'In the fire. Isn't that right?'

'Fired,' I said automatically. 'What happened?'

'My services are no longer required. Signora Ricci told me. The director didn't bother coming down. He had Signora Ricci do it.'

'But why?'

'Why do you think? A word in the ear. It's so different in America?'

'Whose ear?'

'The director's, I suppose. Anyway, someone's. So now it's begun. But so quick.'

'Now what's begun?'

104

'To get rid of me. Now that I've exposed him, what else can he do? Kill me, like my father? He'd like that, but now it's not legal.'

'You think Gianni had you fired?'

'I know it.'

'I'll talk to him,' I said, angry.

'No, it doesn't work that way. He won't know anything about it. No one will. But I'll be gone.'

'Then how do you know it was him?'

'I saw his face.'

'When?'

She turned away from the window and put out the cigarette. 'I'm embarrassed to tell you. It was – I don't know, just something I did. Not thinking. I just went.'

'Where?'

'To the hospital. Signora Ricci told me to leave and I *knew*. Not the end of the week, leave today. I knew what it meant. Who else would do this? Make me go away, that's what he wants now. No more – incidents. I thought, he can do this, make trouble for me just by picking up the phone. But I can make trouble for him too – I know what he did. So I went there, all the way to Campo Zanipolo, and then I thought, what am I doing? I'm going to run into the hospital? They'll think he's right, a crazy. But what do you do? Take your purse from the desk and thank Signora Ricci and just disappear? That's what he wants.'

'So what did you do?'

'Nothing. I just stood there, by Colleoni on his horse. I didn't know. Go? Stay? What? And then he came out. Not alone. With two others, out of the hospital. And they cross the campo – talking, you know – and suddenly he comes near and he stops. It was all there, in his face – no surprise, he knew why I was there, expecting it even, and you know what else? A fear. He was afraid. That I was waiting there for him. I wasn't. Another two minutes and I would have been gone. But he didn't know that. Remember I said how I should do that, just be there, at his parties, everywhere? He thought I *was*.'

'What did you say?'

'Nothing. I just looked at him. And him? Nothing, just a look. But it was there, in his face. And the others, the men with him, they don't understand it at all. Why he's staring at this woman by Colleoni. Who doesn't say anything to him either, just a look. And when they start again, I hear one of them say, 'Who was that?' And he says, 'Nobody.' And one of them turns back to look and I could see he's thinking, So why did he stop? But how can Maglione explain it? So it's the beginning. He wants me dead. Gone, anyway. I saw it there, in his face.'

'In one look?' I said, trying to coax her out of it.

'Yes, one look. I know. I've seen it before.'

'Maybe you're overreacting,' I said gently.

'No, the same. You know how I know? Because it frightened me. The way it always did. Like a knife at your throat – so close, when? So now he's afraid of me, just the sight of me, and I'm afraid of him. We know each other. Maybe it would have been better if I'd never found him. Now how does it end?'

I went over to her. 'You go away and live happily ever after.'

'Ha. Leave. So he wins.'

'No, you do. Just forget about him. Look what it does to you, just passing him in the street. You're all—'

'What?'

'Nerves.'

She shrugged. 'No, I'm better now.' She looked out the window again. 'And how is he, I wonder?'

'Claudia—'

'I know. Forget it. All right – forgotten.' She brushed the air with her hand. 'But I'm still out of work. No job. Nothing.'

'Don't worry about it,' I said, coming nearer. 'I'll take care of you.'

'Like a whore.'

'No,' I said, turning her around, lifting her chin with my finger to make her smile. 'Like a mistress.'

'Oh, there's a difference.'

'Mm. More expensive.'

A small smile. 'Yes? How much?' she said, playing back.

I kissed her. 'Whatever it takes.'

'Any price – how nice for me,' she said.

'How about dinner at the Danieli?'

She pulled back, smiling. 'So that's my price? A dinner at the Danieli.'

'Why not? You don't get fired every day.'

In the end we settled for a drink at the Danieli. The big gothic dining room was almost deserted, quiet as a church, waiting for tourists and spring. Waiters stood near the wall gazing towards the lobby. The few diners spoke in whispers. Nobody was celebrating anything. We had a Prosecco in the bar and slipped back out to the Riva.

The moon was out and the air was sharp. We held hands going over the bridge to San Marco, still happy to be out of the hushed dining room.

'I'll talk to Bertie,' I said. 'Maybe he can do something.'

'No. Anyway, I don't want to go back there.'

'Where, then?'

We were strolling past the empty cafés.

'I don't know. Maybe I'll go to Murano and make glass. Maybe Quadri's,' she said, pointing to the frosted windows. 'Somebody must do the dishes.'

'Not tonight,' I said, looking in. An old woman in a fur coat, nursing a drink. Two men at the bar.

We went under the arcade and out of San Marco, past the back basin where the gondolas tied up. Guido's was a small restaurant, cozy in the winter, with windows overlooking the Rio Fuseri and a long antipasto table filling the far end of the room. In the summer it would be filled with foreigners, sent by the big hotels with walking maps, but now it was only half full, romantic with shaded lamps and a pleasant murmuring of Italian.

Claudia saw them first. I was handing the coats to a waiter near the door, the eager maître d' hovering nearby, and felt her grab my arm. Gianni's back was to us, so it was my mother who looked up, startled for a second, then smiled.

'Darling, what a surprise. Look, Gianni, it's Adam.' She stopped, finally taking in Claudia, her eyes darting nervously to the rest of the room, uneasy. 'I wish I'd known,' she said in her social voice. She motioned her hand over the table, only big enough for two. 'But maybe they can move one.'

Gianni turned in his seat, then got up slowly, hesitant, not sure how to react. It was, as Claudia had said, a kind of fear. But of what? An awkward moment in a restaurant? Her face had hardened, and she was glaring at him. For a few seconds nobody moved, not even the maître d', waiting to see how we wanted to be seated.

'Adam,' Gianni said. 'You brought her here? Why do you do this?' Annoyed, but keeping his voice even so that no one around us heard anything unusual in it. He looked at Claudia. 'What do you want?' he said, almost pleading, exasperated.

'From you, nothing.' She turned, gripping my arm more tightly. 'Let's go.'

'Darling,' my mother said, drawing it out so that it was like a hand reaching over, insistent. She looked around the room again, then at me, a signal to behave. 'It's no trouble. About the table.'

Now her voice reached Gianni, stopping the unguarded look on his face and bringing him back too. He stared at Claudia for another second and then nodded to my mother, trying to please her, or deciding that the only way to deal with the situation was to pretend it wasn't happening.

'Yes, join us,' he said, a little unsteady, still not sure, but gesturing graciously to the table 'I can recommend the polenta. If you like that.' Now even a polite, forced smile.

'With you, never,' Claudia said, her voice low.

Nearby the maître d' waited. Gianni looked around. No one was paying attention. We were still just a group of foreigners saying hello.

'But perhaps you would rather be alone with your friend,' he said to me.

'Oh darling, this would be such a chance to talk things out,' my mother started, then stopped, caught by Gianni's sharp glance, the first time I had ever seen him look at her that way.

'Grace,' he said, cutting her off.

'Is that what you want?' I said. 'To talk about things? Old times?'

Before he could answer, Claudia said something in Italian, her voice still low but edgy, even the sound of it unpleasant. Gianni's face clouded. The couple at the next table looked up.

'Adam, don't,' my mother said. 'Please.'

'She lost her job today,' I said to her, then looked again at Gianni. 'Want to talk about getting it back?'

'Why Gianni?' my mother said. 'What *are* you talking about?'

'Tell her,' I said to Gianni.

Claudia said something more in Italian, rapid-fire, too fast to catch. Gianni's face darkened again.

'Enough,' he said in English. 'First the father, now your job. Everything that goes wrong in your life you blame on me? Why?'

'You made the call, didn't you?' I said. 'Tell her.' I nodded to my mother, then put my hand on Claudia's back, ready to go.

'Listen to me,' Gianni said before I could turn, almost in an undertone, just English to the rest of the room. 'We are almost finished. We will take our coffee elsewhere. Sit over there with your friend. In a few minutes we'll be gone. No scenes.'

'Do you think I would stay in the same room with you?' Claudia said to him in English.

'I am sorry for your confusion,' he said deliberately. 'A misunderstanding. Some other time we will discuss it.'

'Darling, do please stop,' my mother said. 'I don't know what this is all about. Gianni doesn't even know her. I told you.'

'Is that right?' Claudia said to him. 'You don't remember me? Shall I describe it for her?'

'Adam, you can see what she's like,' Gianni said. 'Take another table. People are beginning to look.'

'You don't remember her?' I said.

109

'Go to the table,' he said in a hard whisper.

'That's right. You forget things. You don't remember her father either, your friend from med school. Do you remember the Villa Raspelli? Your friends there? I found somebody today who remembers you.'

'Adam, really . . .' my mother said, but the rest of it faded, only a sound in the background, because at that instant I saw Gianni's face shift. Not just a scowl, a narrowing of the eyes, but a look of such pure hatred that for a second I couldn't breathe, trapped in it, the way a victim must feel just at the end. He wanted me dead. In that one look I saw that everything Claudia had said was true, that he was capable of it. What I hadn't seen in the photographs or behind the smiles over a lunch table: the eyes of someone who could kill. Steadily, without hesitation, just getting something out of the way. And then it was gone – the eyes blinked, adjusting themselves.

'I remember the Villa Raspelli,' he said, staring at me, then shifted again and bowed, an elaborate courtesy. 'I'm sorry you can't join us. Perhaps another time.' He sat down, turning his back to us. The effect was to make people look at us, wondering why we were still standing there.

'Oh, Adam,' my mother said quietly, dismayed.

'Ask him about it over coffee,' I said to her. 'Since he remembers.'

'Sit down,' she said, almost hissing.

'No, we're leaving,' I said, turning to the puzzled maître d' for our coats.

'You don't want a table?' the maître d' said, flustered, sensing a moment gone wrong.

I shook my head. 'I'm sorry,' I said, taking the coats. 'Tomorrow.'

Since this made no sense to him, he just stood there watching us go. Everyone watched, in fact, except Gianni.

In the street I gulped some air, then helped Claudia into her coat and pulled up the collar. Guido's had an antique lantern over

110

the door, and we stood in its light for a minute, breathing streams of vapour in the cold air.

'Never mind,' I said. 'There's another place near La Fenice.'

'He thinks I'm following him,' Claudia said.

But it was Gianni who followed us, suddenly opening the door, coatless, and stepping into the lantern light.

'Who told you about Villa Raspelli?' he said.

'What does it matter who? Why don't you tell me about it?'

'You think you know something. You don't know anything.'

'But I'll find out.'

'More fairy tales,' he said, looking at Claudia. 'Why do you stay in Venice? With your bad memories. Or you,' he said to me. 'Go home. You are making trouble here for no reason. Go and live your own life. Leave us in peace.'

'You sent me away once,' Claudia said. 'Do you think you can do that again?'

'Me? I don't send anyone.'

'But you could arrange it. Like that,' Claudia said, snapping her fingers.

'Yes, like that,' Gianni said, nodding, a kind of threat. 'Easy.'

'Not so easy this time. This time we don't go like sheep. We know.'

'More melodrama. Why do you listen to her? Such a scene.'

'Is that what you came out here for? To tell us to leave town?'

He looked at me steadily, then sighed. 'No, for your mother. To make peace.'

'Peace.'

'I'm a patient man, but not a saint. She wants that, but you – what do you want? I wish I knew. Not peace. To make trouble maybe between us. So I will tell you something. You will not stop this marriage. You will make your mother unhappy, but you will not stop it. Do you think I would let these stories get in the way of that? She will leave Venice,' he said, indicating Claudia. 'So will you. And your mother and I will live here. If you have sense, you will go back and sit and talk to her. Apologise for making a scene.'

111

He looked at Claudia. 'You, I don't care what happens to you. I'm sorry for your trouble, but now it's enough craziness. Leave me alone. Go away.'

'Where would I go? To Fossoli again? You didn't think anyone would come back. But one did.'

He looked at her, cool, absolutely calm, then turned to me. 'Don't do this again. It upsets your mother.'

'Tell her about Villa Raspelli. Then see how she feels.'

'And what would I tell her? I was a doctor doing his duty.' He narrowed his eyes in the same menacing stare I'd seen in the restaurant. 'You think you know. You don't. But you will not stop this marriage.'

He brought his hands up to straighten his tie, and I watched, fixated, as he tightened the silk. Large, square hands, a sharp pull on the fabric. For an instant, oddly, I saw my mother's soft throat in the Monaco lounge, imagined him putting his hands around it. Not in violence, not some improbable tabloid crime, but strangling the life out of her, choking her spirit bit by bit until only a gasp was left. He looked at me, with his hard eyes, and I realised he was capable of this too, a different killing. With no one around to interfere.

He glanced back through the glass of the door. 'Your mother is waiting.'

'What will you tell her?'

'That you are embarrassed and she is mad,' he said, glancing towards Claudia. 'The truth.'

'The truth,' Claudia said. 'The truth is that you sent me to die. Sent me to be a whore.'

He patted his tie, then looked at her, weary. 'No. That's something you did yourself.'

CHAPTER SIX

BERTIE REFUSED TO help at the Accademia.

'You overestimate my influence. I couldn't. Not now. Anyway, I wouldn't. She may be the most wonderful thing since sliced bread, but she's been terrible for you. Just look at this mess – Grace all weepy and Gianni snorting around like a wounded bull. And for what? Some whim of yours.'

'She's telling the truth.'

'I don't know that. And neither do you. You're just thinking with your pants. It's one thing in the army, that's all anyone thinks about, but you're not in barracks any more. So much for a civilising influence.' He waved his hand towards the city outside his long windows. 'And if you ask me, the sooner you get yourself out of her clutches, the better.'

'Her clutches.'

'Her charm, then. I must say, she's the most unlikely siren,' he said, pronouncing it *sireen* for effect. 'Still.'

'He put her in a camp, Bertie. Her father died.'

'He did. Himself.'

'Don't split hairs.'

'Rather important hairs, don't you think?'

'Not if he'd done it to you.'

'Oh, Adam, first he's after Grace's money, now he's working with the SS. Does he look like SS to you? This is all mischief.'

'Why does everyone want to protect him?'

Bertie peered at me over his glasses. 'Nobody's protecting anybody. Nobody's proven anything, either.'

'I will.'

'How, may I ask?'

'I still have friends in the army.'

'Meaning?'

'Meaning they like to know who kept company with the Germans. They keep lists. Testimony.'

Bertie looked at me for another minute, his face slack with surprise. He got up and walked over to the window. 'Well, isn't that lovely? What do you intend to do, put him on trial?'

'He didn't do anything, according to you.'

'Never mind according to me. Keep me out of it. I can tell you now that nothing's going to come of it but tears and more tears. Adam, for heaven's sake, let them be. They're going to marry, whether you like it or not, so let them get *on* with it.'

'You don't think I'd let him marry her.'

'Well, as you keep failing to grasp, he didn't ask you and you haven't accepted. The invitations are out, you know.'

'Help me, Bertie. She's your friend.'

He sighed and opened the window to his balcony. Outside, the winter sun was bright on the Grand Canal, noisy with boats.

'What does she say about all this?'

'Nothing. She refuses to talk about it. She spends all day getting her dress fitted.'

'So I heard.'

'What?'

'Mimi. She's in a perfect snit about it. The dressmaker. None of her friends can get a look-in and there's the ball coming up.' He turned and smiled at me. 'I know, all very silly. And here you are, still fighting the good fight.' He opened the window wider. 'Oh, how I wish you'd go.'

114

'That's what Gianni said. He can't wait to get me out either.'

'Not just you. All of you. Even Grace. She's a darling, but look at her now. Everything all *fraught*. You make everything so messy, all of you. I hate it.'

'No, you don't. You love it.'

'Oh, for five minutes' gossip? You think so? I don't, really. I'm selfish. I suppose it's wrong, but I can't help it now. Look at that,' he said, waving at the view down the canal. 'Did you ever see anything so beautiful? The first time I came here, I knew it was all I wanted in my life. To see this every day, just be part of it. And then you all come charging in, making messes right and left. In a way I think I preferred it during the war. Nobody came.'

'Except the Germans.'

'Well, yes. All right. The Germans,' he said, the phrase taking in more. 'And now you want to bring it all back. God knows why.'

'Things happened here, Bertie. You can't make them go away just because they spoil the view.'

'That's where you're wrong. They will go away. Nobody wants to live with them, over and over. Why do you? They did this and they did that – you don't even know who they are, you just know who you want it to be. I don't like this, Adam, any of it. I don't like what you're doing. Neither will you, in the end. Ach.' He stopped, out of steam, and closed the window, his eyes glancing over to see how I was reacting.

'Will you talk to her?' I said calmly.

'Oh, and say what? "You might reconsider, darling. Your son thinks he's Himmler."'

'She'll listen to you.'

'You keep saying. I don't want to be listened to. I want to be left alone.'

'With your view.'

'Yes, with my view.' He came over to the coffee table and lit a cigarette. 'All right. All right. Getting married. You'd think once would be enough for anybody.'

'They'll find it, Bertie. Evidence. It's there somewhere.'

He looked at me. 'Let's hope not.'

The next day Claudia's landlady asked her to leave. An official from the housing authority had come to inspect. There had been reports of immoral behaviour.

'That's you,' Claudia said with a wry, fatalistic smile. 'You're the immoral behaviour.'

'He can't do this.'

She shrugged. 'Venice is famous for denunciations. You can still see some of the boxes where they put the notes. For the doges.'

'Five hundred years ago.'

'Well, for me, this week.'

'She can't just put you out.'

'She was frightened – an official coming here. So I have till the end of the week. At least it's better than the Accademia, not the same day. He asked if she'd seen my residency permit. So they're going to make trouble about that.'

'Don't you have one?'

'Everything was taken at Fossoli.'

'So get another. You were born here. They'll have records.'

'Yes. In the end, I'll get it. But meanwhile . . .' She opened her hand to show the weeks drifting by.

'He's not going to get away with this. Stay here. I'll be back.'

She touched my arm. 'I'll go with you.'

'Not this time. My mother wants us to talk, so we'll talk.'

I zigzagged my way past the Arsenale and through the back-streets of Castello towards the hospital. Over the bridge at San Lorenzo to the Questura side, where a few policemen were loiter-ing in the sun with cigarettes, not yet ready for their desks inside. Did it only take one call here too? Maybe the policeman we'd met at Harry's, ready to do a favour. San Zanipolo and its dull red brick, then the vaulted reception room of the hospital, following the guard's directions down the stone corridor to the doctors' offices. Not running, but walking so fast that people noticed, thought maybe I was hurrying to a deathbed. I brushed past the nurse in the outer office and opened the door without knocking. Gianni was sitting behind the desk in a white coat, his pen stopping halfway across a form when he saw me.

'I want you to leave her alone,' I said.

The nurse rushed up behind, flustered. '*Dottore*—' she started, but Gianni waved her away, gesturing for me to sit.

'What have I done now?' he said.

'Scaring the landlady. Is that your idea of a joke? Charging Claudia with immoral behaviour.'

'I don't doubt it,' he said. 'A woman like that doesn't change. I made enquiries about her, after the party. When she made such a spectacle of herself. I thought maybe she was deranged.'

'She's not deranged.'

'No, a whore. Do you know what she was at Fossoli?'

'Where you sent her.'

'Do you know what she was? Did she tell you?'

'Yes.'

'Yes, the camp mistress. This is the woman you bring to your mother's house.'

'She was forced.'

'No one forces a woman to be a whore. A man like that, at the camp, do you think he would have kept her if she didn't please him? No one had to force her.'

'You really are a son of a bitch, aren't you?' I said quietly.

'Oh, now names. I try to help you, show you what she is, and you call me names.'

'Just call off the dogs, Gianni. The police or the housing authority or whoever the hell you called this time.'

'For your information, I didn't call anyone. Another of her fantasies.'

'Who else would have done it, Gianni? Who else?'

'A landlord finds a new tenant, he gets rid of the old one. It happens all the time.'

117

'Leave her alone.'

'I see. She scratches my face in public. Waits outside the hospital, like a beggar. Makes scenes in restaurants. But I am bothering her.'

'Just call them off. She's not leaving Venice.'

'She has no permit.'

I smiled grimly at the slip. 'Something you just happened to know?'

He glanced away. 'I told you, I made inquiries. It's not for me to decide. It's a legal matter.'

'Not if I marry her,' I said, not even thinking, just returning the ball.

He looked up at me, genuinely shocked. 'You can't marry her.'

'Why not? My mother's marrying you.'

'A woman like that? It would be a disgrace. Think of your mother. It's impossible.'

'What a piece of work you are,' I said slowly. 'You send her father to die. She ends up in the camp, raped, and now she's a disgrace, not fit to enter your house. You did it and she pays? Not any more. I don't know how you live with yourself.'

He stared down at the papers, not saying anything.

'Always her father with you. Over and over. You think you know,' he finally said.

'What don't I know?'

He pursed his lips, then turned and stopped, turning back, a kind of physical indecision.

'You still see his room on your rounds?'

'Lower your voice,' he said, darting his eyes towards the anteroom.

'I don't care who hears. You got away with it, you can live with it.'

He put his hands on the desk, as if he were stopping his body from moving, coming to an end.

'Yes, I live with it. You want to know? That day?'

'I thought it never happened.'

'Come.'

He took his coat from the rack and started out, not bothering to see whether I was following. There was some quick Italian to the nurse, who nodded uneasily at me, and we were in the hall.

'Where are we going?' I said.

'Out of here. I will tell you something that never happened.'

Outside, he turned right on the Fondamenta dei Mendicanti and began walking along the canal, then stopped, as if he had changed his mind.

'An ambulance. Wait.'

Orderlies were carrying a stretcher off the boat, stepping carefully from the deck to the receiving room door. Gianni went over and asked them something, presumably whether he was needed. I stood looking at the boat, waiting. Everything by water, even the sick. Claudia's father must have come this way, on a boat from the Lido. She would have stood here, watching as they carried him in.

'Another one for San Michele,' Gianni said.

'Dead?'

'Almost. Some morphine, that's all you can do now. Pray, if you believe that. Then San Michele.' He started walking again, shoving his hands into his coat pockets. 'Do you know how many dead I've seen? When I was young, I thought I would be helping people, making them better. You know, the nice doctor with the cough medicine, the way a child sees it. That's what I thought it would be, medicine, but no. Death. Seeing it happen, waiting for it. I've spent my whole life in this building,' he said, motioning with his head towards the long brick wall. 'I know when someone is going to die. What are we supposed to do? We help even when we know it won't help. We don't kill them. We don't make that decision. God does, if you believe that. Maybe it's just the cells, giving up. But not you, not if you're a doctor. I never wanted to kill people, I wanted to save them. And then sometimes you have to make a choice.'

'What choice?' I said quietly. We were walking slowly now, almost in time with the waves of the canal hitting the stone walls.

119

'I said I would tell you something that never happened. Now, this once. And then I didn't tell you. It never happened, we never talked of it. If you say we did, I will deny it. And by the way, everyone will believe me. You can never prove what happened. But we must make a truce, you and I. For everyone. Not a peace, you don't want that, but a truce. Before you ruin your mother's happiness. And your own life, with that— Well, she is what she is. You think I made her that way? No. That I don't have to live with.'

'Just her father.'

'Yes. I have to live with that. I'm not proud – this thing that never happened. Are you proud of everything you've done? Well, at your age it's still possible. Not at mine. I'm a doctor, not *assassino*. He was dying. I knew he was dying. Nothing in the world was going to change that.'

'That doesn't mean you had to help. You knew him.'

'Abramo? Yes. He was like her – difficult. Always looking for the slight. But no matter. He was dying. I had to make a choice, so I did. You can't save the dead – only the living. So was I wrong? I knew what would happen to him. But I'm not ashamed, even now. It was the war. You had to choose the living.'

'Choose how? By reporting Jews?'

'They were not there for the Jews. For someone else. I don't remember his name – maybe I never knew it. Anyway, it wouldn't have been real. You know CLN?'

I nodded. 'Partisans.'

'So someone fighting for Italy. That meant something, you know. I wanted to help. A man not sick, wounded. Bullet wounds. You couldn't hide that. How could I lie about bullet wounds? They would have found him. They had a photograph – they knew who he was. And then what? 'How long has he been here, *dottore*? You never reported this? A partisan?' They were attacking Germans then. It wasn't just sabotage, railroad tracks – they were actually killing them, so if you were caught, the Germans would make an example. There was no way to hide him in that hospital.

120

I had to get him out, somewhere else. I had to make them go away, even for a little, get enough time to save him. So I gave them someone else.'

We were at the end of the fondamenta, facing into the wind coming off the lagoon. On the water, a covered funeral gondola bounced on the waves, heading towards the cypresses. Another one for San Michele.

'That's some choice,' I said, looking out at the water.

'Yes,' he said, 'a terrible choice. But not difficult. He was dying. The other man was living. How else could I save him?'

'And yourself.'

He looked at me. 'Yes, myself, it's true. It would have been bad for me if they had known I helped. But you know, at the time I wasn't thinking about that. Of course you won't believe that either. You want to judge – one thing or the other. But it wasn't like that. Good and bad together, how do you judge that? You do things – well, how can you know what it was like? Villa Raspelli, you think I wanted that? How do you think it felt, putting my hands on them? Giving them medicine? Men like that. So you don't look at the uniform, you don't see it. Then you can do it, if it's just a man.'

'So was Grassini.'

'A dying man. So I played God, yes. A sin. That's what you wanted to know. Now you tell me something – what would you have done?'

I stared at the lagoon, choppy in the wind, and it seemed for an instant, as I watched it move, that everything in Venice was like its water, shifting back and forth.

'Why didn't you tell her this?' I said finally.

'What difference would it make to her? Her father's dead. I had a part in that, yes. Do you think she wants to know why? What reason would satisfy her? I'm not making excuses – it happened. But you, it's different. I want you to know. What happened, happened. Or rather, it didn't happen. Not now.'

'Why?'

121

'You think this is a time for explanations? Now it's revenge, set-tling scores. I have a position here. These accusations – anti-Semite, collaborator. Always something sticks, however it was. Do you think people want explanations? No, they're like you, they want black and white.'

'But if you helped a partisan—'

'Not everyone would love me for that, even now. Collaborator. Communist. It's dangerous to take sides here. This one, that one, and someone is against you no matter what you do. So I do noth-ing. Nothing happened. I go on with my life. I don't want the war again.' He looked at me for a minute, then turned towards the fon-damenta. 'I must go back. Anyway, now it's said. Maybe it makes a difference to you, maybe not, I don't know. I thought, a soldier, you'd know how these things were. What happened then, it's hard to judge now. Do I still live with it? Yes, but shall I tell you some-thing? A little less each day. Maybe that's how the war ends. A little less each day until it's over.'

'Not for everybody.'

'No, not everybody,' he said. 'It never ends for them.'

'You talk as if it's her fault.'

'No, but not mine either. I didn't make the war.'

He said nothing for a few minutes, looking towards the houses across the canal, the same patchy plaster and shutters we'd seen that day going to lunch, before anything had happened.

'You know what ended it for me?' he said suddenly. 'When your mother came back. I heard her laugh, and it was a laugh from before the war. And I thought, yes, it's possible to have that life again. And we do. I won't let anyone take that away now. Not that girl. Does she think she can bring the father back? I did what I did. There was a reason – at least for me it was a reason. Now you know it. Maybe it's still not enough for you. But maybe it's enough for a truce. That's why I told you. If it's enough to make a truce.'

'What do you mean by truce?'

'An end. Talk like this, it can make trouble for me. I want her to stop.' He looked directly at me. 'I want you to stop.'

'You mean you want me to leave.'

He held my eyes for a second, then nodded. 'After the wedding.'

Rosa Soriano was blonde and stocky, the weight, I assumed, a matter of inheritance, because she took nothing with her morning tea, not even glancing at the rolls and jam the Bauer had laid out for breakfast. She had a heavy person's surprising grace, her thick fingers barely touching the cup, lifting it in a delicate arc. Only her walk was clumsy, an awkward shuffle, still new to her, her body pitching forwards but held back by the stiff leg she dragged along. 'From the war,' she said when she saw me looking at it. 'A German souvenir.' When she sat down she breathed out, a barely audible sigh of relief, and brought the leg under the table. The dining room was warm, despite the rain spattering on the terrace, but she had wrapped a shawl over a heavy jacket, a huddled, almost peasant look in a room walled with damask. Joe had said she'd wanted the trip, so I apologised for the rain, but she looked at me blankly, as if she hadn't noticed it. She had come ready for business – a folder with papers and a notebook were at the side of the table.

'My mother was German,' she said, when I asked how she knew the language.

'So that explains the hair.'

She shrugged. 'Italians are blonde too. But not many speak German. So it was useful. My mother said it would be. Maybe not this way, working for the Americans.'

'Joe said you recognised his name.'

'The name, yes. Not his. His brother's.'

'His brother? Paolo?'

'Yes,' she said, patting the folder. 'Him I know well. But the other—' She shook her head, then gently put down the cup. 'Then Joe asked me and ha, I thought, another Maglione, maybe that explains it.'

'Explains what?'

'The brother, Paolo, was often at Villa Raspelli. They kept a

123

record of the visitors every day, so we only have to look at the sheet to see who was there. And then, I couldn't understand it, his name was there after he died. How? I thought maybe the records made a mistake, but how do you make that mistake? A ghost signs in? So I look, and the writing *is* different, only the name is the same. G. Maglione.'

'G? Paolo?'

'Gustavo, his first name. That would be the name on any document, so of course the Germans—'

'But I don't understand. He wasn't a doctor.'

'Well, Villa Raspelli wasn't a hospital. It's – how do you say, *casa di recovero*?'

'I don't know – rest home? Recuperation centre, I guess.'

'So, recuperation. You know, an officer is wounded. Maybe tired of the war. He goes to Villa Raspelli. He looks at Lake Garda, breathes the good air, he eats, he gets better. Maybe he has to practise walking. Maybe the arm is like this.' She made a gesture to indicate a cast. 'But no one is dying. It's *casa di recovero*, not a hospital. A club for butchers,' she said, her voice suddenly bitter.

'But then why did Gianni go there?'

She looked over, almost delighted, pleased with me. 'That is an excellent question. A doctor from Venice? From the big hospital? Why not someone in Verona? I have the records. There were no serious illnesses there in this period. And you know, if it was serious they moved them out to a real hospital. This was *der Zauberberg*, a place to rest. But a doctor comes from Venice. So why?'

I said nothing, waiting.

'Of course, it is an excellent excuse. Doctors do go there. Maybe not from Venice, but they go. To make the check-ups. How is the cast? You know. No one would think it unusual if he went there.'

'But you did.'

'Because I know what it was like. He wasn't needed. Still, there he is. Not once, several times.' She pulled out one of the sheets and pointed. 'G. Maglione. Not a ghost. As I say, an excellent excuse, if you were meeting someone. No suspicion at all. You meet the SS at Quadri's, everyone notices. You meet secretly, someone finds out. But at Villa Raspelli no one questions it. You're a doctor. Maybe someone has asked for you. Take a black bag, all out in the open. Wonderful.'

'Wait a minute. Back up. His brother went there. He wasn't a doctor.'

'Well, Paolo didn't need an excuse. They were his friends. You know about him?'

'Only what I read in the papers. A playboy.'

She nodded. 'Yes. Racing cars. Then more games. The Order of Rome. You know that?'

I shook my head.

'A club, for boys like him. Young Fascists. Rich, stupid. For the new empire. Ha. Abyssinia. What did they care about Abyssinia? An excuse to get drunk, be stupid together. Harmless, and then not so harmless. The Germans began to use them. Of course, it was the Duce at Salò, but really the Germans.'

'Used them how?'

'To inform. To help fight the Communists. For someone like Paolo, that's all you had to say. The Communists – that would be the end of everything, wouldn't it? Better to make a bargain with the devil. So they did.'

'Over drinks at the Villa Raspelli.'

'Yes, many times. He was a favourite there – he must have been good company. Still a playboy. And of course there was the work to discuss. No more Abyssinia. Now he was saving us from the Communists. A hero. For Italy. For the Church. He wasn't the only one like that, you know. There were lots of heroes. And now they answer for it.' She placed her hand on the folder, as if it were the prosecutor's case.

'But not him.'

'No, he answered earlier.'

'A car crash.'

She took a sip of tea, calm. 'No, he was killed.'

'I thought it went off the road.'

'It did. After.'

I looked at her, surprised. 'Do you know that?'

'Yes,' she said simply.

I reached for the coffee pot, something to do while I took this in.

'But Gianni,' I said, 'he wasn't – what was it? Order of Rome?'

'No. I only knew about the brother. That's why I'm here. To talk to you about this one.'

'Well, he wasn't that. Like Paolo, I mean. Not a playboy. Not stupid, either. I can't imagine him joining anything. He likes to keep his hands clean.'

'Not too clean. Isn't that why you came to us?'

'That was something else. Not the Order of Rome. In his own way, he—' I looked up from my cup. 'He told me he did it to save someone else. Who was in the hospital at the same time. A partisan.'

She lifted her head in surprise, then tipped it to one side, thinking. 'A partisan,' she said quietly, turning it over another minute. She pushed at her sleeve, an absent-minded gesture, moving the heavy cloth back until a splotch of white appeared, new skin, without colour. I watched, fascinated, as she rubbed her finger over it, idly scratching. Another souvenir of the Germans? There was more of it, running up under her sleeve. How large had the burn been, the old skin blistering, coming off in peels? 'Then he's lying,' she said finally, startling me. I looked up from her arm. Her eyes were certain, not even a hint of doubt, so that suddenly I had to look away, ashamed somehow of feeling relieved, oddly elated.

'Are you sure?'

'The partisans in the Veneto were Communists. Does he seem to you a man who would help the Communists?'

'But not all—'

'Americans. Why is this so hard for you? Yes, Communists. Or people fighting *with* Communists. It comes to the same. Who else

126

was fighting the Fascists? Not just at the end. And when the Nazis ran, who else was there to chase them? Hunt them down.'

'Were you there?' I said, trying to imagine it.

She nodded. 'Of course.'

'A Communist?'

'My parents were. I was named for Rosa Luxemburg – my mother was her friend, in Berlin. So she had to leave, after they killed her, and my father was then in Milano—' She stopped. 'Well, my parents, that's for another day.'

'But not you.'

'Not when I work for the Americans.' She poured another cup of tea, then looked up. 'This matters to you?'

'Just curious. So you were a partisan.'

'Yes, like everyone now. Then, not so many. Why do you think I do this work? I don't forget what it was like, what the others did. The Magliones.'

'Both of them?'

'It's the logic. Follow the dates,' she said, patting the folder again. 'Paolo we know. A bastard. But his brother, no record. Paolo is killed by partisans. And now the brother appears on the guest list.'

'And not before?'

'No, I checked. *After* Paolo's death. So now there's another Maglione at Villa Raspelli. Why? The logic is, they appealed to him. 'Help us avenge your brother.' Does he say no? Then why go back? Not one visit, several.'

'And you don't think he was treating anyone.'

'No, but at first I thought it could be. I only knew about the brother. Not this one, what he does, how he feels. That we have to guess. And then you tell us he's reporting Jews to the SS. A doctor reporting Jews. You know this for a fact?'

'The daughter survived. She saw him do it.'

'Good. She would be willing to testify to this?'

'Yes,' I said, hesitant, wondering where she was going. 'But—'

'So we have a link now. He helps the SS with the roundups.

What else does he help them with? He's not at Villa Raspelli to give aspirin, I think. It's the logic.'

'But not the proof,' I said.

'No, not yet. But I'll get it,' she said, scratching her arm again, excited.

'Proof of what?'

'After Paolo's death, of course there were reprisals. This man was nothing to them, not really, but now he's an excuse. Make an example for the partisans. Show them what happens when they— Well, you can imagine. It's the end, they're desperate, and they were always butchers, so now they're like crazy men. Torture. Terrible things. And it works. They begin to get the partisans, pick them off. Always it's Communist uprisings they're putting down, not the resistance. And once it's very lucky – this time, a whole group. A house. And they burn it, with people inside. An atrocity. And the question is, who betrayed them?'

'But how could Gianni—?'

'No one betrayed them. Not that way. Someone led them to that house. It's possible not even deliberately, not even knowing. I looked at everyone in that house, I made their files. Who would do it? No one.'

Her voice had become stronger, rising towards the end, so that one of the waiters looked over, thinking we were having an argument.

'You were in the house?' I said.

'Yes. Not everyone died. I was burned, but I lived. It's strange, you know, because now I'm always cold. You would think . . .' She put both hands on the table, anchoring herself. 'So I know who was there. But who did they follow? Who did they know to follow? Someone here,' she said, nodding at the folder. 'And now you tell me something very interesting. You pray for them to make a slip. I think maybe he made the slip to you. But I need your help.'

'How?'

'The date. I need the date when he gave them the Jew, when the

128

SS were there. In the autumn, yes, but when? Exactly. Do you know?'

'She would, I guess.'

'Good. When I get the hospital records, I can match the dates to the names.'

I looked at her, puzzled. 'Why? What slip?'

She smiled slightly. 'A man whose brother is Order of Rome, who visits SS, who reports Jews, this same man tells you he does this to save a partisan. How would he know? How would he know a man was a partisan?'

I said nothing. Not just the lie, the kind of lie.

'The man told him,' I said weakly, taking his side to see how it would fit.

'Who would tell him? Do you know how we lived? Other people's names, identities – everything was secret. We trusted no one. And then you tell a man like that? With his sympathies?'

'But how would they know his sympathies?'

'Then you would not trust him. Unless you knew. Not with a life. You would not tell him.'

'But somebody must have.'

'Yes,' she said, lowering her head, 'someone must. It's possible, the SS. If they already knew. "Help us make the trap. Watch him. Tell us when to follow." Of course, it's possible it was someone else. And *he* tells the SS, his new friends. But in the end they know. Who helps them?'

'If the partisan was there at all. Maybe he just made it up – something to tell me.'

'Such a story to make up,' she said. 'A man who wasn't there. It's more usual, yes, to take the truth and bend it a little. Easier to answer questions, if you have to. Anyway, no matter. We'll see if he was there. There were two people in that house from Venice.' She looked up. 'And one of them had been wounded. I didn't know he had been in the hospital, he wouldn't have said. To protect whoever helped him. But I know when he came to us, so we match the dates. I know what name he used. What name did Maglione tell you?'

'He didn't remember.'

'Ah,' she said, 'a patient without a name. Then I find out, who did Maglione see at Villa Raspelli? I look at them, their files. And somewhere there's a connection. If we're lucky, someone alive. A witness. The Germans talk now – they like to tell us what their friends here did. You see? Not just us. It was the war. The Italians were no better.' She nodded. 'We're very close now.' She sat back, pouring more tea. 'And for that I have you to thank. It never occurred to me to track the brother, and then one day Joe tells me he was reporting Jews. It's like a chain, one thing to another, but you were the start.'

I looked out the rainy window, uncomfortable.

'You'll give testimony, yes? And the daughter?'

'You intend to put him on trial?'

'Intend? Hope. It depends what we can prove.'

'You can prove he gave up Abramo Grassini.'

She shook her head. 'Well, you know that was the law, to turn over the Jews. And the proof – whose word? I'm sorry. I don't say it's right, I say what is. But the one thing leads to the other, so it's a help. With you, of course, it's different A credibility. For you to testify against him, what he told you—'

'But it's hearsay. He'll deny it.'

She leaned forward. 'Let me tell you how they work, these trials. The victims are dead. So what do we have? Records, of course.' She held one up, a court exhibit. 'Circumstances. Sometimes a witness. It's difficult. We have to show the chain. The daughter knows something. You know something. A German knows something. Another. We make a chain of circumstance.' She put down the folder. 'Sometimes a chain of lies. He lies to the daughter. He lies to you. Why? And then you see the chain and you pull it.' She moved her hands in a tugging gesture. 'And you have him.'

'But technically—'

'These are special trials. The technicalities are different. It's not the cinema, a murder trial.'

'It's about murder.'

'No. Reputation. Maybe even social justice. There's always that hope. But not murder.'

'Then they'll get away with it.'

'They did get away with it,' she said quietly, so that the words hung over the table. 'There's no retribution after you're dead. But people don't know. And that they won't get away with.' She sipped more tea, watching me over the cup. 'You're worried?'

'No,' I lied, suddenly seeing the tribunal table, my mother in the makeshift courtroom, Gianni glaring at me from the stand. 'But I don't like throwing mud in public either. If it's just mud. I saw it in Germany. Nobody comes out looking good – you get just as dirty.'

She put down her cup. 'Yes,' she said, a quick nod of agreement, 'but I'll still need you there.' She looked over at me. 'It won't be just mud.'

'And if you can't prove it?'

'Well, I think I will. And it's important, to have these trials. Otherwise—'

'Otherwise what?'

'The partisans find their own proof.'

Afterwards I crossed back to the Dorsoduro side, uneasy, feeling things spinning out of control. All I'd wanted was to get my mother out of a mistake. Now it was something else. How could I testify against him? It would be terrible for everyone and justice for whom? Rosa was right about that, anyway. He had already got away with it.

A little past San Ivo a canal was being dredged, a dirty job saved for winter, when no visitors were here to see. Wooden planks dammed each end so big rubber hoses could pump out the water, leaving a floor of mud, just a few feet down, where workmen in boots were shovelling muck and debris into carts. The mud covered everything, spattering the workers' blue overalls, hanging in clots on the canal walls, just below the line of moss. Gianni's great fear: mud would stick if someone dredged it up. I

131

thought of him on the terrace at Lake Garda, having drinks with the men who'd ordered the trains. I'd met them in Germany, men still unsure why they were being accused. But those were the ones in cells, worn and frightened, out of their protective uniforms, awaiting judgement. The others, in the street, just went about their business, so ordinary there was no way to know, no haunted looks, no furtive tremor from unwanted memories. The crime hadn't stuck to them. They had got away with it, free to walk around, even to marry a rich woman. They smiled over the dinner table. Nobody knew. And that they won't get away with, Rosa had said, asking for help.

But a trial. I imagined the courtroom, me on the stand, Claudia on the stand, and I knew my mother would – what, break? No, she was more resilient than that. But a body blow leaves a bruise. You survive, but not quite the same. She had survived my father's death, with a stray look of sadness that never quite left her now. Those first years, bright for my sake, she worked hard at making us happy, putting part of herself aside, as if it were something she could stow away in a closet for later. But of course it was gone, spent on me. And now there'd be another blow, leaving her bruised and reeling again, harder this time to come back, already weakened, never expecting it to come from me. She'd get over Gianni, but not that, not a trial.

But then he'd get away with it again. I watched the workmen sliding in the wet muck. In a few days they'd be finished, the rubbish and the smell gone, and the water would flood back, the surface a mirror again, dazzling, so that when you came to it, around the corner, you felt you were stepping into a painting. I stared down at the mud, unable to move, as if my feet had actually sunk into it, still trying to find a way out.

CHAPTER SEVEN

MIMI WAS LUCKY in everything but the weather. *Il Gazzettino* was already calling the ball the first important social event since the war, the one that would restore Venice 'to her place in international society'. People were coming from London. There had been a gratifying squabble over invitations – our marchesa upstairs, not one of the lucky ones, went to visit her sister in Vicenza. Peggy Guggenheim said she was coming from New York and then didn't, which allowed Mimi to use her name in the columns without having to put up with her. A generator was found to keep the palazzo blazing with light if there was a power failure. The food arrived on time. And then it rained.

She had planned on a spring evening, one of those first mild days softer in Venice than anywhere else, but the air stayed cold and it rained off and on all day. The special torches at the water entrance on the Grand Canal had to be covered, an awning set up. Footmen with umbrellas would help guests from their boats to the door, but inevitably clothes would get wet. The photographers had to be moved indoors, away from the entrance shots with San Marco in the background. All this my mother learned in a series of phone calls that got more frantic as the afternoon wore on. Finally Mimi insisted that my mother go there to dress.

'Like bridesmaids,' my mother said. 'She says my hair will be a

mess otherwise. Can you imagine? A little rain.' But she was helping Angelina with the garment bag, carefully smoothing out any
folds in the long skirt.

'She's nervous,' I said. 'She wants company.'

'Mimi doesn't have nerves. She just can't stand anyone making
an entrance. Easier to have them already there. Well, I don't mind.
To tell you the truth, it *does* frizz up when it's like this,' she said,
touching her hair. 'Anyway, I'd rather see everything. Gianni's
always late, and you can't say a word because it's always medical.
At least this way I won't miss anything. Darling, would you call the
hospital and tell him to meet me there, at Mimi's? I couldn't get
through before. He'll probably be pleased – now he can be as late
as he likes without someone harping at him. But not too late. I
can't dance by myself. Would you?'

'All right,' I said. We were still living in the temporary peace of
pretending nothing had happened.

'I'm taking Angelina, but you can fend for yourself, can't you?'
Mimi had already borrowed the rest of the staff for the day.

'It doesn't matter. I'm going out.'

'I wish you'd change your mind. Everyone in Venice is dying to
be there and you go to the movies.'

'We're not going to the movies.'

'Well, wherever you're going. I can't imagine wanting to miss
this. You know Mimi, if there's one thing she—' She stopped midstream, asked Angelina to take the garment bag away, then turned
to me. 'It's that girl, isn't it?'

'You don't want me to bring her to Mimi's, do you?'

'Well, not if— But I thought all that business was over and
done with. Gianni said it was. He said you'd talked.'

I looked away. 'She doesn't have a dress.'

'Well, you can *borrow* a dress. That's not a problem.'

'Some other time.'

'What other time? A thing like this? She'd probably enjoy it,
you know. Anybody would.'

'I don't think Gianni would.'

'Ask him. If he doesn't mind, then . . .' She looked up at me. 'I'm so glad things are better. I knew if you would just— Well, I'm off. She'll be calling again. Funny how *her* lines never go down. Don't forget the hospital. And I'd ask him about the girl. He might surprise you.'

'All right.'

'Oh, look, it's starting up again. Poor Mimi.' She giggled. 'Well, it is unfair. You know, we used to come to Venice for the *beach*. You never saw a drop one week to the next. And now look.'

An hour later the phones were clear and I reached Gianni in his office, but I didn't ask him about Claudia and I didn't tell him to go to Mimi's. Instead I said my mother wanted him to come for her earlier than they'd planned. And where was she now? At the hairdresser's. Of course. Easy lies. After another twenty minutes of busy signals and scratchy connections I got the hotel where I'd moved Claudia and left a message that I'd be a little late. Then there was nothing to do but wait, the house growing quiet around me, not even the faint sound of maids' slippers in the back rooms.

The rain stopped, then started again, a light drizzle that covered the Giudecca across the channel like a scrim. I stood at the window looking at the Redentore and thinking what to say. I wanted it clear in my mind so that it would come out as easily as a white lie about the hairdresser. One chance to make him believe me, finally put an end to it. Be careful about everything, even eye contact. Still, what choice would he have?

It was a while before I realised the room was getting darker. No more umbrellas on the Zattere, just people hurrying home with packages. A few calles away, Mimi and my mother would be looking into mirrors, finishing their make-up while the maids stood by with their pressed gowns. Mimi's palazzo was just up from the Dario, so the vaporettos stopping at Salute would see the lights coming on, the chandeliers in the great front rooms reflecting out on the canal. You could walk there from anywhere in Dorsoduro in minutes, but everyone would want to go by water and be seen. It occurred to me that Gianni would probably have a boat too,

135

and I went downstairs to open the water gate and turn on the lights in the murky entrance where Claudia and I had kissed that night. Same gondola up on its storage rack, the pile of paving stones under a tarp, the utility boat bobbing outside near the mossy steps. If we'd followed the kiss, just left the house instead of climbing the stairs – but we hadn't.

I left the connecting door open and put on the lights in the hall, once a single room that ran the length of the house, water to calle. Off it were some smaller rooms we never used, presumably old offices or receiving rooms, now just extra work for the maids. Good enough, however, for a conversation. It was already dark upstairs. Why bother with the chandeliers if I was about to leave too? No need to be polite – a few minutes, not even a drink.

I lit a cigarette and sat waiting in one of the chilly side parlours. Where was he? Now that I'd decided what to do, even convinced myself it was right, any delay seemed to stretch out the time, make it seem even longer than it was. I looked at my watch. Always late, my mother had said. I began to fidget, impatient, picking at the fraying upholstery on the arm of the chair. Maybe she'd called him after all, told him to go to Mimi's. And maybe he was just late. I got up and walked towards the water entrance again, moving to keep warm. No sound of rain outside. Mimi might be lucky after all.

The street bell made me jump, the sound bouncing off the marble floors, jarring in the quiet house. Another ring, insistent, to make Angelina run for it. He had his finger up to ring again when I opened the door.

'Adam,' he said, surprised. He looked towards the dark stairs. 'Where's your mother? Am I so late?' He glanced down at his watch.

'No, she went over earlier to hold Mimi's hand.'

'But you said—'

'I wanted to talk to you.'

'Ah,' he said, noncommittal, still at the door.

I opened it wider. He was dressed formally, white tie, everything crisp and shiny. Even in the halfhearted hall light the shirtfront glowed. I had never thought of him as handsome before, but formal clothes brought out the best in him. The slicked-back silver hair, bright eyes, smooth-shaven skin – everything looked dressed up, stage romantic. When he reached into his breast pocket, I almost expected to see a silver cigarette case, but it was only a pack, not yet opened.

'So I'm not in the doghouse,' he said, pulling off the cellophane. 'She says it's terrible how I'm late. You're expecting someone by boat?' He looked towards the water entrance, the dark canal beyond.

'I thought you might hire a gondola – for Mimi's.'

'I don't hire gondolas. I have a gondola. Anyway, I prefer to walk.' He lit a cigarette, peering at me as he closed the lighter. 'What did you want to talk about?'

'I want to make a truce.'

'I thought we had a truce.'

'A new one. Different.'

'Ah,' he said, marking time. He gestured to the staircase. 'You want to talk here?'

'It won't take long. Anyway, you don't want to crease your tails.'

'All right,' he said, displeased. 'So?'

'Here's the way this one works. You're going to leave my mother, end it. I'll take her away – home, if she'll go. Anyway, not here. You won't see us again.'

He sighed. 'What a nuisance you've become. Like a child.'

'I can get her away in a week. Maybe two.'

'And when am I supposed to do this? Tonight, at the ball?' he said, toying. 'Another scene? Will your friend be there? For the drama?'

'This week,' I said steadily. 'Tomorrow, why not? Maybe you realised tonight, it can never be. Two different worlds – you figure out what to say. It wouldn't be the first time, would it?'

He looked away, not rising to this, and started walking slowly towards the water entrance. 'And why would I do this?'

'Because I'm going to do something for you.'

He turned. 'Don't do anything for me. I don't want anything from you.

'You'll want this. I'm going to save your life.'

137

He stopped, staring at me. 'What are you talking about?'

'Your trial.'

'My trial,' he said, toneless, waiting.

I moved towards him. 'You know, none of this would have happened if you hadn't started with the first lie. Your old friend Grassini. You didn't expect it – it was all of a sudden, her coming at you, so of course you'd deny it. Anybody's first instinct. But then you kept lying about it. Now why was that? Strictly speaking, it wasn't even illegal. And you wouldn't have been the only one. But here you are, just her word against yours and everybody happy to sweep it under the carpet, and still you get all excited. Ride it out? No. You try to get rid of her, make her go away. At the time, I didn't think. I was ashamed for you. I thought this is how anyone would feel, to have this known. But you were never ashamed of that. Your reputation would have survived it. Others' have. But you had to get rid of her. Now why was that?'

'This is so hard for you to understand? Talk like that.'

'No, that's not it. You didn't want people talking at all. Looking into it. Grassini meant nothing to you. But think what else they might find, once they started looking into things. That you had to stop.'

He picked up an ashtray from the hall table and rubbed out his cigarette. 'Really,' he said finally. 'What makes you think so?'

'Because I did look into it.'

'You did?'

I nodded. 'With some friends in the AMG. They do fieldwork for war crimes trials. You scoop up a German, you'd be surprised what else swims into the net.'

His eyes widened. 'What else?'

'A brother who ran errands for the SS and got bumped off by partisans. A whole series of cozy dinners at Villa Raspelli – no stethoscopes, just you and the boys in black. They have records. They also have the Germans. Can't stop talking, it seems. Don't care a bit what happens to their old Italian buddies. Happy to help out. See, once you start looking into things—'

138

'Why are you doing this?' he said, his voice quiet, stunned, the earlier smooth polish gone.

'To make a truce,' I said. 'To get rid of you.'

'You hate me so much.'

'All of you. Look at you. Fucking Fred Astaire, and a year ago you were putting people on trains. Ever see what happened to them? I'd take you down in a minute if I could, but I'm not going to let you take my mother with you. So you get a break. Which is a lot more than you gave Claudia's father, and who knows who else. Your famous partisan.'

'You don't know what you're talking about.'

'That was good. You explain away one lie with another. What made you think I'd believe the new one? You killed him too.'

'You're crazy.'

'Had him tracked, I should say. You never pull a trigger yourself. A whole bunch of them this time, thanks to you. They're preparing the case now. Check with the hospital – see if anybody called about the records, first week in October, 1944.'

'But it's not true,' he said, pale now.

'You want to know something? I don't give a shit. I think it is true. And if this isn't, something else will be. One way or another, they'll get what they need. They're good. And you were so close – getting away with everything. Except Claudia came back.'

He stared at me, not saying anything, his eyes still wide.

'The problem is, they want me to testify.'

'Testify? To what?'

'Our little heart-to-heart about the partisan, for one thing. It gives the story a certain heft. Not to mention it's a confession about Claudia's father, which isn't going to win you any friends in court.'

'You can't prove any of this,' he said, panting a little. 'A trial. They can't prove anything.'

'Well, they might. In fact, I'd bet on it. On the other hand, anything can happen in court. I've seen it. You might get lucky. But either way it'll be a circus. You don't want me on the stand, and I don't want to put my mother through it. So this time you really get lucky. No trial. You just go away. No, better – we'll go away. All you lose is the money.'

'Bastard,' he said, trying to control himself. 'Keep your money.'

'I will. I guess the usual thing would be to buy you off, but I figure you're getting a great deal anyway. You go on as if nothing ever happened. Of course I can't say about later – this kind of stuff has a way of coming out. But I can stop it for now, and that'll buy you time. Then, who knows? Things change.'

'Stop it how?'

'I'll get them to close the case. I can do it. I guess it's obstructing justice in a way, but I'll do it. That's the truce. I don't want a trial.' I looked at him. 'And neither do you.'

'*Marmocchio,*' he said, almost under his breath, a rumbling. '*Sei uno stronzo. Cazzo.*'

'Not very nice, I guess. Whatever it is.'

'You shit. No, you know *sciocco*? Fool. You are a fool. I've tried everything with you.'

'Then try this. We'll go away and your troubles will be over.'

'My only trouble is you. Crazy. Maybe that's it, still crazy from the war. Maybe it affected your mind. You think you're still in Germany? Always the Jews. Here, it's another place. Not Germany, not the same. You want to put people on trial? For what, suffering in the war?'

'Not everybody suffered. You look like you're doing all right.'

'It's that Jewish whore. She makes you crazy. A woman like that. How many did she sleep with there? They should put *her* on trial.'

I stared at him, not responding, clenching my hands.

'But right now,' I said finally, 'they'd rather have you.'

'You did this. You made this trouble.'

'No, you made it. But I can stop it. That's the deal.'

He turned to leave. 'You can go to hell. Do you think you can come here and put *me* on trial? Like a criminal? No, it's a farce. You will be the one with the bad name, not me. A shame to your mother. Saying lies – and then, where's the proof? Nowhere. No proof. You can't prove anything.'

'Well, see, that's the thing. They don't necessarily have to prove it.'

'What?' he said, stopping.

'Not the people I talked to, anyway. They prefer it – professional pride. But sometimes, with the right guy, it's enough just to say what they know, go public with it. Somebody else figures out the rest. Old partisans, maybe. Then they take care of it their own way.' He had paled again. 'I told you I wanted to save your life. They did it to your brother. They wouldn't think twice about doing it to you. Not once they know.' I looked at him. 'You don't want this trial.'

'It's lies,' he said quietly.

'Then you have nothing to worry about.'

'You don't understand anything here – what these people are like.'

'I thought they were friends of yours. The one you helped – he'd speak for you, wouldn't he? Or was he in the house that burned?'

'You—' Not finding the word, sputtering.

'Of course, they didn't know about your other friends, over at Villa Raspelli. What are you going to say that was?' I shook my head. 'It's a great cover until the Germans talk. You know how they are, keeping track of everything. Reports to Berlin. Duplicates here. Verona, I guess. Everything that happened. All their little hopes and dreams. Their friends.' I stopped. 'You don't want this trial. They'd knock you off before you were halfway through. I don't want any part of that. Not that you don't have it coming. But I'm not going to be the one to do it. Make the truce.'

'You're threatening me?'

'Make the truce.'

'*Cazzo*, make it yourself,' he said, throwing up his hand as he brushed past me so that it accidentally caught my shoulder. I reacted by flinging up my arm to push it away. A flicker of motion, but enough to trigger an alarm in his head. I didn't even see the hand come up, just felt it on my chest as he pushed me back in a fury, banging my head against the wall. 'Don't you dare raise a hand to me,' he said, panting, holding me.

'Let go,' I said, seeing only the blur of his white front, his hand

141

coming out of a starched cuff. Then his face, clearer now, eyes glaring at me.

'You think I wouldn't do it? Bah.' He loosened his hold, then dropped his hand. 'And make more trouble. So you can run to Mama.'

'That's right,' I said, staring at him. 'You like someone else to do it. Even better when it's official. When it's the right thing to do.'

'Go to hell.' He started towards the door, smoothing back the sides of his hair, then turned. 'I warn you.'

We stared at each other, a stand-off, broken suddenly by the front doorbell. For a second neither of us moved, not yet jolted out of ourselves, then I stepped away from the wall.

'Fix your tie,' I said, brushing past him.

'*Cazzo*,' he said, spitting it, but he went over to the mirror to adjust himself, public again.

I opened the door to Claudia, looking worried, her hair a little scraggly in the moist air.

'So you are here,' she said. 'The lights are out upstairs.'

'Didn't you get my message?'

'Yes, but it's late.' She stopped, seeing Gianni in the hall. 'Oh.'

'Ha, the whore,' Gianni said. 'Now everything is complete. The *cazzo* and his whore. A perfect couple.'

'Shut up,' I said.

'Why is he here?' Claudia said.

'To listen to nonsense. Now I go.'

Claudia looked at me. 'What nonsense?'

'Nothing,' I said, drawing her in. 'Just a little talk.'

'Talk,' Gianni said. 'Nonsense.'

'You're right,' I said, turning to him. He was elegant again, his hair back in place. 'It is nonsense. Why bother? I don't want a truce either. Not any more.'

'No? What do you want?'

'I want to nail you. I want people to know.'

'At my so-called trial.'

'That's right, at your trial. I'm looking forward to it.'

142

'What trial?' Claudia said. 'What are you talking about?'

'More drama for you,' Gianni said. 'You like so much to make scenes. Now you can tell everybody where your bed was at the camp. All your special privileges – how you earned them. He wants you to tell everybody. He wants people to know.'

'Stop it,' I said.

'My lawyer will ask the questions. I guarantee it. At this trial you want.'

Claudia moved from the door, backing into the hall. He followed her with words.

'You think I don't know about you? Someone attacks me, I ask questions. I find out. Vanessi, the man at the camp – you think he would keep a woman out of pity? No. And not once, months. Not forced, a mistress. Someone who liked it. Who liked him, maybe.'

'No,' Claudia said softly.

'So, an actress. Maybe still acting.' He turned to me. 'This is what you want? A wonderful witness. The camp whore.'

'Stop it,' I said.

'No, it doesn't stop, once it starts. How can you stop it? Hold up your hand, like traffic? You think I won't fight back? You make this trouble and then you think you can stop it. No, not when you like. So you shame her and it doesn't stop there. Until everybody's dirty. Then what? Nothing. You will win nothing.'

'I don't have to win,' I said. 'I just have to let them see you.'

He stared at me again for a minute. 'I'm not going to let you do that,' he said finally. 'Understand that. Never.'

His voice was low and steady, the same calm menace I'd heard in the restaurant, and I felt a prickling. It had already started, beyond fixing now, any polite truce.

'That's what you think,' I said.

'Never,' he repeated, his voice still low. 'Go home.'

'I'm not leaving her. Not with you.'

'You don't know how it is. You don't know anything. A fool. Like the father. Just like the father. He saw nothing. Under his nose, still nothing.'

'Saw what?' I said, feeling clenched, as if his hand were pushing me again.

'You think it's the first time, with your mother? You know nothing. The father's son. Another fool.'

A snap in my head, like the click of a safety catch.

'Shut up,' I said. 'Just shut up.'

'Both of you, fools.' Each word like a prod with a stick.

'Shut up,' I said, my hands springing up without my being aware of it, pushing him back, away from me.

The shove caught him off-guard, so he staggered before he could catch his balance, his weight pulling him back towards the wall, his head hitting the edge of one of the sconces.

'Adam!' Claudia said, somewhere out of my line of vision.

Gianni put his hand to the back of his head, then looked at it, streaked with blood. I saw the white of his dress shirt, his blank expression, the smeared hand, everything utterly still, and then the blood seemed to jump, alive, as he lunged for me. I reared back, keeping my throat out of reach so his hand struck my chest. Then we were both falling, his hands now pounding at me, wild. The smell of blood. Claudia yelled something.

'*Cazzo!*' Gianni said, punching me.

I had never fought anyone hand to hand. Combat had always been a few kilometres away, even across a field. Now I could feel his breath on me, that close. I rolled away, not thinking, instinct. Protect your eyes. Get up. Now. No pattern to it, a blur, slaps and grabs and sudden bursts of pain.

I pulled at his shirt, the stiff white front, to draw him closer, immobilise his arms, but he pushed me away, landing one hand on the side of my face. I felt a dull burning and moved back. One of his shirt studs had popped out, opening up a patch of hairy skin in the evening clothes, suddenly primitive, what was real underneath.

I looked at the furious eyes, the dishevelled hair, and saw that he was right, it wouldn't stop now. His hand caught me again, my ear went hot, stinging, and I punched back until both of us were wrestling, close in, falling to the floor again in a heap, pulling each other down the hall, trying to find a position, any kind of advantage. Then his grip loosened and I grabbed a chair, pulling myself up away from him. In a second he was on one knee, then he pitched forwards, pounding me in the side, a throbbing ache that didn't go away, that would bruise.

'Stop it!' Claudia yelled, following us.

'Whore!' Gianni said, as if he were punching her too, finishing all of it.

I grabbed at him again, pushing, but he was ready this time and instead caught me and knocked me down. I dodged a kick, sliding away from his foot, then scrambled up and moved back towards the water entrance, the sound of my own breathing loud in my head. He followed, arms reaching out, implacable, the moving line at bayonet practice. No time to hesitate. Do it.

I jumped at him, my fist aiming at his nose, and smashed down. He howled, weaving a little, his hands to his face, looking up at me in shock. I backed away. There were red spots on the shirtfront now, then a longer drip, blood running out of his nose.

'Stop it!' Claudia said, grabbing his arm. He brushed her away, a gnat, and started towards me, implacable again. But he was slower this time, obviously in pain.

'All right,' I said, panting. 'Enough.' A man my father's age, not a soldier. Already slowing down, bound to get hurt. My father's age. His friend, in fact, betraying him too. Not the first time. I held up my hand. 'Enough.'

But he was looking down at his ruined shirt, bright with blood, not hearing me, dazed and then shaking, excited, everything about him ready to move. And maybe just then I wanted it too, that rush of blood.

He looked up at me, a quick glance, then, before I could move, he rammed his head into my stomach, knocking me over. I landed with a thud on the pile of paving stones poking up bluntly beneath the tarp, so that for an instant, winded, all I could feel was a spasm of pain. Then my head fell back too as he jumped on me, hands on my throat.

'Stop it! Stop it!' Claudia was hitting him on the back, trying to pull him off, but he was oblivious, lost in his own adrenaline strength, tightening his hands on my windpipe. I choked. I could feel the blocks against my back, then the wetness of the tarp. Everything smelled of damp, the slick steps, the canal. I tried to wriggle out of his grip, punching his sides, but the hands didn't budge and now began to shake me, banging my head against the tarp. I looked into his face and found no expression at all, just a kind of strained exertion as he kept his hands in place. Beyond him there were dim lights, the gondola up on its support rack, Claudia flailing at his back, her face frantic now. She pulled on his collar, yanking his head back, and I saw, absurdly, that the white tie was still in place, but then I was choking again, beginning to feel dizzy, without enough breath to shove his body off mine. Claudia was shouting, still pounding on his back, but I couldn't make out the words, indistinct behind the pulse in my ears and the faint wheezing coming from my throat.

Then suddenly a look came into his eyes, hesitant, a question to himself, and I felt the hands loosen, a quick rush of air. I lay still, waiting for him to lift his hands away, and he was blinking, as if waking, still looking down at me in a kind of surprise, unaware of the shadow over him – Claudia, her face pulled tight, a paving stone in her hand now, raised high, then smashing down on the back of his head. His eyes went wide. A grunt, then he fell on me, pinning me under dead weight.

Everything stopped, no sound at all but the soft lapping of the canal against the steps. His head had fallen to the side of mine and I listened for breathing, anything. Then the stone slid off his back onto the floor, a thunk, and I felt blood oozing down his neck. Thick, still warm. I pushed at him, gently at first, then with a heave, until he rolled off, turning on to his back. Claudia stood looking at him, shaking.

'Oh God. I thought—' Her voice was shaking too.

I got up and bent over with my hands on my knees, the air still coming in ragged gulps. How long had it been? One minute? Two? Like a flash of light. One flash and everything was different.

'He was going to—' Claudia was saying.

No, he was going to stop. But before I could say it, Claudia made a sound, a kind of frightened yelp.

'He's not moving. Is he moving?'

I looked down. Eyes closed. A small pool of blood under his head. But not spreading. If his heart were still pumping, there'd be more blood, wouldn't there?

'Oh God. Now they'll—'

I shook my head, rubbing my throat with my hand. 'No, it was a fight.'

'No. No,' she said, a wail. 'They'll say I killed him. I did kill him. They'll send me—' All in a rush, like blood pouring out. She had folded her arms over her chest, holding herself, a protection, as if someone were already there to take her away.

I looked up, catching her eyes, the fear in them, and felt it too, a queasiness in the stomach, both of us in a helpless freefall, using our eyes to hold on. I was still breathing hard, excited, and the fear was like another surge, my skin warm with it, stronger even than sex but like it too, connecting us, because we both felt it. Her eyes were shiny with the fear, letting me in, closer than we'd ever been.

'They'll send me—' she said again, feebly, almost to herself, and I saw what she had already imagined, how it would look: the engagement party, a public attack, then the private killing, driven to it. Nothing else would be believed.

I looked down at Gianni again, not moving, then back into her eyes. Frantic, the way they'd been, standing over him with the stone raised. For me.

'We have to get him out of here,' I said.

'Out of here. But they'll know – he came here.'

'Nobody knows that. Nobody knows you came here either. Nobody. We have to get him out.'

'Out,' she said vaguely, meaning how.

'The tarp,' I said, stepping away from his body to reach the edge of the covering. 'We'll wrap him in this.' Two pieces. One would never be missed.

'Oh God,' Claudia said, not moving.

'We'll have to use the boat.'

'The boat,' Claudia said dully.

'We can't carry him through the streets. We have to dump him in the lagoon.'

'They'll find him.'

'Not if we weight him down. Here, give me a hand with this.'

'But they'll look. They'll ask questions.'

'We never saw him. Quick,' I said, gesturing at the tarp.

'You'll be in trouble too. For me. The police—'

I went over and took her by the shoulders, still trembling under the coat.

'I need you to help me move him. To get him on the tarp. Can you do that?'

She said nothing for a minute, just looked at me.

'Nobody will know,' I said, then let my hands slide away from her. 'We need to roll him over. On to the tarp.'

'There's blood,' she said quietly.

'Take his feet,' I said, still looking at her.

Then she nodded, calmer, almost herself again. She stepped to the other side of the body and bent down to grab his legs. I looked at him again. Shiny leather shoes, white tie, already dressed for burial.

I crouched down and put my hands on his shoulders, ready to push.

'Okay, when I say—'

A groan, faint enough to be a sound out on the canal, then an almost imperceptible twitch in his arm. Another groan, louder this time, and Claudia made a little cry, her hands to her mouth, and jumped away.

'Oh God,' she said. 'He's not dead.'

A stiff body, no longer pumping blood. It had never occurred to me to check. Now I leaned over him, listening, my fingers touching the side of his neck. But what were you supposed to feel? A pulse, any movement at all. If he were alive, there'd be breath. I put my ear next to his mouth. For a second, nothing, then the faint gagging sound again. I looked up at Claudia, our eyes meeting

148

across the body. Alive. To have her arrested, sent – out of the way. Ruin everything. I felt a slight movement in his shoulder and looked back down. Eyes still closed. A blotch of red on his shirt-front. Just dead and now alive again, unstoppable. No expression on his face – maybe the way it had been, nodding at the hospital, sitting on the terrace at Villa Raspelli, calmly leaning over my mother, touching her soft throat. Not the first time. Unstoppable, about to get away with all of it. Get us out of the way. I looked up at Claudia again, the same shiny eyes, and then grabbed his shirt-front and began dragging him to the steps.

'Adam,' she said, but what I heard was the scrape of his clothes across the stone floor, another whispered groan. The back of his head left a smear of blood behind. Unstoppable.

I dragged him over to the steps, then, kneeling, pushed his head into the water and held it there, forcing it down, my arms clenched, shaking. Do it. A whimper from where Claudia was standing. I felt the wet creep along my legs. Nothing moved in the water, then a few bubbles appeared, rising out of his mouth, and the body began to twitch, maybe an unconscious reaction, a last gasp. Not thrashing for life, just a series of twitches. I held his head under by the throat, hearing my own blood in my ears, watching the bubbles. How long? Then suddenly his body shook and his eyes flew open and I felt they could see me through the mirror of water, knew it was me leaning over him with my hand on his throat, choking him, until the water finally rushed in and forced out the last bubble. I held him for another minute, until nothing moved at all, then stood up slowly, my arms dripping with water. His eyes were still open, rigid now, not focused on anything. I took a deep breath and for a second expected the fear again, the free fall in my stomach, but what I felt, dazed, was the ease of it. A matter of a minute to kill. In the war we always wondered if we could do it, stick the bayonet in. And now I had, with no more effort than it would take to nod.

I turned to Claudia, but neither of us said anything. I could hear a ship's horn – the moist air in the lagoon was probably thickening to fog. Easier to hide. I nodded at the wall switch.

'Get the lights. We don't want anybody—'

Claudia glanced down at Gianni, his leather shoes sticking up incongruously on the water stairs, then went over to the wall.

With only the lamps from the indoor hall, we had to work in shadows. I looked across the canal to the neighbouring buildings. A few upstairs lights, the rest of the windows dark. No one seemed to have noticed anything. Even the marchesa was away. I pulled the boat around.

I laid out the tarp, then dragged Gianni up to it by the feet, hearing thuds as his head hit the stairs. I pitched him forwards so that he was sitting up, then started to take off his jacket, struggling with the arms.

'What are you doing?'

'We have to wipe up the blood. I don't want to use anything here. They might miss it. That's it. Okay, use this, then we'll throw it in with him.'

She hesitated for a second, not understanding, then looked at me, dismayed. I nodded. She waited another second, staring, then shivered and took the wet jacket and began mopping the floor around us as I moved him on to the tarp. We threw the jacket over him and weighed it down with paving stones, then rolled the tarp over and tied it at each end with some rope I found near the water gate. I didn't think anyone could see us in the half-light of the room, but we worked quickly, making sure the blood was gone, then lugging the heavy bag towards the steps.

'Here, let me steady it, we'll just slide him in.'

Claudia was sweating, her face flushed from the lifting, and when she looked up, waiting for me, I felt the closeness again, not fear this time, something more intimate, in it together.

I was lifting the rolled tarp over the gunwale when the phone rang. We froze. Two phones ringing, one upstairs, one in the hall. Looking for him. Drawing attention to the house. I stood still, as if any movement might be seen through the water gate, eyes peering around the edge of curtains, curious about the phone. When it stopped, I realised I had been holding my breath.

150

I took up the tarp again. 'On two,' I said, and she lifted with me and he was in, the boat rocking from the sudden movement. I steadied it with my foot and reached out my hand to help her in. She stopped, a small panic in her eyes.

'I can't swim,' she said.

'Do you want to stay?' I asked.

She glanced quickly at the dim entryway, then shook her head and stepped in, clenching my hand until she sat.

'It's cold. You'll need a coat,' she said, motioning towards my jacket, wet at the sleeves.

'No time,' I said, untying the boat and pushing off into the canal. 'We'll have to use the oars until we get farther out. The motor's too loud.'

As we floated quietly towards the Zattere, it occurred to me, a stray thought, that nothing ever changed in Venice. Muffled oars, a body taken away in the night. I looked across at Claudia. Over fans at La Fenice.

The rain had left a heavy mist over the water. When we reached the Giudecca channel, there were a few distant shafts of yellow lights from boats and a much stronger wind that cut into my wet sleeves. I lowered the small outboard motor into the water and jerked hard on the starter cord. A sputter, not much more than a grunt. How long since it had been used? Was there even gas in the tank? Another pull. Why not just dump him here? The Giudecca was a deep channel, not one of the shallow city canals, but too near. The tides that flushed out the city could flush things back in. I imagined Gianni stuck just a few feet underwater in a side canal, waiting for the dredgers. Better to get him out into the lagoon, even if it meant rowing. But that would take hours. I pulled on the cord again. A louder sputter, as if it were choking on itself.

'Adam.'

I turned. A vaporetto had pulled away from its stop on the Giudecca and was heading across towards us, its headlights growing brighter through the mist. I pulled the cord again. The pilot would see us, not run us down. And then be curious – what would anybody be doing out at this hour, in the cold? A witness.

I let the cord sit for a second, not wanting to flood the motor, then yanked it. A louder sputter, almost catching, lost under the noise of the vaporetto. The light was closer. I yanked again. A small cough, then another, settling into a series of spitting exhaust noises as the motor came to life.

'Hold on,' I said, then let out the choke and swung us away from the approaching boat into the dark, close enough to feel a lift from its wake.

I had no idea where to go, except away from the city, some-where beyond the lights. The open sea, past the barrier islands, was too long a trip and in the dark too dangerous. The lagoon itself was a maze of currents and shallow water – you heard stories about visitors who ended up stuck on an unexpected mudbank. You were only safe if you followed the channel markers.

I turned at the tip of the Giudecca and went behind San Giorgio Maggiore, putting the island between us and San Marco. It was darker here, the thick mist broken only by tiny marker lights, a few bobbing on buoys, the others on those fence posts the Venetians use to outline their water roads. If other boats were out, they'd be here too, hugging the safety of the channel, but what choice was there? In the mist, without even starlight, to drift away from the markers would be to circle in complete darkness. With a dead man in the boat.

I glanced down at the rolled-up tarp, the first time I'd even thought about it. A dead man. Would the blocks be enough to hold the body to the bottom, or would the tides dislodge it? What if they never found him at all?

I moved the boat out of the main channel, keeping parallel to it, the markers in sight. Boat traffic might churn up something from the bottom – this distance could give it a small margin, let it lie undisturbed. The mist was gathering in patches now, almost fog. I squinted, afraid of missing any of the markers. Behind us San Marco had disappeared, just a vague light source without defini-tion. Claudia was bent over in the prow, looking down, arms wrapped tightly around herself, and I realised that it must be cold,

152

that I should be shivering in my damp jacket and instead felt flushed, still excited, the boat trip somehow just an extension of the fight, not yet over. I saw my hand on his throat underwater, the eyes come open. What I'd never had to do in the war, kill a man. I swung the boat away from a buoy that seemed to have come from nowhere. Pay attention. Think later. Now just get rid of it. This was far enough, somewhere between the city and the Lido. What if he washed up on the beach? Where they'd met.

I idled the engine, but it stalled, gave another cough, and then went quiet. Suddenly, without the throb of it, the silence around us had the quality of mist, opaque, opening up slightly for the faint bells on the buoys. There was just enough light from the marker to see her face, staring at the tarp, then looking at me.

'Adam, if we do this, the body, it's a crime. We can't explain—' She looked away, unsure how to finish.

'It is a crime. I killed him.'

She glanced back at me, her eyes suddenly fierce. 'No, both. Both of us,' she said, her voice steady. And I thought of her that first afternoon, in the hotel near the station, opening a button.

I looked across at her for another minute, not saying anything, then nodded.

'Hold on to the sides. Keep the boat steady.'

She placed her hands on either side. I knelt forward, took up the front end of the tarp, and lifted it over the edge. It didn't matter where you grabbed it. It was no longer a body, just something heavy wrapped in tarp, pushing the boat down with its weight. Claudia shifted to the other side, as if she could counterbalance the slide.

'It won't tip,' I said. 'Don't worry.'

And then, before it could settle, I heaved up, lifting the back end with a grunt and swinging it around until its own weight was pulling it over and all I needed to do was push, then quickly right the boat as the tarp plunged into the lagoon. There was a splash, rocking the boat. For a few minutes we just sat looking over the side, as if the body would bounce back up again, but then the ripples died down and the water was smooth all the way to the buoy, just a gentle lap at the side of the boat. I looked around. No other boats. Claudia was still staring at the water.

'So,' she said.

I didn't say anything, suddenly tired, as if the adrenaline were draining away, a kind of anemia.

'How long before we know – if it's down?'

'It's already down.'

'What do we say? We have to think what to say.'

'Nothing. We never saw him.'

'But they'll ask. Where were we?'

I pulled the cord, grateful the motor started right away, not wanting to talk. I hadn't thought beyond the body, getting rid of it. But of course we weren't rid of it. People would ask, the police would be called, we would be part of it. You called him at the hospital. When did you see him last? Where were you? The body was only the beginning.

Now I did feel the cold, the wet air hitting my face in little stings, then harder ones as the mist turned to rain again. Almost as cold as Germany, the terrible sharp wind and people fighting over pieces of coal. You didn't think about anything except staying warm. Not bodies, not what you were doing there, just getting in out of the cold. The black water streamed past the side of the boat, pelted with rain. We'd be coming up to San Giorgio soon.

I slowed the boat, unable to see more than a few yards ahead. Claudia hunched down under her coat, shivering, folding herself up against the rain. I followed the markers, still looking around for other boats. But who would be out now? No fishermen, no water taxis. Only someone who didn't want to be seen, hidden by the emptiness of the lagoon.

I wiped my eyes, feeling the cold rain seeping down my neck, the shocked alertness of a cold shower, no longer caught up in a blood heat. What were we doing? A body wrapped in a tarp, dead, not an accident. I saw the tarp sinking, dragged down by stones, deliberately made to disappear. What explanation could there be now? Claudia was right – we had to think what to say. They'd look for him. He had

154

a daughter. Doges in the family. Why would a man disappear? They'd hear about the engagement party. They'd talk to Claudia. And somehow it would come out. Somehow. Only people like Gianni got away with murder. I felt queasy again. But she hadn't hesitated. Both of us. There was a sudden burst of rain in my face; it was really coming down now, sheets of it. Mimi's party would be chaos.

The trip back was longer, and by the time we reached the Giudecca channel we were soaked through, my fingers frozen on the rudder. I killed the motor when we were almost at the Zattere, letting the boat bob for a minute, then rowing back under the footbridge to our canal. The sound of the rain now covered the splash of the oars. I didn't have to let the boat drift. Claudia lifted the coat off her head and looked around.

'It's okay. No one's out,' I said.

'I won't go back to that camp,' she said, as if she hadn't heard me, another conversation.

'No.'

'Never. No matter what.'

'It's not there any more, Claudia,' I said quietly.

'That one. Another. Any of them.'

'Ssh,' I said. 'No one's going anywhere.' I put a finger to my lips, then pointed at the lighted window across the canal. I used the oar to swing around to our gate, catching the mooring pole and tying the boat before I helped Claudia out. She was shivering, her lips moving involuntarily. I helped her up the stairs, then closed the grilled door on the canal. She was standing near the pile of paving stones, staring at the tarp. I looked down to where the blood had been, just a streak of wet now.

'Come on, let's get you dry,' I said, taking her arm.

She was still looking at the tarp. 'What are we going to do?'

'A bath. You're freezing.'

'No, I mean, what are we going to do?' She motioned towards the pile.

'I know what you mean. A bath. Then we're going to go to Mimi's.'

155

She looked up. 'What?'

'I've been thinking – it's the safest thing we can do. Hundreds of witnesses. When anyone asks, we were at Mimi's.'

'Are you crazy?'

'We can do it. People will be late. Everything'll be a mess in the rain. We go in the back. Then we're in the ballroom, dancing. That's all anyone will remember.'

'Dancing,' she said, shocked. 'After we just—'

I took her arms. 'I know what we just did. And now we're going to Mimi's.'

'I can't.'

'We have to,' I said, still holding her. 'Otherwise, where were we?'

'How can we go?' she said nervously. 'Like this? What do we wear?'

'Borrow something of my mother's.'

'I couldn't.'

'Claudia,' I said, gripping her now. 'There isn't time. I'll run the bath. We'll pick something out. It'll be all right. It has to be.'

'But my hair, it's all wet,' she said, putting her hand up to feel it.

'Your hair.'

She stopped, hearing the absurdity of it.

'Everybody'll be wet,' I said. 'Come on. We have to hurry.'

She didn't move.

'We can do it.' I looked towards the tarp. 'We can't let anyone know.'

'And we're supposed to smile? After this?' She shook a little.

'Yes. As if nothing happened.' I took her shoulders again. 'Because nothing happened.'

She looked at me, then nodded, still shaking.

'All right. Hot water. Come on. Leave the lights. I want to check later. If there's any blood we missed.'

'Oh,' she said, stopping. She looked back towards the steps, her face slack.

'You all right?' I said softly.

She nodded. 'It's just – I forgot about the blood.'

CHAPTER EIGHT

THERE WAS ONLY enough hot water for one bath, so we took turns. While I was drying off near the space heater, Claudia went through my mother's closet, her head wrapped in a towel, her skin flushed from the warm soak.

'You're young. That already puts you ahead. Wear anything.'

'To a party like this? It's easy for you.'

'If it still fits,' I said, picking up my jacket from the bed. 'I haven't worn it in three years. That's nice.'

She was holding up an evening gown with a scalloped neck, as creamy and soft as lingerie.

'It's from before the war.'

'Here, let me help.'

She slid the dress over her head.

'It's loose,' she said.

'This much?' I pinched in some fabric at the back. 'We can pin it. You'll look wonderful.'

'Oh, wonderful,' she said, flouncing out her damp hair. 'Everyone will see it's old.'

'They'll still be looking at you. That's all we want.'

'Look at all this. Powder, everything. How can she have so much?'

I left her at the mirror, patting her face, and went to dress, hurrying, even managing my tie in a few minutes. Then I headed downstairs to check the water entrance, running a flashlight along the edge of the tarp. There were a few dark splotches of dampness on the stone floor, possibly from our dripping clothes, but nothing that looked like blood. One more check tomorrow in the daylight. What else? The ashtray in the hall. Not even a trace. When I got back to my mother's room, Claudia was still at the dressing table, putting her hair up.

'We have to hurry.'

'There's nothing else I can do with it,' she said, ignoring me. 'This way it doesn't matter if it's wet.'

I saw the white back of her neck, like a girl's, then looked into the mirror as she blotted her lipstick. The room was warm now, close with the smell of perfume and powder.

'You look beautiful.'

She met my eyes in the mirror, then looked down, suddenly upset.

'I can't do this. All the time thinking—' She stopped, then reached for another tissue and raised her head to look at me again. 'Where are the pins?'

It needed only two, which I covered in the back with the sash. The shoes were more difficult – we had to stuff wadded tissue into the toes to make them fit.

'So,' Claudia said, standing in front of the mirror, smoothing the skirt. 'It's okay?'

'Almost.'

I went into my mother's closet and pulled out the false panel in the glove drawer that hid her jewel case. You had to lift the top tray of rings out to get to the bigger pieces. I took out a necklace.

'I can't wear—'

'She's not wearing it,' I said, fastening it behind her neck. 'She won't mind.'

She fingered the stones, just gazing into the mirror for a minute.

'My God. Are they rubies?'

'I don't know. Garnets, maybe. Anyway, they suit you. Your colouring. Ready?'

But she stood there, still looking, then made a wry grimace. 'All my life I wanted to go to those parties. In one of the palazzos. With jewels. And now – like this.'

Mimi's ground-floor layout was similar to ours; a long hall stretching from the Grand Canal to a calle, flanked by old offices and storerooms converted tonight into cloakrooms and little parlours. As I'd expected, there was a crush at the water entrance, a swarm of flashbulbs and dripping umbrellas and harried maids running back and forth. Most of the maids were new, borrowed from friends or hired for the evening, and none of them recognised me. We were just part of the crowd in evening dress streaming in from all directions, handing over wet coats, adjusting hair in powder rooms, stamping our shoes dry on the marble floor. In the confusion of arrival, with everyone talking at once and music coming from upstairs, no one noticed us. We might have come in at any time. I glanced up to see if Mimi was on the stairs, receiving, but she had evidently already joined the party. Better still.

At the top of the stairs was a landing, an ante-room before the main *sala*, a place to catch your breath and gather your skirt, and for a moment we stood there, dazzled. Mimi's ballroom was one of the grandest in Venice, as large as the Rezzonico's, and tonight every inch of it seemed alive with light. The centre chandeliers were electric, but the walls were lined with sconces holding real candles, hundreds of them, backed by mirrors, so that the effect was watery, constantly in motion, the night-time equivalent of sunlight reflected off the canal. At the end of the room the high windows tapered to gothic points, but the walls themselves were rococo, panelled Arcadian scenes framed in gilt, mouldings of swirling plaster. Waiters passed trays of champagne. Women glanced at themselves in mirrors. After the dark lagoon, the bulky tarp splashing over the side of the boat, I felt we had stepped into another world – not this one, maybe the one the room had been meant for, not real even then.

'Adam, you did come.' Mimi after all, standing guard at the

door. Her hair, swept up, was sprinkled with jewels, not a tiara but tiny diamond pins, bits of starlight. Could she see it on my face? Washed now, but still somehow streaked with his blood? I felt my hands shaking and dug my nails into the palms. We could do this, had to.

'Hours ago,' I said, nodding towards the crowd below.

'And you've brought Miss—'

'Grassini,' Claudia said.

'Yes, I remember. So glad,' she said, shaking hands, her eyes sweeping down to take in Claudia's dress. She turned to me. 'How nice you look. Out of uniform.' A raised eyebrow. 'I thought you didn't have evening clothes. Grace said you couldn't find—'

'And then I did. I hope it's all right.'

'Darling, don't be silly. I'm desperate for young people. Half the men here seem to have canes. When did we all get to be such an age?' She paused. 'You're supposed to say, *You* didn't.'

I lifted my head, focusing, digging my nails in again. 'You didn't.'

'Charm itself, isn't he?' she said to Claudia. 'And so quick. I don't suppose you've brought Gianni?'

'No. Isn't he here?' I said, not looking at Claudia.

'Not yet. I don't know how Grace puts up with it. I wouldn't. He'd be late to his own funeral.'

Claudia moved involuntarily, catching Mimi's eye. 'Well, a doctor,' she said.

'Yes, but at this hour. Oh dear,' she said, looking over my shoulder towards the stairs. 'Count Grillo. I never thought – the stairs.' I turned to see a white-haired man making his way up slowly, gripping an attendant with one arm and the banister with the other. 'Maybe I should have him carried. But so embarrassing. My God, when I think how he used to—'

'An old flame?'

'How he used to *dance*. Don't be fresh. Go and be conspicuous. Maybe you can get the orchestra to liven things up a bit.' She turned to Claudia. 'We'll talk later. I'm so glad you came. You look

160

lovely.' She moved over to the head of the stairs. 'Ernesto, how marvellous. No, don't hurry. Oodles of time.'

A waiter came by with champagne.

'They're going to start wondering where he is,' Claudia said, looking at her glass. She shuddered suddenly, like someone caught in a draft.

'Cold?'

She shook her head. 'I'm nervous. I don't know why. Not before, not even in the boat. And now here, a place like this.'

'Have some champagne.'

'Oh, just like that. Champagne – as if nothing's happened.'

'I want people to see us having a good time,' I said, spreading my hand, steady now, towards the ballroom. 'He won't be missed for hours. He's a doctor. They're like that. Things come up.' I put down my glass on a little table. 'So let's be conspicuous. Dance?'

She looked up at me, biting her lip. 'It's my fault, all this.'

I held up my arms, ready to dance.

'And now for you, this trouble. What if you had never met me?'

I took the champagne glass out of her hand. 'Yes, what if?' I said, then put my arm behind her back and moved her into the room.

The orchestra, in formal cutaways, was playing 'Why Do I Love You?' but slightly off-rhythm, as if they were sight-reading, more familiar with Strauss than a twenties show tune. Not that it mattered. The dancers were moving at their own pace, peering over shoulders, the music just an excuse to look around at one another. Everything gleamed – jewels, the huge mirrors, even the long parquet floor, polished probably for days. I thought of Byron's famous party, when they threw gold plates into the canal.

'So you can dance too,' Claudia said.

'Miss Hill's dancing class. We all had to go. The boys hated it.'

'And the girls?'

'They liked to get dressed up.'

She glanced around the room. 'So nothing changes. Look at the clothes. Is it all right, the dress?'

'Perfect.'

'Ha, perfect. The poor relation.'

'Not too poor,' I said, putting a finger to the necklace. Off to the left I caught a quick flash of light, stronger than a candle.

'Jewels. If my father could see me—' She looked away, frowning. 'Maybe it was for him, what happened. For him.'

But at that moment, my face suddenly warm, I knew it wasn't. Not for him, not even for Claudia. I'd wanted to do it. I wasn't in the cold boat any more, unable to think. I'd wanted to do it. Even now I could feel the odd excitement of it, my arms shaking as I held his head under.

'What's wrong?' Claudia said.

'Nothing. Just a little warm. Dance over there – I want them to take our picture.'

Another flash went off, and now the heat drained away from my face, as if my blood were running back and forth, like the tide in the lagoon.

'Adam? What are you doing here?' My mother was standing with a couple at the edge of the dance floor. I leaned over and kissed her cheek.

'I decided you were right, so we borrowed a dress. Your idea, remember?'

My mother was taking in Claudia, giving a surprised glance at the necklace. Then she smiled, extending her hand, not missing a beat. 'Claudia, how nice.'

'I hope you don't mind.'

My mother waved this away. 'Wonderful what being twenty years younger can do for a dress. It's perfect on you.' And I saw in her smile that she thought some other bargain had been struck, an end to the trouble, our coming a promise of smoother days ahead, more precious than rubies. Her face beamed with a kind of warm relief. 'Oh, but let me introduce Inspector Cavallini. Signora Cavallini.'

'Inspector?' Claudia started, not expecting this, but the Cavallinis, half turned to the dance floor, missed the flicker in her eyes.

'Signorina Grassini, isn't it?' my mother went on. 'I've become so bad at names. And my son of course you know. I think you met at Harry's.'

There were the usual nods and handshakes, something to fall back on while I collected myself.

'Yes, I remember,' I said quickly, a signal to Claudia. 'I hope you're not on duty tonight.'

'Only as an escort,' he said, smiling. 'It's my wife who brings me.' Signora Cavallini nodded, accepting this. She had the grave, long face of someone invited for her family connections.

'Well, if Gianni doesn't get here soon you *will* be,' my mother said. 'I'll have to send you out to find him.'

'Ah, if every woman did that when the man is late, the police would never sleep.'

'Adam, you did call him.'

'Yes. At the hospital. I told him to meet you here. He's probably around somewhere. It's a mess downstairs. We were here for ages before we found you.'

Claudia looked away.

'No, it's not like him. Well, it is like him, but not this much, if you see what I mean.'

'Excuse me, would you turn this way, please?'

The photographer stepped back on to the dance floor, motioning with his head for us to stand closer. A flash went off and there we were, evidence, Claudia and I standing next to the police. For one wild moment I wanted to laugh, caught by the unexpectedness of luck.

'Perhaps you would not worry so much if you were dancing,' Cavallini said. 'May I?'

After a nod to Signora Cavallini, he led my mother out to the floor, leaving us to make small talk with his wife. It was a pity about the rain, but the ball was lovely, the way Venice used to be. So much food. Of course, it was easier for foreigners. When even this ran out, I looked at my mother, chatting happily while she danced, and I felt queasy again.

163

Signora Cavallini, whose English was poor, must have been as bored as we were, because she led her husband away before he could ask for another dance. They drifted into the next room, where supper would be served later, picking up glasses of champagne along the way.

'My God, what a country. Even the policemen go to balls. Imagine at home,' my mother said.

'How does Mimi know him?'

'His wife, I think. Of course, with Mimi you never know. She casts a pretty wide net. Look at them all,' she said, waving to the room. 'And she was so worried. "They won't come out in the rain" Well, they'd come out in a monsoon. You'll never guess who's here. Celia de Betancourt. I thought, the war really must be over if she's back. Venezuela all this time. Imagine the boredom of it.'

'Who?'

'Darling, you remember. You were fascinated by her when you were little. On the beach. She would just tan and tan.'

I made a helpless gesture.

'Well, anyway, she's here. Still brown as a berry too. Of course it's sunny there, I suppose. That's her, over with Mimi. Remember?'

I looked across the floor at a woman in a strapless taffeta gown, her dark neck entirely covered in diamonds.

'That's some necklace.'

'The jewels are past belief. I think even Mimi was stunned. They said the war would put an end to all this, and just look.'

'I hope it's all right,' Claudia said, touching hers. 'About the necklace.'

My mother said nothing for a minute, her face soft and pleased, then put her hand on Claudia's. 'It's lovely, isn't it? Adam's father gave it to me. Awful to think of it just sitting in a box somewhere. It's nice to give it some air.'

'Like a pet,' I said.

'You know what I mean. What's the point of having them if you don't wear them? Anyway,' she said to Claudia, 'I'm glad you did.'

She turned to me, her eyes moist. 'You look so like your father in those clothes. So like. He loved to dress up, you know. Parties.'

While you were – where? I thought, then felt dismayed for thinking it.

'So handsome. Well,' she said, and then, making a connection known only to herself, 'You know, it's not like him, not really. I'm worried. It's all very well that policeman pooh-poohing, saying men are late, but he wouldn't be late for this. What did he say to you?'

'Just that he'd see you here. It's not that late,' I said, glancing at my watch. 'He'll be here.' Suddenly I wanted a cigarette, anything to steady the jumping in my stomach.

'But I called his house. He left hours ago.'

'Maybe he stopped for a drink somewhere.'

'A drink. And then fell into a canal, I suppose,' my mother said, dismissive. 'Tonight of all nights.'

'The inspector didn't seem to think—'

'Oh, I know what he thinks. Some woman. Why else would a man be late? A little stop along the way. I wouldn't put it past *him* – he practically winks at you when he talks. But that's not Gianni.' She put her hand on Claudia's again. 'I hope Adam explained things. What he's like. He wouldn't hurt a fly, you know. He wouldn't know how.'

Claudia moved her hand, looking away.

'Anyway, you've come to dance, and I'm just fussing and ruining things. Off you go. I'll wait here like Penelope with my weaving.' She made a shooing motion with her hands towards the dance floor.

The orchestra had switched to a piece of generic ball music, lilting and sweet without being recognisable as anything in particular, something to talk under as we danced. People were passing back and forth between the ballroom and the food tables next door, balancing little plates of hors d'oeuvres.

'What are you going to say to her?' Claudia said when we'd moved away from the edge.

'Nothing.'

165

'But if they never find him – think how it will be for her. Never to know.'

'If they never find him, we'll be safe. She'll be—'

What? All right? Frantic? Waiting for some word, the phone to ring. How long before a disappearance becomes painless, just a mystery? I looked at Claudia.

'We can't say anything. You know that, don't you? We can't.'

She nodded.

'I'll get her to go away somewhere. Maybe Mimi—'

'She won't leave now. She'll look for him.'

'She can't look for ever. It'll pass,' I said weakly, not even convincing myself.

We stared at each other for a moment, not talking, just moving our feet in aimless circles to the music, then her eyes grew shiny and she turned her face away.

'Oh,' she said, a moan, cut off, turned suddenly into a kind of nervous giggle that caught in her throat. She pitched her head forwards on to my shoulder to stifle it, steady an unexpected shaking.

'We have to get through this,' I said. 'Then we'll be all right.'

'Can't we leave now? Everybody's seen us.'

'If they find the body, they'll try to fix a time of death. People have to think we were here all night.'

'How would they find it? You said he'd go to the bottom. In the lagoon.'

'If they find it.'

'Oh, God. And then what?'

'Then we were here all night. Having a good time.'

I pulled her hand to me, bending my head to kiss it, then saw my own fingers and froze. There were little rims of rust under the nails. No, blood. When I'd clenched my hands earlier, had I dug them in so deep? I opened my hand. No marks on the palms. His blood. Where anybody might see it if he looked closely enough. Cavallini hadn't noticed, shaking hands, but what if we met again? I might be lighting a cigarette, bringing my fingers up, the rims suddenly visible, unavoidable. The smallest thing could give you away.

I turned Claudia's hand over, spreading it. 'Let me see. No, you're all right.'

'What?' she said, startled, clutching her hand.

'I'll be right back,' I said, letting my arms fall. 'Have some champagne. Right back.' Turning away, not even waiting to see her expression, to explain anything. Time enough later.

The nearest men's room was on the other side of the stair landing, unmarked but guarded by a footman placed there to direct ladies down the hall. Inside, another servant was acting as washroom attendant, turning taps and handing out towels. Count Grillo stood in front of the toilet bowl, still supported on one arm, his pee a trickle that barely made a sound as it hit the water. I dug my fingernails in again, waiting.

When he finished, flushing and then slowly buttoning up, I stepped forward to take his place, but nothing came out. I was too anxious now even to pee. But I had to – otherwise why had I come? And then the attendant turned on the tap, the sound of gushing water like a cue, and it was all right. I slumped a little, my breath spilling out too.

Count Grillo took for ever to dry but finally shuffled away. I rubbed my hands around the bar of soap, lathering them, keeping my back to the attendant. My knuckles were raw, not broken but scraped – what happened to hands in a fight. I ran one nail under the others and dug at the dried blood. More soap. When I rinsed, there was just enough blood to stain the water, a thin pale stream. I stood for a minute staring at it, light rust, like something that might have come out of an old water pipe. There all along. Shaking hands with Cavallini, with scraped knuckles and blood under my fingernails. But he hadn't seen, hadn't thought to look. And now it was too late, the red running into the soapy water, then out some ancient drain to the lagoon. Safe.

'*Prego.*' The attendant had leaned forward, holding out a hand towel, the word loud in my ear. Had he been close enough to see?

167

It didn't have to be Cavallini. Anybody. Just one glance at the basin, the eye drawn to the unexpected stain.

'*Momento*,' I said quickly, turning my shoulder to block his line of sight. What if any of it had stuck to the porcelain? But I couldn't wash the bowl, not with him standing there. I lathered once more, then rinsed, holding my hands out for the towel but keeping the water running, a last chance to let it wash away. The attendant reached over and turned off the tap. Not looking at the water, busy now with the towel, taking it from me and putting it in the hamper. Involuntarily I looked down at my hands. Pink from all the soap and water, but no more rims, no evidence. When I looked up, I found the attendant staring at me, his eyes a question mark. I dropped my hands, folding the rough knuckles out of sight. He kept staring and for a minute, feeling chilled, I thought he had seen, was trying to decide what to do, but then he held up a clothes brush and I saw that he was just waiting for me to turn around so that he could dust me off, make the rest of me as clean as my hands.

An hour later we called Gianni's house again, this time using Claudia to speak Italian.

'*Non in casa*,' my mother said, 'that's all I can get out of them. Well, I know he's not at home.'

Claudia took the phone and spoke rapidly for a few minutes, but learned nothing more. He'd left the house on foot before eight. Dressed for the party. Did he say he was going anywhere first? No, he said he had to hurry, he was a little late.

The hospital knew even less. He'd left at the usual time. For home? Yes. And he hadn't been back? No, he was going to a big party.

My mother now fidgeted, genuinely worried, as if Claudia's Italian should have produced different answers.

'But it's ridiculous,' she said. 'No one just vanishes.'

'No,' Claudia said. 'So he must have a reason.'

I looked at her, expecting to see her eyes dart away, but she met mine evenly, no longer skittish, her balance restored somehow by having to lie to my mother. Or maybe the lies were becoming real to us, what had really happened.

'Maybe he did fall into a canal,' my mother said. 'You think I'm joking. Bertie says it happened all the time during the war, in the blackout. Several people *died*. Funny, isn't it? The only war casualties. No bombs. Just people falling into canals.'

'Where is Bertie, anyway?'

'He always comes late. Always. He doesn't dance, you know. He just turns up for supper and a good look around.'

'Maybe that's it. Maybe he's coming with Bertie.'

'Gianni? Why would he do that? They're not chums, really. No, something's wrong. I know it. Seriously, what should I do?'

'I don't know. Where else would he be? With friends?'

'Darling, instead of me? Something's happened.'

'Maybe you should talk to Inspector Cavallini,' Claudia said.

I looked at her, but she ignored me, concentrating on my mother.

'Yes, but what do I say? I don't want to ruin Mimi's party.'

'Ask him to call the Questura. If there has been an accident. Somebody in the canal. Anything like that.'

My mother hesitated, frowning. 'They'd report that, wouldn't they?' She nodded, thinking to herself, and turned away, touching my arm absent-mindedly as she left.

'You're sending her to the police?' I said, watching my mother head into the other room.

Claudia shrugged. 'He won't do anything. But maybe he'll remember. That we went to him before anything was wrong.'

Inspector Cavallini, indulging my mother, made the call to the Questura. Nothing had been reported, no accident, no body stumbled over in a dark calle. He asked someone to check the hospitals for anyone brought in with a heart attack, a stroke, anything sudden, but Venice had been quiet, huddled in out of the rain.

'You know, she'll make it worse,' he said, drawing me aside, his voice confiding, man-of-the-world. 'A man stops somewhere,

169

sometimes it's difficult getting back. Maestre, perhaps, somewhere on the mainland – many go there. And then a delay, the train is late. So, the arguments. Often this happens. A part of life.'

'He wouldn't go to Maestre in white tie.'

'He was in white tie?' Cavallini said, looking at me.

'I suppose so,' I said quickly. 'They said at the house he was dressed for the party. I just assumed . . . Anyway, too dressed for Maestre.'

'Somewhere in Venice, then. A visit. It's usually the case.'

'Or someone sick. A medical emergency.'

'Perhaps,' he said, dubious. 'But then he would call, yes?'

'I don't know. Maybe he's sick himself.'

'Then someone will find him. Meanwhile, make your mother easy. Maybe sick, yes, but maybe delayed, a simple matter. Ah, Signora Miller,' he said as my mother came up. 'Nothing has been reported. So I think it's a matter for the patience.'

'But they'll call you here if anything—'

'Yes, I asked them to do that. Don't upset yourself. I think next you'll hear the apologies.'

'Thank you,' my mother said, still frowning, concerned.

Then Mimi was with us.

'Grace, I've been looking—. Is anything wrong?'

'No, no,' my mother said, brightening.

'Don't tell me he still hasn't shown. It's Maggie and Jiggs. You need a rolling pin. They're all stinkers, aren't they? Have you had supper?' she said to the rest of us. 'There's lovely food. I'm going to borrow Grace for a minute.' She took my mother's arm. 'Come on. Ernesto's in a pout, and you always know what to say to him.'

She was moved off, a boat in tow, and we were alone with Cavallini again.

'Thank you for doing all this. I'm sorry – at a party.'

He shrugged. 'These things happen. She'll be angry, yes? When he comes.'

'Yes.'

He gave a sly smile. 'Yes. Another night would have been

170

better.' An old hand at slipping out. I wondered if he kept a girl in Maestre, in a small flat near the factories, for visits.

'Dance?' I said to Claudia, eager to get away.

The orchestra, looser and more confident, finally upbeat, was playing Cole Porter. It was the music everybody had wanted, what they'd flirted to on the Lido, and the floor was crowded. Soon the older guests would begin to drift away or settle themselves with plates of food, but just now the whole room seemed to be dancing, moving back and forth in flickers, like the candles. The stairs were empty. Everyone who was coming had already arrived. How long before even Cavallini became alarmed? He was watching from the edge of the floor, a knowing smile still on his face. Knowing nothing. And I realised then that no one knew, not anyone in the bright, crowded room, and the secret carried with it a kind of perverse pleasure. No one knew. We were a couple dancing to 'Night and Day', that was all – something for Cavallini to gossip about later with his well-born wife.

'Not too much longer,' I said.

'All right,' Claudia said, preoccupied. She moved with the music for a few more minutes, then said, 'What will she do?'

'She'll go back to Ca' Venti. She won't stay here. Not with Mimi. But we don't have to wait. We should do what we would normally do.'

'Can we eat something first? It's terrible, I know, but I'm so hungry.'

Food had been available all night, passed on trays and anchoring long tables in the next room, but now a new buffet had been set up, a lavish late supper, hot in silver chafing dishes, with waiters to carry your plates to a table. There were glass bowls of caviar and carving trolleys of roast veal, fruit arranged in pyramids. It was, in its way, more opulent than the ball itself, as if rationing had never existed, imaginary. Even in Venice, which had had an easy war, it was disturbing to see so much food.

'You go,' I said to Claudia. 'I want a smoke first.'

I went over to the balcony windows facing the canal, lit a cigarette, and almost at once became nauseated, the queasiness I'd felt all evening suddenly lurching in my stomach. It might have been the close room, the sight of the rich food, the smoke on an empty stomach, but I knew it wasn't, just what was left of the nervous energy that had started when I'd pushed him against the wall. Everything up and down, the freezing rain in the lagoon, then a ballroom hot enough for bare-shouldered gowns; pushing his head down in the water, my fingers still streaked with blood, everything in me pumping, willing me to do it, then polite evasions, the puzzled, hurt look on my mother's face. I opened one of the windows and gulped in some air. It was surprisingly cold, like the air in the lagoon, stinging on my warm face. Below, a vaporetto heading to Salute was passing Mimi's water entrance, still busy with lights and boats tied to the striped poles, gondoliers waiting on the dock with cigarettes cupped in their hands. A murder had been committed, and no one knew. I took another breath, then drew on the cigarette again, steadying myself. He was gone. This is what it felt like – not remorse but a grim satisfaction, and this tension in the stomach. No going back. A constant tremor on the surface of your skin, alert, because all that mattered now was not getting caught.

Getting caught. My stomach lurched again and I found my shoulders shaking, my body heaving, not bringing anything up, just gasping for air. He wasn't going to come late. I'd choked the life out of him, the last breath. How could it not be in my face, a red stain? My shoulders moved again. Somebody would see. I'd give everything away, out of control.

'Adam, whatever is the matter?' Bertie said to my back. 'Are you all right?'

I tossed the cigarette and gripped the window frame, willing my shoulders to be still. Nothing escaped Bertie. I nodded, keeping my back to him.

'I just felt funny for a minute. Some air.' I drew some in, making a point.

'Funny?'

172

I looked down again at the men on the dock. The rain had let up. You could hear the music coming from the ballroom. It might be hours before anyone asked for his boat. One of the gondoliers passed a bottle, something to hold off the damp. No one knew.

I took another breath and forced my mouth into a smile so that it was in place when I turned. 'Too much wine, probably.' Taking out a handkerchief to wipe my forehead, avoiding his eyes.

'Hm,' Bertie said, still staring. 'You sure?' But when I nodded, he let it go. 'Is that where you've been hiding, at the bar?'

'No, in plain sight,' I said, then stopped, disconcerted by his white shirtfront, almost a duplicate of Gianni's. I smiled again. 'Dancing.'

'By yourself.'

'No, Claudia's here.'

'Ah,' he said flatly. 'I thought you weren't coming.'

'And miss this?'

'I'll have one of those,' he said, glancing back at the room while I got out another cigarette. 'No, you wouldn't want to miss this. Mimi's had her ball, hasn't she? I don't suppose people will talk about anything else for months. Extravagant, my God. Even for Mimi. Celia de Betancourt's here, did you see? She can't get over it. And you know there's no one richer than a South American. Forty of them own everything or something.'

'They're lining up at the trough,' I said, gesturing to the food tables. Claudia seemed to have been swallowed up in a swarm of gowns. An old man with medals on his chest, an operetta figure, was pointing to chafing dishes as a waiter filled his plate.

'Well, the food,' Bertie said. 'I don't want to think where she got it all. Flown in, someone said. But it can't be legal, not all this. Rosaries for days, that's what it would cost me.'

'The Church doesn't seem to mind,' I said, pointing with my cigarette to a heavy-set priest filling his plate.

'Ah, Luca,' he said. 'Well, the Church takes the world as it finds it.'

'I'll say,' I said, watching him spoon cream sauce over his plate, then looked away, still not sure of my stomach.

'It's only the next, you know, that concerns them. Poor Luca. It's a weakness, all that hunger.'

'Maybe he should see real hunger. The kind in this world.'

'Adam, if you're going to start, I'm leaving. Here, of all places? You can't be serious. *In* your nice formal clothes. Eating Mimi's caviar. Oh dear,' he said, catching a glimpse of the priest wolfing down a bulging mouthful, a comically greedy moment.

I made a sound, trying to laugh. 'Who is he? One of your monsignors?'

'No, no, just a father now. A Maglione before.'

I turned. 'A relative?'

'A cousin, I think. It's impossible to keep track here. They branch and branch. Just assume everyone's family and you're safe. Why, do you want to meet him?'

'No, I was just curious. A priest in the family—'

'Ah, of course. And now yours. I hadn't thought of that. I knew we'd get you a priest somehow. Well, if he is a cousin. Let's ask Gianni.'

I shook my head. 'He's not here.'

'What do you mean?' he said, looking up sharply.

'He's late.'

'Don't be ridiculous. It's nearly midnight. He's not *late*.'

'Well, he hasn't turned up. We asked the police to check – you know, if any accidents had been reported.'

'We who? Grace?'

I nodded. 'She talked to Cavallini. He's here.'

'Yes, the wife,' Bertie said, an absent-minded response, dotting *i*'s.

'He seems to think Gianni stopped off somewhere on the way. Got delayed somehow.'

'Stopped off? Where?'

'To see somebody. A lady friend. An old Venetian custom, according to Cavallini.'

Bertie stared at me. 'Are you out of your mind? Do you think Gianni—'

174

'I don't know, Bertie. But he's not here.'

'Something's wrong,' Bertie said, serious.

'Cavallini called the Questura. They checked the hospitals. Nothing.'

'And Grace is—?'

'Putting a good face on it. She doesn't want to ruin Mimi's party.'

'Oh, these ladies. And he's probably lying in an alley somewhere.'

'Bertie, for God's sake.'

'*Sick*. Of course it would never occur to you. At my age, it's the first thing you think of. Happen any time – just walking down the street. You feel a little queer and—' He gave a small shudder to finish the thought. 'Well, you'd better get your mother home. She won't keep putting a good face on it.'

'But we don't know there's anything wrong,' I said, hearing myself, genuine.

'Of course there's something wrong.' He puffed on his cigarette, thinking. 'Has there been any trouble between them?'

'Between who?'

'Gianni and your mother,' he said, stressing each word. 'Don't be dense.'

'I don't think so,' I said, thrown by this, an unexpected idea.

'Well, it has happened before, you know. Cold feet at the altar. Still, not at the biggest party of the year. He simply wouldn't. Ah, Luca.'

The heavy priest had lumbered over. There were introductions, the Maglione connection established, but I scarcely paid attention, jittery again, wondering if Bertie would notice. Then two more minutes of aimless chatter. 'But where is Gianni?' Father Luca said, finally out of conversation. 'I've been looking for him.'

'He was called to the hospital,' Bertie said quickly. 'A shame, really. To miss a party like this.'

'Yes, very splendid. Such food. Not since the war.' Just the thought of it seemed to send him back to the table. 'You'll excuse me? I think a little coffee before I go.'

'Why did you say that?' I said to Bertie.

'What do you want people to say? If they start wondering, they won't talk about anything else, and Mimi'll never forgive her. Have some sense. Even so, you ought to take her home.'

'You act as if it's some kind of scandal.'

'Not yet.'

'Anyway, I can't. I've got to get Claudia home.'

He had another puff, brooding. 'Lovely for her, at least.'

'What do you mean?'

'That he's gone missing. Not exactly her favourite, was he?' He studied me. 'You weren't best fond, either.'

'Missing. You talk about him as if he were dead,' I said evenly. 'He's not dead.' My voice steady, not a waver.

'All right, all right, never mind. Here she comes.' He nodded towards Claudia, carrying a plate. 'Looking pretty, I must say.' He peered at me over the tops of his glasses. 'Calmer, I hope.'

'That's all over.'

'Really,' he said, neutral. 'And with everyone waiting for a rematch.' He was already reaching out for her free hand. 'Claudia. So pretty.'

'Signor Howard,' she said, tentative, not trusting the smile. 'You've just come?'

'Late, yes, I know. Mimi's already scolded me. But I'm not the only one, I gather.'

'No,' Claudia said, looking directly at him. 'How is it at the Accademia?'

Bertie ignored this, staring frankly at the necklace, not even pretending to hide his curiosity. 'It's wonderful. Wherever did you get that?' he said.

Claudia touched it. 'Adam's mother gave it to me.' She caught his raised eyebrow. 'For the evening.'

'And rubies, no less. You can always tell.'

'Yes, it's beautiful. It was so kind.'

'Well, it's all in the family, isn't it?' Bertie said, putting out his cigarette in an ashtray. He looked at me. 'I'm glad to see everyone's getting along so well. I'd better see what I can do about Grace. You two enjoy yourselves. I'll get her home.' He lifted his hand in a little wave as he left.

'He thinks something's wrong,' I said.

Claudia looked up from her plate, heaped with food. 'What did he say?'

'Nothing. Don't worry, he doesn't know anything. Just that something's wrong.'

'Oh,' she said, putting the plate on the table.

'Not hungry?'

She shook her head.

'Eat something. You can't put down a full plate. People will notice.'

She shook her head again and I picked up the plate and forked some veal.

'Why would he think that?'

'Why not? Something *is* wrong. He just doesn't know what.' I was eating quickly now, almost gulping the food down, no longer nauseated, surprised to find that I was hungry.

'Did you see the way he looked at me? Someone from the back rooms. Not someone who wears necklaces.'

'He's just jealous.'

'How can you laugh?'

'I don't know.' I put the plate down. 'I don't know how I'm doing any of it.'

But suddenly it was easier. I felt another surge, warm and full of food, a primitive well-being, filling up with life again after hours of empty dread.

'All right, one more dance to show you off, then we'll go.'

'Yes?' she said eagerly.

'If he's not here by now, whatever happened must have already happened. While we were here.'

She looked at me, unsure, but followed me back to the ballroom.

Bertie, near the door with my mother, was leaning over to talk quietly, presumably arranging to go. The floor had thinned out but was still lively.

'You know what he was thinking?' Claudia said, looking at Bertie. '"What is she doing here? That type. Ha. Looking for a rich American."'

'And you found one,' I said, smiling. That was safe now too, something I hadn't thought about before, my mother protected. I glanced towards the door. She and Bertie were talking to Mimi, heading for the stairs. 'That's better,' I said. 'You want them to see you smile.'

She looked away, then danced closer, putting her head next to mine, trembling again. 'What kind of people are we? To smile now.'

'Don't.'

'Now I've done everything. I thought before it was everything, but now there's this too.'

I pulled back to face her. 'Think what he was,' I said.

She didn't say anything.

I had said one dance, but then it became two, another. My mother had disappeared, and with her any talk about Gianni. We drifted with the music. I could feel the heat of her through her dress. Maybe this is what happens after, I thought, every sense stronger than before, as if we'd taken some extra portion from the dead. Food, touch, just being alive. In Germany, after combat, the troops were ravenous. Rapes happened then. Relieved not to be dead, proving something.

Around us, the beautiful room spun by in slow circles. Claudia had put a hand behind my neck, pulling us close, so that everything smelled of her. We were no longer pretending, with one eye to the others.

When we left, the crush for coats and umbrellas had begun, so that we were lost again in the crowd. No one noticed us leave, no one looked at the time.

We avoided the boats and walked back through San Ivo, the way Gianni would have come earlier. The calles were nearly

178

empty, just the occasional umbrella bumping into ours in the narrow passages. Claudia was quiet, leaning against me. When we reached San Polo, she stopped under an arch near the hotel.

'Here,' she said, reaching behind and unclasping the necklace. 'Take it.'

'You don't—'

'No, it's hers. What if something happens? If I lose it.'

'If you lose it,' I said dubiously.

She held it in her hand, looking down at it. 'So. No more Cinderella.'

'There's no rush.'

She pushed the necklace into my hand. 'Listen to me. We can't do this. I knew when he looked at me, Signor Howard. Tomorrow everybody asks questions. The ball, that's finished now. And who do they question? How do I explain all those things? That night, everybody saw me with him. My job, all those things. Where is he? And who's the one to suspect? Me. The easy one. Who else? Even if they don't find him.'

'Without a body they can't—'

'What's the difference? It's still me. And then you.'

'Stop it,' I said, grabbing her. 'Don't talk like that. No one is going to suspect anything.'

Her eyes were darting. I put my hand to the side of her face, as if I could stop her thoughts by touching it.

'They'll come for me.'

'They're not going to come for you.'

'Yes, they will. They'll come.' Her eyes were wide, staring at me.

'No. They can't. They can never get you.'

'Yes.'

I put a finger to her lips. 'Never. Don't you see? You were with me.' I moved the finger slowly along her lip, then rested it on her cheek. 'I'll be your alibi.'

She started to shake her head, turning it into my hand, but I held my finger there so that her eyes couldn't move away.

179

'And you'll be mine,' I said. 'We'll be safe.'

She stared at me for a minute more, then lowered her head.

'They'll come,' she said, barely audible.

I brushed my hand down her cheek. 'No,' I said, as quiet as she had been. 'No,' I said again, a murmur, then suddenly a door slammed, someone leaving the hotel, and she jumped, startled, and reached for me.

'Oh.' A muffled sound, no louder than the water dripping in the passage. She pulled me close to her, turning her face away from the light, holding on to my coat until we heard the footsteps grow fainter in the campo, heading off towards the Rialto.

'It's no one,' I said, my mouth close to her ear, but she was holding me even tighter, her arms around me, then one hand behind my neck, bending me towards her, kissing my face in a kind of rush, tasting it.

'Oh, I don't care,' she said, still kissing me, as if the slam of the door had been a shot and she were running away from the evening, from whatever was going to happen. 'I don't care.' Clutching me to her. I felt her breath and then my mouth was open too, moving down to her neck, excited, both of us panting, the promise at the end of the evening, everything finally letting go, feeling the flush in my face again.

'We can't,' I said, my face in her hair.

'Stay with me,' she said, moving her neck so I could kiss it again.

'I have to know what's going on there tonight.'

'No, stay,' she said, kissing me. 'What we would do. That's what you said.' She pulled me closer until I knew she could feel me against her, already hard. 'A party. And then you didn't come up?' Moving now, pressing into me.

'Is that what we would do?' I said, kissing her again.

'Yes,' she said, her hands on me, holding me. 'Don't you want to?'

All evening, every sense working up to it. Spurting blood. The bundled tarp splashing into the dark water. My mother's dressing

180

room, warm with powder. The white skin at the back of her neck.

'The hotel clerk will say we were together,' she said.

'Claudia—'

'I know, I know. How can we do this? After. And I still want to. I want to,' she said, her breath on my face again.

'I can't stay all night,' I said, my voice sliding away, skidding. 'I have to get back. We have to be careful.'

'Yes, careful. A little while then.' She pressed her face against my coat. 'Before they come.'

'Nobody's going to come.'

My mother was still up when I got back, coiled in a chair near the space heater, a full ashtray on her lap.

'You're a sight,' she said, raising her eyebrows, as if she could see through the rumpled jacket, the loose collar, to the rest of me, still sticky.

I stood in the doorway to the sitting room, surprised to see Inspector Cavallini on the couch. At this hour his presence was beyond the call of any duty. Was he waiting for me, the body already found, questions raised?

'I thought someone should be here,' he said, answering whatever he saw in my face. 'So Signora Miller would not be alone.' Courtly to women, a man who visited Maestre. A brandy snifter was on the table near the couch.

'I'm sorry I'm late,' I said. 'Any news?'

'Nothing,' my mother said. 'Something terrible's happened.'

'Signora, we don't know that,' he said gently.

'Of course it has. What else could it be? What's awful is not to know.'

Cavallini looked at me with an open palm of resignation. 'I've sent a man to Dr Maglione's house. He will call if—'

'He comes home? He won't. Something's happened,' my mother said.

'No word at the hospitals? Anywhere?'

'No. So a great mystery. But, let us hope, with a simple explanation. The best thing now would be to sleep,' he said, turning to my mother.

'Sleep,' she said. Her face was pale but not splotched with tears, just in retreat, her eyes distant, the way they had been after my father died, days of it, not crying, away by herself. 'I don't see what we're waiting for. Why can't you trace his movements? He left the house, we know that. For Mimi's. Unless he forgot and came here.'

'No, I was here. Until we went to Mimi's.'

'But darling, I called. There was no one here.'

Inspector Cavallini looked up from his brandy.

'Oh, that was you?' I said quickly. 'Somebody called, but I didn't answer.'

'Darling, you *might* have picked up. It rang and rang. I mean, even in the shower—'

'I was busy,' I said, my voice a little clipped, nervous. But Inspector Cavallini took it for embarrassment, his eyes amused over the glass.

'Busy?' my mother asked.

'Signorina Grassini was here as well, perhaps?' Cavallini said.

'Yes.'

'Well, I still don't— Oh, darling.' She stopped, flustered. 'Really.'

'Getting ready for the ball,' Cavallini said, having fun with it.

'Yes. Anyway, he didn't come here.'

'Well, he must have gone somewhere,' my mother said. 'Somebody must have seen him. You have to ask.'

'Signora, at three in the morning who should I ask?' Cavallini said. 'You understand, my hands are tied in this. What is there to investigate? We tell everyone to listen for the accidents, a sickness, but that's all we can do. It is not a crime to miss a party. Even such a party.'

'What do I do?' my mother said. 'Officially. Do I fill out a form?'

'Not tonight,' Cavallini said, putting his empty brandy glass on the table. 'Tomorrow I will make more inquiries. So we see. And you, signora, please, some rest. If I need you to help me.'

'Help? How?'

'You are his fiancée, yes? So who knows him better?'

'Yes,' my mother said vaguely.

'Till tomorrow, then,' he said, taking my mother's hand. 'Make yourself easy.'

'Thank you. I've kept you so late.'

He made a small 'it's nothing' gesture.

'I'll see you out,' I said, leading him to the stairs.

'You have some pills for her? To sleep? Tomorrow will not be pleasant.'

'What do you mean?' I said. We were walking down the stairs, then through the hallway where Gianni and I had fought. Without thinking, I glanced up at one of the sconces, as if it might be dripping blood, but everything was in shadow, kept dim by night-lights.

'She's right. A man like that – why would he run away? He wouldn't. So why is he missing?' He left it open, a question that answered itself.

'Let's hope not,' I said, opening the door for him, reaching up to the old handle, then quickly dropping my hand, moving the raw knuckles behind me.

'Yes, we can hope. Meanwhile, some sleep, I think. You too.' He turned in the doorway. 'The maid? She doesn't answer the phone?'

My hand went farther back, as if it were moving on its own.

'Yes. Oh, you mean tonight. They all went to Mimi's to help.'

'So you were alone in the house.'

'Well, not alone.'

'I meant you and Signorina Grassini.'

'Yes, why?'

'I'm sorry to ask before, in front of your mother. I know how it is. An opportunity, yes? How do you say, the mice play when the cat's away?'

'Yes.'

183

He shook his head, amused, then patted my arm. 'To be such an age.'

I leaned against the door after I'd locked it, looking down the hall, my forehead sweaty. One slip was all it took. I needed to go through everything tomorrow with Claudia. Exact times. When she had left her hotel, how long it had taken to get here. The rest was safe, playing while the cat was away.

'You don't have to wait up,' my mother said.

'He's right, you know. There's nothing we can do tonight. You should get some sleep.'

'I know. I just want to sit for a bit.' She was picking at her gown, the black velvet skirt now flecked with ash. 'I'm frightened.'

'I know.'

'He could be hurt. Dead.'

'Yes.'

She looked up. 'Well, that's a change anyway. Cavallini – the man's impossible. Every time I say something, he just tut-tuts and pours another brandy.'

'I said could be.'

'And now I'm supposed to help. How? I don't know where Gianni goes, what he does. It's funny, isn't it? You know somebody, and then something like this happens and you don't. I mean, I know him, who he is, but the details . . .' Her voice trailed off.

I reached into my pocket, pulling out the necklace, and handed it to her.

'Here. Before it gets lost.'

'Yes,' she said, looking at it. 'You know, I never thought. What a night for a robbery. Everyone at Mimi's. No one home. Perfect, wouldn't it be?' She paused, her eyes still on the necklace. 'You're serious about this girl?'

'Yes.'

She sighed. 'Not the best time to talk, is it? I can't think about anything.'

'I know.'

184

'Of course, it doesn't matter what I say, really.' She reached out her hand to cover mine. 'You know that I'm always—'

I leaned over and kissed her forehead. 'It can wait. Get some sleep, huh?'

'But, Adam, if it's . . . I don't know what I'll do.'

'You'll be fine. You're always fine.'

'I'm not always fine, you know,' she said, looking down at her lap. 'Not always.'

I stood there for a minute, uneasy, not knowing what to say. Then she patted my hand. 'Well, look at the time. Off to bed.'

'Do you want a pill?'

'No, I don't want to miss anything,' she said, without irony.

'All right,' I said, flustered. 'I'm going to have a bath.'

'Darling, you'll wake the maids.'

'A short bath.' I leaned over to kiss her forehead again. 'Don't sit up too long.' As I left, I lifted my head towards her. 'That's some dress.'

A faint smile, acknowledging the gesture. 'It was all right in the end, wasn't it?'

'Mimi couldn't take her eyes off it.'

She nodded, a wry grimace. 'Hm. But I didn't wear it for her.'

'No,' I said, meaning, 'I know, I'm sorry,' whatever she wanted it to mean, more an embrace than a word.

There was enough hot water for a soak, and everything that had happened began to drain away as my head grew logy with steam. Every part of me ached with a different exhaustion – my shoulders from rowing and lugging the tarp, my legs from the party, my back just from being on edge. But it was going to be all right. My mother would be all right too, though she couldn't know that now. I washed away sweat, whatever else my skin had picked up. Clean. While the cat was away. Who was to say otherwise?

I looked at my hands again. No rust. But I grabbed the brush anyway and ran it over my nails, pulling the skin back to get the bristles in under the rims. Back and forth, scouring, until they were pale. I sank against the tub, relieved. It was gone; I'd caught it in time. What else? I closed my eyes for a second, back in the dim light of the downstairs hall, seeing everything again, the brocade chair I'd used to pull myself up, the sconce where he'd hit his head, the smug face over the white shirtfront.

I sat up, eyes wide open. The smallest thing could give you away. I got out of the tub quickly and towelled off and grabbed a robe. No time to dress. The maids would be asleep anyway. I went down and crossed through the piano nobile. No light was coming from the sitting room – my mother must have finally gone up. Down the main stairs, grateful for the carpeting, steps that didn't creak.

The marble in the hall was cold on my bare feet. I walked over to the door of the room where I'd waited. Reconstructing. He'd had his cigarette here. But I'd already cleaned the ashtray. I'd backed him into the wall there – exactly which sconce? I took a handkerchief and wiped both, looking for any smears, flakes of blood. What if one of the maids came? Then he'd pushed me here. I walked slowly, trying to move with the fight in my head to the spot where he'd lost it, where the shirt stud had popped out. A tiny thing, not even thought of until the bath, but lying here somewhere, waiting to give us away.

I got down on my hands and knees and felt along the dark floor under one of the side tables. It might have rolled, might be anywhere. Every inch, if I had to. They'd know it was his. I patted the floor in front of me. If I turned on the lights, someone would get up, come down to investigate, and then I'd make up something else and someone would ask about that and – an endless spiral of detail, easy to slip up.

I moved my hand in front of me, barely touching the marble, hovering over it like a mine sweeper. The stud must have rolled until it hit the wall. I ran my hand along the edge of the room, then stopped, thinking I'd heard a sound upstairs. I held my breath for a minute, listening, but there was only the water lapping outside, the faint creaking of the boat pulling against its rope. Yes, we'd been near this end, the stud popping out of the shirt. Maybe with blood on it – even more damaging.

I kept feeling my way along the floor, carefully sweeping around the table legs, the crevices where it might hide for ever, until they found it. And then there it was. Round, smooth metal, the gold warm even in the dim light. I snatched it and looked at it. The smallest thing. I went to put it in my pocket, then decided to keep it in my hand, to feel it until I could get rid of it in the deep water off the Zattere. Then everything would be all right again.

I put my left hand up to my forehead, surprised to find that I was sweating again, even with my feet cold on the floor. But my whole body was awake, and I knew then what it was going to be like, even when it was all right, a wariness that took over your life, what happened to animals, who either killed or became prey.

CHAPTER NINE

IL GAZZETTINO HAD two full pages on Mimi's ball, mostly pictures of women in gowns and couples standing together, but nothing about Gianni. Cavallini, however, had started his investigation, already up while the rest of Venice slept in, grey and hung over from the night before. His men badgered Gianni's household staff, questioning them over and over to hear what they'd already heard: Dr Maglione had left before eight, dressed for the party. He went in the direction of Santo Stefano, presumably headed for the Accademia bridge. He had been in good spirits.

Policemen made some random checks of the canals along the route, but no body had been spotted, no suspicious object had bobbed to the surface. Gianni's daughter had been called in Bologna and, bewildered, asked if she should come right away and was told to wait until they had more information. His assistant at the hospital was asked to go through his patient list to see if there was anyone he might have stopped to visit. In a small city like Venice, only a few calls from the Questura were necessary: by midmorning everyone knew Gianni was missing. The police had now begun questioning the hotels.

'The hotels?' my mother said. 'Why on earth would he go to a hotel?' She was back in the chair beside the ashtray, looking haggard under her fresh morning make-up.

'It's a procedure, signora,' Cavallini said. 'We always ask the hotels, for everything that happens in Venice.' He stopped, putting down his coffee. 'It's not for him, you see. But you must prepare yourself for this – if there has been a crime, there are two people to look for, not just the victim. There is the other. So, anything suspicious.'

'Crime?' my mother said, whose imagination up till now had ended with a heart attack.

Cavallini spread his hands. 'We don't know, signora. Perhaps he *saw* a crime, a burglary, and then someone had to—'

'But were there any? Burglaries, I mean. Surely that would have been reported.'

'Not as yet,' Cavallini said. He looked at her, his voice soothing. 'We don't know.'

I sipped my coffee, trying not to show any expression. Hotels. Burglaries. No suspicion at all. The desk clerk would confirm what Claudia said, the time she left, the time she came back. With me. Who later was seen by Cavallini himself – a perfect circle.

I had expected to spend the day in a void, dreading any knock on the door, but now I saw that Cavallini's personal interest gave us a peephole at the Questura – what they were doing, what they were saying, looking everywhere but here. When he left, promising to report later, I took a few minutes to look over the water entrance. Maybe a film of blood had stuck to the canal steps like a bathtub ring, maybe some stains had soaked into the marble. But everything was clean, even tidy, the paving stones piled neatly under the tarp, no smears on the damp floor. Nothing on the boat outside, washed by rain. One of the cleaning women would do the entrance hall today, swabbing down the marble floor, wiping away every mark, every trace. I went back upstairs.

'You don't have to stay,' my mother said, feet up under an afghan now that Cavallini was gone.

'Of course I'll stay.'

'No, don't. I know you. You'll moon around and treat me like bone china. And I'm not, you know. I won't break.'

189

'Somebody has to answer the phone.'

'Oh God, it's going to start, isn't it? All the friendly little calls. And we can't not answer,' she said, shooting me a glance. 'What if it's the police?'

So I spent the rest of the day at home, making cups of tea while my mother retreated into herself. She made no pretense of passing the time by reading or playing cards. She was waiting. She would walk over to the window, then back, absorbed in a world of her own, not even hearing the phone. She smoked and drank tea, thanking me in a voice so abstracted it was almost a monotone, like that of someone who'd taken painkillers and become vague. I fielded Mimi and Bertie and everyone else who called, an after-noon of them, all eager for news, sniffing drama. 'She thinks he's left me,' my mother said when Celia called. 'Walked out on me.' So far from what Celia or anyone was thinking that for a second I wondered if she had, in fact, taken pills.

I looked at *Il Gazzettino* again. Mimi with stars in her hair. The man she called Ernesto, evidently someone important. Not the picture of us with the police, but Cavallini would remember it, which was all that mattered. When exactly had my mother called? While we played and someone else rowed out to the lagoon.

Inspector Cavallini stopped in at the end of the day, in time for drinks, but had nothing new. None of Gianni's patients had heard from him. No accidents had been reported.

'Imagine,' my mother said, her voice flat. 'You can just disap-pear. I didn't know it could be so easy.'

'I'm sorry, I must ask. Do you have any thoughts yourself, sig-nora? Something he might have said to you?' My mother was shaking her head. 'Anyone who might have wished him some harm?'

I glanced up, but his eyes were on my mother, not even taking me in.

'Of course not. Why *would* anyone?'

'In this life, every man has his enemies.'

'Why do you think it's someone – why not a stroke?'

190

'Because we would have found him by now. A man falls in the street, he would be seen. So of course the possibility is that someone put him somewhere.'

'Where?'

Cavallini shrugged. 'The usual place in Venice is the sea.'

I went over to the drinks table, an excuse not to look at him. I heard the tarp splash in.

'The sea? But then—'

'Yes, it's difficult. We cannot dredge the lagoon. A canal, yes, but not the lagoon. It's too big. We have to wait for the sea to give him up.'

'Give him up,' my mother said quietly. 'You mean his body.'

Cavallini said nothing.

After he left, I made two drinks, but my mother waved hers away. Angelina had lighted a fire and my mother sat next to it, staring, listening to the sound of the burning wood. The phone had stopped. The servants, sensing a kind of illness, had gone silent in the other rooms. I sat pinned to my chair, unable to break the quiet, feeling it like a weight around me, pressing. My mother kept staring at the fire, her eyes dull. I knew it wouldn't always be like this, that it would pass, but while it was here, the terrible quietness between us, I felt it squeezing, worse than Gianni's hand on my throat.

At dinner we sat at the same end of the long table. The cook had made a risotto dotted with shellfish, but my mother only picked at it, barely sipping her wine, still talking to herself somewhere else. Finally she put down the fork and lit a cigarette instead.

'Adam,' she said, 'that business at the party.'

I looked up.

'You know, when Claudia . . .' She stopped, waiting to see if I was following. I nodded. 'It's because she thought Gianni had worked for the Germans, you said.'

I nodded again, waiting.

'That's what you did in the army. Investigate people like that.'

'Yes.'

'And you thought so too. Because she said?'

191

'No, because he did. All Claudia knew is that he reported her father.'

She took this in without moving, wanting to see it through.

'So if it's true –' She hesitated. 'There would be this hate.'

'She didn't hate him enough to—'

My mother looked at me, puzzled, then waved this away. 'Darling, not her, the *others*. Inspector Cavallini asked, who wished him harm and I thought, well, if it's true, there might be people – they'd wish him harm. But that was the war. I thought all that was over. I mean, who goes around now . . . ?' She paused, taking another sip of her wine. 'He's the last, you know. His brother was killed in an accident.'

'No. He was killed by partisans. For collaborating with the Germans.'

She flinched. 'What a lot you know.'

'I had his file pulled.'

'You investigated his brother?'

'And Gianni. I thought we should know.'

She looked down, flustered, busying herself putting out the cigarette. 'You had no right to do that, Adam. No right.'

'Mother—'

She raised her hand to her forehead. 'I know, I know. But the point, darling,' she said, taking a breath, controlling herself, 'is that if he did those things, or people *thought* he did, by mistake or something, then they might have a reason . . .' She drifted off, letting me finish.

'Yes, if they thought he did,' I said, making it easier.

'It just doesn't seem possible somehow. That he would. You know, I've known him, my God, all my life. Almost all my life.'

'People change.'

'Yes. But they don't, really.' She looked down at her glass. 'He was in love with me, you know, even then.'

'And you?' I said, staring across.

'Me? Oh, no. I was in love with your father. I was, you know. And then I came here – I don't know why, really, I wasn't looking

192

for him – and there he is and he's still in love with me. All those years. It's funny, the curves life throws at you.' She raised her head. 'Did he really do that? Work with them?'

'Yes, I think so.'

'Maybe he had to. They forced people, didn't they?'

I said nothing.

'But that would be a reason. For somebody to—'

'It's possible.'

She thought about this for a minute, then started brushing the tablecloth, a nervous movement. 'Oh, what's wrong with me? Here we are burying him and we don't know anything. He could be in a hospital somewhere, anything.'

'Yes,' I said, squeezed again, almost out of breath.

'It's just, if he's not—' She stopped her hand, looking at the table. 'I don't know what I'm going to do.'

She went to bed early, or at least went to her room. I saw the sliver of light under the door, heard the creak of the floorboards, until finally it was quiet there too and I imagined her, still dressed, lying exhausted on the bed. The fire in the sitting room had died down and I sat in the cold, wanting to go out but feeling I couldn't leave. How long would it take to get through this? Being with her, lying to her, was worse somehow than what had happened – there was no end to it and no going back. I thought of her after my father died, holding herself together for me. You'll feel better soon. He wouldn't want you to be sad. You'll have to take care of me now. All the lies for my own good.

When I woke I was hunched in the chair, cramped, and the light had begun to come in. The electric bars of the space heater, glowing orange, had been going all night, an extravagance, but the room was still cold, the damp seeping in. I switched off the heater and went to the window to see the sun come up behind the Redentore, my old early-morning view. It was going to be a nice day, shiny after the rain. A walk. Nobody would miss me if I went out now. I'd be back in time for the morning vigil, but at least with some air in my lungs.

I crossed over to the San Marco side, away from the house and Mimi's and the last two days. The sun was already filling the great piazza. I went behind the basilica, taking the route to Santa Maria in Formosa, not going anywhere in particular, just going. Through the campo, then stopping in the street – if I kept going this way, I'd reach the Questura, where Cavallini's clerks might still be looking through the patient lists. I turned left instead, through the narrow calle and over the bridge to Zanipolo. Past the equestrian statue of Colleoni, where Claudia had stared at Gianni. A few people were going into the hospital – nurses, maintenance men, none of them looking at the rows of arches along the façade, the mosaic Gianni had pointed out, charming a visitor. Along the fondamenta, an ambulance boat was delivering a patient to the side door, just as one had when we'd walked here, Gianni explaining why he'd had to – lying. And then I was at the end, nothing but the open lagoon and the chimneys of Murano. In America you could walk and never stop, never run out of land, but here you met yourself within minutes – a bridge, a canal, then abruptly an end, water or a blind alley.

I looked at the ambulances moored on the quay. What kind of doctor had he been? There must have been a time, cramming for exams, when it had been about saving people, being on the side of the angels. Do no harm. And a few years later he could condemn someone with a nod. What had happened in between? But doctors in Germany had taken the same oath and then nodded and nodded, killing everybody. Maybe nothing had happened, just opportunity. A matter of degree. Think of him young, on the Lido, betraying my father. Or saying he did. I stared at the water. He was off there somewhere to the right. And here at the hospital, everywhere I looked. You could walk all day and never put him behind you.

Cavallini was waiting on a chair in the downstairs hall when I got back.

'Signor Miller, you're out so early.'

I stopped, hesitating. How long would every question sound like an accusation?

'I couldn't sleep.'

'Yes, it's understandable,' he said, getting up. 'Your mother, she's very tired, I think.' Raising his eyes towards the stairs, indicating that they'd already spoken.

'There's news?'

'I thought I would come myself. A courtesy. The telephone, it's—'

'What's happened?'

'A body has been found.'

'What?' How? The rope slipping out of its knots, rocked by the tide? What if the tarp were still there, a match for the one in the water entrance? Why hadn't I got rid of it? But then someone would have noticed.

'You're surprised?'

'A body. You mean he's dead?'

'Yes.' He raised his eyes again. 'I've told your mother. So at least now she knows.'

'I'd better go up.'

'No, she's resting. The girl – Angelina? – is with her. Maybe now she can sleep. I was waiting for you.'

'Waiting for me?' I said, feeling a tingling along my skin.

'Yes. I thought – I don't like to ask your mother, but it's a formality. We can't reach the daughter, you see. Another early bird, perhaps. There's no question, I think – the same description, in evening clothes – but it's necessary for the formality.'

'What is?'

'To identify the body. It should be family, but you are almost a son. And it's not good to wait. The condition of the body – he has been in the water. You don't mind?'

'All right,' I said, not knowing how to refuse. 'You know him. Couldn't you just—?'

'No, no, I am police. It must be someone else. You understand, for the formalities. And now the crime report.'

'Crime report.'

'Yes, he was killed.'

'How do you mean?' I said, manoeuvring through this, some-one who didn't know.

Inspector Cavallini made a smashing gesture with his hand. 'A blow to the head. So they tell me. I haven't seen the body yet. We'll go together, to San Michele. I'll call the Questura for a boat. Would you open the canal gate?'

'The canal gate,' I repeated vaguely, looking towards the damp room, the steps where I'd dragged him. 'Yes,' I said, catching myself, 'all right. Just let me run upstairs for a second, see if she's all right.' To get away, even for a minute. 'You can phone in there.' I pointed to the room where I'd waited the other night.

'Thank you. And for this help. I'm sorry to ask you.'

'He was killed?' I said again, because I should be dumb-founded.

'Yes.'

'You mean, not by accident.'

'No, by murder.'

I stared at him, no longer acting, the word itself like a jolt, what it had really been.

'You're sure? It couldn't be a fall?'

'No. Not according to San Michele. Of course, I will look myself.'

'But who – I mean, where—?'

Inspector Cavallini shrugged. 'We only know where he was found.'

'In the water, you said.'

'Yes, the lagoon. A fisherman, only this morning. The body was caught on a channel marker. Otherwise . . .' He opened his hands.

'So he could have been put in anywhere.' Far from here.

'Not anywhere. You know, there are channels in the lagoon, like rivers. The tides follow a path. You can see on the charts. This was the major channel from San Marco, behind San Giorgio, out to the Lido. Usually that would mean this side of Venice. But it's more likely that a boat took him, so the murder itself could have been anywhere.'

196

'A boat?' I said, my head spinning with charts and currents – this much already known, before the body had even been identified. And then they'd find out the rest.

'Yes, because of the distance from San Marco. It's unlikely it would float that far in a day. Well, but this is all early, a speculation. First we must see the body. To make sure.'

My mother was sleeping, Angelina indicated with a finger to her lips, worn out by the waiting and now able to go into full retreat. I washed my face and held on to the sides of the basin until my hands were still, looking in the mirror to see what Cavallini would see. Maybe that's what he wanted – to watch my expression when I saw the corpse, some sly police trick. The smallest thing could give you away. But this was being jumpy. Why should he suspect anything? We'd been photographed together.

When I got back downstairs, he was already at the canal entrance, walking by the tarp, looking up at the gondola. I felt a small tremor in my hands again, then steadied myself.

'You don't use the gondola?' he asked.

'No.' I opened the gate, my back to him. On the canal, the rowboat was bobbing idly at its mooring post.

'Ah, you're an oarsman,' he said, spotting it.

'Well, not in this weather,' I said quickly. 'I haven't been out yet. Maybe in the spring.' Why say that? What if somebody had seen? Any contradiction would be suspicious. Two things to explain.

'It's very fine, this one,' Cavallini said, pointing to the gondola. 'Old.'

I looked down at his foot, almost touching the tarp. 'It came with the house,' I said. 'Of course, the lucky thing about Venice is that you don't really need a boat. You can walk anywhere.'

He nodded, distracted, lifting up the edge of the tarp, used to looking over a room. 'Yes, so many boats at Ca' Maglione, and yet he chooses to walk.'

'Maybe they were put up for the winter too,' I said, raising my eyes to the gondola.

'No, no, all in use.' So he'd already checked. 'Many boats,' he said, taking pride in it, a tour guide praising a landmark. 'I've seen them. My wife, you see, was a cousin of his wife.'

'Oh,' I said, not knowing what to say, what connection he felt this gave him. The endless genealogy of Venice. He was running his hand over the paving stones.

'Yes, a very old family.'

'Everyone in Venice seems to come from an old family,' I said, still looking at the stones. Where was the police boat?

'Well, not all. My family, you know, were simple people. Still, Venetians, educated. But not Magliones.'

And then he had been counting the boats in Gianni's garage, an in-law invited for tea. I saw him for a second as he must have been – young, the curious eyes over the moustache, smiling at the long-faced girl, moving up.

'You're making some repairs?' he asked, letting the tarp fall back.

'The owner. We lease the house.'

'You see those stairs?' He pointed to the water's edge. I turned my head slowly, almost expecting to see a streak of blood. 'How the sides are weak? You should make the repairs soon. In Venice—'

'I'll tell the owner.'

'Yes, of course, the owner,' he said, suddenly embarrassed. 'Excuse me, I forgot you would be leaving.' I looked at him blankly. 'After the wedding.'

The police launch had a motor so loud that we would have had to shout over it, so we made the trip without talking, backtracking up the Rio dei Greci to the Questura, then out past Santa Giustina to the open lagoon. San Michele, the cemetery island, was the first thing you could see from this side, just across the water from the hospital – hadn't Gianni joked about that? – the low brick mausoleums lined with dark cypresses. We were met at the dock by some of Cavallini's men, who steered us away from the graveyard paths to the morgue. I pushed my feet one after the other, as if we were wading. There seemed to be no sounds, not even birds, a funeral quiet.

Inside, it could have been any hospital building, white plaster and tile, except for the smell, so heavy and cloying that not even disinfectant took it away. We were led down a corridor by a man in a white coat with a clipboard. He stopped at a heavy double door and said something in Italian to Cavallini.

'He wants to know if you've seen a dead body before.'

'Yes.' How many now? Stacked in piles, left in fields by the side of the road, just left, waiting for someone to cart them away. Mouths open, limbs missing. At first you stared, shocked, and then you stopped looking. Five years ago it had been possible never to have seen the dead – a grandfather maybe, lying on a bier. Now you couldn't count how many.

'You know, for some it's difficult.'

We paused just inside the door, stopped by the cold. The body was on a gurney, covered with a sheet. His feet were sticking out, not tagged as they were in the movies, just naked and exposed. What would he look like after a day in the water? Eyes still open, staring at me? But it was Cavallini's eyes that would be open, watching every move. Just walk over to the table. Now.

An attendant pulled back the sheet, drawing it down, and for a terrible second I thought he would keep going, until we saw all of him, his genitals, like an unwelcome glimpse in the shower, without a towel. They had removed his clothes, so there was only skin, pasty and bloated from the water, the hair on his chest matted like bits of seaweed. Someone had closed his eyes, or maybe it was part of the general swelling, the puffy blur of a face, not peaceful, just inert. Pale lips. That grey that only the dead have, not even a colour, a warning not to touch. I took a shallow breath, trying to ignore the chemical smell in the room. Grey, awful skin, pouching at the sides.

'You can identify him?' Cavallini said.

I nodded.

'You must say, for the record. This is Giancarlo Maglione?'

'Yes.'

199

'And you must sign a statement.'

But for a second I couldn't move. I stared at the body, not Gianni any more, just a body, utterly still, separate now, something left behind, like moulted skin. We always forget what it means, becoming nothing. How long had it taken? A minute, two, water displacing air, and now irretrievable. How did the workers here stand it, day after day, seeing the grey bodies, the terrible reminders? All that we left. The frightened Egyptians thought we'd come back for our bodies if we kept them ready, with pots of barley and hunting scenes painted on walls.

'Signor Miller?' Cavallini said, touching my elbow.

But we never come back. This was all there was, grey skin and fluids to drain. I'd taken the rest. And then gone to a party. But hadn't he done the same? How many times? Except he never had to see them afterwards.

'Signor?' the doctor said.

'Yes,' I answered, raising my head. 'It's Gianni.'

'You would sign over here?'

He was leading me away, signalling to the attendant to cover Gianni's face. We went over to a desk, where he handed me a clipboard and a pen. A long form, as elaborate and unwieldy as lira notes.

'Now what?' I said to Cavallini as I signed.

'Now they make the autopsy. For the cause of death.'

'I thought he was hit on the head.'

'Another formality. In the case of a crime. To be precise, you know, it wasn't this,' he said, tapping the back of his head. 'The doctor says drowning. But now he has to say officially.'

'Drowning? Why would he say that?'

'The water in the lungs. If he had already been dead—'

'You mean someone put him into the lagoon alive?' I said, appalled, forgetting the bubbles now, imagining him struggling in the tarp, fighting his way out.

'They may have thought he was already dead. You know, *basta*.' He hit his palm with his fist, a hard smack. 'Then in the lagoon.

But it was the water that killed him. Of course, to the law it will make no difference. Are you all right?'

'Maybe a little air,' I said.

Outside, warmer than in the morgue, I lit a cigarette. 'I'm sorry. I'm not usually squeamish. It's different when it's somebody you know.'

'Yes, it's not pleasant for you, I know. Still, a great service to me.'

'Anybody could have—'

'Yes, but since it's you, now there can be no question about an investigation.'

I looked at him, trying to make this out.

'No question of an accident,' he said, taking out a cigarette of his own.

'But it wasn't. You said.'

'No. You saw the skull in the back? Not a fall. But how much better for everyone if it had been. So, maybe a temptation.'

'To whom?'

He shrugged. 'Poor Venice. The war, finally it's over, and they start coming back. The visitors. Not soldiers – your mother, her friends. It's good for Venice. You look at the buildings and we – well, maybe we look at you a little. But no one comes if they're afraid, if there is crime. A murder? Not in Venice. But now look who identifies the body – one of the visitors. Who sees it's not an accident. So I have my investigation.'

I drew on my cigarette, my stomach sliding again.

'But surely you would have—'

'Yes, but now I can be certain. Something that involves the international community? The Questura will want to act. To solve it. Men, whatever I need. And we will solve it.'

'I hope so.'

Cavallini reached over, reassuring, and patted my arm. 'We'll find him, don't worry.'

I nodded, feeling the weight of his hand.

'I know it's a loss for you. But you'll help me.'

'Me?'

'You knew his character. With a Maglione, sometimes it's easier for foreigners than for our Venetian families.'

'But I hardly knew him. I mean, your wife must have—'

'No. A blood tie only, not a friendship. But you, your mother . . .' He let it drift, waiting for me to pick it up.

'Well, yes,' I said. 'We'll do anything we can. Of course.' I paused. 'Do you have any idea who—'

He withdrew his hand, shaking his head. 'No, it's early for that. First we get the facts, from in there.' He jerked his head towards the morgue. 'Then we look at the life. Who profits?'

'You think it's someone who knew him? Why not a robbery?'

He smiled. 'A hit on the head, grab the wallet, push him in the canal? But he still had the wallet. Also his watch. What thief leaves a watch? No, some other reason. So, who profits? You see how lucky I am to have you.'

'Me?'

'In a murder you look at everyone. Him? Him? What motive? Who profits? But with you, it's the opposite. No profit, a great loss. After the wedding, perhaps, I would have had to suspect you too. But now you are the only man in Venice I can't suspect.'

A trap? Another step through the looking glass? 'Why not?' I said quietly.

'Why not? Who throws away a fortune? He would have been your father.'

'Yes,' I said, waiting, my voice neutral.

'Your father,' Cavallini repeated. 'One of the richest men in all of Italy.'

I looked at him, then caught myself and turned to the water before he could see my face.

CHAPTER TEN

GIANNI'S FUNERAL SERVICE was held at the Salute, so close to Mimi's that it seemed a grimmer version of the ball, with the same crowding at the landing stage, people being helped up the broad steps, all in black this time, with hats and veils. The waiting gondolas stretched up the Grand Canal, as in a Canaletto, filling up the canvas, all of Mimi's guests and more, enough for a state occasion. When the funeral boats arrived, a cortège of bobbing hearses, people lingered on the church steps to stare at the coffin, draped with flowers. We had become part of a news story: a violent death, an old family, the foreigners who drank at Harry's. Across the campo, people watched from windows.

Claudia hadn't wanted to go.

'I can't. You go. I'll stay here,' she said, gesturing at the rumpled bed.

We were always together now, a kind of hiding, making love in her room, wanting each other even more because no one else was part of the secret, a new intimacy. Sometimes we went out for walks and talked about it, the only ones who knew, but mostly we stayed in, sex another way of talking, something else we could say only to each other. When she held me afterwards, her fingers would move over my shoulder, making sure I was still there, and I would put my arm around her as if I were folding her up in a cape, making the world go away, both of us safe.

'No. We want them to see us.'

'How can I sit there? What will people think?'

'That you're part of the family. Cavallini already thinks it. He thinks we're *Gianni's* family. Almost, anyway.'

'Ha.'

'He asked if his wife could call on my mother. Like something out of—'

'Yes,' she said impatiently, 'very Venetian. The old manners. And you trust that?'

'You're going for her sake. He'll expect it. He'd notice if you didn't.'

'My God. His family. Am I going crazy?'

I put my hands on her shoulders. 'Just this, then we'll go away.'

'Leave Venice?' She reached up, grabbing my arm. 'You think they know something?'

I shook my head. 'No, nothing.'

'Then why?'

'Because we're the only ones who can give us away now – if we slip, say something. So the sooner we leave—'

She looked at me, silent for a minute. 'Yes, the only ones,' she said finally. Then she turned away, out of my hands. 'But first this. Am I supposed to cry too?'

'Just as long as Cavallini sees you with the family.'

But in fact there was some question about where to seat us. The ushers led my mother to the front, the widow's pew, and then stopped short, placing us a few rows behind, on the right. My mother, dry-eyed behind her veil, seemed not to notice, still enveloped in that eerie calm that had settled in after Cavallini's first visit. But someone must have told the ushers, decided on the protocol. It occurred to me then that I had no idea who had arranged the funeral, taken care of all the details that only seem to happen by themselves. A full mass at the Salute. A gondola banked in flowers. A reception at the Ca'

Maglione. All organised, down to where to seat the almost-widow.

I looked at the front pew. Just behind, Cavallini and his wife sat next to the priest from the ball, presumably a row of relatives. But in the front itself there was only an old woman leaning on a girl, who must be the daughter, finally arrived from Bologna. Or had she been here for days, ignoring us, going about her father's business? I noticed then that the church was divided, the faces I recognised from Bertie's on our side, Venetians on the other, my mother separated from the family by an aisle.

I stretched my neck, trying to see the daughter's face, but she was looking straight ahead, to the high altar, where the priest had appeared with upraised hands. We stood, and the backs of the relatives now hid her from every angle. Music echoed through the vault under the dome as the pallbearers brought the casket forwards. When we were sitting again, I felt Claudia rigid against me, staring at the coffin. I put my hand over hers and looked past the altar, hoping to draw her attention away. To the left was the sacristy with the Titian ceilings, but they were lost in the space, distant and dim, while the coffin sat right in front of us, inescapable. Down in the first row, the daughter had bowed her head.

The service took hours. I had never attended a mass in Venice – for me, the churches were poorly lit galleries – and the spectacle of it took me by surprise. Busy altar boys in white surplices, Latin chants and candlelight, hundreds of people answering in unison – the whole vast church seemed to be in movement, except the women on either side of me, Claudia still rigid, my mother simply quiet, looking vaguely at nothing in particular. At one point Cavallini turned his head slowly, as if he were counting the house, caught my eye and nodded, but otherwise we were left to ourselves. Nobody stared, more interested now in the theatre of public grief. The eulogy, in Italian, was long enough to cover Gianni's entire life. A choir sang. People streamed down the aisle for Communion.

Who were they all? Patients? Neighbours? There seemed, beyond the formalities, to be a genuine sadness in the room, or at least a sombre reserve. What had he been to them? A friend? Or just someone with a doge in the family, respected out of long habit? Or maybe a dinner companion at Villa Raspelli, drinking the last of the good Soave. Don't forget what he was. I looked down towards the daughter. Did she know? A law student, after all, not a child. But maybe he was still Papa, affectionate at home. People saw what they were supposed to see. Cavallini thought Gianni was rich, what any poor cousin would think, having even less. But the daughter's grief was real enough. Her shoulders were moving now, shaking with discreet sobs, the only person in the great church actually crying. The old woman – an aunt? the nanny? – put an arm around her. I looked away.

Outside, there was confusion. People loitered on the steps, waiting for a cue. Were we supposed to follow out to San Michele? I remembered my father's funeral, the long line of black cars, lights kept on, heading slowly towards Long Island. Here they would be gondolas, another ordinary ritual made fantastical by water. Or was the burial private, by invitation? Everyone looked at the daughter, climbing now into a gondola, away from the boat with the casket. Thin, her face still indistinct behind a veil, but perfectly erect, a girl from a good convent school. Her gondola headed up the canal towards Ca' Maglione.

Cavallini came up to us and took my mother's hand in a silent condolence, then nodded to Claudia, standing at her side – exactly what I'd wanted him to see.

'Is there a burial?' I asked, looking towards the hearse gondola.

'Yes, but not here. The country house. They'll take him there, and then tomorrow the family . . .' He let the rest explain itself. 'Today, it's for Venice.'

'The country house?'

'Yes, on the Brenta. It's very well known. For the Giorgiones.'

'Oh,' I said, surprised. 'He never mentioned it.'

'Yes, he did, darling,' my mother said, her voice flat. 'You just didn't listen.' She had turned to Cavallini. 'Thank you so much. You've been kind again.' About what?

'They were not, you know, evidence. And of course Giulia agreed.'

'After you asked.'

'No, no, she agreed. She has them for you.' He looked at me. 'Photographs. Of sentimental value, for your mother.'

Not evidence. But something he'd looked over, going through Gianni's things, already on the case.

'Grace.' A gloved hand appeared out of nowhere, along with Celia de Betancourt's eager voice. 'How awful for you.' She nodded towards the logjam of boats at the bottom of the stairs. 'You're not going back to the house?' she said, somehow making it ordinary, a dusty ranch, not a palazzo on the Grand Canal.

'Yes. His daughter's there.'

'You don't mind if I take a rain check, do you? All this.' She waved her hand to the church behind us. 'I feel done *in*.' She paused, catching up. 'His daughter. You've made up?'

'There's nothing to make up. She's been at school.'

'That's not what Bertie says. He says she—'

I looked up, curious, but my mother was patting her hand, stopping her.

'Celia, I can't. Not today.' She looked down. 'Not today.'

'Oh, sugar,' Celia said, distressed. 'This mouth. I don't mean anything by it. You know I wouldn't—'

'I know,' my mother said, patting her hand again.

'Not for the *world*.'

'You're old friends,' Cavallini said, a polite intervention.

'Since the Bronze Age,' Celia said, herself again, glancing at him. She hugged my mother. 'Don't mind me. I just get funny in church. Everybody being so good. You know.'

'Signora Miller,' Cavallini said. 'He's waving to you. It's your boat?'

'Yes, thank you.'

'So you took down the gondola,' Cavallini said to me.

'No, it's hired. The marchesa doesn't want us to use hers.'

'Just the other boat.'

'Maybe,' I said. 'When the weather's better.' Making a point of it, consistent, but Cavallini seemed not to have heard, busy now with Celia.

'May I offer you a ride somewhere?' he said, courtly, making Celia smile.

'God, would you? Just across. I'm going to swim to Harry's if I don't get a drink soon.'

'A long morning,' he said, his voice pleasant but his eyes, just for a second, flecked with disapproval. I looked around for his wife, but she seemed to have gone ahead on her own, leaving Cavallini to the foreigners. 'You permit?' he said, taking Celia's elbow, suggestive, but I saw that the point for him was the flirtation itself, nothing more, a game to distract. There hadn't been a girl in Maestre either. And he'd already gone through Gianni's papers.

'What did she mean about Giulia?' I said to my mother.

'Nothing. Just some idea of Bertie's. About the engagement.'

'You mean she didn't approve?'

'I didn't say that. She just didn't come to the party. A cardinal sin in Bertie's book, of course. You can imagine.'

'But didn't she?'

'Darling, ask *her*. Gianni never said so. You were the one he was worried about.' She stopped on the stairs, lifting her veil and staring for a minute across the water. 'You know, children never like things to change. But they do.'

We joined the flotilla of boats heading up the canal to Gianni's house, Claudia fidgeting beside me, restive, wanting it to be over. The sun had come out, the early Venetian spring that had eluded Mimi, making the buildings shine, scrubbed fresh by the rain. At Ca' Maglione footmen lifted us on to a floating dock between striped mooring poles, like Mimi's ball again, without the umbrellas. A long staircase lined with candelabra led up to the piano nobile, the usual Venetian layout. The ballroom was not as pretty as Mimi's but just as large, done in red damask and heavy gilt chairs, like a version of La Fenice. Everything gleamed, spotless. How large a staff did it take to keep it going?

'I thought you said he had no money,' Claudia whispered to me, looking around.

'I didn't say broke.' But in fact the room made me uneasy. It was not what I'd expected. No frayed upholstery, no chipped pieces. Nothing needed repair. The war might never have happened.

A long table had been set out with plates of biscotti, coffee cups, and thin glasses for Vin Santo – spare but appropriate, a reception, not a party. People spoke softly. Near one end Giulia was being kissed by an old man, just a movement to the cheek, hands placed over hers. When he moved back, she turned to the next in line, so that her face was towards us. I stopped. She had the kind of delicate features that went with the convent school posture, but her face, soft and composed, was slightly long, the one trace of her mother's family. Otherwise, she looked exactly like Gianni, the same wavy hair, broad-set eyes. She was wearing a black dress with a small white bow at the neck, and for one awkward second I saw Gianni in his cutaway, arriving to take my mother to the ball, even the same quizzical look in his eyes. The look, at least, was real. I realised I must be staring and turned away.

'There's Giulia,' my mother said. 'Come and meet her.'

'Later,' I said. 'I want some coffee. You go.'

'There's nothing wrong, is there? You look all white.'

'No, I just need some coffee.' Eager now for her to leave.

'You'll be nice,' she said, looking at me, a question. 'You know you were almost brother and sister.'

'Yes, almost.'

'What's wrong?' Claudia said to me when my mother left.

'She looks just like him.'

Claudia peered down the table at her. She was greeting my mother now, not with a kiss, but polite. 'The eyes, a little.'

'All his features.'

'No, I don't see that. The eyes, yes. His eyes were like that.' She looked away, then reached over and picked up a coffee cup. 'What a pair we are. Standing here talking about his eyes, a man we—' She took a sip of coffee, still looking down.

'I'll have to say something to her.'

She was leading my mother out of the room.

I looked around. 'Who are they? Do you know any of these people?'

'From the newspapers. *Il bel mondo*,' Claudia said.

'What did the eulogy say?'

'A humanitarian. A saviour of men.'

'Christ.'

My mother was back in the room, carrying a brown envelope. Of sentimental value.

'So, another meeting.' Father Luca was leaning over the table to pick up a biscotti. 'A very different occasion,' he said sadly, looking at it as if he were referring to the food.

'Yes, very different. A beautiful service, though.'

He nodded. 'Father Prato,' he said, 'always excellent.' A professional appraisal. He bowed to Claudia, who acknowledged it, then glanced away, uncomfortable.

'He will be buried tomorrow?' I said, making conversation. 'In the country, not at San Michele?'

'Yes, of course, the country. All the Magliones are buried there.'

'I didn't realise he had a house there.'

He looked at me, stupefied, as if this were too absurd to answer. 'Yes,' he said finally, 'they always preferred it there. Not Gianni, he loved Venice, but the others . . .' He waved his hand. 'Always this love of land. Well, you can see how lucky it was for them. Poor Venice. The trade declines, what do the families do? Buy more ships. But the Magliones? Land. And now the other families are gone. How many of these are left?' he said, indicating the palazzo. 'In the family? Not a hotel. Not a museum. Still Ca' Maglione. It's because they bought land. It's an irony, yes? A house in the water, still here, all because of land.'

'How much do they own?'

He looked at me again. 'You mean exactly? I don't know. These are private matters, family matters—'

'I'm sorry. I didn't mean it that way. Just in general. It's a farm?'

'A farm? But Signor Miller, the Magliones are the largest landowners in the Veneto. Surely you knew that.'

'No,' I said, disconcerted.

'Yes, from the Brenta . . .' He started spreading his arms, then stopped. 'Well, considerable property. Of course, Giulia, the first wife, also had property. Near Ferrara.' He paused. 'His first – his wife, I should say. Now she will be the only one.' He placed his hand on my arm. 'I am so sorry for your loss.'

I looked at him, then nodded, a silent thank-you. 'I wish I'd known him better.' Something to say.

Surprisingly, this seemed to move him. He gripped my arm tighter. 'Your mother. She's—?'

'It's hard for her.'

Father Luca shook his head in sympathy. 'To lose a man like that. And think of the family. Always taking care of everybody. Paolo, everybody. Even as a child you could see it – the head of the family.'

'But I thought Paolo was older.'

'Yes, but Gianni was the head. Even then. Boys. Well, we were all boys. And now? A tragedy, a tragedy. So much evil in the world now.'

'More than before?' Bertie said, coming up behind him. 'I wonder. Luca, I have to drag you away. Hello, Claudia,' he said, his voice cooler. 'What a surprise.' He met her eyes for a second, then backed away, turning to me instead. 'I promised Luca a proper lunch. You must be famished,' he said to him, glancing at the table. 'She's the mother's daughter, isn't she?' He sighed. 'Be lovely to pay a little attention to the living.'

'But this is traditional.'

'Oh, I'm sure it's perfect. Just right. The mother was like that too. And you never had a decent meal in her house.'

'Signor Howard,' the priest said.

'Oh, I know. Very bad of me. Anyway, come to lunch. Adam, you ought to get Grace home. It's a strain, a thing like this.'

'She seems all right.'

'Mm. It's all this holding herself together I don't like. Much better to collapse with a good weep and get it over with. Much better in the end.'

Father Luca took my hand. 'If you ever want to talk, I knew him very well.'

Bertie threw me a 'What are you up to' look, then turned to the room. 'Aren't people extraordinary?' I followed his gaze to the crowd in suits and black dresses, idly talking, sipping coffee. 'You'd think he'd had a heart attack.'

It was Giulia who finally found us, smoking out on the balcony, pretending there was more sun than there was. 'You're Adam,' she said simply, extending a hand. I introduced Claudia, who moved back against the railing, suddenly skittish, but Giulia nodded graciously. There was no sign of recognition, the engagement party scene apparently not known to her. Another relief, something already fading, no longer gossiped about.

'I saw you looking at me before,' she said.

'I'm sorry. It's just, you look so like your father.'

'You think so? Most people think my mother.'

'Well, I never knew her.'

'No,' she said, suddenly embarrassed. 'Well, the eyes maybe. Everyone says that.'

But her eyes had none of Gianni's sharpness. They were soft, almost hazy, as if she had just taken off glasses and were trying to focus. 'You went to San Michele,' she said, her voice flat, so that for a second I wondered if she resented it, felt it was an intrusion.

'The police asked me.'

'Yes,' she said quickly. 'I am so grateful. To see him like that—' She stopped herself. 'I gave your mother some pictures. From his youth. They knew each other then, before – before the others.'

'Yes.'

'So it's a romantic story. I didn't know.'

212

'He never told you?'

She looked down. 'We didn't talk about it, no. Well, maybe he tried.' She lifted her head, clear-eyed, no longer soft or unfocused. 'You know, it's not easy to say this. I disagreed with him about this marriage. I thought he was bewitched.'

I smiled to myself. A word never used in conversation. Despite the perfect English, foreign after all.

'But now, I meet her and I see I was wrong. Not the fortune hunter. An affair of the heart.'

'Fortune hunter?' I said, thrown by the unexpectedness of it.

'I'm sorry, I don't know how to say it. You know, with my father there was always that danger, so it was natural . . .' She paused. 'A mistake. I apologise to you.'

'No, I just meant—' But what did I mean? That she would appreciate the irony? That it was the other way around? I put out my cigarette, stalling. 'I wish we'd met earlier.'

'Yes, I apologise for that too. Of course I had examinations, but that was an excuse, really. Anyway, I didn't come. So that was the last thing he said to me. "Good luck with the examinations."' She looked out at the canal, where a vaporetto was passing, catching the faint sun on its white roof.

'You're going to be a lawyer?' I said, bringing her back to somewhere neutral.

She smiled. 'In Italy? A woman? No. They let me study – well, because of my father. But in the courtroom? They wouldn't like that so much.' This to Claudia, who gave a thin smile back.

'So what will you do?'

'Oh, it was to work with my father. Like a son, you know? He used to say that to me, "You're my son." So it's a good thing to know, law, to run the businesses. My father used to trust everybody, and of course they cheated him. So now his son is there, a lawyer, they don't cheat so easily.' Not soft. Gianni telling me exactly what would happen at the trial he'd never have. She stopped, smiling shyly. 'I'm sorry, it's boring to talk about this.'

'No,' I said automatically. Businesses, not just land.

'We should go in. It's getting cold,' Claudia said, folding her arms across her chest and starting for the door.

Giulia glanced into the room, still filled with people. 'Yes, they can't go until they tell me how sorry they are. It's the form. Over and over, how sorry.'

'Who was the woman with you in church?'

'My grandmother.'

'Gianni's mother?' I said, a nervous twinge in my stomach. A child killed – nothing was worse. Not just dead.

'No, my mother's. She's the only one left now.'

I opened my hand to indicate 'After you', expecting her to follow Claudia through the door, but she hesitated.

'Wait,' she said. 'A moment. I don't know how to say it. I want to talk more. Will you come to see me?'

'Yes, if you'd like.'

'It's strange, you know, but there's no one else. I mean, we're not family, but we might have been. So it happened to you too, this death. Death – murder,' she said. 'Murder,' she said again. 'They won't even say it. No one else will care the way we do. You're the only one I can ask.'

'Ask what?'

'For your help.'

'My help?'

'To find the murderer.'

I stared at her. 'But the police—'

'Ouf, Cavallini. Filomena's husband, that one.'

'He's still the police.'

'They'll never find out. They'll look and then they'll stop.'

'But you won't,' I said quietly.

'Never,' she said, her voice Gianni's again, sure. 'I can't. I'm the son.' She looked at me. 'And you.'

'The way she looks at you,' Claudia said later, in bed.

'Like a sister.'

'Ha.'

214

'Jealous?' I said, smiling at her.

'No, careful. One slip, you say, but who's talking? The priest, then the daughter. I thought I would scream. I thought we'd never leave.'

I smiled again, but my mind was elsewhere, in the polished high room with the gilt furniture. Not a fortune hunter.

'But we did,' she said, putting a finger on my chest, bringing me back. 'So it's over, yes?'

The largest landowners in Veneto.

'Everyone saw us. That was the point,' I said.

'Everyone saw us at the ball.'

When I got home, my mother was looking through the photographs, the brown envelope next to her on the couch. I turned on a lamp and went over to the sideboard to make a drink.

'Want one?'

She pointed to her half-filled glass on the end table.

'You know, I don't remember wearing my hair this short,' she said, peering at a snapshot, 'but I suppose I must have.'

'What businesses did Gianni own?'

'Oh, darling, I don't know, a little of this, a little of that. Wines. He was always talking about that. Why?'

Giulia mentioned the family businesses. I was just wondering what they were.'

'They own part of a bank. I expect that's what she meant. And bits of things. He said it was safer that way, spreading out your chips.' She looked up. 'Not munitions, if that's what you mean. He wasn't that.'

'No, I didn't mean that. Just curious.'

'Well, the wines he used to mention. He said there was no such thing as a bad year during the war. So much demand. But I think it was more a hobby, really. The rest was through the bank.'

'But he was rich?'

'Darling, what a question. What's this all about?'

'Cavallini said he was one of the richest men in Italy.'

'Well, the family. They always had pots.'

'But he *was* the family.'

'After his brother, you mean. Yes, I suppose. But darling, you knew all this. Anyway, what does it matter now?'

'It doesn't, I guess,' I said, sipping my drink. 'But you knew?'

'Well, of course I *knew*. He always had money. I don't know how much exactly. I didn't ask to see his bank balance. I'm not Peggy Joyce yet.'

'I didn't say that.'

'You might as well.' She looked away. 'I admit I thought about it. Well, who wouldn't? But I was fond of him, you know. I really way. It wasn't just the money.'

I hesitated, taking this in. 'I didn't know it was the money at all. I thought you were in love with him.'

'I never said that,' she snapped, annoyed. 'I said I was fond of him. Though why any of this should matter to you now, I haven't the foggiest.' She put the photographs aside, unfolding her legs, restless. 'I must say, you pick your moments. I've just buried the last husband I'm likely to have and you want to talk about his finances. Accusing me of I don't know what. All right. So we're crystal clear. I was never in love with Gianni. I've told you this. I was in love with your father. But Gianni – well, after all these years, I never expected that. And then there it was, and yes, I thought, Well, this is lucky, everything will be all right now. But I was fond of him. I never deceived him about that,' she said, her voice finally breaking. She reached for a handker-chief. 'Now look. I get through the whole funeral and now I start to puddle.'

I stared at her, my mind racing, connecting dots. 'What do you mean, everything will be all right now?'

'What? Oh, the money. That's what we were talking about, isn't it? Anyway, that's gone now. It really doesn't matter how much he had, does it? I won't see any of it.' She sniffed into the handker-chief.

'So what? You have your own. We'll go back to New York.'

But she was shaking her head. 'It's not going to stretch there. I can do it here. Why do you think I came? You can still live here. You have no idea what New York is like now, just the simplest things.'

'Stretch?' I said, looking at her, trying to follow. 'What about Dad's money?'

'I've been living on it. I'm still living on it – I never said anybody was *starving*.' She moved away. 'I don't know how much you thought there was. Those last years, when he was sick, it just went through your fingers. All the nurses, everything. It goes. And every year there's less. So you have to be careful. Look, I can do it. It's just I can do it better here. And I thought, well, you have that little trust from your grandfather – and you were always so independent anyway. I'm not going to be a *burden*, you don't have to worry about that. But New York just eats it away. You get worried. You just keep hoping something will turn up.'

'And something did.'

'Yes, something did.' She looked at me. 'I didn't *plan* it. I went to Paris, not here.'

'I know.'

'But the way you look. So I came and it was lucky, and shall I tell you something? We would have been happy. We would have taken care of each other. He wanted to marry me so much. Why? I don't know, but he wanted it. We would have been happy. It wasn't just the money. I was fond of him.' She fingered the brown envelope on the couch, then turned to me. 'But you never saw that. Always so—' She cut herself off, then shook her head. 'You made it so difficult, Adam, you really did. We didn't deserve that, either of us.' Her voice dropped, finally out of steam, and she moved towards the door. 'What shall I tell Angelina? Are you in tonight?'

'Yes, all right.'

'Not for me, I hope,' she said. 'I don't want that, Adam. I don't mind being alone.' Her shoulders moved, a small shrug. 'Anyway, I'd better get used to it.' Almost casual, making peace.

'No,' I said, trying to reassure her with a look. 'Something will turn up.'

She nodded, smiling weakly. 'Twice.'

After she left I went over to the couch and picked up a few of the pictures. On the beach, with her short hair, in a group. Gianni as a teenager, grinning, then as a young man, sitting with people in cafés, posing in San Marco, in a racing car with his brother, in front of the hospital – all smiling. Giulia must have raided the family album to find Gianni as my mother would have known him, young, unattached. Even in the later pictures his wife was missing – at home, or maybe just outside the frame. Smiling, happy, exactly the man my mother described. Not the one I knew. But they must at some point have been the same. When had everything turned inside out. If it had.

My face felt warm, as if my mother's words were stinging it. All I'd wanted to do, the start of everything, was to protect her. But he'd been rich, not after her money, not even thinking about it. I dropped the pictures, my hand shaking a little. What else had I been wrong about? I tried to think what his face had looked like when he hadn't been smiling, when he had been reaching for me in the hall. Malevolent, or just angry, frustrated? Maybe Claudia's landlady had wanted the rooms back. Maybe the Accademia was cutting staff. Maybe I'd killed the young man in the photograph, imagining he'd become someone else. Held his head underwater until the life went out of him because I had got everything wrong. Not just murder, murder for no reason at all. I sat for a few minutes more, my chest suddenly tight, taking in gulps of air, then went over to the phone and placed a trunk call to Rosa Soriano.

CHAPTER ELEVEN

'WELL, NOW YOU have your answer,' Rosa said, tapping the news-paper lying on the folder next to her. We were at the Bauer again, at the same breakfast, except that sunshine had replaced the rain outside. '*Una cospirazione comunista.*' She smiled a little, shaking her head.

Gianni's funeral took up half the front page, with a big picture of the casket being carried down the Salute steps, the veiled Giulia just behind, held by the elbows for theatrical effect, a scene ready for La Fenice.

'Why Communist?'

'Why not? A political killing, very convenient. You don't scare the tourists and you get to blame the Communists for something else. You see it says here "rumours." In other words, they don't know, but now people have the impression the Communists did it.'

'But why would they want to?'

'An old Venetian family, a doctor, a "saviour of men," every-thing that's good – naturally they'd want to get rid of him.' She pushed the paper aside. 'Who knows why? As long as they did. So now they're like gangsters, even worse than people thought.' She sipped her tea. 'It's not a political city, you know. Whatever's good for business.' She smiled. 'When the Allies came in – from New Zealand, did you know? Venice liberated by New Zealand – they

219

were still serving German officers at Quadri's. Not in uniform. Civilian clothes. They hated to leave. One last coffee. So the waiters kept serving. That was all right. It was *after* – when the partisans acted. For the crimes, all those years. People shot. That was terrible, worse than the Germans. You see how it says here about the brother?' She tapped the paper again. 'A tragic family. Again this violence. So they make the connection. Another killing, like the brother. Partisans again. Now Communists, the same thing to them.'

'But maybe it was a partisan.'

She looked at me over the rim of her cup but didn't say anything.

'You said they acted on their own sometimes. If the trials—'

She was nodding. 'Yes, it was the first thing I thought, when I heard. Like *Il Gazzettino*,' she said, giving a wry glance at the paper.

'But now you don't?'

'A feeling only. Why now, so late?' She took the cup in both hands, warming herself. 'You see, when the Germans left, there were killings like this. A season of bad blood – avenge this one, that one. You know, this happens. A part of war. But then it stops. It's enough. And the way he was killed—'

'What do you mean?'

'So clumsy. Like a thief. With the partisans, it was a bullet. A *military* action, not a crime. Oh, such a look. You think it's the same? It's not the same to them. These are not criminals. Soldiers. They were fighting for their country. But the war's over. So why now? It's only for us,' she said, waving her hand back and forth between us, 'that the war doesn't end. With our files. For the others, it's late.' She paused. 'But also too early. You know, when I said they act, they find their own proof, it's for justice. Because I couldn't do it with this.' She placed her hand on the folder. 'But there hasn't been any trial. They don't have to make their own justice yet. It's too soon.'

'Maybe someone didn't want to wait.'

'Maybe, but there's no talk of this. You know I have many contacts. Old colleagues,' she said, raising an eyebrow, almost conspiratorial. 'No one says anything.' She sighed. 'But what's the difference now? He got his justice anyway.'

'You found the proof?'

'Proof?'

'The fire. The house.'

She looked away. 'The house, no. No proof. The dates don't work.'

'What?'

'The man who was in hospital, Moretti, he was released on the fourth of October. That's the date you found, yes? It's too early. The raid, it's not until the fifteenth. Why would they wait? And he doesn't come to us. A week in Verona, a safe house there. I thought at first it must be – such a coincidence, Moretti in the hospital, if he had just come from Venice, but no. First to Verona. If they tracked him, why wait?'

'For someone else to come to the house,' I said faintly.

'No one else came. Couriers, people who had been before. None of them were in the house when the Germans attacked. None were picked up later. So who were they waiting for? Of course, maybe there's something in the German records – you know, in all the confusion, some are missing. But still, why wait? It's not characteristic. The dates don't work.'

I stared at her, gripping the edge of the table, stepping into the outer swirl of an eddy. 'You mean he might not have done it?'

'I mean we can't prove it. For a trial Except it's not a question of that any more. He's dead.'

'But how do we know—?' I stopped, one thought tumbling over another. 'What if he didn't do it?'

'If not the house, something else. He was a collaborator, no? Isn't that why you came to us in the first place? He was what he was.'

'But what, exactly?' I said, mostly to myself.

She looked at me, surprised.

'I mean, we should know. Now that we've started.'

'But he's ended it, Signor Miller. He's dead. The file is closed. I can't investigate the dead. There's no time for that.'

'But he was killed.'

'Well, now it's a police matter.' She paused. 'That's what's troubling you? You feel guilty?'

I looked at her.

'Yes, I know,' she said. 'I know what you think. We open the file, start looking, and someone hears. Aha, so it's Maglione, he thinks. And he decides to act. On his own. Because we started this.' She put her hand across the table, not quite touching mine. 'We can't blame ourselves for this. I make files, that's all. The files don't kill people. Maybe it was always going to happen. Maybe this *is* the justice. Anyway, it's done.' She moved her cup aside, finished.

'But if a partisan killed him, wouldn't you want to know?'

She looked straight at me. 'And what? Bring *him* to trial? No. My justice doesn't go that far. And how did he know? Because we started this. Then it's our fault too? So we all killed him? That's what you want to think?'

'But what if we killed the wrong man?' I said, shaky, finally there, near the centre of the eddy.

She stared at me for a moment, then put both hands in front of her, fingers touching, making a point. 'Signor Miller, he's dead. If he did terrible things – well, it's good, yes? If he didn't, he's dead anyway. What do you want me to do? Get proof and condemn him in the ground? Or no proof – then what? Rehabilitate him? Make a good reputation for him? In *Il Gazzettino* he's already a hero. What more can he want? Let it go now. Close the file.'

'But then we'll never know if he did it.'

'It's so important to you, this?' she said. 'What do you want to prove? That he deserved to die?'

I looked away, for a second seeing again the grey skin on San Michele, pasty and inert.

'Lieutenant Sullivan said it was like this with you,' Rosa said. 'Personal. In Germany, every case.'

Had it been? Is that what Joe had thought? Folder after folder. 'I hate to walk away. That's all.'

'Yes, but there are so many others. The point is to make a trial. To make it known. There's no trial here,' she said, putting her hand on the file. 'Not any more. It doesn't matter to me how he died. There's no trial.' She was silent for a minute, waiting, then began to gather up her things. Case closed.

'But I have to know,' I said, the words jumping out of me, trying to hold her in her seat.

She looked up at me, startled.

'Want to know,' I said, correcting myself. 'I want to know what he did. So do you.'

'It's not personal with me, Signor Miller. I don't have the time.'

It was at that moment, everything swirling again, that I saw Cavallini, a glimpse over Rosa's shoulder, circling into my line of vision across the room – the moustache, then the side of his face, then his back, sitting down. I craned my neck, looking around her. Was he meeting someone? No, alone. At the Bauer. Talking to the waiter now, opening a paper. Why not at work at the Questura? Unless he was at work, keeping me in sight. The one man in Venice he could trust.

'Look,' I said, dropping my voice, as if he could actually hear it across the room, 'all I'm asking you to do is keep checking the German files. There has to be something, and I don't have access. You do that and I'll work the rest from this end.'

'Work what?'

'I'll finish that,' I said, pointing to the file. 'The hospital, the times, how it happened.' I hesitated. 'The other members of the group. Not to nail them. I promise you, if it turns out—'

'Don't promise me anything.'

'If it was a partisan, it stops here. You won't know. Nobody knows.'

'Except you,' she said, tilting her head slightly, as if another angle might explain things. 'Then why do it?'

Why. Because there had to be a reason for the bubbles in the

223

water. But why else? Something I could say that she could believe. Over her shoulder, the waiter was pouring Cavallini's coffee.

'Because it wasn't a partisan. You don't think so and neither do I.'

'No?'

'We can't stop now. You've already done the spade work – now you're just going to give it a pass? An atrocity everybody knows about? There *should* be a trial.'

'Signor Miller, he's dead,' she said, her voice weary but her eyes intrigued, assessing me. Think of something. Quickly. Cavallini would turn in his seat any second, make an elaborate show of coming over. Rosa's help lost for good. I'd never know.

'But not everyone is. Whoever killed him isn't.'

'Not a partisan,' she said slowly.

'No. And if I find him,' I said, nodding at the file, 'then you're back in business. So it's worth a chance.'

She had leaned forwards, her whole body listening. 'Back in business?'

'Well, there's always somebody else, isn't there? Always. But nothing ever came out. Then all of a sudden you're investigating Gianni – you know something, you're getting close. So if you were the somebody else, it might be a good time to get rid of Gianni,' I said, rushing now, believing it myself, the way it should have happened.

'Another collaborator.'

'Who set up the raid.' I opened my palm, an offering. 'Your trial.' And then, before she could say anything, 'Could you get me a list of everyone you talked to, who knew you were doing this?'

Because there had to be someone who knew about Gianni, who could tell me.

'Besides you and Lieutenant Sullivan?'

'Everyone. At the hospital, whoever you talked to. It had to be someone who knew this was happening, that you were opening the case.'

'But they might have talked to others.'

'I know. We'll follow it as far as we can.'

'Oh, *we*. I told you—'

'*I*. You just work on the Germans. I'll take care of that,' I said, reaching over for the file.

'You know I can't. It's Allied property.'

'Joe would do it for me.'

'And me? When they ask me?'

'Files get lost. Misplaced. Even the Germans lost files,' I said. 'It happens. And then they turn up again. You want to know what happened too, don't you?' She raised her hand, letting the file slide away, then pushed up her sleeve and scratched the white skin on her arm. 'We both want to know.' I kept looking at her as I pulled the folder towards me.

'And you're going to do this all by yourself? One man. Talk to all these people, in Italian. How? I can't take the time.'

'I know. We made a deal. Just work the German side.'

'But you can't—'

I glanced over her shoulder again. The one man he could trust. Not even an idea, an impulse, grabbing at anything, unable to stop now, the eddy in control. 'Yes, I can. I'm going to get the police to help.'

We had to pass Cavallini's table to leave the dining room, so there was no avoiding a meeting. He sprang up when we got near, as if he'd been waiting.

'Ah, Signora Soriano. They said you would be here.' He took her hand. Waiting for Rosa, not me.

'You know each other?' I said.

'Who said I would be here?'

'I telephoned your office.'

'Ah, looking for the Communists,' she said, pointing to the paper in front of him, mischievous. 'You know I can't help you with that. I don't know any.'

'No one does,' Cavallini said, smiling back. 'Sometimes, you know, I think we make them up.'

Rosa looked at him. 'Sometimes you do. But they're useful, no?' She nodded to the paper.

'Some coffee? You can join me?' He offered a seat.

'No, it's impossible. I'm late. If I'd known – it's important? You came here to see me?'

'I don't like to interrupt,' he said, motioning towards the table where we'd been.

'What is it?' Rosa said, direct.

'Not the Communists,' he said, picking up the paper. 'The victim. You have so much information about our Venetian citizens. I thought perhaps – you know, we have to look everywhere in a murder case.'

'Ha, so this is your help?' she said to me. '*Come due gocce d'acqua*. What's the English? Not drops of water – peas?'

'Two peas in a pod,' I said, not really following.

'Both of you, so interested in Maglione,' she said to Cavallini, then pointed her thumb at me. 'Talk to him. You know I'm not allowed. Only if Lieutenant Sullivan—'

'But you can tell me – is there a file?'

She kept her eyes on him, away from the folder in the newspaper under my arm.

'A murder case, signora.'

'All right. I'll look,' she said evenly. 'But now I should go. You're finished with me?'

'It's not an interrogation,' Cavallini said, smiling.

'There's a difference, with police?' she said, but pleasantly, easing her way out. 'I'll call you,' she said to me. 'Good luck.' This with a move of her eyes to Cavallini.

'So you know the famous Rosa,' Cavallini said as she left.

'She works for a friend of mine. Why famous?'

'During the war, in the resistance. Brave, like a man. The Germans never got her. A Communist, you know.'

'She says not.'

He shrugged. 'They all say not. So, why good luck? The peas in a pod?'

'We both asked her about Gianni.'

'Ah,' he said, noncommittal.

'Look, you said on San Michele that I could help. Maybe I can.

226

This is what I did in Germany, with her boss. The army's not going to talk to you – they like to keep things to themselves. But he'll talk to me. I can find out what they have.'

'So there is a file.'

'Yes.'

'Why?'

But maybe he already knew. 'Because I asked them to start one.'

He looked at me for a moment, then at the waiter gathering up cups. 'I must get back. But it's so nice today. Perhaps you'd walk with me? Part of the way?'

Outside, we stopped in front of San Moise, the rococo stone dark with grit even in the bright sun.

'You asked for this investigation?'

'Yes. Didn't you know?' I said, probing.

'Your mother mentioned something,' he said casually. Known all along. Take nothing for granted.

'Then you also know why.'

He nodded. 'The incident with Signorina Grassini, I think. Several have mentioned this.' Why? I felt warm, a rush of blood. Had he been asking about her? Running through his checklist, rumours and times I left the hotel and who had seen what? But the engagement party had been bound to come up. It had happened. And so had the ball, when we'd spent the evening with him, having our pictures taken. Just move the party off his checklist, away from Claudia. 'An embarrassment for you.'

'And for her now,' I said, starting to walk, the narrow calle feeling suddenly like a tightrope. Keep your balance and don't look down. 'You know, when something terrible happens, you look for someone to blame. Anybody. And Gianni was there when they were taken. You don't always think, you just – then later you realise it's a mistake. You can't blame someone personally. Of course, Gianni was nice about it. I suppose for my sake. So they made a truce.' The same word he'd used when he lied to me on the fondamenta, maybe a word that was always a lie. 'In the end they were both relieved, I think.'

'But you asked your friend – Lieutenant Sullivan? – to investigate him.'

'I wanted to reassure her that Gianni was all right. That she'd made a mistake.'

'And did it? Reassure her?'

'Yes,' I said, looking at him, 'because I didn't tell her what they found.'

He was quiet for a minute, thinking, then he stopped. We were near the turnoff for Harry's, standing next to one of the stores. Shoes and handbags and cashmere, with Harry's at the end of the calle, my mother's Venice.

'But you want to tell me?' he said, a question, not a request, his eyes slightly apprehensive. I remembered the broad smile that first night at Harry's, pleased to see Gianni.

'Yes. But only you. It wouldn't be fair to his daughter. To my mother, for that matter. Nobody has to know. Not yet. They're only suggestions. Not proof, suggestions.

'What suggestions?' he said calmly.

'That he was working with the Germans. That he betrayed partisans.'

'You believe this?'

'I don't know what to believe. People have to do things in wartime – it's hard to judge. So maybe yes. But the point is that if he *did*, then there's a motive. Why would anyone want to kill Gianni. But if he betrayed them, or if they thought he did . . .'

He was nodding to himself. 'Yes, there were such cases. Rosa knows this. And yet she runs away when I ask.'

'She doesn't want it to be a partisan.'

'That's your idea, that it was a partisan?'

We started walking again, past the jewellery stores and into the deep shadow of the arcades.

'You know, Signor Miller, everyone worked for the Germans. We don't like to say now, but what could we do? This was an occupied country. Even the police worked for them.'

'Not like this.'

228

'Like this,' he repeated, waiting. 'There was a suggestion—'

'That he was an informer for the SS. There was a raid, an atrocity.'

'A fire.'

'So you know about it.'

'I thought it must be that. With Rosa.'

Just then we came out of the arcades into the bright open piazza, that exhilarating first moment when the space of San Marco dazzles. Even Cavallini stopped, looking across at the campanile and the domes of the basilica.

'It seems impossible, doesn't it, that such things could happen,' he said, 'where it's so beautiful.' I glanced at him, surprised. 'Look at this,' he said, genuinely moved. And in fact the piazza was spectacular, flooded with spring light, the sun flashing off the gold mosaics, the pigeons swooping up and around in the soft air. 'Imagine,' he said, 'to be a Maglione in this city.' He turned to me. 'I hope you're wrong, Signor Miller. So many years, and then a disgrace like this on the name.'

'I hope I'm wrong too. For my mother's sake.'

'Yes, forgive me,' he said. We started to walk across the piazza. 'I forgot what this would mean to her. I was thinking of my wife's family. An indulgence. Do such things happen? Who knows better than a policeman? Of course you're right – we must know. I'm grateful to you for your help.'

'Maybe we can help each other.'

'Yes?'

'I can find out what Joe Sullivan has – well, Rosa, really. But if we want to take this any further, there are hospital records to check, and I'd need your authority for that.'

'My authority? But the Allies have all the authority you need.'

'For war crimes. But now he's dead. They're not interested in trying a dead man. What would be the point? So it's a police matter. Your case.'

'My case,' he said to himself, as if he were trying out the phrase. He looked up at me, a faint grin under the moustache. 'And you want to be the Dr Watson? The partner? It's not usual, such an offer.'

'Just an assistant. If it would help.'

'Oh, I accept, I accept. An experienced investigator? For you it's like old times, maybe. More Germans.'

'No, no trials this time. I just want to know whether he did it.' I looked at Cavallini. 'And then we'll know why he was killed.'

Unexpectedly, he extended his hand. 'I am so grateful for your help. At the Questura, do they want this? To know why? With you, it's a family matter, they say to me. You see, you can understand that. But the others? They just want it to go away. For everything to be normal. The tourists will be here soon.'

Around us, as a kind of live illustration, the waiters were putting out more tables at Florian's, even one day's sun an excuse to start the season. In a few days the musicians would be back, playing waltzes, and everything would be the same. I watched for a second, uneasy, even the white-jacketed waiters carrying chairs suddenly surreal. I was supposed to be one of the people sitting down for coffee, reading an English newspaper, writing postcards. Not lying to policemen, who were grateful for my help.

'Will you come back to the Questura?'

'I can't now,' I said. 'Anyway, I'd better call Joe. Get you the file.' After I'd read it first, decided what to pass on. 'So we can start.'

'Yes, thank you,' he said, but the idea seemed to darken his mood again, a reminder. 'I remember the incident of the house very well. Those were the worst times, near the end. I don't know why.'

I shrugged. 'The losers are desperate and the winners aren't accountable yet. So it's open season. It was the same in Germany. At the War Crimes Commission, most of the cases were recent.'

'War crimes,' he said. 'Sometimes I think everything in the war was a crime.'

I looked at him, surprised again. 'And nothing. That's the problem. It's war, so it doesn't count.'

'Well, now it's over,' he said, taking one last look at the piazza, still filling with chairs. 'Now it counts.'

CHAPTER TWELVE

'ARE YOU CRAZY?' Claudia said.

'Maybe. But this way we know everything they're doing.'

'Help them. What are you going to do? Help them catch us?'

'The closer I get, the more they look somewhere else. I'm *making* them look somewhere else.'

'No, digging a grave. Two. Not just yours.' Pacing now, drawing smoke in tight gulps, as if she were angry at the cigarette too.

'We *want* them to look somewhere else. You don't want them coming back to that party.'

'Back to me, you mean.'

'Back to either of us,' I said, looking at her. 'Either of us.'

'And now they won't – because you're there? Maybe they ask themselves, why does he do this?'

'Look, I was a kind of cop. Something like this happens in my family, they expect me to take an interest.'

'Not your family.'

'Close to me, then. They expect me to help. Cavallini asked me. Giulia asked me.'

'Oh, Giulia. The pretty sister. Now, not a sister. So there's a convenience.'

'Stop.'

'What do you want to do, make it up to her? "I'll find out who did it." Ha. Not as difficult as she thinks.'

'Claudia.'

'Maybe you want to show her what he was like. "Here's your father. SS." You think she'll thank you for that, your little sister?'

'Are you finished?'

She turned her back to me. 'You said we would leave Venice.'

'We will.'

'Oh, but not yet. Not until it's too late.'

I put my hands on her and turned her around. 'Listen. This is how it works. I show Cavallini what Gianni did. I prove it. So it's the logical answer, the *only* place he looks. Not here, not at you, not at me. Some partisan, someone Gianni betrayed.'

'And when there is no partisan?'

'But they'll think there is. Maybe dead, maybe still out there – they don't know exactly, we never find out, but we know who it has to be. The kind of crime. So they're satisfied – it couldn't be anyone else. And maybe it's just as well they can't get him. That way nothing has to come out about Gianni. No scandal. No disgrace. All covered up. Like his brother. All they want is an answer to what happened, something plausible. They don't want to open anything up. Nobody wants to know.'

She was silent for a minute, then moved away, carrying her cigarette to the table. 'Only you,' she said, putting it out. 'You want to know.'

'Don't you? I want to be sure.'

'Sure of what? You want to use the police to prove he was guilty? Why? So that it was right for you—'

'I want to lead them somewhere else.'

'No,' she said, shaking her head. 'You'll lead them back to us.'

'The closer I am to them, the safer we are.'

She looked up. 'Yes? Unless they use you.'

We stopped then, too tired to go any further, but the argument went on in different ways, a general prickliness that began to seep into the days.

Claudia had found a job in a lace shop near San Aponal.

'You don't have to work.'

'Yes, I have to. What do I do, sit and wait? Besides, after the Accademia, maybe they think I have a grudge. No job. So it's better.'

'No one suspects you.'

'Maybe I want to do it anyway. What else? Sit with your mother, waiting for her to guess?'

So we saw less of each other, busy being careful in public. I went through reports at the Questura – a staff member to translate, a desk that wasn't officially mine but was always available – and Claudia made a point of not asking where I'd been. One night, leaving her hotel, I realised that we'd made love because we were expected to, as if our comings and goings were still being monitored, even sex now part of an airtight alibi, something noted for a file.

On Sunday the weather was still fine and we went to Torcello, an excuse to get away. The vaporetto wasn't crowded – a few families going out to Burano and two American soldiers in Eisenhower jackets who sat inside with half-closed eyes, out late the night before.

The military had been a light presence in Venice during the occupation, and since the official changeover in December soldiers were even less visible, more like tourists passing through than conquerors. In Germany it had been rubble and jeep patrols and lowering your eyes when a soldier passed, keeping out of trouble. Here, in the close quarters of the boat, the Burano families stared openly, curious, as if they were sizing up customers. I thought of the Germans finishing coffee at Quadri's. Now the Allies. Who might like a little Burano lace to send home.

Surprisingly, however, the GIs got off with us at Torcello. I looked at the sluggish canal, the lonely marshes beyond, and wondered if they'd made a mistake, but after a quick glance at a map they went straight towards the piazza. Claudia hung back, letting them go ahead. No one else was around. Somewhere on the island,

233

on one of the farms, a dog barked. Otherwise it was quiet, no summer insects yet, just the wind moving through the reeds. By the time we caught up with the GIs, they were standing in the piazza, a worn patch of grass, looking as melancholy and lost as the shuttered buildings around it.

'There's supposed to be a restaurant here,' one of them said. 'Locanda. You know where that is?'

I pointed to the closed-up inn across from us.

'That's the one Harry's runs?'

'Yes, but only in the summer,' I said. 'It's too early.'

'Well, shit,' he said, then dipped his head towards Claudia, an apology to a lady.

'They didn't tell you?'

'I never asked. I just heard about it. Shit.' He looked around the empty island. 'What's the rest, a ghost town?'

'No, people live here. Farms. It's just a little early in the season. You're welcome to have some of ours.' I pointed to the picnic bag.

'That's okay, we'll just catch the next boat.'

'That'll be a while. You check the schedule?'

He shook his head, then grinned. 'Never thought to look.'

We opened the wine and shared out the salami sandwiches, sitting on the steps of the Greek church, Claudia slightly away from us, uncomfortable. They were on furlough, trying to see something worth seeing before they headed back to Stuttgart. It was the usual service talk – where I'd been stationed, where they were from, when their separation papers were coming through.

'And I can't wait,' he said. 'I mean, I can't fucking *wait*. They can keep the whole thing.' He spread his arm to take in all of Europe, then remembered Claudia and dropped it, embarrassed. Instead, as if it would explain things, he pulled out his wallet and showed us a picture of his wife, Joyce. Head tilted for the camera, blonde, ordinary, holding a baby in her arms.

'A boy?' Claudia said.

He grinned back. 'Jim junior. Haven't seen him yet. Just this.'

'Well, but soon, yes? They're sending everybody home now.

234

We saw it in the newsreels,' she said. 'All the boats.' Thousands of waving soldiers, the skyscraper shot, then running down the gang-plank, arms open.

'You from here?' he said, intrigued by her accent, maybe the first Italian he'd met. He looked around. 'What is this place, anyway?'

'It was the first Venice, where it started.'

'So what happened?'

'The canals silted up. Malaria too, I think.'

He gave her an 'I'll bet' look. 'Anything here to see? I mean, you came out, and you knew the restaurant was closed.'

'The basilica is very old, eleventh century. The original was seventh,' Claudia said. 'The mosaics are famous.' But she was losing them. They were already looking away, uninterested. 'And, you know, for walks.'

'Right,' he said, nodding. 'Walks.' A smile, just a trace of a leer. 'And here we are, in the way.' He brushed off his trousers, standing up.

'But you don't want to see inside?'

'Tell you what, you take a look for me. I never know what I'm looking at anyway. We'll just go wait for the boat, let you be.'

'It's a long wait.'

'Not in this sun. I could just soak it up, after Germany.' He grinned. 'Fucking sunny Italy, huh?'

They took a photograph of us, then headed down the canal path to the pier, turning once to wave.

'So that's who comes to Cipriani's,' Claudia said, amused.

'Not usually,' I said, leaning back. A favourite of Bertie's before the war. 'I wonder how they heard about it.'

'Oh, how do people hear about anything? Somebody tells them.'

'Yes,' I said lazily, closing my eyes. 'And who tells him?'

'Somebody else.'

'And him?' I said, playing.

'I don't know. Maybe Cipriani.'

235

I smiled, letting the thought drift, then sat up, taking a cigarette out of my pocket. 'So who told Gianni? I mean, how *did* he know?'

She looked at me blankly.

'Rosa said he wouldn't know a partisan – somebody would have to tell him. Not the SS. If they already knew, why use him? Somebody else. Maybe I've been looking at this backwards.'

'How do you mean, backwards.'

'We've been tracking what happened *after*, and we're getting nowhere. But what about before?' I bent over, lighting the cigarette, then saw her confused expression. 'Look, the only one in that house who'd been in hospital was a man called Moretti. If there was a connection to Gianni, he'd be it. But he was discharged more than a week earlier. So where was Gianni all that time? There's nothing to prove he was involved at all.'

'So maybe he wasn't,' Claudia said calmly.

'No proof,' I said, not listening. 'A few visits to Villa Raspelli. But if he did know about Moretti, *how* did he know? Maybe that's what we should be looking for. The link before.'

'And if you don't find that either?'

I exhaled some smoke. 'Then we can't prove he did anything.'

'He gave them my father.'

'But there's no proof he did.'

'No,' she said, 'only me.'

'I didn't mean—'

'Just my word. And now he can't answer. So how can you prove it? Maybe I made it up. The camp too. Maybe it's all in my head.'

'I didn't mean—' I said again.

But she was gathering things up, finished with it. 'Let's see the church.'

I put out my cigarette, still thinking, and followed her inside. Santa Maria Assunta had been built before churches became theatres – the walls were austere and the air was damp. We could see our breath in little streams. Venice was still primitive here, the island a mudbank with reeds again, the world full of mystery and fear. But then there were the mosaics at the end, cold and glittering, spreading over the chancel in an arch of coloured light. People would have knelt here on the rough stone floors, dazed.

'You see the tear on her cheek?' Claudia said, pointing. 'Mary crying. It's unique.'

We studied the Apostles for a while, then walked slowly back to the west wall and the big mosaic of the Last Judgment, the afterlife arranged in tiers, a medieval sorting out, with hellfire on the bottom. Dying wasn't enough for the early Christians – there had to be punishment too. Claudia stood before it with her arms folded across her chest, working her way down through the levels of grace to the figures on the lower right, engulfed in flames.

'So this is what happens after,' she said. 'But they didn't want the Jews to wait. They burned us here.'

The chill of the old stone followed us out into the piazza, not quite as sunny as before. We took one of the footpaths leading away from the canal, waving to the GIs, who were still waiting on the dock for the Burano boat. 'Why are they laughing?'

'They think we're going parking.'

'Parking?'

'Kissing. In a car. People drive somewhere to be alone.'

'America,' she said. 'Everyone has a car.'

'Will you like that? You'll have to learn to drive.' An unexpected thought, jarring, because I had never imagined us beyond Venice, anywhere outside her room.

'Drive,' she said, maybe jarred too. 'Here, no one does.'

Except Gianni's brother, I thought. Who had actually pushed him off the road? Maybe a connection. Something to ask Rosa.

We passed the farm with the dog, then turned on to a path that led down to the water, a cleared patch of dry land that looked back through the reeds to the campanile. In summer, lovers would come with picnics. Now we pulled our jackets tight against the wind.

It was only after his brother's death that Gianni had made the house calls to Villa Raspelli. Younger, but head of the family, Father Luca had said. His brother's keeper.

'So you're thinking again,' she said. 'Why is this so important to you?'

'I don't want to be wrong.' I turned to her. 'Then it's just personal – something I did for myself.'

She stopped in the path. 'He was trying to kill you.'

I looked over the reeds. His eyes, hesitating, about to stop, then the slippery stairs, my hand underneath, getting cold as I held him there, my breath ragged.

'What?' she said.

'No, I wanted to do it,' I said finally. 'I wanted to do it.'

She came over to me. 'You know what he was.'

'If he was. I was wrong about him and my mother. He was never after her money, never. Anyway, it turns out there isn't any.'

'No?' she said, then started to smile, raising her hand to brush at my hair. 'So it's lucky I found the lace shop.'

'I was wrong,' I said, not letting go.

She brushed my hair again. 'It doesn't matter now. It doesn't change anything.'

'Of course it matters.'

'Why? So you can blame yourself? And then what? For you it's like the mosaic.' She tossed her head towards the church. 'Always a judgement. There is no judgement. No one is judging. No one is watching.' She stopped, dropping her hand. 'No one is watching.'

'Then we have to,' I said.

'Oh, like he did,' she said, annoyed, moving away. 'Play God. Of course, a doctor, they're used to that, aren't they? Then he plays it with my father. Bah.' She waved her hand. 'But that's not enough for you. How guilty does he have to be? Before it's all right?'

She walked to the end of the clearing where it was sunny and faced the water, using her back to put an end to the conversation. I went over to her, not saying anything.

'That's Jesolo,' she said, pointing, meaning nothing, not expecting a response.

238

I took out my cigarettes and offered her one, waiting for her lead. But she seemed to enjoy the silence, turning her face to the sun, then squatting down to test the ground for dampness, sitting, and lying back. I sat down next to her.

'This is better. All week in the shop, never any sun,' she said.

I stretched out, leaning on my elbow to prop up my head as I looked at her.

'You don't have to work there,' I said, going along. 'I mean, with your English. They're always looking for translators. Joe would hire you in a second.'

'For the army? No, not even yours. Not carabinieri either. Or police. No uniforms.' She glanced over. 'I don't work for the police. One of us is enough.'

I turned and lay on my back, squinting at the bright sky. In the distance was the faint sound of a boat's motor, maybe the GIs' vaporetto. 'What's wrong?' I said. 'All week. It's not Cavallini, not really. What?'

'I don't know.' She paused. 'I'm worried.'

'About what? I'm telling you, they don't know.'

She shook her head. 'Not that. It's different between us. At first, it made us closer. And now, already we're quarrelling.' She turned to me. 'You can't change it. What it is. You want to make it better. Nothing makes it better.'

'I know.'

'But you keep thinking, maybe. It's in your head.' She lay on her back again.

'Nothing's different between us. I just want to know about him, that's all. It's important.'

She closed her eyes, another way of turning her back, and said nothing for a few minutes, then sighed, not much louder than the moving reeds.

'They have sun in Georgia?' she said. 'Where that soldier lives?'

'Nothing but.'

'So he's happy there. But not you,' she said, thinking aloud. 'You don't want to go home.'

239

'I'm happy here.'

'No. Something else. Those men on the ship – in the film, remember? So excited. It's over for them.' She turned, opening her eyes. 'But not for you.'

I said nothing, remembering Rosa wagging her finger between us, both of us still with files.

'Maybe it takes an ocean, and then it's gone,' she said. 'Oh, I want—'

I looked over at her. 'What?'

'What? What do I want?' she said to herself. 'I want to be Joyce. The girl in the picture. Make curtains. Wait for the ship. Feed the baby.' She stopped, her voice drifting off. 'Think how wonderful, not to know about any of it. Not any of it.'

'And that's the life you want,' I said, teasing. 'Joyce.'

'No.' She turned. 'Anyway, I can't. No babies. So that's something you should know,' she said, her voice tentative, waiting for a response.

'Oh,' I said finally, trying to sound easy.

'Do you mind about that?'

'No.'

'No?'

Another pause, this time waiting for her.

'I got rid of it myself, in the camp. I knew that if he found out, he'd send me. And there was no one to help, so I did it myself. That's why.'

I looked at her for a minute, not saying anything. Then she moved to brush off a blade of grass, pushing at her sleeve, and for an instant I saw Rosa's arm again with its jagged patch of white. Visible scars, reminders. But what about the others, the ones you couldn't see? Years of them, nobody unblemished now.

I reached over and touched her hand. 'I don't want Joyce.'

'So it's lucky for me.' She closed her eyes. 'But now there's this. Maybe you enjoy it, being police. But it's both of us they'll catch. Why do you have to know?'

'I held him under, Claudia. Me. What if—?'

For a minute she didn't say anything. Then she took a breath. 'When it happened, I thought you did it for me. So they wouldn't take me. I thought my heart would stop. Imagine, someone doing that for me. Everyone else wanted me dead, and you—' She moved her hand away and sat up. 'But now it has to be something else, I don't even know what. You can't change what happened, whatever he was. Say you did it for me. Isn't that enough?'

'Yes,' I said quietly.

'But you still want to know.'

I sat up, looking straight at her. 'I saw the body. What he looked like after. I can't explain – it's different when you see what it really means.' I dropped my head. 'It won't take long. Nobody suspects.' I ran my hand over the grass. 'How else are we going to live with this?'

She smiled slightly, giving up, a movement of the lips, not really a smile at all. 'Oh, how. You can live with anything. Anything.'

'What was Paolo like?'

'Paolo? A puppy,' Bertie said. 'Why Paolo all of a sudden?'

We were having coffee in Santo Stefano, a chance meeting on my way to Ca' Maglione, where Giulia was waiting with Gianni's papers. The sun was bright enough for umbrellas at the cafe tables, but the air was still cool. Bertie was wearing a three-piece oyster-coloured suit, perfectly pitched, like the weather, somewhere between winter and summer.

'I don't know about him. About any of Gianni's family, for that matter.'

'*Now* you want to know?'

'It might help.'

'Who? Your friends at the Questura? I hear you're thick as thieves. Is this an official visit?' he said, his voice rising slightly, like an arched eyebrow.

I smiled. 'I'm just trying to help. It was Giulia's idea.'

'Oh, Giulia's idea. The fair Giulia.' He looked over at me, then tilted his head, his eyes beginning to twinkle. 'No, it's too penny dreadful. Still.'

'Having fun?'

'I admit it's a little novelettish, but think how suitable.'

'Well, don't.'

'And Grace the dogaressa after all.' He giggled.

'Bertie.'

'Oh, I know, I know. Very bad. It's just a *thought*. Anyway, you're otherwise attached. As we know. There'd be that to contend with, wouldn't there?' His voice casual, Claudia still an inappropriate affair to him, unaware we were joined by blood now, our hands streaked with it.

'Yes, there would.' I leaned forwards, serious. 'Bertie, tell me something. What happened at the Accademia?'

'Me? Why ask me?'

'Because you know.'

'I don't always, you know. Better not to. Venice is a very small town. You don't want to be telling tales out of school – people don't like it.'

'Tell this one.'

He looked at me, then nodded. 'I don't want any *reactions*, please. It's not perfect, the world, not even here.' He glanced around the sunny campo, the terracotta planters sprouting bits of white, the first spring flowers. 'Some attitudes – not very nice, but they just don't go away overnight, either. And at first, of course, no one thought to ask. There'd never been any, you know, not in the curatorial department.' He let it hang, awkward, and took a sip of coffee.

'Are you trying to tell me they fired her because she's Jewish?'

'I didn't say that,' Bertie said quickly. 'And I don't want you saying it either. I merely said they didn't think she was – suitable.'

I thought of the Montanaris. Just a look.

'Who didn't?'

'Oh, what does it matter? All right, old Buccati, if you must know. He's nearly ninety. At that age, all you've got is old ideas, whatever they are. Mostly he just naps away the afternoon, like an old tabby, but this time he pricks up his ears and makes a fuss.

And of course it *is* Buccati, so they can't very well say no. *What* a
tear. Even me, if you please. Because I'd recommended her. Which
I only did because Emilio asked. I thought, a cousin. And then not
even that. I had no idea—'

'But how did he hear? Buccati?'

'Hear what? About her? Well, who didn't, after that awful
scene?'

'But Gianni didn't say anything?'

'Gianni? Adam, what are you talking about?'

'I thought Gianni might have had something to do with it.'

'What, at the Accademia? Gianni never looked at a painting in
his life. I doubt he'd ever been inside, much less— What? Do
you think he was prattling away to old Buccati? What for?'

'To get her fired.'

'Well, I wouldn't have blamed him – so unpleasant, that business at the party – but no. No. Nobody's even suggested it. This
was Buccati's own particular nonsense, and what a mess. I'm sorry
about the girl, of course, but think of me. And the staff. Nervous
as hens now that they see what he's really like.'

'So you don't think it was Gianni,' I said, partly to myself.

'No, I don't,' he said steadily. 'And I would have heard.'

I finished the rest of the coffee, thinking. 'He showed me some
frescoes once,' I said.

'And? Adam, I'm having a little trouble *following*.'

'You said he never looked at pictures. But he knew these.'

'Where?'

'At the hospital.'

'Well, the hospital. And Ca' Maglione. I'm sure he knew every
wall. And I'd still bet he'd never been inside the Accademia. Adam,
he was a doctor. They're all a bit Home Counties, really, aren't
they? He was a very conventional man. He wasn't really interested
in . . .' He waved his hand to take in the city. 'You know, this.'

'But he loved Venice.'

'As property. Not as – this extraordinary thing. No eye, none.
He was just a conventional man.' He paused, putting down his

243

cup. 'Except for Grace, I suppose. I've been thinking about it since – well, since – and you know, she's the one thing that does-n't make sense in his life. He does his work. He cares about his family – oh, that dreary wife, the marriage must have been a *penance*. Everything what it should be. Except for her. Maybe she was this for him,' he said, waving his hand again at the campo. 'This whole other side that must have been there. I never saw it, but it must have been, don't you think? Mad for her, even years later. I think she was the only idea he ever had about – whatever it was that was missing.'

I looked out at the square, the faded red and melon plasterwork warm in the sun. This extraordinary thing.

'You're a romantic, Bertie.'

He smiled. 'Oh, I don't know. Maybe I just like a good mystery story. It's the ultimate mystery, isn't it? People. Not who done it. Who they are. Of course, you're one of the "done it" people, you and your friends at the Questura. Somebody done him in. Well, yes, but who was he? That's what I want to know. Here's a man I've known for – well, if I did. Anyway, who wants to know his doctor? And it turns out I didn't. Sometimes I think we're all little mysteries, whirling around.' He moved his finger in a circle. 'And none of us has the faintest clue about the other. Think of it. Gianni in love. I didn't know he was capable of it. But I suppose he was. Then murdered. What could he have done to make somebody want to do that?'

'That's what they're trying to find out.'

'Are they? Well, good luck. Cavallini couldn't catch a fly.' He shook his head. 'And you. Such nonsense. You'd be better off getting Grace out of here. Mooning about with Mimi and Celia and probably getting sloshed, if I know my Celia. Talk about the bad penny turning up. Oh, I know,' he said, seeing my look, 'her heart's broken, but it so happens I don't believe in broken hearts.' He peered over his glasses. 'I'm not that romantic. What she needs is a change. But here you are, playing Father Brown. What a world.'

'How do you know Cavallini?'

'I had to report during the war – all the neutrals. I've told you this. All present and accounted for, you know. Actually, he was nice about it – he'd come to me. Of course, that was right up his street. He's a policeman who likes a canal view.'

'Maybe he's better than you think. He's talked to everybody. I've seen the reports.'

'Oh, I've heard. The poor servants, over and over. I suppose one conked Gianni on the head in a fit of pique. He can't be serious.'

'He's just being thorough. The house, the hospital. He's doing the patients now. He'll probably get around to you any day,' I said, teasing.

'As a suspect?'

I smiled. 'As someone who knew him.'

'But why should it be anyone who knew him? A thief wouldn't—'

'Because it wasn't robbery. He still had his money on him. His watch.'

'Really,' Bertie said, then looked over at me. 'What else?'

'All we know is what it wasn't. And if it wasn't robbery, then it was about *him* somehow. Who he was.' I fiddled with my coffee cup. 'Your little mystery. We need to know more about him.'

'Such as?'

'Anything. Paolo, for instance. Tell me about Paolo.'

'Oh, we're back to Paolo. But he didn't count for anything. Awful thing to say, isn't it? But he didn't. Simply didn't matter.'

'But Gianni was upset when he died. Everyone says so,' I said, trying it out.

'Do they?' Bertie looked away, thinking. 'I suppose he was. Family, after all. That was important to him, probably more than Paolo was, really. But now that you mention it, he did take it hard. Went all quiet and monkish for a while. But they do that here.'

'So they were close?'

'Only in the sense of Paolo's being there all the time – we're talking about the early days now. He was always around. You know, at the beach, parties, whatever.'

'Like a puppy, you said.'

'Yes. Whatever Gianni wanted, he'd *fetch* it. It was like that.'

'But he was the older brother.'

'Well, what's there to that? I'm an only child and I've always been sociable. Anyway, he didn't seem to mind. He looked up to Gianni.' He reached over to the cigarettes on the cafe table and took one out. 'Is that what you want to know? I can't think why.'

'So Gianni was distressed when Paolo died?'

'Well, yes,' Bertie said, striking the match and cupping it at the end of the cigarette. 'Why wouldn't he be? Awful way to go, a crash like that. So young. And so typical, I must say, so careless, although of course one *didn't* say it.'

'You know there are rumours that it wasn't an accident.'

Bertie looked at me through the smoke, not saying anything.

'That he was killed by partisans.'

'And?'

'And if he was, there might be a political angle to this murder too. Gianni's murder.'

'Oh, *both* now. Very *Il Gazzettino* of you. Is that the line you're taking down at the Questura?'

'Did he ever say anything to you about Paolo's death?'

'No, he didn't,' Bertie said, tapping the end of his cigarette, his voice prickly. 'And if he had, I wouldn't have listened. I don't listen to rumours either. Political angle. I don't listen and I don't know. All I want is to be left alone. I have *no* politics. None. I'm the most neutral man in Venice. And it's very wrong of you to go on about it. Badgering people. Even Cavallini didn't do that. And that was during the *war.*'

'I wasn't asking about your politics, I was asking about Gianni's,' I said quietly.

He leaned his head back, reprimanded, or surprised at his own reaction.

'Well, how would I know?' he said.

246

'Because you do,' I said, looking at him.

He made a face, peevish. 'Well, as a matter of fact, I don't. Oh, Adam, *what* politics? Gianni didn't have any politics. He just blew with the wind. We all did. The only party he ever cared about was the Maglione family. That was his politics.'

'His brother worked for the Germans.'

'Do you know that?'

I nodded. 'And so did Gianni.'

He looked away, then put out his cigarette and picked up his hat from the table. 'I'm sorry to hear that,' he said finally. 'But it's got nothing to do with me.' He lifted a finger. 'And it's got nothing to do with you, either. Watch you don't make a mess of things. All this huffing and puffing. Shall I tell you something? You will never understand this society. This isn't even Italy. It's Venice. Nothing has been real here since Napoleon. Nothing.'

'But it happened anyway. He worked for the Germans. He was killed. It happened.'

'Not where I live.' He stood, putting on his hat and looking out on to the square. 'You see this? It's like a jewel box. Beautiful. And nothing gets in.'

'And you're the jewel, I suppose.'

He smiled. 'You could do worse. Anyway, it's what I like. Just the way it is. As far as I'm concerned, Paolo was a slow-witted boy who drove too fast. Gianni was a perfectly respectable man who gave the most boring Sunday lunches you can imagine. Once would do it. And that's all. If they weren't, I don't want to hear it. Politics. Murk. You want to make everything murky. Well, I don't. Not here.'

Gianni's papers took no time at all. His businesses were all in the hands of managers, and Giulia, his heir, had already been to their offices, looking through the accounts.

'I thought it could be someone afraid of being caught. Everybody took a little during the war, to survive. But not enough to kill.'

How much was that? I wondered, but let it drop, not really interested in the businesses anyway. But the personal papers were disappointing too – a neat drawerful of bank statements and house accounts; another of official documents, birth, death, and accreditation, crowded with elaborate seals; some hospital paperwork; a few letters, none revealing; a small pile of receipts; a programme from La Fenice; clipped articles from professional journals put aside for a rainy day. A blameless life, anybody's.

We sat at the big mahogany desk in the library, a dark room that backed onto a side calle, away from the canal. Giulia had turned on the desk lamp, making the polished wood gleam. The house was as perfectly waxed and still as it had been after the funeral, maybe the way it would always be now, a convent quiet.

'But did he keep everything here?' I said, rummaging through the deep bottom drawer.

'Yes, I think so. And the albums over there on the shelf. Where I found the pictures for your mother. Maybe you should see the rest. What are you looking for?'

'I don't know. Him. People he knew.'

'There's an address book,' she said, bringing it over.

For a few minutes we looked at it together, flipping pages. 'That's a patient, that one,' she said, and so, I assumed, were the others. And friends and dinner partners and tradesmen, all Italian. But what had I expected? Extension numbers at the Villa Raspelli? Combination letters, a coded secret life? I closed the book.

'Any diaries, anything like that?'

She shook her head. 'No, only the Maglione books, from the old days.' She pointed to a shelf behind her, scrapbooks and odd-shaped journals, some bound in leather, others in gathered-together, yellowing folios. A few boxes, meant to look like books, for stacks of letters bound with ribbon. 'They kept everything. For their history.'

'It must have stopped with him.' I closed the drawer.

248

'Well, my uncle did the notes. I remember him writing. My father was too busy for that.'

'But letters? There must be *some* letters. Your mother?'

'No. They never wrote. Or they're gone.' She looked over at me. 'Before – I never thought about it. They didn't love each other. Maybe that's why.'

We looked at the photo albums – stiffly posed grandparents, then the Maglione childhood, Gianni and Paolo in sailor suits, the usual. Then the book from which she must have got my mother's pictures – sunny days on the Lido in wet wool bathing suits, groups lolling in front of changing cabanas.

'Which is your mother?'

'They didn't meet till later. Look, Luca, before he became a priest.' A plump boy with a grin, years from piety. 'I don't know this one.' Standing next to Gianni.

'That's my father,' I said.

'Oh.' She looked up at me. 'Yes, I see it now. It's strange, our parents together. Like the same family, but not the same.'

My father was squinting into the sun, but both of them were smiling. A day at the beach, a casual snapshot, no hint at all of anything to come, their lives twisted together.

'But where's Paolo?'

'He was always taking the picture, I think,' she said, smiling. 'No, here, the tennis one. My father didn't like tennis, so maybe it was his turn with the camera.'

I took the picture out of the album and brought it nearer, looking at it closely. No hint here either – no Order of Rome, no politics, none of Bertie's murk. He was standing against the net in tennis flannels and a white sweater with a chevron neck, his arm draped over the shoulder of another player, both of them holding their rackets at their hips.

'It's sad to look at them,' Giulia said, moving away. 'Everyone so happy. Does that make sense?'

I nodded. 'What was he like?'

'Paolo? *Uno vitaiolo.* You know, always for the pleasure. Tennis.

249

Those cars. Of course, when I was a child I thought this was wonderful. Another child, you know?'

'And then?'

'And then I wasn't a child any more.' She turned, facing me. 'He was a Fascist. You're surprised I say that? I know. Today, no Fascists. We were all in the resistance. I think we even believe it.'

'How do you mean, Fascist?'

'Fascist. He liked Mussolini. He liked the parades, dressing up, all of that. He was on committees – you know, they liked him because of his name. Of course no one listened to him, but it made him feel important to go to meetings. And after, the tennis. So not so serious – how could Paolo be serious? And then it's the war, and everything's serious. He's too foolish to see what is happening to us, that it's a catastrophe. He thinks the king will save us, make peace with the English king. Because he's a king too. Imagine the foolishness of it. Well.'

'And after that?'

'After that, the Germans. And Paolo? He supports the Salò government, against the CLN, the partisans. It interests you, Italian politics?'

'It confuses me.'

'Yes,' she said. 'But at the end it's not difficult. If you're with Salò, you're with the Germans. So Paolo was too. Sometimes I think it was good that he died, before it was a disgrace to the family. Even for my father it was too much. Paolo was his brother, so that's something sacred to him, but it wasn't the same between them. The Germans, that's something my father would never forgive.'

I looked over at her, expecting irony, but she seemed utterly sincere, guileless.

'They had a fight?'

'A distance. Maybe a fight, I don't know. I was at school. And of course I wouldn't speak to Paolo then. You know, the students, the way we felt – I was too angry with him. Maybe ashamed, too. My own family. So I didn't speak.' She came back to the desk and looked down at the picture. 'And then after he died, I remembered him like this. When he was so nice. My father too, I think. So quiet, days like that. You know, whatever he did, still a brother.'

'What about your father, his politics?'

She smiled. 'Was he this, was he that? Nothing – he wanted to survive them. That's what he used to tell me. Stay out of it. Keep your head down. So of course we would quarrel. You know, at that age. He was afraid, I think, that I would get involved in the resistance. So many of the students—'

'Did you?'

'No. I wanted to, of course, everybody did, but in the end – I don't know, a coward maybe. Too much a lady, my friend used to say, my mother's daughter. So maybe she was right.'

'But not your father's?'

'Oh, a little bit. I think secretly he admired the resistance too. But he was afraid of it. For him it was simple – the family, Venice. The Church – well, maybe that was for my mother. He believed in those things. And what was the resistance? Maybe a threat. Something else to survive. So he kept his head down. No sides.' She turned at a soft rap on the door, an even quieter opening. 'Ah, Maria,' she said, 'thank you.' Not surprised.

The maid, in a starched linen collar and apron, carried a coffee tray to the table in front of the reading chairs. The cups and pot lay on a white doily, also starched, as if it had been meant to match her uniform. Shy smiles and murmurs in Italian, part of the ceremony of getting the tray on the table.

'I'll pour, shall I?' Giulia said, at once dismissing Maria and taking up the pot in her hand, poised, her mother's daughter.

I sat on the other side of the low table. It was the funeral all over again, nothing extra, everything as it should be, sure of its own taste. Even her dress, I noticed, was suitable, black without any purple frills, a discreet mourning – mourning because I had held his head under. Now we were drinking coffee, polite.

'But it must have been hard in the war, not taking sides,' I said.

She took a sip, then held the cup in her hand, thinking. 'Of

251

course in the end you do. It's your country. I didn't have the courage, maybe, but I had money. So I helped with that. We were alike that way. Keep your head down, but do it anyway. No sides, but he helped the partisans.'

'He told you that?' Maybe as plausibly as he'd told it on the fondamenta, but why?

She shook her head, then smiled. 'Well, I didn't tell him about the money either. But I know. He made it a question of medical ethics – what's the right thing to do? You know, they do this in the law school too. So it's good training for me. But this is his way of telling me. A man is brought in with a gunshot wound, a man you know. The law says you must report all such wounds. But you know that the only way he could have been shot is in the fighting, a partisan. If you report it, the government will kill him. If you don't, maybe it goes badly for you, for helping a traitor. The man begs you – "Help me, don't give me up" What do you do?'

'And what did he do?' I said quietly.

'We agreed that the first obligation must be to save the man.'

'Even if he's a traitor.'

'But if the government itself is illegal—'

'And who decides that?'

'Yes, who? You see how it goes on? He liked these questions. Well, I liked them, so he would ask.'

'And how did it end, this one? What did he do?'

'Oh, he said you can make it complicated if you like, but the simple fact is, if you know a man, you can't give him up. So I know he didn't.'

I put down my cup. 'What if you gave up someone else instead?'

'Someone else?'

'To save the first. Your friend. If you gave up someone in his place.'

She looked at me for a second, then down at her cup. 'What makes you ask this?'

'It's a question he once asked me.'

'And you think,' she said, stirring her cup, still not looking up, 'this was his way of telling you something.'

For a minute we were quiet, still enough to hear the clock.

'Do you think he did that?' she said finally, sitting up straight, braced.

I hesitated, then sat back, moving away from it. 'I think it was just a question.'

'It's a terrible thing.'

'Yes.'

'Why would he ask that?'

'As a moral dilemma, maybe. An impossible choice.'

'But you can't choose someone's death.' She was looking at me now, her face longer, more severe, like her mother's again. 'That's murder.' Sure, admitting no exceptions.

I said nothing, kept quiet by her stare. Then her face began to change, no longer as properly arranged as the tray, and I saw that she was distressed, waiting for me to say something.

'He wouldn't do that,' she said. 'You knew him. Do you think he would do that?'

'I think it was just a question.'

'Then why—'

'Something may have put it in his mind. Something that actually happened. The story about the partisan – when did he tell you that?'

'When? Last year,' she said, composed again, interested.

'After the war?' I said, confused.

'No. I mean the year before. Forty-four. When he came to see me. I remember he told me at lunch.'

'When was this, exactly?'

'Autumn. October, maybe.'

'Why did it come up? I mean, why do you think he told you?'

She smiled a little, shaking her head. 'Maybe to make me like him. Always we were arguing then. So maybe this was his way of saying, You see, Papa's not so bad. I'm on the right side too.'

'But he never actually said he'd done this.'

'No, but that wasn't his way. He never talked about himself. Maybe he thought it wasn't dignified. He was private, a Maglione. My mother was like that too.'

'Secretive?'

'No. Private,' she said, making a distinction to herself. 'I never knew what he was thinking. But what does a child know? All those years, here we are in this house, a family, and I never knew.' She leaned forwards, placing the cup on the tray. 'Maybe a little secretive. A doctor has to be, you learn that. You don't talk about your patients. I used to ask him things and he'd say, "That's not my secret to tell." Always somebody else's secret. "I won't tell," I'd say, and he'd wag his finger, like this,' she said, demonstrating, so that I looked up, seeing Gianni. 'You know the old saying.' She lowered her voice, becoming him. 'Two people can keep a secret, if one of them is dead.' She paused. 'So I didn't ask. And then it turned out he must have had one of his own.'

'What do you mean?'

'He was murdered. Do you know why? No. So it's still his secret.'

I sat back, looking around the room to avoid her gaze. 'Well, it's safe here. There's nothing else? Files?'

'At the hospital. His real life was there, I think,' she said, her voice wistful. 'Not here.'

There was an awkward pause.

'I should go,' I said, getting up. 'Maybe there'll be something in the patient files. That's next. He seems to have erased himself everywhere else.'

'Yes, he was good at that. He didn't like to keep things.'

I smiled, glancing around the old library, virtually an archive.

'Oh, this was Paolo. Poor Paolo, Papa erased him too. Threw out his books. You know, he was always writing in those books – *appunti* for the family history, and Papa said they were rubbish. Well, what did he expect? Mazzini from Paolo? But, you know, now it just stops. Unless I write it, I suppose,' she said, her voice diffident, as if she were talking to herself, suddenly alone.

254

'Wait. Paolo kept notebooks and your father threw them out?'

'Not all. Just the ones with his activities. "What will people think later?" he said. It was an embarrassment for him.'

'But where are they?'

She gestured towards the shelves.

'Paolo kept them here?'

She looked at me, puzzled. 'It was his house.'

'Yes, I forgot. But you all lived here?'

'Of course. The family.'

'All during the time they—?'

'Yes. There was an agreement – no political talk at dinner.'

I imagined them sitting at the starched table, private, talking politely, each one whirling in his own mystery.

'Can I see them?'

'Yes, of course,' she said, walking over to the shelf. 'I'm sorry. I thought, my father's papers. It didn't occur to me. These are Paolo's.' She ran her hand along a line of leatherbound spines.

The books weren't histories so much as diaries, the kind a fourteen-year-old might write, full of underlinings and exclamation marks, the world a theatre, with himself, luckily, at centre stage. Even with my poor Italian, I could understand Gianni's reluctance to have them fill the family library's shelves. But here they were, not all of them thrown out. Why not?

I skimmed through a few, trying to get a sense of why these had survived. Innocuous? But here was Mussolini, a trip to Rome with friends to hear a speech, dinner afterwards at the Eden – a time-capsule mix. Not embarrassed here, at any rate, by the Fascism or Paolo's comments. The speech had been inspiring, Rome itself a new city. A nightclub after dinner had featured Somalian dancers. Venice now seemed a backwater, dowdy. I flipped pages. Less exalted excursions – a drive to Asolo, dinner in a villa. The Maglione history now mostly idle days. Committee meetings, just as Giulia had said. Recording it all for posterity. The war, sombre fourteen-year-old's thoughts on what it would mean. The Albanian fiasco. The Allies in Sicily. And then it stopped. Gaps here and there before, then nothing after 1943. A war with no Germans at all. But why the earlier gaps? What else had Gianni culled out?

Giulia had been hovering next to me, reading as I flipped, no doubt taking it all in more quickly. 'But what do you see?' she said.

'I don't know. Nothing, I guess. Can I borrow these? Just the last few?'

'You want to read them?'

'I want to see where the gaps are. Look, here, for instance, he just ripped the pages out. So why here and not there?'

But before she could answer there was another rap on the door, and this time Maria was carrying an old telephone with a long cord, her eyes wide with apprehension.

'*Polizia*,' she whispered, pointing to me, then plugged the cord into a jack behind the desk.

Had Cavallini tracked me here? I picked up the phone and then must have registered the stunned dismay I felt as he spoke, because when I hung up, Giulia said, 'My God, what is it? What's happened?'

'Cavallini,' I said, my own voice an echo, hollow. 'They've arrested somebody for the murder.'

CHAPTER THIRTEEN

THE QUESTURA WAS like Gianni's hospital – functional, even ordinary inside. Cavallini's office could have been anywhere, a room with a desk and a phone and pale green institutional walls. There was a large map of the lagoon along with a few photographs of Cavallini shaking hands with various officials, but it still felt scarcely inhabited, as if he had just moved in, waiting for a new paint job. Today, at least, it was crowded with people – assistants delivering telephone messages, two policemen standing near the door waiting for orders and a tall man in a suit conferring with Cavallini, stroking his chin in thought. I saw all this in a blur, my mind still numb with dread.

'Signor Miller,' Cavallini said, smiling. 'Good. My superior wants to meet you.' The tall man turned to me. 'I have told him how it started with you.'

We shook hands, with a few polite words in Italian, then he rattled off something to Cavallini.

'So everyone is very pleased,' Cavallini said. 'I thank you for this.'

He put his hand on the beige folder, Rosa's file. 'Of course, it's a question of police work too,' he said, directing this to the tall man, who smiled blankly, clearly not following. 'The one helps the other. *Una collaborazione.*' At this the other man nodded, said

257

something more in Italian, and left, dipping his head towards me, almost a bow, as he went out the door. The two waiting policemen followed him.

'You see? Very pleased. So again I thank you.'

'But who did you arrest?' I said.

'Moretti,' he said, patting the file again. 'Rosa shows us where to look and we find him.'

I leaned forwards, holding the desk. 'But he's dead. You mean he didn't die?'

'Yes, he died. That's it – a vengeance killing. The son.'

'You think Moretti's son killed Gianni? Why?'

'But Signor Miller, it's as you say. The connection is the house, what happened there. I didn't know this. But once you look.'

'But Rosa never said—'

'No, but she's not a policeman, you know,' he said with a little smile, almost smug. 'Still, she suspects. And she's right. One man in that house was in hospital. His doctor? Maglione.' He held up a light blue folder in illustration. 'And Maglione is working with the SS. She makes this connection.

'But he was released days before they—'

'So she goes to see his son. She is an old friend of the father. How long was the father in hospital, when did he leave, did the boy see him – also Carlo, like the father. And of course he wants to know why, and she tells him she suspects Maglione of betraying his father. And what happens? He becomes *agitato*. "It's my fault," he tells her. "I killed him." Why? Because *he* went to the house, so maybe they followed him. And Rosa tells him, "No, you were there before, people never followed you." He was a courier for them, you see. Imagine using a child that way. A Communist, of course, the boy too. No, he tells her, this time he was also bringing medicine for his father, from Maglione. A trap. So now it's his fault. And Rosa tells him it's foolishness – he can't blame himself for this. They already knew somehow. But she's troubled. She hadn't known about the medicine, you see.'

'How do you know all this?'

258

'Some from him, some from her. So she leaves,' he said, picking up the story. 'And he's still *agitato*. An unstable boy anyway, according to the neighbours.' Police work. Collecting gossip, like a noose. 'The father's dead and he's to blame. No, somebody else. Somebody still alive. This is a boy who worked with the partisans, someone who *acts*. What could be more natural?'

'So he had a motive,' I said. 'But that doesn't—'

'A strong motive. Very strong. It's as you predicted – a political crime, but also a personal one.' He walked out from behind the desk, a courtroom gesture, enjoying himself. 'Of course, we're hoping for a confession. And it's possible. This kind of case – so much remorse. I've seen it before. It's a kind of relief for them.' He glanced at me, amused. 'Signor Miller, such a face. We're police, not SS. We *hope* for a confession. We don't torture, we ask questions.'

'And if he doesn't confess?'

Cavallini shrugged. 'It's still a very strong case. He has no alibi.'

'No?' I said weakly, sitting down to hear the rest.

'No. The night of the murder, where is he? Out for a walk. In that weather. You remember that evening, the rain? And where did he walk? Around. Along the Riva, then he's not sure where. Who walks like that in Venice? Tourists.'

'No one saw him?'

'No one. Then the *cine*. Except the ticket girl doesn't remember.'

'That doesn't necessarily—'

'No, not necessarily,' he said, looking at me. 'So, you act the defense? Good. We need to think of everything. But no one sees him, that's the point. So, his word only. Next, his profession? He works on one of the delivery boats from the Stazione Marittima. Not just to Venice, also the outer islands. So, familiar with the lagoon.' He paused. 'Even in fog.' He sat on the edge of the desk. 'And after the murder, what does he do? We have witnesses to this, his behaviour. Drunk, in the bar he goes to. With the news-paper. He keeps reading it and drinking. "For once, justice," he says – we have a witness to this. "What are you talking about?" the witness asks. "He deserved it, he deserved it," the boy says, "a toast to justice." And then what? Tears. Unstable, you see. More than one saw this.'

'The newspaper,' I said, almost to myself. 'So this was after the body was found? Not before?'

Cavallini looked at me, uncomfortable for a second, weighing this, then decided to ignore it. 'Yes, after it was found. Celebrating.'

'But why would he do that, draw attention that way? Why would he be happy they found the body? Wouldn't it be better for him if they never found it?'

Cavallini sat back, a twitch of annoyance in the corner of his mouth. 'Nevertheless, that is what he said. A toast to justice. Of course, really to himself. We have witnesses to this,' he said again, then paused. 'It's not always the logic that rules the head in these cases. A boy who blames himself, then who kills – you're surprised he gives himself away?'

'It just doesn't make sense.'

'But it will. Don't worry. We will make a case.'

I looked up at him. Held together by nothing except his will. But convincing, a solution to everything, delivered by Cavallini to a grateful force.

'You're troubled?' he said.

I shrugged, not knowing what to say, swirling again. A case any defense lawyer could pick apart, but would he? Who was the defense? What were trials like here? It wasn't America. Maybe a different set of priorities, with Carlo Moretti, whoever he was, satisfying all of them. Gianni's killer.

'But why?' Cavallini said. 'It was you yourself who suggested the motive. You said it would be someone exactly like him. And it is.'

'It's just—' I stopped, my heart sinking. Someone exactly like him. You yourself suggested it.

He waited, frowning a little, surprised now at my reluctance. And why should I be?

'It's just – you know, to prove it in court, you'll have to prove that Gianni did betray them. An informer, all of that. It'll have to come out.'

'Ah,' Cavallini said, 'I see. But Signor Miller, it's a case of his murder.'

'But can you prove it? About Gianni?' What I'd wanted in the first place, just to know.

'Well, as to that, we only have to prove that Moretti believed it. A doctor prescribes medicine, the boy delivers it, his father is betrayed. Because he is followed? Perhaps not. But *he* believes it, so he acts.' He paused. 'Dr Maglione's reputation need not be in question. Only Moretti questioned it.'

He met my eyes, an explanation that was also a bargain. Perfect in every way. Justice done. A family's honour held intact. A promotion for him. A kindness to Giulia, to my mother. Gianni a victim, like Paolo.

'Yes,' I said, thinking, 'and what if he was wrong – if we were wrong?'

'How do you mean?'

'For the sake of argument,' I said, getting up, 'what if Gianni didn't do it? It explains the gap. He treats Moretti, he releases Moretti, nothing happens. A week – longer, ten days. He prescribes medicine. Why? If he wanted to betray Moretti, why not do it earlier? Why wait? What if the son is wrong? What if Gianni never meant the father harm?'

Cavallini got up and walked back behind the desk. 'Then he killed him for nothing.' Another pause. 'Signor Miller, I am confused. Do you think Dr Maglione was innocent? After all, it was you . . .' He let the words drift, his eyes simply curious, the way they'd been at the water entrance, asking about the boat.

'No, no,' I said quickly. 'But if we can't prove it, then it's very difficult to prove the motive.'

'Well, that's for the lawyers,' he said, dismissing this. 'And you forget there is still the confession. Would that satisfy you?' He smiled again, a kind of tease. 'It was like this in Germany? Always the proof?'

'Not always,' I said. 'But in capital cases—' I stopped. 'What happens in Italy? To the boy, if he's guilty.'

'Execution.'

I looked down, suddenly winded, the air rushing out of me. Execution how? Hanging? Shooting? An innocent boy. Worse than murder. I caught my breath, aware of Cavallini's stare. 'Then we have to be sure.'

'Don't worry, Signor Miller. We will be. Ah, again,' he said as the telephone rang. 'All morning it's like this. Excuse me.' A complaint he'd make later to his long-faced wife. A man of importance.

I picked up Moretti's blue hospital folder and glanced at the form while Cavallini talked. A fake name, but presumably him. Date of admission, release, address and personal information, also presumably fake. An attached chart with what looked to be blood pressure and temperature readings. Diagnosis and report, in longhand, Gianni's familiar signature on the bottom, the attending nurse, blood type, everything except what had happened. *Iniezione antitetanica*. Injection against tetanus? Well, there would be.

'Still looking for the proof?' Cavallini said, hanging up.

'This is him? How did you know the name?'

'The boy told us,' he said, almost amused.

'What's *ferita puntura* – bullet wound?'

'No, *ferita da pallottola. Puntura* is puncture. It's very close.'

But not the same. Not reported. I held the folder for a few seconds, taking this in. You don't report someone you know. And he hadn't. Unless he had lied to Giulia.

'A bullet would have to be reported to the police, you know,' Cavallini said. 'Even now. It's the law.'

'And if you don't?'

'Usually it's a question of the medical licence. Then, under the Germans, who knows?'

'So he would have reported it to his friends in the SS. But if he told the SS, why falsify the police report? It came to the same thing in those days, didn't it?'

262

Cavallini nodded stiffly, not sure whether to be offended. 'If it was a bullet,' he said.

'It had to be. How else would he know Moretti was a partisan? What does the son say?'

'This is important?'

'If he knew it was a bullet wound and knew Gianni didn't report it, he'd think Gianni was *helping*.' Plant any doubt, some confused opening Moretti's son might use. 'Why would he think Gianni betrayed him?'

'He didn't. Until you and Rosa suggested it,' Cavallini said calmly, not even raising his voice, no louder than a door closing. I felt blood draining from my face.

Cavallini sighed. 'Signor Miller, how you worry. What if? What if? Why not a simple answer? A man betrays, his victim is avenged. It has happened a million times before. What do you want to prove? That the boy is innocent?'

I looked up. The inescapable other question – then who is guilty? I dropped the folder on the desk and walked over to the window. Below in the Rio San Lorenzo a freight boat passed, loaded with bottles. Maybe a boat just like young Moretti's. Someone who knew the lagoon, even in fog.

'I just don't understand why he didn't report the bullet wound.'

'It's a detail, yes.'

'I mean, it would be terrible if we were wrong.'

'Yes,' Cavallini said, 'and for Moretti's son. He murdered a man for this. Imagine, if it was a mistake.'

I turned, my stomach churning again, but there was no sense of accusation in his voice, no sense that it even mattered. Moretti's son had murdered Gianni. The rest was details.

'Don't worry, Signor Miller,' he said, confident. 'We will learn everything, now that we have him.' He flipped open the folder on his desk, as if having it there were proof, something tangible.

'Is that him?' I said, nodding at the photo on top.

'Yes. The usual bad picture. So dark.' He shook his head. 'Our police photographer. But we can't let him go. His wife is—'

He handed me the photograph. Wild eyes and uncombed hair, the scowl of a mug shot, guilty just being there. But something more. Exactly the same eyes, the shape of the nose. I imagined the hair brushed over, the face clean and smiling – the same boy in a V-necked tennis sweater, his arm over Paolo's shoulder. The son, then. So Moretti was someone Gianni knew. But what did it mean? Someone you knew, you wouldn't turn over. Not in a moral question, anyway. But someone had. I started to speak, then caught the sound in my throat. Would it make it worse for Moretti, another connection for Cavallini to use against him? I looked up to see the inspector watching me.

'He's just a kid,' I said, my voice suddenly distraught. I stared again at the picture, everyone's solution to the crime.

'Yes. But not a child. A man.' Making a legal distinction. 'You know, it's often like this in police work. People like to help catch and then—' He made a snapping noise with his hands. 'They realise there's also the punishment. That's more difficult for them. The cold feet, you say, yes?' he said, still genial, sticking his chin out so that for a half-second he looked like Paolo's hero in Rome. Not a joke in the end, either. He took back the picture. 'He's young, yes. But think of the crime. Think how Gianni would feel. Grateful, I think, for your help.'

Before I could answer, Cavallini's door, only half shut, swung open and his secretary came in, arms held out, being pushed by Rosa, who was screaming in Italian. 'Ah,' Rosa said, spying Cavallini, moving the secretary aside and wagging her finger theatrically.

He yelled back, but she cut him off, flinging her hands now. There must have been some physical resistance in the outer office, because her cardigan, usually wrapped tight, seemed a little disheveled, and her hair was spilling out of its tidy bun.

'Oh, you too!' she said, seeing me, switching to English. 'What a pair. What a pair. How can you be part of this? Give me that.' She reached over for the beige file. Cavallini put his hand on it. 'It's property of the Allies. Not yours,' she said.

'And now evidence in a murder case.'

'*Basta*. What evidence?' She turned to me. 'You see how they use everything? We investigate Maglione, not some poor boy. And now they use that because he's Communist. Anything to discredit the Communists. Where is he? I demand to see him.'

'He's being questioned. He has a lawyer.'

'Ha. Picked by the Questura. Wonderful.'

'Let him pick another, then.'

'Don't worry, he will. My God, what a fool you are. Always the same. The father was a hero. The boy was a hero. While you were – what? Keeping *order* for the Germans. And now you want to destroy him? Take everything he says and twist it – no, worse, everything I say. It was to help get Maglione. Why? Because he has to know.' She pointed her thumb at me. 'So I help, and now you want to use that? Against an innocent boy? Shame. But then, when were you ever ashamed?'

'Innocent boy,' Cavallini said scornfully.

'Yes, innocent, of course innocent.'

'How do you know?'

'Because I do.'

'Ah. And that's his defense. No wonder you came. How did you know he was here, by the way?'

'Oh, you think maybe someone here told me? Good, start the search. A Communist in the Questura. Yes, that must be it. You'd better look everywhere. Under the desks. Do it to your own – see how they like it.' She turned to me. 'You see what they're trying to do? You think this boy killed Maglione?'

'No, he agrees with you,' Cavallini said, mischievous. 'He's been trying to convince me the boy is innocent.'

Rosa stopped, thrown by this.

'But he hasn't,' Cavallini said, with a small smile for me.

'Be careful what you say here,' Rosa said to me. 'It's not justice here. Politics. Nothing changes.' She looked at Cavallini. 'When can I see him?'

'Make a request,' Cavallini said. 'While he's being questioned, his lawyer only.'

'One hair,' Rosa said to him. 'If you touch one hair.' She turned to me. 'And you – you know what Maglione was. They're the same. And now you work with them.'

'Is that the purpose of your visit?' Cavallini said, mock-formal. 'To criticise the police?'

Rosa raised her head. 'No, to warn you.'

'Oh, to warn me.'

'I know you, what a coward you can be. You want to make the Communists look bad? Go ahead. But not with this boy. You know me too. You think I survived that house to let you have Moretti's son? I warn you, I will fight you with everything.'

'Except your own evidence. That fights for me.'

'Evidence can change.'

'But not the truth,' Cavallini said, pompous, actually raising a finger, the whole conversation a series of gestures, a visible squaring off.

'Truth? You're a fine one—'

'*Che cosa succede qui?*' a policeman said. He had stopped at the door, the secretary trailing behind.

'*Niente, niente,*' Cavallini said, then to Rosa, 'This behaviour is for the streets, not the Questura. You want to see the prisoner, make a request.'

'The prisoner? He's formally charged?'

'He's answering questions,' Cavallini said, not answering hers.

'So. Then wait for his lawyer. Already sent for, already sent for,' she said, anticipating him.

'Tell him to hurry,' Cavallini said, smiling again. 'We are expecting a confession any minute.'

'Bah,' Rosa said, flinging her hand.

There was a noise in the outer office – more people, including the man I'd met earlier, Cavallini's boss. When I looked at Cavallini, I caught a flicker of anxiety, a worry perhaps that he'd be blamed for the commotion.

'Come on, Rosa,' I said, taking her arm.

To my relief, she nodded and moved with me to the door, then turned one last time to face Cavallini. 'Remember,' she said, 'not one hair.'

Outside on the fondamenta she stopped for a second to look across the canal to San Lorenzo. I gave her a cigarette, a peace offering, surprised to find my hand shaking, still rattled.

'I didn't know—' I started, but she cut me off with a wave.

'They're going to charge him.'

'No, they're not. They can't prove anything. He didn't do it.' Trying it out, wanting to believe it myself.

'You're so sure?' she said, looking up at me but not waiting for an answer. 'Anyway, when did they need proof, this bunch?'

As we neared the bridge, Claudia ran towards us from the calle side of the building, glancing nervously at the police guards in front. She was clutching her open coat, as if she'd left too quickly to button it.

'Thank God. You're all right?' she said, touching my arm.

'Yes, fine. What—?'

'Cavallini called, looking for you. He said they arrested some-body.' She looked again at the Questura.

'It's okay, calm down. They didn't arrest *me*,' I said, trying to make a joke of it and signal her at the same time. 'Meet Rosa.'

The introductions were offhand, not much more than an appraising glance, each of them too distracted to be interested in the other.

'But who—?'

'A boy. His father was in the house with the partisans.'

'But how can they think—?'

'He's got a motive,' I said quickly, looking at her. 'And he can't explain himself.'

'A motive?'

'Yes, we did that for him,' Rosa said grimly. 'He never even thought about Maglione until I talked to him. So now it's our fault.'

'But he didn't do it,' I said.

267

'Yes, and who's in there?' Rosa said, jerking her thumb towards the building.

'What are you going to do?' Claudia asked quietly.

'We're going to find out who did do it,' I said to Rosa, ignoring Claudia's stare. But who? A phantom, a better story.

'No, I'm finished with this business. Look how it is already. They don't want anyone else. He's perfect for them. So now the lawyers will have to save him, not the file clerk,' she said, pointing to herself.

'Help me.'

'Do what?'

'Find out what happened. None of it makes sense. Gianni faked a medical report. Why? Risked his licence for Moretti, maybe saved his life. Does that sound like Gianni to you?'

'Anything's possible.' She dropped some ashes and rubbed them with her shoe.

'Tell me about Moretti. Was he a Communist?'

'A patriot.'

'And a friend of Gianni's brother.' She looked at me, not surprised to hear it but surprised I knew. 'I saw an old picture. But he was a Communist?'

She shrugged. 'Many came from good families. With them, a matter of conviction.'

'Was he involved – when Paolo was killed?'

She pulled on the cigarette, saying nothing.

'Rosa.'

'Don't ask me this.'

'For Chrissake, why not? It was during the war. What does it matter now?'

'It would matter to the son. He's already heard enough. Let it go. It's the past.'

'Why? It would make him a hero, wouldn't it?'

'A hero. Do you know what that meant, in that kind of war? It's not the army. Everything is permitted. It's good to lie. To kill. And then it's over and it's the opposite.'

'Yes,' Claudia said unexpectedly. Rosa looked at her, not sure how to respond, then back at me.

'I'm not going to tell his son.'

'All right. Tell me.'

She dropped the cigarette and took a few steps towards the canal, wrapping her sweater tighter. 'Paolo was a fool, but he was careful. Maybe people were careful for him. So, to get him, they had to trick him. Moretti knew him – an old friend, as you say.'

'He set him up?'

'You want to know the details? What's the difference? He betrayed him, he helped to kill him. Paolo trusted him, so it started with him.'

'Then why would Gianni help him?'

'He didn't know. Who was going to tell him, Moretti?'

'But—'

'That's right. He kills his old friend and then lies to the brother to save himself. Not the way a hero acts. I told you, it was that kind of war. Anything was right.'

'Who else killed him? Who was also in the house – besides Moretti.'

'Also in the house? Just one,' she said, looking straight at me.

I held her eyes for a second, then dropped my gaze to the pavement, thinking. 'So there's no other connection. And Moretti leaves the hospital and nothing happens. Gianni helps him.'

'A wonderful man.'

'But it has to be him somehow.'

'Well, now there's a life at stake. I have to help the lawyers. I leave the doctor to you.'

'Why fake the report?' I said, moving absentmindedly in a small circle. 'Start with that.'

'You start. I have to go now.'

'Wait. What about the attending nurse? I just remembered. She signed the report too, so she must know something. Please. I need someone who can talk to her. In Italian.'

269

Rosa was quiet for a minute, shifting on her bad leg, physically wavering.

'I speak Italian,' Claudia said, breaking the silence.

Rosa looked at her, then nodded. '*Brava*,' she said, starting to move away. 'You talk for him.'

'Rosa—'

Claudia glared at me. 'I'll talk to the nurse,' she said, her words deliberate, like a hand on my arm. Let her go.

'Maybe we can get him out,' Rosa said, gesturing at the Questura. 'Before they charge him.'

Without even looking at us, she headed for the corner, barely limping now, in a hurry.

'Why did you do that? She would have stayed if—'

'Yes,' Claudia said, 'and then what? More detectives. You don't want her help. Not now. The police *have* somebody, so why are you still looking? That's what they'll think, why is he doing this? And then they look at you.'

'But Rosa doesn't—'

'You think she's your friend, but nobody's your friend now. The police, her, it's the same. One slip, that's what you told me. At least it's over with Cavallini, this business. He doesn't need a part-ner any more.'

I nodded, reluctant. 'No. I have to do it without him.'

'No, you have to *stop*. They *have* somebody. Now what reason can there be for you—'

But I was only half listening, thinking of Cavallini strutting behind his desk, chest puffed out.

'We can't just walk away. We can't let this boy—'

She reached up, touching my arm. 'Yes, walk away, before it's too late.'

I looked at her, surprised. 'You don't mean that,' I said quietly. 'You can't.'

She turned her head, letting her hand drop.

'Claudia, what happened with Gianni, that was one thing. But this – they'll hang him.'

'But they can't prove he did it. We *know* they can't prove it.'

'They may not have to. They might convict him anyway. They'll try. They won't want to admit they made a mistake. Not now. They just solved the case.'

She looked down at her foot, moving it, something to do while she took this in. 'So now we have what we wanted,' she said finally, her voice distant. 'A perfect alibi.' She looked at me. 'Better than the party. Even better than that. Now someone else did it.' She walked away, towards the canal. 'Until you show them he didn't.'

'Claudia, he could die.'

I stopped, caught by the sound of some policemen coming out of the door behind us, their shoes clumping on the pavement, voices loud. Claudia didn't turn, just kept staring down at the canal water, as if not moving would make her invisible. When we heard them cross the bridge to San Lorenzo, she spoke without raising her head. 'So it gets worse,' she said. 'Another one, unless we help him. And then what? Then who did it? And now you want me to help you. What, catch myself?'

'We'll find them someone else.'

'Someone else,' she repeated.

'Who could have done it. Another possibility. Just so long as it's not him. We need to make a story. Something so close to what really happened that they can believe it. Just make a little change. The way Gianni did, remember?' Walking along the fondamenta, making the truce.

'Ah. Now like Gianni,' she said, her voice tight.

I looked at her, then let it go. 'But we have to know what really happened.'

She turned from the water. 'We already know what really happened.'

'I mean at the safe house. It's in Cavallini's head now. It's too late to use anything else. He thinks Moretti has a motive. But who else would?'

'And the nurse is going to tell you?'

'A piece, anyway. If I can talk to her.'

At the hospital, Claudia didn't even bother to translate. On my own I might have managed some kind of conversation, helped by gestures, but Claudia and the duty nurse spoke in a rush that swept me aside, unable to pick up even the occasional word. It was easier just to lean against the glass front of the nurses' station and watch them speak. I thought of Moretti, lying upstairs with his puncture wound. The nurse would have had to know. Now this one was writing something down, motioning with one hand, giving directions.

'The one we want just retired,' Claudia said in the high gothic hall. *'A great* friend of Maglione's. He was that kind of man? With the nurses?'

'I don't know. I never thought so.' But then, so much else had been wrong.

'And who sleeps with retired nurses? Young nurses, yes. So maybe it's just this one's idea.' She nodded back towards the nurses' station. 'She thinks they were lovers because he helped her find a place to live – what else could it be? After all those years together, devoted to him, what does she get? Two rooms in Castello. Put away somewhere so he can marry his American. Typical, the man does as he likes, while the woman . . .' She stopped, shaking her head. 'And maybe, she thinks, the nurse didn't like it. Who would have a better reason?'

'To kill him?'

'She reads magazines.'

We had left the hospital and were walking across the campo past the equestrian statue.

'And who dumped him in the lagoon?'

'She's not that far. Still with the romance. They worked together for years, and not a hint. Only now, when she's old and he helps her. And this one believes that.'

'Were there rumours – other nurses?'

'Of course not. He was a saint,' Claudia said, her mouth turned down. 'A saint.'

'A saviour of men.'

'Yes,' she said, still grim. 'Except my father.'

We followed the directions through several back calles of hanging washing to a house whose plaster front had peeled off in patches, leaving irregular pockets of dark brick, like Dalmation spots. Anna della Croce was on the second floor, up a staircase that smelled of cat and listed to one side. When we rang the bell, we could hear a series of locks being turned, as if the room had been barricaded against the rest of the sagging house. Then the creak of the door, a pair of eyes peering into the stairwell. It was only after Claudia mentioned Gianni's name that the door swung open. For a second no one said anything, adjusting to the light. Then Claudia's eyes widened, and her whole body went rigid with surprise.

Voi,' she said softly.

The woman looked at her, wary again. '*Che cosa volete?*'

'What is it?' I said to Claudia.

'It's the same nurse, the one with my father. Look, she has no idea. No memory at all. I'm someone new to her. She watched them take me away, but she never saw me before. It meant nothing.'

'You're scaring her. Speak Italian.'

The woman had drawn closer to the door, stepping slightly behind it, as if it were a shield.

'Imagine. Nothing to her,' Claudia said, her voice almost dreamy.

'Claudia,' I said, touching her shoulder. 'Ask her about Gianni.'

She looked at me, coming back, then smiled wryly. 'Yes, that's right. Something she'd remember. *Scusi,*' she said, turning to the woman, reassuring her with a spurt of Italian that I couldn't follow but that got us through the door.

We went into a tidy small room filled with porcelain figurines, Claudia still talking. We had got the address from the hospital, she

273

said it was so nice to see us, it had been a tragedy about Gianni, and then I lost the thread again. I was given a straight-backed chair with upraised arms and a velvet-covered seat, formal, the kind that's kept for visiting priests.

The nurse sat primly on the edge of the daybed, a severe-looking woman in her sixties who still seemed to be wearing a starched uniform, her eyes sharp and suspicious, even now on the lookout for sloppily made bed corners. I could see that she would never have spoken to me, but Claudia, another woman, had some-how put her at ease. Tea was made, an excuse for small talk to find out why we had come, whether we could be trusted. This time Claudia did translate, first paraphrasing their conversation, then finally with nearly simultaneous answers so that it felt as if we were all really talking.

'She's worried about her pension. But I told her it's to solve the murder, so that's different.'

'Because he was a saint.'

She nodded. 'The best man she ever knew. Would this hurt his reputation? And I said no, now everyone would admire him for this.'

'So it was a bullet wound?'

'Yes. She helped him remove it, just the two of them. He said he would take the responsibility – he didn't want her to get in any trouble. Always thinking of others, you see. But of course she wanted to help him. So they took out the bullet and cleaned the wound and then she dressed it so no one else would know, not even the other nurses. Then they made out the report.'

'Had he done anything like this before?'

'No. But he knew the man. A family friend. And Dr Maglione told her, "I can't refuse him. I have to help. But no one has to know."'

'He came into the hospital with a bullet wound and no one else knew?'

This involved a longer answer, filled with what sounded like medical details.

'You couldn't tell. The wound was shallow. Not much blood. But of course the bullet had to be taken out. Maglione saw him right away – and after, all people knew was a bandage. Except for Anna,' she said, nodding to the nurse.

'Why would Moretti take the risk?' I said to myself. 'If it wasn't serious. Going to a hospital.'

'The bullet still has to come out. You need a doctor. And this one he knows. She says they were friends – Maglione liked to talk to him.'

'About what?'

A shrug. 'She assumes old times. They hadn't seen each other in years.'

'No, they wouldn't have.'

'But the risk.' The nurse was shaking her head at the memory of it. 'She was worried the whole time. But with him it was always the patient. When he found out Moretti had left, he said it was too soon. It needed more time.'

'But he discharged him.'

'No, he left. In the night. Like a thief in the night.' Hunching her shoulders, stealthy. 'Because he was so grateful. The Germans came one day and he saw that it was a risk for Maglione. How long before someone found out? So he left in the night. He didn't wait.'

'But the medical report—'

'They had to say discharged. What else? Escape? Then everything would come out. So he was "discharged" and she signed it, and that was the end. Until now.'

I went over to the window, a view across the calle to another window, shuttered. 'So Gianni couldn't have had him followed,' I said. Wrong about this too. Moretti had gone without Gianni's even knowing. Then the report had been faked to protect him, all witnessed by a sharp-eyed nurse.

'There's no doubt about this, any of it?'

'You don't want me to ask her that. She'd be offended.'

'The Germans who were there – soldiers or SS?'

'SS. They were looking for Jews.'

'And did they find any?'

Claudia looked at me, but translated. The nurse nodded, lowering her head.

'There was nothing they could do. The Germans knew. Grini, maybe, the informer. That was his speciality, hospitals and mental homes.'

'But he wasn't there that day.'

'No, but they knew. Dr Maglione was helpless. He used to say, "The Germans are like wild animals. You have to be careful with them. If you frighten them, they'll bite. You can't get too close."'

For a minute no one said anything, the only sound in the room a teacup clinking on its saucer.

'Anything else?' Claudia said.

I shook my head. 'I thought there'd be something. Something she'd seen.'

'Oh, and she'd tell you? She sees what she wants to see.'

She started again in Italian, calm, almost in a monotone, so the nurse's reaction seemed all the more abrupt, a shocked expression, head jerked back.

'What?' I said.

'I told her someone said Gianni helped the SS. That he pointed out Jews.'

'Claudia.'

'She was there, wasn't she? See what she says.'

A flood of words, angry. I waited, watching Claudia.

'Whoever said that, it must be his imagination. The doctor would never do that.'

'She might not have seen it,' I said quickly.

'She saw everything else.'

'It's not the same,' I said. 'He wouldn't want her to see that.'

'I saw it.'

The nurse, still angry, was looking from one of us to the other, listening to the volley in a foreign language.

'She'd never admit it now anyway. Ask her when this was, when the Germans came.'

276

Claudia said something in Italian.

'The fourth of October.'

When Claudia and her father were taken, when Moretti was being protected, just as everyone had said. Exact, an excellent witness. The story everyone agreed on, except for the nod. I looked at Claudia, the other witness.

I moved in the chair, stuck. Why would the nurse lie? The fake report had become a badge of honour, her war story, helping Gianni do the right thing. So we had to assume he had.

She said something in Italian, her eyes on me.

'She wants to know how you knew about the bullet wound.'

'Tell her Gianni told me.'

'Ah,' the nurse said.

'I told her you're the American woman's son,' Claudia said, explaining. The nurse was taking me in now, somebody in Gianni's world, not just a foreign voice. 'She wants to know if she can talk about this now. It's no longer a secret?'

'Not any more. Better tell her the police might ask. No surprises.'

They both got up as they spoke, the meeting over.

'She wants to know who did it.'

I shrugged. 'The police think young Moretti.'

The nurse turned to me, speaking Italian, forgetting for a second to go through Claudia.

'She says, why would they think that? Dr Maglione saved his father's life.'

'Tell her we don't think he did it either. That's why we came,' I said, one more blurred half-lie.

I looked around at the shelves of knick-knacks. The rooms he had helped her find. Not enough to buy anyone's silence, even assuming there was silence to buy. And why would there be? She still thought he was a hero, and she'd been there.

'Are you finished?' Claudia said.

I nodded, feeling deflated. Finished with no next place to go, and still no way to connect Gianni to the house.

We said goodbye, a thousand thanks, most of it by rote, my mind elsewhere. Then Claudia spoke in Italian, and the nurse stopped, taken aback.

'I said to her, "Do you know you look familiar to me?"' Claudia said.

'What are you doing? Leave it.'

Claudia's eyes flashed. 'I want her to remember. I remember – why shouldn't she?'

The nurse studied her for another minute, then shook her head. 'She says maybe from the hospital. So many people come and go, it's hard to keep track.' She looked down, her lips in a forced half-smile. 'So many people come and go. And I'd know her face anywhere.'

We started for the door, the nurse still talking.

'She says it's like that in the hospital,' Claudia said, airy now, the nurse prattling. 'So many people. After a while you don't notice.' She looked at me. 'So that's all it meant for her.'

'Maybe she wasn't there,' I said. 'Right then, I mean.'

'No, she was in the ward. Or do you think it's my imagination too?'

Could it have been? A question so faint it was almost unnoticeable, like a hairline crack in porcelain.

'Do you? Yes, it must be. The doctor would never do that,' she said, playing the nurse again.

She turned to her and said something in Italian, without translating, but it must have been asking whether she was sure, baiting her, because the nurse squinted at Claudia's face again, then shook her head.

'Claudia. We didn't come here for that.'

'No, to make sure he did something else. It's not enough, what he did. But maybe he didn't even do that. *She* didn't see it. So how do you know?' Asking something else, her voice angry, all of it still alive to her, not yet just a white splotch of skin. Real, more accurate than memory.

'Because you said so,' I said calmly.

278

She turned away, embarrassed, so that my eyes went to the nurse at the door, watching us closely, maybe the way she'd watched things in the ward, not really understanding what they meant. People coming and going.

'By the way,' I said, 'ask her if she was there when the son came for the medicine.'

'What medicine?' the nurse said.

'That he sent to Moretti.'

'Why would he send medicine to Moretti? There was no infection.'

I looked at Claudia, my head suddenly light.

'For pain maybe?'

She brushed this away with her hand. 'Then? In the war? Who had such medicine? There wasn't even enough for the ones who were suffering. Moretti hadn't had any in the hospital – only at first, to take out the bullet. After that, no, he didn't need any.'

'But Dr Maglione sent him some,' Claudia said to her. 'The boy said so.'

'No, it's impossible. He didn't need medicine.'

'He didn't need medicine?' I said, wanting to be sure.

'No, I told you. Anyway, how could Dr Maglione do this? The man left in the night. Dr Maglione didn't know where he was.'

'No,' I said, following the thought right to the house, 'but his son did.'

CHAPTER FOURTEEN

CARLO MORETTI MAY have been legally adult, but he looked years younger, smooth and wide-eyed, barely adolescent, features that must have given him a useful innocence in his courier days. Now they made him seem childlike, a frightened boy waiting to be taken home.

Rosa was finally allowed to see him that evening, and Cavallini, improbably, allowed me to go with her, maybe as a kind of unofficial watchdog for the Questura. She had brought the new lawyer, and most of the time was spent going over what the police had said to him and what he'd replied. The lawyer took notes. The boy glanced at me from time to time, but his attitude was more bewildered than suspicious – I was no more surprising than anything else that had happened. No, the police had not used any force, just questions. Had they promised him anything? No, but they said a confession meant a more lenient sentence, if it came early, before physical evidence was collected, prints, bloodstains. They wanted to know about his boat. Given Gianni's probable route on foot, Moretti must already have had it waiting. Where? 'They're looking for witnesses,' Rosa said, 'to put you on that boat.' 'But surely there was someone who could verify that you hadn't taken one out,' the lawyer said. 'You couldn't just take a boat.' No, it was easy enough. They weren't guarded at night. If you did it carefully, you could get out to the lagoon and no one would know. I looked away.

'Did they ask you whether he was dead when you put him in?' I said.

Rosa and the lawyer turned to me.

'Cause of death,' I said. 'The official cause was drowning.'

'How do you know this?' the lawyer said, beginning to write on his notepad.

'Cavallini told me when I identified the body. Check the coroner's report.'

'Yes,' the lawyer said, 'it's an interesting technicality. Maybe useful, the actual cause.'

'What difference does it make?' Moretti said, his voice sullen.

'Listen to me,' Rosa said. 'Everything makes a difference. It's going to be all right.'

'No, it's not,' he said, looking down.

'We've found a witness,' she said. 'For that night.'

'You should have told me,' the lawyer said, surprised.

'The man with the umbrella,' Rosa said, still looking directly at Carlo. 'You remember, he offered you an umbrella. When you were walking. In front of the Londra Palace. By the statue of Vittorio Emanuele.'

'The man with the umbrella,' Carlo said numbly, not understanding.

'Yes, he remembers the time exactly. How wet you were. If you think, you'll remember him,' she said, tapping her finger on the table.

He glanced at her in recognition, then shook his head. 'It won't make any difference. It's what you used to say – don't get caught. Once they have you—'

'That was different. That was the war,' Rosa said.

Moretti shrugged, all the answer he could manage.

'Talk to him,' Rosa said, pointing to the lawyer. 'Every detail. So he can help.'

'To find another technicality?' Moretti said. 'What does it matter to them? They've already decided. They want to put me in prison.'

281

'No,' Rosa said, suddenly stern, a kind of slap. 'They want to kill you. That's the punishment.'

He stared at her, his face pale, all the defiance seeping away, then rushing back in a flash of panic as she pushed back her chair and stood. 'So talk to him.'

'Where are you going?' he said.

'Talk to him now. He'll tell you what to say. I'll be back tomorrow.' She reached over and put her hand on his. 'Listen to me. You didn't kill your father. They did. Do you think I would let them do this to you?'

He lowered his head. 'And if it was my fault?'

'I was in that house too. Do I blame you? I blame *them*. No more. Just talk to him.' She placed her hand now on the lawyer's shoulder, then motioned for me to get up. 'Come,' she said, shooing me away with her. 'Too many ears.'

The abruptness of it surprised me, so my question seemed blurted out. 'Did he give you the medicine himself, or did someone else?'

Moretti looked at me for a second as if he were readjusting a dial, going back to an earlier programme. 'He did.'

'So you knew him?'

'No, I'd never met him. But I knew my father had been in the hospital, so I wasn't surprised.'

'He called you himself?'

'Yes. "Come to the hospital. Tell your father I have his medicine" – you know, as if he thought he was at home, in bed. So I went. And he gave me the pills. "Does he have any fever?" he said. No. "Tell him one more week with these." As if I knew all about it. So I said all right, and I took them and that was that.'

'And you took them to the safe house?' Next to me I felt Rosa stir, annoyed that I was going back over this.

'No, I didn't know exactly where he was. I thought Verona. But then when he wasn't there, I tried the house.'

'Was he surprised? To get the medicine?'

'Yes. He said it was nice of the doctor to worry, but he felt fine.

Maybe somebody else could use it. It was hard then to get anything, even aspirin. But there was no label on it, so we didn't
know what it was for. How could we use it?'

'No label?'

'No. That's when I thought, you know, he knows what my
father is. He doesn't want it found – to be connected.'

'Did your father take any?'

'Yes, one, to see what it was. He said he felt the same. It wasn't
the medicine that killed him. Not that way.'

'Not any way,' Rosa said, putting her hand on his arm again.
'Are you finished?' she said to me.

'And then you stayed the night?' I said, still trying to make a
picture.

'No, never there. Back to Verona.'

'Not Venice?'

'Not with the curfew. I had to leave the house after dark, so
there was only enough time to get to Verona.'

'To a safe house there.'

'Yes.'

'And you'd done this before?'

'Many times,' Rosa said. 'He was the best.'

'Yes,' Carlo said, 'except this time.'

Rosa was still angry when we left the Questura.

'What are you trying to do, make him crazy? You can see he
blames himself. And how do we know they followed him? Do
they come while he's there? No. The next morning? No,
another day. So who knows? Maybe a tip. Maybe they already
knew.'

'Then why did Gianni send his father medicine he didn't need?'

She looked away, stymied. 'A fine thing we did. You know, a
boy who blames himself for one thing, sometimes he takes the
blame for another. I've seen this. A confusion in the mind.' She
was quiet for a minute, folding her arms across her chest as if she
had caught a chill. 'You know that if it's true, it strengthens
Cavallini's hand. It gives him a case.'

'He already has a case. That's why it's important to know what really happened there.'

'If it's connected. It's too many ifs now – there's no time for that.'

'Just inventing witnesses.'

'Why not? The police are inventing a case.'

I said nothing. For a few minutes we pretended to look at buildings as we crossed over the bridge to Santa Maria in Formosa.

'It's the only way it makes sense, you know,' I said finally. 'If he was followed.'

'Yes,' she said, half aloud, as if it had been pulled out of her.

'What happened to the house in Verona?'

'It was betrayed. Not then,' she said quickly. 'Later. Everything was betrayed eventually.' She thought for a second. 'Why did they wait another day?'

'To see if he went anywhere else. When he came back to Venice, they knew he'd delivered the medicine. So it had to be that house or Verona.'

'And it had to be the house, or he wouldn't have gone there – just stayed in Verona. So they came.' She stopped, looking away from me, towards the far end of the campo. 'You know what they did? First they poured the petrol. And then they were all around the house, with machine guns. So if you came out, they shot you. Then the matches. So you had a choice. Run out to the guns or stay inside. And of course people stayed – at least you had a chance. Nobody was burning yet. But then the smoke got you, and after that you burned.'

I looked down at her arm. 'But you got out?'

She gave a weak smile. 'I'm afraid of fire. I ran into the guns.'

'And they missed?'

'No, they shot me. Twice. They left me for dead. So that's how it happened.' She turned to me. 'He knows this. Carlo. He knows how his father died. And if it were you who led them there? How would you feel?'

*

284

'I don't even know what I'm supposed to be looking for,' Claudia said.

We were in Gianni's office at the hospital, going through a stack of blue folders.

'Anything that happened that week.'

'How do you know anything did?'

'It must have. Otherwise, it's a contradiction. He takes in a partisan, swears his nurse to secrecy, fakes a medical report. He saves him. Why set up his son?'

'Because Moretti escaped. He didn't know where he was.'

I shook my head. 'Then why not send up a red flag right away? No, I think he meant to help him. He never changed the report. He brags to his daughter, tries to make himself look good for helping the resistance. Days go by. Over a week. And then all of a sudden he sends the boy out with some phony medicine so he'll be followed. That part's right – it has to be. So what happened in between? Something happened.'

'And you're going to find that here?' she said, touching the files.

'I want to know everyone he saw that week. Anything that might explain it.'

There was a tap on the door frame. The night duty nurse stood just outside with a coffee tray, an excuse to see what we were doing.

'*Dottore*,' she said. 'Some coffee. You're working so late.'

She placed the cups on the desk, glancing at Claudia. Had she been listening? But the desk outside was empty, the nurses' station farther down the hall. Was there anything else we wanted? Staring openly now at the folders as she left.

'So now you're the *dottore*,' Claudia said.

'They call everybody that.'

'No, only the stepson,' she said, smiling to herself. 'They all know. She thinks you *look* like him.'

'She thought the old nurse killed him, too.' I sipped some of the coffee. 'We need to be him for a week,' I said, rubbing the arms of the chair, as if just touching his things could put me in his place. 'Everything he did. Something happened that week.'

'With the patients?' she said, picking up a folder.

'I don't know. Here's his calendar. Meetings at the hospital, mostly. Then the appointments – I'm cross-checking those with the medical files. Did they really show up? What happened?' I looked over at her, an appeal. 'You know how to look at these. You're a doctor's daughter.'

She took the appointment schedule and began shuffling through the stack to pull out files. 'It's crazy what you're doing,' she said.

An hour later the nurse came in with more coffee. Claudia was smoking, her feet propped up on the edge of the desk and folders in her lap, and for a second I thought the nurse, almost scowling with disapproval, would protest, but she merely raised her eyebrows at me, the new *dottore*, and sniffed. Claudia, unaware, just kept turning pages, absorbed in Gianni's medical day. When she reached over for her coffee, she kept her eyes on the page.

'And?' I said, lighting a cigarette, signalling a break.

'So many ulcers. Gastrointestinal, a good specialty in the war. The bad food, the fear – think how busy.'

'So he was good?'

She nodded. 'Yes, you would think—'

'What?' I said, leaning forwards to get her attention.

'No Germans.'

'They had their own.'

'Well, in the army. But a specialist, that's different.'

'Maybe he wouldn't see them.'

'You didn't refuse the Germans, if they asked. But they didn't.'

'Would they see a local doctor?'

'The soldiers, no. But the officers? You have to remember what it was like. It's not a camp, it's Venice. They sit in San Marco, take a gondola – what everyone does in Venice. Parties. With Venetians, too. How do you think my father survived? Getting rid of their

286

babies. At least it was safer for the girls, a real doctor. They were – here. Restaurants, everywhere. It's their city. So if you get a stomach ache, why not go to the doctor? But they don't.'

'Why not?'

'I don't know. You asked me what do I see, and I see he's the only man in Venice who never sees Germans. Clean hands. At least in public.'

'And in private he saves a partisan,' I said, another dead end.

'A partisan,' she said dismissively. 'No. He saved a friend.'

I stared at her, the words clicking into place like cylinders in a lock.

'Paolo's friend,' I said, another click. Tennis sweaters, arms slung over shoulders. 'Because he was Paolo's friend. Wait a minute,' I said, reaching for the phone.

'What?'

'But then he sends young Carlo to where Moretti had to be.'

I asked the hospital operator to put me through to the Bauer. Rosa had just come in and, given the slightly groggy tone in her voice, must have had some wine at dinner.

'Do you never stop?' she said.

'Just one more thing. The group who killed Paolo – there was someone else, besides whoever was in the house.'

'He's dead.'

'Dead how? I mean, in the fighting?'

'No, the Germans captured him. They killed him.'

'Which means they probably tortured him.'

She was quiet for a second. 'It's possible. But it doesn't matter. He didn't know about the house – where it was, anything. He was never told. It was a protection for us. And him. It couldn't have been him.'

'But he knew who killed Paolo.'

'Signor Miller, he's dead.'

'When he was captured – any interrogation files?'

'No. Of course we looked for that.'

'How long was he kept?'

'We think two days. They hung his body in Verona. In Piazza Bra.'

'Remember who the commanding officer was? The German?'

There was a silence, so long that I thought I had lost her. 'Yes, I remember,' she said finally. 'Like here. Bauer.'

'What happened to him?'

'He went back to Germany. With the other butchers.'

'He's alive?'

'I don't know.'

'Any files here on him?'

'No. Destroyed. Not that it mattered to us. He wasn't an Italian case – he was already in Germany. Anyway, maybe it's good. I don't want to know what they did to Marco. What good would it do now? He's dead. And he didn't know about the house. So you're wasting your time.'

'Marco. You have a last name?'

A pause. 'Soriano.'

Now it was my turn to wait. 'Your brother?'

'My husband. And he didn't know where the house was. Try something else,' she said, hanging up before I could say anything more.

Claudia, who'd been watching, said nothing, waiting for me to explain. Instead I got the hospital operator again and asked her to put me through to Joe Sullivan in Verona.

The call took a few minutes, but the connection was clear.

'We've got a trial tomorrow and I'm down one investigator. Now you?'

'I need a favour.'

'From me? Send Rosa back and then we'll talk. You weren't supposed to fucking steal her.'

'She's here on her own business. A small favour.'

'What?'

'Army still have a priority line to Frankfurt? I need to call Germany.'

'So pick up a phone.'

288

'Come on. The civilian lines'll take days.'

'I can't patch you through from here.'

'No, you make the call. Get Schneider in Frankfurt – remember him?'

'And?'

'And ask him to run a check on Bauer, SS out of Verona, probably Hauptsturmführer level.'

'You don't have to call Schneider. I know Bauer. A real sweetheart.'

'But you don't know his files. Rosa said they were destroyed.'

'Rosa said.'

'He captured her husband. So she took a personal interest.'

He was quiet for a minute. 'She wasn't supposed to do that. He's out of our hands – Frankfurt's problem.'

'Do they have him? Is he still alive?'

'No idea. What's your interest, anyway?'

'The files here were destroyed, but the SS duped everything for Berlin, so maybe copies are still around.'

'Doubtful.'

'Or better yet, Bauer himself. If he's facing trial, he'll want to do anything to catch a break.'

'Like tell you all his secrets? Which one in particular?'

'He interrogated her husband. The husband told him who killed Paolo Maglione. So who did Bauer tell?'

'You want to explain this to me?'

'When you have more time. Just ask Schneider if he can lay his hands on the files – start with September nineteen forty-four. I'm not sure when they captured him, Soriano interrogation.'

'Rosa know about this?'

'No. She doesn't want to. He was tortured. Then they strung him up in the street.'

'Jesus.'

'I know. But before they did, I think he talked.'

'Which opens up another can of worms.'

'Right.'

'Is there going to be anything for us once you open it?'

'I'm not sure. That's why I'm asking.'

'Because you're not official any more, you know. You want the army to do all this for some private deal?'

'Think of all I've done for them.'

'Fuck.'

I waited. 'It's not a big favour, Joe. I'll tell Rosa you miss her.'

'Fucking drowning here, and I've got to waste time on this.'

'It's a good deed. I promise you.'

'Yeah, the last time you checked on somebody, the guy ended up dead.'

'Maybe we can do the same for Bauer. Tell Schneider where he can reach me, okay? If he comes up with anything.'

There was a growl for an answer and a click on the line. I glanced over the desk at Claudia, still immersed in a folder.

'What makes you think he told them anything?' she said without looking up.

'If he was tortured by SS? They all did – even things they didn't know.'

'And Bauer told Dr Maglione?'

'That's the way it makes sense. Gianni saves an old friend of the family – how could he not? – and then finds out the friend killed his brother. It explains the about-face. It didn't matter to him whether or not they were partisans – that just made it easier to get someone else to do it for him. Keep his hands clean.'

'His new friends at Villa Raspelli.'

'Including Bauer, I'm betting. It had to be that way. We're close now.'

She said nothing, then closed the folder. 'I didn't know about Signor Howard. I'm sorry.'

'Bertie? What?'

'He didn't tell you? He has cancer.'

I looked at the blue folder in her hands. Other people's secrets. 'No, he never said anything.'

She tossed the folder back on the pile.

I stared at it for a minute. Something real, not part of a story for Cavallini. Living in his jewel box, not wanting to be disturbed.

'Does he know?'

'He must.'

'God, what do I say?'

She shook her head. 'Nothing. He would have told you, if he wanted that.'

Giggling about Giulia at the café but discreet about anything real – his assistants, his death.

'Do you want to do more?' Claudia said, her voice weary.

'Let's finish.'

She took another folder. 'So you can make a story.'

'We have to.'

'Do you know what I think?' she said, looking up. 'When it started, I thought you wanted to prove that he was a bad man. That it made some difference to you. But now it's—' She stopped.

'What?'

'It's not for the police, this story. It's for you. You want to believe it. That someone else did it.'

CHAPTER FIFTEEN

MIMI GAVE MY mother her farewell lunch party. No one called it that – Celia was going to Paris to buy clothes and had asked her along – but all of us knew, I think, that she wouldn't be back. They would take a water taxi to the station after lunch, slightly tipsy, and in a week or two she'd call to have the rest of her things sent on and leave me to close up the house. She had run out of reasons to stay. I had counted on her usual resiliency, but instead she'd turned listless and vague. Bertie said the trip would do her good, and in fact she seemed to rally at lunch, laughing with Mimi, her voice rising with some of its old buoyancy, but there were sidelong glances too, private moments when her mind went somewhere else.

It was a large party, too large to seat everyone in the dining room, so people passed down the long buffet table and then stood in small groups or huddled around the tea tables that had been set up all over the piano nobile. I spent most of the time watching Bertie, expecting him somehow to look different, tired, thinner, but there were no signs yet that anything was wrong. His illness, like my mother's sadness, was locked away somewhere, not for public display.

'What's this I hear about the police arresting somebody?' he said to me.

'Moretti's son. You must have known him.'

'No.'

'The father, I mean. He was a friend of Paolo's.'

'Oh, that Moretti. Well, a long time ago. Childhood, practically. But they didn't stay friends – you never saw him around.'

'No, he became a Communist.'

'Really? Paolo's friend?' He smiled faintly, then shook his head. 'And his son killed Gianni? Why?'

'He thinks Gianni betrayed his father to the SS.'

'Gianni? You don't actually believe that, do you?'

'The police do.'

'Oh, nothing they like better than a good vendetta. And how is this one supposed to have started?'

'I don't know. Paolo's death, probably.'

'Paolo again,' he said, his voice resigned. 'All that's supposed to be over. And look how it goes on.'

'Somebody I knew in Germany said it would be interesting to follow one bullet, see where it finally stops. You think it ends in somebody's body, but really it keeps going, the people he knew, the way it changes things, on and on.'

'Poor Paolo. And he was so good-looking,' he said, as if he hadn't been listening. 'Not a thought in his head, but so good-looking.' He glanced over his glasses, back with me. 'No, it doesn't stop, does it? Look at Gianni. It didn't stop with him. Your mother's a wreck. Clothes with Celia, the new collections. They'll probably have to roll the two of them off the train. And the lovely Giulia – what's to become of her? One of the vestals, I suppose, keeping the flame going. You, of course, have already lost your mind. Our little policeman. Still, I suppose if you've caught him.'

'I didn't say I thought he did it. I said the police did.'

'Oh?' he said, interested, wanting to hear more.

But what more could I say? I looked at Bertie, his lively eyes, suddenly wishing that we weren't talking about it at all, that everything was back to the way it had been before I tiptoed around everything I said. I wanted to talk about his being sick, what it would mean. Is that why he wanted us all to go away, so we wouldn't see? When all the gossip would be beside the point, not worth the effort? But he was staring at me, not that sick yet, waiting for an answer.

'They've made their usual leap to the wrong conclusion, is that it?'

'I didn't say that.'

'Hm. Now you even sound like them. Never mind, I'll ask Cavallini myself. If I can pry him away from Mimi.'

'He's here?'

'Just. Made a beeline for our hostess. You don't think he suspects—' He smiled to himself. 'No, not possible. Celia, yes, I wouldn't put it past her. But Mimi? Anyway, it was her party. When would she have found the time?'

'I heard that,' Celia said behind us. 'Wouldn't put what past me?'

'Just about anything, darling,' Bertie said, kissing her cheek. 'Ready for the train?'

'It's hours. Come have a drink. I never see you. Wait.' She fingered the lapels of his jacket, smoothing out his back collar. 'There. Adorable. Sugar, you look more like Jiminy Cricket every day.'

'How I'll miss you,' Bertie said.

'Adam, go say goodbye to your mother while we're all still standing.'

Instead I went to find Cavallini, talking to Mimi.

'Something wrong?' I asked.

'Oh, they want to grill everybody again.'

'So you'll tell them?' Cavallini said, nodding to me as he spoke to her.

'Yes, yes. But after lunch. You can see, I've got a houseful.'

'Of course. After lunch.'

'Don't tell your mother,' Mimi said to me. 'It's the last thing she needs.'

'What is?'

'Starting all this up again. Who was where when. I thought you'd got him.'

'We like to be certain,' Cavallini said blandly, telling me with his eyes to be quiet. 'Till later then.'

294

He bowed to her, signalling me to follow.

'What?' I said as we headed for the stairs.

'Walk with me a little.'

'Something's happened.'

'A witness.'

'Somebody saw Moretti?' I said, imagining Rosa leading him into the Questura.

'No. Somebody saw Dr Maglione.'

We went out the calle entrance and walked away from the Grand Canal, as if we were headed to my mother's house.

'Saw him where?'

'On his way to the ball. Come, I'll show you. It's important, where.'

We turned right on the Fondamenta Venier, bordering a canal so still it seemed to have no outlet. There was the faint, stagnant smell of wet plaster.

'She was there,' he said, pointing up. 'The window looks to the bridge from San Ivo, so it's busy here. She likes to watch the people. Of course, what she says is that she just happened to look out.'

I followed his finger to the window, then to the bridge. A few people were walking down its steps. The way Gianni would have come, turning right at the end towards my mother's house.

'And she saw him?'

'Yes, in his formal clothes, that's what interested her. She knew there was a big party. She wanted to see the clothes. You understand the importance of this? Now we have a time. And where. Before, we knew only that he left his house. Then what? It could have been anywhere. Now we have him seen here.'

'She's just telling you this now?'

'She's an invalid, she practises the economies. A friend saves the papers for her and then she reads. She says the delay doesn't matter – anything important she hears from the street.'

'They must have talked about Gianni being missing.'

'Yes, but not what he looked like. For that, she had to wait for the papers. So now we know he came from Accademia through San Ivo. Along here, and then at the end, left to Signora Mortimer.'

He turned, facing the point where the fondamenta split, his eyes fixed in Mimi's direction, as if he were actually following Gianni, listening for footsteps. But they would have echoed off to the right, on their way to Ca' Venti. Without thinking, I looked towards the calle he'd really taken, then realised Cavallini had noticed and was now looking with me, thinking.

'Unless he was going somewhere else,' I said, forcing it out, waiting to see his response.

He kept looking for another minute, working it through, then shook his head. 'But you called him at the hospital, yes? Go to Signora Mortimer's. Where else would he go from here? I thought, you know, maybe a stop at the Incurabili – a doctor, after all – but he would have turned earlier in San Ivo. No, if he came this far, he was going to Signora Mortimer's, just as you said. Now the question is, where was the boat?'

'The boat?'

'The boat is important. There had to be a boat, to take him so far into the lagoon. If he was killed here – right after the woman saw him, it would have to be, but I don't like to tell her that – then the boat was also here. There is only this canal and that one, where it connects. It's lucky, this part of Dorsoduro, so few. Anywhere else in Venice . . .' He spread his hands, indicating a web of canals. 'But here they fill in the old canals. So it's just this one.'

And what would happen when they turned up nothing? Another idea, just down the street in the opposite direction? I had to move him away.

'But he could have been put in a boat anywhere,' I said.

'It's possible. But if he's already hit, they don't like to drag him far. Somebody sees.' He paused. 'Of course, it's possible he is killed after he gets into the boat.'

'After.'

'Yes. And I thought, but where is that likely to happen? Signora Mortimer's. Boats coming and going. Moretti's waiting with a message – he's needed urgently. So he gets in the boat.'

'And that's why you want to talk to the servants again.'

'Yes, everyone at the landing stage. Although I will tell you frankly, I doubt it was that way. Very risky for Moretti to show himself to so many people. It's more likely that it happened here,' he said, pointing back down the fondamenta. 'After the corner, I think, where it's quiet. But that would depend on whether he found somewhere for the boat.' He smiled at my expression. 'I can see you're not a Venetian. It's not so easy to tie up in this district – look, so few spaces. So we talk to people – what was free, who was gone? And if we're lucky, someone saw. Then we have him.' He looked down the canal again towards the turn to Mimi's. Where Gianni must have gone. 'I will tell you,' he said, smiling, 'some in the Questura will be surprised. There have been discussions.'

'They don't think Moretti did it?' I said, alarmed, unaware that any doubts had been raised. Had they already started looking else-where?

'Well, it's more accurate maybe to say they would prefer some-one else. The kind of trial this will mean, once the newspapers – They want something simple. Not a show trial. So they're suspi-cious of you.'

'Of me?'

'Making these trials. This is what you did in Germany, yes? They don't want that here – it brings shame to people. Look at Rosa. She's Italian and she makes this trouble for Italians. But you – I say to them, it's not for trials, it's personal with him. Like me. Rosa, that's something else. But you don't want to make trou-ble. Look how careful you were about Moretti. Be sure, be sure. So now maybe we can be sure. We find where he kept the boat.' He shook his head. 'It's a gift, this woman. Now we know when he was last alive and we know where to look.'

'I don't suppose there's any chance she made a mistake? Old woman, anybody in formal clothes—'

'No, no, sharp eyes, you know how they are, these women. Once she saw the picture, she knew. She identified Signorina Grassini too.'

'What?' I said involuntarily, like a twitch.

'In the funeral pictures. At Salute. That's how I knew the eyes were sharp. She said she saw her the same night. Right here, coming from San Ivo, like Maglione. Half an hour or so later. And that's right – it's as you said. So I said, oh, she was going to the party too? No, no, she says, not dressed up at all. *Normale*. So that was accurate, because she dressed at your house, you said.'

He looked at me, the faintest hint of a question.

'That's right. A dress of my mother's.'

'Yes, I remember. Very beautiful. And the necklace. Well.' He raised his hand, glancing up at the building. 'So, an accurate witness. Maybe watching now, who knows?'

He went on to San Ivo, and I started back along the narrow stretch of pavement where Gianni was supposed to have been attacked and bundled into a waiting boat. What would happen when Cavallini didn't find the boat, when there were no more old women with sharp eyes? I looked to my right up the calle. But our house wasn't visible from here – you had to make another turn, go deeper into the maze. There were no straight lines in Venice. Maybe if you lived here long enough your mind began to work that way too, seeing around corners, making leaps out of sequence, until you arrived at the right door. But Cavallini had turned left, to Mimi's, the logical route. I looked down at the grey, sluggish water, my stomach turning. He wouldn't stay there, though. The servants wouldn't know anything. The boats would all be accounted for. It was personal with him. And now he had something to prove at the Questura. He'd see, finally, that it was a dead end and turn around to look somewhere else.

I got back just as Celia's bags were being put into the taxi. My mother was standing at the water entrance with Bertie, and when she turned and hugged him for a second, I thought I saw him wince, pressed too hard maybe, where he felt sensitive. I wondered if he'd told her yet. But the embrace had been quick, fleeting, two friends at the station, not someone who thought it might be the last. Then he said something and she laughed and they were back in their own time again, cocktails and patter songs, before the war.

'Just in the nick,' my mother said, seeing me. 'I thought I'd miss you.' She kissed my cheek. 'Don't get into any trouble.'

'Don't buy any clothes,' I said back.

'All right,' she said, smiling, 'a little trouble. Celia says I haven't given Paris a chance. Not really. She says I left too soon.'

'So you might stay for a while.'

'Well, we'll see. It's odd here for me. And the trial. They'll want to take my picture, and why? I have no position, really. I'm just someone he knew,' she said, her voice drifting a little.

'Don't worry about anything. I'll take care of the house.'

'You know all the papers are in my desk? I don't know why I'm talking like this. We've got the house through spring, and I'll probably be back in a week. It's just – well, what's here now?' She touched Bertie on the arm. 'Except me pals,' she said in stage cockney.

'You'll miss your train,' Bertie said, giving her another peck. 'Have fun. Just don't try to keep up with Celia. And no *cinq à septs*, please. It's unseemly at our age.'

'Yours, you mean,' she said, laughing. Then she looked around, swiveling her head to take in the line of palazzos across the canal. 'It is so beautiful, isn't it?' Then she was hugging people and getting into the launch with Celia, waving to friends and settling in beside the stacks of luggage, leaning out the side of the boat for a last look as they headed up the canal.

I turned to Bertie, whose eyes, surprisingly, were moist.

'And you'll be next, I suppose,' he said.

'Not yet.'

'That's right,' he said airily, turning back to the house. 'Otherwise engaged.' He started walking again. 'You stick, I'll give you that. Where is she, by the way? I thought she'd be here playing daughter.'

'Couldn't. She's working.'

'Working? Where?'

'In a shop.

'A shop,' he said. 'Adam. Really.'

She'd left the shop early, however, called back to the hotel. When I got there, she was already packing, moving things from the wardrobe to the bed, stopping in between to look out the window, her movements anxious and darting. A cigarette was burning in an ashtray on the end table, half forgotten in the rush.

'What's going on?'

'The police were here. Back again, about that night. You think Cavallini's a fool? Maybe not such a fool.'

'But I just saw him. It couldn't have been him.'

'Another one, then. What's the difference? They know something.' She went to the window and peeked out. 'Why come again? The same questions. What time did I leave? They know.'

I walked over to her, taking her by the shoulders. 'Calm down. It's not that. They don't know.'

'How do you know? Are you inside their heads now?'

'Just listen. They turned up someone who saw Gianni that night. That's what I came to tell you. An old woman. She also saw you.'

'Saw me?'

'On your way to the house. At exactly the time you said. They're just checking with the hotel to verify *her* story. Nobody suspects you of anything. They just want to make sure it all fits.'

Her shoulders, tense under my hands, softened a little.

'Yes?'

'Yes. Calm down.'

She went over to the night table and picked up the cigarette. 'She saw him? Where?'

'Where she saw you. San Ivo. Out her window. She's an invalid, watches the street.'

'Then they know where he was going.'

'It's also the way to Mimi's. Depends which way you turn.'

'Oh, so he turns one way and I turn another? You believe that?'

'They believe that.'

'And when it occurs to them that he could have gone the other way, like I did?' She started walking to the wardrobe, then turned back, her pacing like visible thought.

'It won't. He went to Mimi's. You came to me. That's all there is to it.'

'No, not all. They're looking again. They're looking at me. Who hated him. Who follows him to your house – yes, that's all the woman proves, that I was there too. Who better?'

'But you were with me.'

'Yes, doing what? How long before they see it?' Another move to the window, still anxious.

'Listen to me,' I said quietly, lowering my voice. 'I've been over everything – the hall, the canal gate, the boat. Every inch. Everything's been scrubbed. There's nothing there, no evidence at all. Nobody saw him. Nobody can prove he was there except us.'

'So maybe there's another invalid.'

'Nobody except us. All we have to do is keep our heads.'

'Oh, and I'm losing mine, is that it?' She went over to the wardrobe, turning her back to me. 'It's me they're asking questions about, not you.'

'They're just making sure about her,' I said calmly. 'That's all. They don't suspect you.'

She kept her back to me, staring at the wardrobe, then reached in, pulled out a dress, and carried it over to the suitcase on the bed. 'Yet. And now what?'

'Come home with me.'

She shook her head.

'My mother's gone. She's not coming back.'

'I can't.' She looked up. 'I can't stay here, in Venice. Today, I thought, It's getting closer. Oh, I know what you say, but I can't help it. They'll find out somehow. If I don't leave now, I'll never get out. So maybe it's true they don't suspect. But how much longer? And then we're trapped here.'

'What do you mean, "leave now"?' I said, the only phrase I'd really heard.

'Now. Just get on the vaporetto and go to the station. Unless they're watching,' she said, jerking her head towards the window. 'But then at least I'd know.'

'I can't leave now.'

'No,' she said, going back for another dress, then folding it into the case. She tucked a toiletries bag into the side, then looked around, the room suddenly bare, just a few hangers dangling in the wardrobe. 'Look how easy it is when you don't have anything. Remember how we left San Isepo? Not even an hour. You can pack up your whole life and leave.'

'And go where? It wouldn't make any difference, you know,' I said, trying to keep my voice emotionless. 'You'd have the same papers. If they really wanted to find you—'

'They would, I know. But then it's easier to run. Where can you run in Venice? It's a prison here. And they're always look-ing. And, who knows, maybe someday they ask the right question: What if he turned the other way?' She stopped, then closed the lid of the suitcase. 'Today it was like a warning. If I stay here—'

'But if you leave without me, they'll wonder.'

'No, they'll be happy for you. A woman like that, a *puttana*? What else would she do? That's the way it is with them.'

'Stop it.'

'Then come. It's our chance now, before it's too late.'

'And leave Moretti to them? You could do that?'

She walked over to the window. 'Today it's him. Then some-thing else. And we stay and stay. Under their noses.' She gestured out, as if the police were lurking beneath a tree in the campo. 'This cat-and-mouse. Waiting to be caught.' She turned. 'Maybe that's what you want, to be caught. There are people like that. They want to be caught.'

I said nothing, waiting it out.

'But I don't.' She looked away, then busied herself closing the wardrobe and checking the bathroom, her silence itself a kind of apology. When she came back to the window she looked up, across the roofs of San Polo to the campanile of the Frari. 'And now it's going to rain,' she said, weary, a last straw.

'Come and sit,' I said, moving the suitcase.

But she stayed at the window, looking out. 'If I don't go now, it'll be too late. I'll get caught in the rain.' She paused. 'Listen to me. What difference does the rain make? I'm talking with my nerves. No sense.'

'No one's going to get caught,' I said evenly, as if I were stroking her arm.

'But I'm afraid.'

'You? You're not afraid of anything.'

'Yes, now I'm afraid all the time,' she said, facing me, moving away from the window, her hands so jittery that she folded them under her arms, holding herself to stay still.

'Of what, exactly?'

She began pacing again, but near the bed, in tighter circles. 'Everything. That I'll say something.' She stopped in front of me. 'No. That you'll say something.' She lowered her head. 'I'm afraid you'll say something.'

I looked up at her, stung, and for a minute neither of us spoke, everything fragile, even the air. 'All right,' I said finally. 'Then marry me.'

'What?'

'A husband can't testify against his wife. Isn't it that way here too? They could never use anything I say.'

For a second she froze, then her shoulders twitched, that peculiar shudder that moves between laughing and crying, unable to settle on either. She sank down on to the bed next to me.

'Wonderful,' she said. 'Marry somebody to keep him quiet. To protect yourself.'

'No,' I said, reaching over and brushing back her hair. 'For all the other reasons. The usual ones.'

'The usual ones,' she said, looking down at her lap. 'With us, after this, the usual ones. But also just in case. Just in case. *Brava*.'

I dropped my hand. 'I just meant you'd never have to worry.'

She stared at her lap for another minute, then got up, turning to me. 'No, and then neither would you. Is that why you want to?' She went over to the night table and lit a cigarette, her eyes avoiding me. 'A wonderful marriage. Because we're afraid of each other.'

'You know what I mean.'

'Just the way I always imagined it.' She went back to the window, blowing smoke and staring out, letting the quiet settle over the room. 'I was right,' she said finally. 'Now it's raining. Where did your mother go?'

'Paris.'

'So you want me to come to Ca' Venti. Yes, why not. I can't stay here.' She smiled wryly. 'I was going, but—'

'You can still get a train if you want,' I said, staring at her. 'You can do whatever you want.'

She came over to the bed and put her hand in my hair. 'Oh, no strings.'

'No.'

'No. But it's too late for that, isn't it? We're tied now, with this thing. No matter what. So why not Ca' Venti? Maybe it's my fate.'

'What is?'

'You. I never thought, when it started—' She took her hand away. 'But that was before.'

We waited until the rain stopped, not saying much, then took a vaporetto to Accademia and walked the rest of the way home. In the downstairs hall she hesitated for a moment, looking through to the water entrance, and I saw that she was imagining Gianni there again, his head on the steps. But then Angelina appeared, wanting to take her suitcase, asking her where to put it, making us feel, oddly, as if we were checking in to a new hotel.

Without my mother, the house seemed even larger than before, and instinctively we avoided the big reception rooms, staying in the sitting room with the space heater. At one point Claudia wandered out to the room where the engagement party had been, but it was empty and gloomy, barely lit, and there was nothing to see, not even in memory. She fiddled with the radio for a while, the static somehow like our own strained jumpiness, then made drinks. When we weren't talking, you could hear the clock.

Dinner was roast chicken and a creamy polenta, nursery food, and afterwards we sat with a fire and listened to the house quiet down, footsteps in the upstairs hall, running water, then nothing.

When we made love later, I thought of how it had been after the ball, the clutching, everything unexpectedly exciting. Now it was more like having too much to drink, a grudging pleasure that made it easier to sleep. We stayed in my room, Claudia curled beside me, just what we'd always wanted.

We both slept fitfully. Claudia tossed next to me, restless, and I drifted in and out, sleeping and then lying on my side with my eyes open, making out shapes in the dark room. Nothing was wrong – we were safe – but my eyes stayed open, my mind picking over things at random. Moretti, who had to be saved somehow. Cavallini, searching the canal for the right mooring. Claudia in the hotel room, anxious, looking out the window to see if they were coming to get her.

I turned on to my back and looked up at the ceiling and the faint moving reflections of the moonlit water outside. It was back again, the uneasiness of those first weeks, waiting for the sun to come over the Redentore. But that had been the dread of being suddenly at loose ends, a kind of decompression. This was a formless worry. Claudia moved next to me, rolling to her side. Not formless. I saw her again in the hotel room, turning to me. *And then neither would you.* I'd always thought of it one way, me reassuring her, safe as long as I held her. But of course it had to work the other way. I was only safe as long as she held me. And now she was frightened, ready to run off, sure they knew. Afraid I would say something. Afraid she would say something.

She moved again, rolling farther away, and I slid quietly towards the edge of the bed, slipped out from under the blankets, and tiptoed to the closet, grateful that the marchesa had scrimped on the squeaky parquet floors, a luxury for the public rooms. Here, on noiseless carpet, I could get my clothes and leave the room without a sound. I stopped at the door, checking, but Claudia hadn't moved. I dressed and made my way to the stairs, not even aware of the dark, everything familiar from the sleepwalking nights.

But why would she say anything? For that matter, why would they believe her? I had lost a fortune – the one man in Venice

Cavallini didn't suspect. Unless he wanted to. Nothing was predictable. You met a girl at a party, and the next morning, on a boat, you have the first clear idea you've had in months. I thought of her as we pulled in to Salute, intrigued, the start of it. Then looking out the hotel window for shadows. Lying in the same bed now, afraid of each other. But these were four-in-the-morning thoughts, irrational, gone in the daylight, like mist burning off. I turned the door latch carefully, making only a click as I stepped into the calle. Nobody was going to say anything.

It was breezy on the Zattere and my head felt clearer, wide awake now. Across the channel the giant brick Stucky factory loomed over the gardens of the Giudecca. There were shouts and clanging sounds up ahead at the warehouses behind the maritime station. The city would be awake soon – bakers, the first dog-walkers, everything normal. I would check in with Cavallini. Maybe Rosa's lawyers had managed to get Moretti out. If we could just get Cavallini to back away, the boy might not even be tried. A case any defense could fight, a trial nobody wanted. Then we could leave, go anywhere Claudia liked. I went into the workers' cafe opposite San Sebastiano, feeling better. Nobody would say anything. The barman nodded, as if it had been a day, not weeks, since I'd last stopped in, and handed me a coffee still foamy on top. I stood at the window, looking across at the church. Veronese's church, the dreary stone façade, then the riot of colour inside.

She must have been standing outside the steamy door for a few minutes, hands stuck in her pockets, before I noticed the movement in the corner of my eye. She was biting her lip, not sure whether to smile, pleased with herself for having found me but slightly embarrassed. Or maybe waiting for me to be pleased. Then someone opened the door and she was in anyway, standing next to me.

'I thought you were asleep,' I said.

'I thought you were.'

'Coffee?'

She shook her head, then glanced around, taking in the other customers in their blue overalls and caps.

'What is this place?'

'It opens early. I come here sometimes.'

'What's wrong?'

'Nothing. I couldn't sleep, that's all. How did you find me?'

'I looked out the window. I saw you on the Zattere. I didn't know what to think.'

'I went for a walk.' I paused. 'I was coming back.'

She looked away. 'I just didn't know where you were going. I was worried.'

I held up the coffee cup. 'Sure?' She shook her head again and I finished it. 'Come on,' I said, guiding her with a hand on her back. A few of the men turned, amused, making up their own stories.

'I didn't want to be alone in the house,' she said outside, explaining. But it wasn't the house. 'It's so stupid. To be like that,' she said, shaking a little, just as she had in the hotel.

'You're cold.'

'There's only the coat,' she said, drawing it closer. 'I didn't have time to dress.'

I glanced at her. Once it would have been fun, nothing underneath, our secret in the café, something to laugh about when we got back to bed, warming ourselves. Now I thought of her throwing it on, racing down the stairs, making sure of me.

'Come here,' I said, folding my arms around her. 'You'll freeze.'

She let her head fall against my neck, so I could feel her breath, quietly shaking like the rest of her.

'I'm sorry,' she said, then tipped her head back, and I saw that there were tears, the shaking stronger.

'Claudia—'

She took a breath. 'Nothing. It's nerves.'

'Ssh,' I said, moving her closer. 'It's the cold, that's all.'

She rubbed her face against my coat. 'I didn't want to be with anyone again. Remember, I told you? At La Fenice? I was afraid of that. And now? I'm afraid when you're not there. So the joke is on me, yes?' She wiped her eyes.

'No joke,' I said, lifting her head. 'I'm not going anywhere.'

'No? So it's what you wanted. You wanted us to be together.'

'Don't you?'

'Oh, me,' she said, brushing the question away, another tear. She looked up. 'You're still so sure?'

'Yes,' I said, suddenly filled with it, a certainty you could touch. Seeing her face at the water gate, her eyes looking at me as we moved the tarp. And after, at the hotel, clutching each other, no one else, no doubt at all.

'Yes, and at the nurse's, I saw your face. You thought for a minute – yes, you did – is it all a story? Something I made up. The hospital. The camp. What if she's—'

What I had thought, just for a minute.

'Why would I make it up? But you thought that.'

'Claudia, I'm not going anywhere.'

She looked down. 'So we can watch each other.'

'No,' I said.

She raised her head, waiting.

'I'm not going anywhere, I said again.

She looked at me, then nodded, a kind of concession, her eyes moist again. 'No, we can't. Not now. It doesn't matter why, does it? It's the only way we're safe.'

'That's not—' I said, but she was leaning into me, away from the wind off the Zattere.

'I know. It's all right,' she said, her voice muffled. 'So come home.' She turned, crooking her arm through mine, something she'd done a hundred times before, and suddenly I felt as if we had been snapped together. I looked down at the arm, curved around mine like a link in a chain. Tied now.

CHAPTER SIXTEEN

CLAUDIA AND I were married at a magistrate's office in a ceremony that lasted less than fifteen minutes. Mimi and Bertie were
the witnesses, and because there was no party, no real wedding,
they insisted on taking us to lunch afterwards at the Gritti. I had
called my mother and told her not to come, and after a squeal of
protest I think she was relieved not to have to make the trip. We'd
have a proper celebration later, she finally agreed, but why the
rush? Claudia wore an off-white silk dress with a coral belt that we
bought in the Calle Frazzaria, off San Marco, and Bertie somehow
miraculously found a corsage of hothouse flowers that set it off like
a giant tropical brooch. A man took souvenir pictures after we
signed the register, and we are all smiling in them. It was not the
wedding any of us would have imagined, but Venice made up for
the missing bridesmaids. The weather was beautiful, warm enough
to eat outside on the Gritti's floating dock, with all the canal traffic going by. We joked that Salute, gleaming across the water with
its marble icing, was our wedding cake.

'And you're already here for your honeymoon,' Bertie said.
'Think of them all, pouring out of the station. All swozzled and
cranky before they even begin. Well, cheers.' He lifted his champagne glass. '*Auguri.*'

'What do you suppose they do?' Mimi said.

Bertie sputtered, smiling. 'Mimi, dear—'

'During the *day*. I mean, you don't want to look at Tintorettos on your honeymoon, do you?'

'Gondola rides,' I said. 'With accordions.'

'What does Signora Miller want to do?' Bertie said, tipping his glass to Claudia.

'Signora Miller,' she said, trying it out. 'It is, now, isn't it?'

'Mm,' Bertie said. 'I'm a witness.'

'It started with you, you know,' I said. 'Your party. You introduced us.'

'I wish you'd introduce someone to me,' Mimi said.

'Oh no,' Bertie said, holding up his hands. 'Anyway, as I recall, Adam, you introduced yourself. Bold as brass. And now look.'

'Yes,' I said, looking at Claudia, pretty with her flowers, the bright sky behind her.

'Signora Miller doesn't want to do anything,' she said, as if Bertie had been waiting for an answer. 'She's happy to sit right here.' She looked over the blue midday water to the palazzos on the other side. One of the traghetto gondolas was weaving its way across, graceful as a dancer on point. 'I could sit here for ever.'

'Yes,' Bertie said, following her gaze. 'Wouldn't it be nice?'

We finished the wine, talking idly, then Bertie excused himself and a few minutes later I followed. In the men's room he was leaning on the marble counter, dabbing his face with a cold towel.

'Everything all right?'

'Yes, certainly. Why wouldn't it be?' He looked at me in the mirror, then blotted his face again.

'I mean, are you in pain?'

A longer stare now in the mirror, then a resigned look away. 'Somebody's been reading medical reports.' He wiped his hands on the towel. 'It's all right now. It won't be soon. Does that answer it?'

'No. Talk to me.'

He shook his head. 'There's no point. If you've read my file, then you know everything I know.'

'I don't know what it means.'

'It means enjoy the beautiful day outside. I intend to. And that doesn't mean going on about things that can't be helped. Or things that – well, things. So let me enjoy it, please. I mean it, Adam. And not a word to Grace, either. Rushing back on trains and making me a *cause*. I know just what she's like.'

'Bertie—'

'No,' he said, putting his hand on my arm. 'Now let's not ruin the day. It's supposed to be the happiest day of your life.' He looked up at me. 'Hers, anyway.'

'Did you get another opinion?'

'Yes, I've been through all that. Gianni was a perfectly competent doctor, you know, whatever else you may think he was. If he was.' He turned away. 'Find anything else in his files?'

I shook my head. 'Just you.'

'Serves you right. Snoop.' He threw the towel in the wicker hamper underneath the sink. 'Better go before Mimi comes in after us. Don't think she wouldn't.' He started for the door, then stopped. 'I almost forgot. Here.' He took an envelope out of his breast pocket and handed it to me. 'For the happy couple.'

'Bertie.'

'I know, I shouldn't have, but I did. Now put it away before you-know-who sees it.'

I stepped closer and put my arms around him, surprised a little when he hugged back.

'All right, all right,' he said, breaking away, touched. 'It's not a funeral, it's a wedding. Such as it is. So let's have a drink, and if you're good, I'll get Mimi away and you can have the day to yourselves.'

It took two drinks but then they were gone, taking their conversation with them. We sat quietly for a while in the sun, rocking on the wakes of the passing boats. The waiters, paid by Bertie, had disappeared inside.

'Is there anything you'd like to do?' I said. 'See Tintorettos?'

She kept facing the water, squinting a little against the sunlight.

'I'd like to see my father,' she said finally. 'Would you mind?'

I shook my head, waiting, not knowing what she meant.

'But it's so far to walk. These shoes. Do you have money for a taxi?'

I patted my jacket pocket. 'We're rich. Bertie gave me a cheque. Where?'

But she was already getting up and walking over to the landing platform. A bellman helped her into the motorboat, then I followed, both of us sitting back against the cushions as the boat headed up the canal. The motor was too loud to talk over, so we watched the city go by – under the Accademia bridge, past the turn where Ca' Maglione stood, brightened now with pots of geraniums on the balconies, then up the busy stretch to the Rialto, the water crowded with delivery boats. The view from Bertie's window. What would happen to the house? I wondered. One of the assistants, perhaps, unseen but devoted, there in the end while the rest of us were kept away. Bertie's real life, whirling in its own mystery.

We got out at San Marcuola and walked the rest of the way to the ghetto, Claudia's high heels clicking loudly on the pavement. Away from the canal the streets became sombre and dingy, and people stared openly at our clothes, the corsage almost startling here. Then up the narrow calle where her aunt used to gossip window to window, and over the bridge, ducking our heads in the low *sottopasso* to the open campo, as stark as before, the trees just beginning to bud. She stood for a minute, looking. No one passed us, the only campo in Venice that seemed lifeless, left behind.

'I always say I'll never come here again, and then I come back,' she said.

We went over to a bench in front of what had been the old people's home. She sat for a minute with her back against the wall, then leaned forwards and took off her shoes.

'*Mama mia*, these shoes. What?'

'*Mama mia*,' I said, grinning. 'A real Italian.'

'Ha, like the others,' she said, rubbing her foot. 'At Signor Howard's, speaking English. You don't know real Italians.'

'I married one, didn't I?'

She stared at the campo. 'I don't feel Italian here. Something else. They didn't think we were Italian when they came for us.' She sat back, frowning. 'Why do I come here? It's always the same.'

'Maybe that's why.'

'No, it's foolish. But at the Gritti I thought, what am I doing here? My father can't see me here.'

'But he can here?'

'No, that's why it's so foolish. But I wish he could. I thought, Today I wish he could see me. This dress. These shoes. Married. Just to show him I am alive. He never expected to see that.' She paused. 'Well, did I? I never thought I'd leave that place. And now, flowers,' she said, touching the corsage. 'So maybe I came to see myself. All dressed up. Show off to the neighbours.'

I lit cigarettes for us. 'Maybe you will see somebody. You never know.'

She shook her head, the empty campo its own answer, then pointed across to one of the tall buildings. 'That's where it would have been, the wedding. See the windows on the third floor? There. And then after, a party somewhere. Big, with everybody. He liked parties.'

'Would he have liked me?' I said, just making conversation.

She shook her head, smiling. 'No.'

'No?'

'No.' Laughing now, a private joke.

'Why not?'

'You're not Jewish.'

'Part.'

She waved this away. 'Americans. It's different.'

'How?'

'It's different.' She turned, a new idea. 'And now me. I'm American too, yes? Passport, everything?'

'Everything.'

'I forgot about the passport,' she said. 'Now I can go anywhere.'

'Almost worth getting married for.'

'He would have liked that, anyway. You know, for him, that generation, America was like a dream.' She looked again at the synagogue windows. 'He would have made a big fuss. Introducing you. All the relatives.'

I kept looking at the campo, saying nothing.

'Well,' she said, moving somewhere else in her mind.

'Are you sorry it wasn't like that?'

'Me? I'm supposed to be dead. Sometimes, at the Gritti, it's easy to forget. Then I come here and I see it again.' She opened her hand to the square. 'We're all supposed to be dead. Not married, dead.' She paused. 'And now who's dead? The man who killed him. So that's one thing I did for my father.'

'He can't see that either,' I said.

'No, but I'm glad. I'm glad it was me.'

'It wasn't you,' I said quietly.

'Yes, both of us. Do you think they'd take one of us without the other?'

I glanced at her, suddenly back in the registrar's office. 'Nobody's taking anybody.'

'No. Well,' she said, getting up, dropping the cigarette, 'not today. Anyway, such talk. On a wedding day. Of course, it's not that kind of wedding, is it?' she said, nodding towards the windows again, where the relatives would have been.

'What kind is it?'

She ground out the cigarette with her toe. 'Our kind.'

We walked towards the station, intending to get a taxi back, and in a few minutes were on the Lista di Espagna, crowded with people just off the train.

'Let's go back there,' she said, pointing to the hotel on the side street where we'd first made love. 'Do you want to?'

'Do you?'

'Yes. Not your mother's house. There.'

The desk clerk raised his eyebrows at Claudia's corsage, as if we were newlyweds from Maestre who'd wandered into the wrong place, but he gave us a key. Claudia was playful on the stairs, backing me against the wall on the landing, the way we'd been that first time, too eager to open the door. But the room was different, stuffy, in the back, and we had to draw the blinds against sun this time, not the cold rain that had made us feel hidden away, illicit. When she took off her clothes, first unpinning the flowers, I thought of her unbuttoning her blouse that day, the jolt of it, before anything happened. Before we were different. She felt it too, I think, that sudden moment of everything being different, because she looked for one second as if she might dart away, but then she stepped over to me, naked, and pressed herself against me, and that was the same again, different but the same.

We made love in a kind of rush, grabbing, so that our minds were free of everything but what was happening to our skin. You could feel it being pushed away, every thought crowded out by physical excitement, gathering speed, until sex was something happening to us, not in our control at all. When she came, a ragged burst of gasps in my ear, the sound seemed dragged out of her, involuntary, and then I was coming too, almost surprised by it, as if I'd been caught in some unwilled convulsion. I stayed in her afterwards, not sure it was over, then finally rolled off, blinking at the ceiling, returning, still not thinking about anything. The way she'd once described it, something to prove you're alive, just feel-ing it. When she'd told me it could be anyone, as long as you could feel it.

Now she was leaning over me, propped up on one arm, touch-ing my face.

'We still have this, don't we?' she said, not waiting for an answer, bending down to kiss me.

'You're all red,' I said, reaching up and running my hand over the tops of her breasts, still flushed, as if she had a birthmark.

She smiled a little, feeling my fingers, her eyes on mine. 'You should marry me.'

'Okay.'

'We could spend our wedding night here.'

'We could,' I said, my fingers still tracing a line across her chest.

For a second she gave in to the stroking, closing her eyes. Then she opened them again and stared down at me. 'You're not sorry?'

I shook my head, turning my hand over, brushing her with the back of it. 'I'll marry you again,' I said. 'Would that do it?'

She nodded. 'For all the other reasons. For those.'

I let my hand drop, then reached up with both arms and pulled her to me, kissing her, and for a while it really was the same again, but different.

We tried to sleep, lazy after sex, but the voices from the Lista di Espagna funnelled into the calle, seeping through the window like dust, and neither of us really wanted to stay. Instead, like real honeymooners, we took a gondola, winding through the back canals until we lost our sense of direction, content to watch people crossing bridges over our heads, moving at their land pace while we drifted below. Sometimes they stopped to look at us, pointing at Claudia's corsage, so that, mirror-like, we became part of each other's scenery. By the time the gondolier got back on the Grand Canal the sun was setting, the water gold and pastel, and he threw out his arms in an *ecco* gesture, as if he had arranged it for us, a wedding gift.

After the Gritti lunch, it seemed extravagant to go out, but the house in Dorsoduro felt confining, filled with ghosts, and Claudia said she wanted to do something American, so we ended up going to Lucille's, just behind Campo San Fantin. The club had opened during the occupation, a little piece of home, and the customers were still mostly soldiers, on leave from bases in the Veneto or attached to one of the Allied offices that hadn't yet packed up and gone. It had the borrowed, pretend quality of places like it in Germany – America till you walked out the door – and most of the locals avoided it.

When we got there, it was only half full. The band was finishing its first set, so the house lights were down, the other customers just shadows in the smoky darkness. At the table next to ours everyone was in uniform, drinking beer. Lucille, the coloured singer who fronted the place, was doing 'Easy Living', trying to pass as Billie Holiday, with a flower in her hair. The soldiers next to us stared at Claudia when we sat down, someone approachable, the kind of girl who went to jazz clubs, and for a second I stiffened, then laughed at myself, a cartoon reaction: *That's my wife.*

Lucille finished, and through the applause I heard one of the soldiers say, 'Hey' – not flirting, trying to get our attention.

'Hey,' he said again, 'remember us?' Moving his finger between him and his friend. 'The island that was closed. Jim and Mario.'

'Torcello,' Claudia said, smiling. 'Yes. You're still here?'

'Last day,' one of them said. 'Hey, let us buy you a beer.'

Claudia held up her left hand, wiggling her ring finger. 'Ask him,' she said, nodding to me.

'What did I tell you?' one said to the other, then leaned forwards, taking me in. 'That's great. When?'

'Today.'

'Today? Fucking A,' the GI said, then dipped his head in apology to Claudia. 'Congratulations.' He signalled the waiter, then moved his chair closer, half joining us at the small club table. We shook hands.

'I have to tell you, I knew it. I said to him, what else would they come out here for? I mean, with the restaurant closed. We cleared out, remember?'

'I remember.'

Claudia, who seemed to be enjoying herself, shook hands with both of them.

'Mario?' she said.

'Calabrese. My grandfather.'

'Ah,' she said, pointing to herself. 'Romana.'

The beers arrived, hers in a glass. She lifted it to them. '*Salute*,' she said, smiling, the party we hadn't had at the Gritti. 'So they sent you here? You speak Italian?'

'Two words, maybe. My father didn't want us to—'

He stopped, afraid of offending, and just then Lucille stood up again, this time for a comic, sexy version of 'The Frim Fram Sauce', flirting with the audience, coating each word with innuendo. Claudia tried to follow it, taking her cues from Jim and Mario, who laughed at all the right places, but inevitably her reactions were late, one step behind, foreign.

317

'What's *chiffafa?*' she asked Mario as we applauded. 'A vegetable?'

He laughed. 'It's just jive,' he said, almost shouting. The band had started playing, without Lucille, so people talked above it, the small room noisy. He pointed at Claudia's wedding ring. 'So does this mean you're going to the States?'

'What do you think, will I like it?'

'Like it? You're gonna love it. It's the States.'

'Yes? Which one are you from?'

I sat back watching, not really listening. New York had everything – the big shows, everything. It never stopped, not like here, where they rolled the streets up – well, canals, rolled the canals up. Jim laughed, trying to picture this, then both soldiers turned to Claudia to tell her about things she had to see, things she'd like because they liked them. GI talk. America now a movie to them, shinier than anything they'd ever known. And why not? I smiled to myself, enjoying the breezy descriptions, Claudia's face as she listened, pretending to be wide-eyed, the sort of girl they might want to take back themselves. There were more drinks. Mario asked her to dance, if it was all right with me.

'You're a lucky guy,' Jim said, stuck with me now. 'Want us to clear out?'

'No, she's having fun,' I said, looking at her on the floor, doing a foxtrot with Mario.

'Some place, huh? Like being home.'

I looked at her again, my chest suddenly tight. My wife. Of course we'd have to go back some time. But even in this ersatz version in San Fantin she seemed out of place. America was about easy happiness, chiffafa, as casual as picking up a girl in a club. I thought of the look in her eyes that afternoon as she had stared across the empty campo. What would she do with it there, her old life? Pretend it didn't exist, like Bertie, until it started to grow inside her?

Mario finished with a surprise twirl, so they were laughing as they came off the floor. When her laugh stopped suddenly, cut off, we all looked at her, then followed her gaze towards the back of the room.

'See a ghost?' Jim said.

'No, no, sorry,' she said, sitting down. 'It's nothing.'

But my eye had caught him now too, the moustache neatly brushed, sitting against the wall in a double-breasted suit, on the town. A woman was with him, her back to us, and I tried to look away before he saw me. Not Signora Cavallini. Maybe a friend from Maestre. Lucille's was a kind of Maestre – no one his wife knew would come here. I felt embarrassed, as if I had opened the wrong door by mistake.

'He's coming over,' Claudia said.

I turned, expecting some version of a man of the world wink, an elbow nudge, but instead he was smiling, delighted.

'Signor Miller. So you like the jazz too? All the young people, it seems,' he said, waving his hand towards his table, where the woman had turned to face us.

Giulia. For a second I simply stared, too surprised to move, then she was nodding and I had to nod back. She was dressed for a night out, lipstick and earrings, no trace of mourning. To see Cavallini? In a place where no one would see them. But neither of them seemed disconcerted by our being there. Cavallini was taking Claudia's hand, greeting her.

'Please, you'll join us?'

'Oh, but . . .' Claudia fluttered, spreading her hands to Jim and Mario, clearly unnerved by the idea of sitting with Cavallini.

'That's okay,' Mario said. 'We were just having a beer. You go sit with your friends. I mean, what the hell, your wedding day.'

'How?' Cavallini said.

'Claudia and I were married today,' I said to him.

He looked at me, speechless for a moment, then fell back on form, taking up Claudia's hand again with a flourish. 'Signora Miller. My very best wishes,' he said, the English sounding curiously like a translation. He turned to me. 'So. You didn't wait for your mother?'

'We didn't wait for anybody. We just thought it was time.'

'Yes, I know how that is. Everything for the family, and really you want to be alone.' I thought of his wife, an unlikely candidate for elopement. 'And now here we are, more people. But at least have some wine with us to celebrate?' He glanced at the table of beer bottles.

'That would be nice,' I said, shooting a look at Claudia.

Cavallini extended the invitation to the GIs too, but they begged off, so it was just the four of us at the little table in the back.

'Giulia, what do you think? Married today,' Cavallini said, waving his hand at us, then summoning the waiter for more chairs.

'Yes?' Giulia said to me, taken aback. And then, for an instant, a look that was more than surprise, a question mark, a change of plan. 'So. That's wonderful. You didn't tell anyone?'

'Ah, no secrets from the Questura,' Cavallini said, joking. 'You see how we find you out, even here.'

I laughed, but Claudia barely managed a smile. When the chairs were brought, she sat at the edge of hers, as if she were afraid of accidentally touching Cavallini's leg. It was an awkward table. Giulia talked about jazz, popular at the university because it had to be clandestine, almost a link with the Allies. Cavallini asked about the wedding. Finally the bottle arrived and Cavallini made a toast to our future.

'Yes, the future,' Claudia said, edgy.

'And what will it be?' Cavallini said pleasantly.

Claudia shrugged.

'You don't know? But women always know. They're the ones with the plan. The men . . .' He opened his hand, all of us feckless.

'America, I suppose,' she said. 'It depends on Adam.'

'Ha, already a wife. My wife too. Everything depends on me, as long as it's what she wants,' he said, raising his glass to Claudia.

I glanced quickly at Giulia, surprised he'd mentioned his wife. Maybe not a girl from Maestre after all.

'You could leave Venice?' Giulia said. 'You know, I thought I could, and then at university I missed it. *Terra firma*, nothing moves. I missed the water.'

'Not everyone likes the water,' Cavallini said. 'Maybe it's

different for Signora Miller.' He nodded at her new name. 'When you can't swim—'

'How do you know that?' Claudia said, off-guard.

'I'm sorry,' he said, genial. 'It's not true?'

'No, it's true, but how do you know? You asked someone that?'

'No, no, Signor Miller mentioned it. We were talking about boats. He said you didn't like boats, only the vaporetto.'

'She's getting better,' I said, jumping in. 'Today we took a gondola ride and she wasn't nervous at all.'

'So you think I'm always the bloodhound?' Cavallini said, amused.

'Your men were asking questions at the hotel,' I said, explaining. 'Checking times.'

'My men,' he said, blushing a little, as if he'd been accused of being clumsy.

'Any news? About the boat?' I said, moving him away from Claudia.

'No, it's very difficult.' He sighed. 'But not tonight. Tonight the bloodhound is not official. Just a wedding guest. The bride will permit me a dance?'

He held out his hand, smiling, so Claudia had to raise hers and get up before she could think of any excuse not to. She glanced at me, then let Cavallini take her elbow, following him to the dance floor like someone being led away for questioning.

Giulia took out a cigarette and waited for me to light it.

'You really like jazz?' I said.

'You mean, what am I doing here? Don't worry, it's not what you think.'

'It's none of my—'

'I asked him to bring me here. He wanted to have dinner – you know, where everyone can see – and I thought, no, why not here instead. I like the music, and alone, it's not possible for me to come.'

'Why dinner?'

'Oh, he said to explain to me what was happening. About my father, the man they caught. Of course, the real reason—'

321

'I can guess.'

'No, it's not that,' she said. 'Just to be seen. Be helpful. You know his wife is my mother's cousin, so he thinks he's a Maglione. I'm the family now, the son. It's useful for him if people think I want his counsel, that he has influence with me. You know, he has political ambitions. So it's useful.'

'He does?' I glanced towards the dance floor, where he was chatting with Claudia.

'He's always been ambitious. Why else would he marry Filomena?'

'You mean she's rich?'

'No, but a good family. A step for him.'

'Maybe he married for love.'

She looked at me. 'Did you?'

I said nothing for a second, thrown by the directness of it, her eyes on me.

'Yes.'

She tapped her cigarette on the ashtray. 'Then it's good. You'll be happy.' She glanced up. 'I hope you will be,' she said, softer now, a kind of apology for having asked.

'So Cavallini gets seen with the Magliones. And what do you get out of it, a night out?'

'Well, a friend in the police, it's always good. And to thank him for solving the murder. Of course, I know it was because of you. But he listened to you. Would the others have done that?'

'Do you really think this case can be tried? You're a lawyer.'

'Not for crime. Business, you know. Contracts. Anyway, in this case I'm a Maglione. The police get the man, *brava*. But now the important thing – well, that it all goes the right way.'

'What way is that?'

She leaned forwards, businesslike. 'The best, of course, is that there's no trial at all. He confesses, it's an end. But if it has to be, then I want *him* on trial, not my father.'

'What do you mean?'

She shrugged. 'A tragic mistake. My father gives him medicine –

322

a humanitarian act, at that time even a brave one. And he *thinks* it's a betrayal. Foolish, but he acts.'

'But the defense will say it was a betrayal.'

'And the more they say it, the more they make him look guilty. Vittorio says—'

'Vittorio?'

'Inspector Cavallini,' she said, surprised I hadn't known his name. 'He says this is the trap – if they talk about my father this way, it gives Moretti *more* motive. So maybe they won't.'

'They have to say something.'

'They'll say the police are mistaken. That it's political, the government is trying to put the Communists on trial. And of course it's true – a convenience for them, a case like this. But at least then my father's name—' She broke off, crushing her cigarette, her mouth drawn, as if putting on lipstick had hardened it, aged her. I thought of her at the memorial service, pale, when her father's good name had not even been in question.

'You've thought about this.'

'Of course. It's my name too. That's why it's so important, with Vittorio. To make it all go right. So I make him feel part of the family.' Her eyes slightly amused but determined, Gianni's face at the Monaco.

'By bringing him here.'

'Well, I'm the son but not the son. I know what people say. We go to Harry's and I'm his mistress. Nice for him, maybe, but not for me. So I bring him here. Who will know? Some soldiers.'

'And me.'

'Yes, now you. But you know everything. You're the other son. He thinks of you that way, you know.'

I made a noise, shrugging this off.

'You almost were.' She smiled to herself. 'Maybe it's close enough for him. He has a great respect for money.'

'Then he's wrong again. I don't have any.'

She picked up her wine glass. 'Then she married for love too,' she said, not looking at me, casual, as if the phrase were a stray thought.

323

I waited a minute. 'I hope so.'

She finished her wine, then looked at the dance floor. 'It's true, you're going to America?'

I opened my hands. 'I'm American.'

'You know, if things had turned out differently – if my father had lived – I think he would have offered you a place in his business.'

'I doubt it,' I said easily. 'I don't know anything about business.'

'But I do,' she said, looking up. 'I know everything about our business. I was raised for it.'

A trumpeter stood up on the bandstand, holding a note, the end of the song. No one spoke, so that the moment seemed suspended. Giulia's eyes were still, and I felt an almost physical pull, being drawn in, like Cavallini. Making us both part of the family so things would go right. The father's daughter.

'More than Gianni did, then,' I said, trying to be light.

'No, he knew. Often he did things – because of the business,' she said, her voice remote, something she was still debating with herself.

People on the dance floor were applauding the trumpeter.

'Anyway, I'm not his son,' I said. 'So—'

'But you avenged his death,' she said quickly. 'I'm grateful for that.'

'No,' I said, shaking my head. 'Maybe Moretti's just convenient for everybody. A feather in your cousin's cap. But what if he's innocent?'

'You don't believe it's him? Why did he say he was glad, at that bar?'

'I don't know – a million reasons. Maybe he hates businessmen.'

She put her hand over mine. 'How you defend him, my father. Better than a son, maybe. You think he couldn't have betrayed this man? He could. He betrayed everybody. My mother. Everybody,' she said fiercely, almost spitting out the words. She moved her hand away and grabbed at her glass to steady herself. 'You didn't suspect? No, like me. All my life I thought he was a good man. A moral dilemma – save a partisan? Ha, once. That he tells me about. And what about the rest of it? What was he saving then? The business? Well, he saved it for me, I should be grateful, yes? I should be grateful.'

She lifted her head suddenly, as if she'd been caught talking to herself, then reached for another cigarette, something to do. For a moment I sat still, afraid I'd startle her away, then struck the match and lit it for her.

'What?' I said gently.

'It's in the notebooks.' She glanced up at Claudia and Cavallini coming towards us, only a table away.

'You figured out the gaps?'

'Yes,' she said. 'But not now. Nothing to Vittorio.'

'But if they prove Moretti didn't—'

'No, they prove he did.'

'They can't,' I said involuntarily.

She looked at me, surprised, but before either of us could say anything more the others were sitting down, the table a party again.

'I dance like an elephant,' Cavallini said, laughing at himself, and Claudia politely said no, he was good on his feet, and we all drank more wine. Claudia had given me a 'Let's go' look, but now I couldn't, not until I finished with Giulia, so I ignored it. Instead we drank, a new bottle exchanged for the old. Cavallini drummed his fingers on the table to the music. Finally Claudia got up, saying she'd promised Jim a dance, and left the table, shooting me another look. The dance was obviously a surprise to Jim, but everyone was a little drunk now and he waved a salute to me, grinning. A minute later I led Giulia on to the floor. 'These Foolish Things', slow enough to talk, my hand barely touching her back.

'What do you mean, they can't prove it?' she said, still turning this over.

I hesitated, trying to think, feeling the sweat at my hairline. 'They're Paolo's journals, aren't they? He was already dead when the house was attacked. So how could they prove anything?'

'Oh, I see. No, they don't say my father gave Moretti the medicine. But of course we know he did. Moretti said so.'

'So what do they say? You figured out the missing pages?'

She nodded. 'I found the other books.'

'But he destroyed them. Didn't you say?'

'Well, a Maglione. He gave them to Maria to be destroyed. The maid, you saw her.' Entering nervously with a phone. 'Loyal to Paolo, it turns out. Maybe the only one.'

'She read them?'

'No, she doesn't read. She can write her name, that's all.'

'But she kept them.'

'You know you forgot to take the books away, the day Vittorio called. So that night I was looking through them. The missing pages, what did they mean? And she saw me and said, would I like to see the others? My father had told her to burn them, but she thought, these are Paolo's, the history of the family, and they're not my father's to burn.' She smiled. 'He wasn't the first son. She thinks that way.'

I nodded, encouraging her to go on, but there was no reluctance now, almost a rush to get it out.

'Once I had those, it was easy enough to guess the rest. Because I know my father's businesses so well.'

'His businesses?'

'Yes, it was always about that. I don't know if that makes it better or worse. If he had believed in something – anyway, he believed in this.'

Over her shoulder I could see Claudia signalling me.

'You had to work with the government,' Giulia said. 'Everything was like that here. Licences. Friends.'

'It's like that everywhere.'

'Yes, but here it was Fascists. And then the Germans.'

'He sold arms? My mother said he didn't.'

'No, not that. One factory in Turin, it makes forks, then it makes forks for the army. Little things, not the Agnellis. Uniforms. Electrical pieces. Many things. So, the Italian army, that's one thing, it's still your country. But then the Germans come. Not your country, but you supply them too. Ha, one partisan. My wonderful father.'

'He worked with the Germans? Paolo says so?' I said, trying to keep my voice calm, finally there.

'Paolo worked with them. Paolo was perfect. The older brother. It was his name on the companies, the ones that were all ours, not just a piece. He was already friendly with them – a puppet, like everybody in the Salò government. The worse things got, the happier he is in the books. "I presented our proposal to Donati." So who is "our"? Him? No, my father. "I met with Rohrer and told Gianni that the plan had met with approval." His plan? No. So busy now, so important. Head of the family. Even his brother praises him, confides in him.'

'Uses him.'

'Yes. It's my father who's working with them. But no one knows that. They only see Paolo.'

'And kill him for it.'

She looked away for a minute, just shuffling to the music.

'I don't blame my father for that. Paolo did that to himself. I don't know, did Paolo have to do everything he did for the Germans? Help them with – whatever they asked. I think with my father it would have been different. But Paolo didn't know where to stop. He was important, he liked that. So, you know, it's his fault too. I don't blame my father.' She looked up. 'But my father did. He blamed himself. Now I understand it, how he was when Paolo died. His fault.'

'And now there was no one to run interference.'

'No. Now he had to deal with the Germans himself. It was too late to back out. If he wanted to. I don't think he did. He hated the partisans for killing Paolo. Maybe he hated the Germans too. But it was the end, they would be gone soon, and he was still safe, if he was careful. No one knew. He was a doctor, a good man. You know, when the trials came right after the war, no one even thought of him.'

I remembered Rosa at the Bauer, her face filled with excitement, a new quarry.

'Work with the Germans? That was Paolo, it all died with Paolo. So my father survived the Germans, then he survived you.'

327

She waved her hand a little, taking in the rest of the room, the Allied occupation. 'With his good name. My God, and now an American wife. And all the money. The money Paolo earned for him.' She looked down. 'Sometimes I think I should admire him. It's not so easy to survive. But then look what he did to Paolo.'

'And this is all in there? The Germans he worked with?'

'That Paolo worked with, yes. And him. I'll show you. You have to know how to read them, how the businesses are connected.' She paused. 'Are you still trying to defend him?'

'I just want to be sure.'

'You think I want this to be true? I wasn't even going to tell you about them. But it was your idea, wasn't it? Look through the papers. And what did we find? A man who sells his brother to the devil.' She paused. 'And maybe Paolo had his revenge. His friend comes to the hospital. Such a small thing, and then it starts . . .' She drifted, following the bullet that didn't stop, her chain of events, unaware that it had been an even smaller thing, a mere nod. I saw Gianni's face twisted with fury in the entrance hall, thinking I was about to ruin everything because of something so small it hadn't mattered to him.

'So this is who he was,' she said, her voice unsteady, eyes filling.

I glanced down at her. What I'd wanted to know, but not this way, making another wound.

'Part of who he was,' I said, trying to salvage something.

'Oh, because he was Papa? Well, which part do you pick? You think they're all the same, all equal?'

'No.'

'No. Those people in the house are dead. Who knows, maybe others. What part was that?'

'We still don't know he did that,' I said. 'Just because he did business with the Germans. It doesn't prove—'

But she wasn't listening. 'For me, Paolo, that's the worst. His own blood. My blood. And I never would have known. Nobody would.' She looked up. 'And nobody has to know now. Just the family. They can never put him on trial now. Moretti saved us all from that.'

For a second, the back of my neck prickling, I thought how easy it would be to let it happen, let Moretti save all of us, just by being guilty.

'But now there's his trial,' I said. 'It'll come out.'

'Not if he confesses,' she said, her eyes firm, not flinching, maybe the way they were when she talked to Cavallini. Family matters.

Mario cut in on me at the end of the song, so that both girls were now on the floor with the soldiers. Behind them, others were standing with their drinks, waiting a turn. The band, surprised to find a party, didn't even break before moving into the next number.

'Well, I'm glad for this,' Cavallini said, watching the dancers. 'I wanted to talk to you. That business at the hotel, asking questions about Signorina Grassini – I'm sorry for that. An absurdity. I assure you, not my men.'

'No? Then who?'

'I told you, some at the Questura, they're not happy about Moretti. It's politics, of course, but they don't say that.'

'So they're investigating Claudia?'

'No, no. Please don't upset yourself. Reviewing the case, they say. Going over everything. Why? A waste of time, but there's Moretti's lawyer, making trouble for them. So there has to be the pretense. Looking at everything. I tell you this because I know they called your mother.'

'In Paris?'

'Yes, such an expense. And for what? What they already knew in the report. If she mentions it, tell her it's nothing – some foolishness here, that's all. She's well?'

I nodded. 'But what do they want to know?'

'If I made a mistake, that's what. A time wrong, anything. Then they can discredit me. This is typical of the Communists. But do they find anything? No. It's just as it is in the report. No mistakes.'

'They haven't talked to me.'

'They will,' he said easily. 'This is how things are now. A man

329

who has been like a partner to us. You know, if it were up to the Questore – he knows your service. But even he . . .'

'I understand. They're just being careful.'

'Still, an inconvenience. And after all, what can you tell them? You were with me.' He laughed, a joke on the Questura.

What could I tell them? I smiled back at Cavallini, but my mind was racing, the new questions a chance, maybe, to raise doubts about Moretti, open just enough space to let him wriggle free.

Cavallini patted me on the shoulder, a kind of reassurance. 'Well, it's a question of patience. I tell you frankly, though, I don't like these delays. The longer it goes on, the more this boy becomes a symbol. I told the Questore, we should move him. Jesolo, maybe Verona, a facility somewhere out of sight. As long as he's in Venice, the parties throw him at each other. This is a crime, not politics. And look how people use it. Well, here come the ladies.'

But they came trailing suitors, so there was another dance before they sat down and another round of drinks before I could rescue Claudia by asking her to dance.

'If you don't take me home, I'm going to scream,' she said in my ear.

'I thought you were having a good time,' I teased.

'No. You're having a good time. All your favourite people. The police. The wonderful Giulia. You think no one can see you, with your heads like that? So much to talk about.'

'All right, just a few more minutes.'

'What do you talk about, anyway?' she said. 'Her father?'

'Actually, she was offering me a job.'

'What?' she said, the word catching in her throat, the beginning of a giggle.

'In the Maglione businesses.'

'A job? His daughter offers you a job?' she said, shaking now.

'Ssh,' I said, but she pulled back, putting her hand to her mouth, laughing, then gulping, her eyes shiny, and I realised that she was tipping out of control, pushed by drink and tension to somewhere easier, funnier.

330

'His daughter? His daughter wants to give you money? A reward?'

'Ssh, they'll hear you.'

'What about me? Do I get something too?'

I pulled her close to me. 'Stop it. Go to the ladies' room – put some water on your face. I'll get your coat.'

'And go?'

I nodded, my face against hers. 'Just don't say anything. Understand?'

'I know what job. Son-in-law. Ha, too late.'

'Claudia—'

'I know. Ssh.' She put her finger to her lips.

I got her off the floor to the ladies' room, then stood outside for a second, shaken. Wasn't this the way it always happened? All the answers, the cross-checked times, destroyed in a careless moment? I went over to the table for her coat.

'Sorry, but we'd better go.'

'She's all right?' Giulia said.

'A little too much to drink, that's all.'

'I'll go see if—' she said, getting up.

'No, it's fine. Goodnight. And thank you,' I said, taking her hand, looking directly at her, our secret.

'Yes, but I am the one who pays,' Cavallini said smoothly, a smile in his voice. He held up his hand before I could say anything. 'No, I insist. A wedding gift. Here, let me tell the *cameriere*.' He led me away from the table, ostensibly to find the waiter but really to move out of earshot. 'You see how remarkable she is. After losing a father.'

But I wasn't thinking about Giulia. I looked towards the ladies' room door, wondering what was happening inside. Was she talking to someone? Being sick? My forehead felt moist again, nervous sweat.

'And now more trouble. But at least we can protect her from this.'

'Protect her?' I said, distracted.

331

'This investigation – your Rosa. We had to start there, yes, but now it's of no importance. He takes the medicine, he blames Gianni. What else matters?' I looked at him. Already making sure it went right. 'These suspicions about Gianni. Imagine how it would hurt her.' He nodded towards the table where Giulia, alone, was lighting another cigarette.

'But the defense is bound to bring it up. They'd have to.'

'Well, if there is a trial.' What neither of them wanted now. 'Let's hope, for her sake . . .'

He let the rest of the thought float towards the table. She was looking out through the smoke at the band, and suddenly I saw her as she would be, one of the ladies sitting alone at Harry's or Florian's. Rich, attended by Cavallini or someone like him, a curiosity, finally, for the tourists. How long would it take? Years, one layer of money at a time, the way varnish is spread over a painting to fix the colours. I squinted, as if I were really looking into crystal, waiting for the blur to clear, show me my own future, but nothing appeared, just Giulia sitting alone at Florian's.

'These trials,' Cavallini was saying. 'Who wins but the lawyers? You're surprised I would say this? But I've seen it many times. One question, then another, something that doesn't matter to the crime, and now it's public. An embarrassment, worse. A reputation ruined – I have seen this – and for what? Think of Signorina Grassini – excuse me, Signora Miller.' He smiled, tipping his head slightly.

I turned to him, confused, not sure what connection he was making. 'Claudia?'

He put his hand on my arm. 'These are simple people, in the Questura. The obvious, that's all they can see. In the end, what comes of it? Nothing. But meanwhile, it's a trial, so they bring up everything.'

'Like what?'

'Excuse me, I don't say this myself. I know she had a difficult time in that camp. And then to have to talk about it.'

'But why would she?'

'The way Vanessi died – you understand, these are simple

people. Everything to them is suspicious. Of course, nothing was ever proven. But still they ask their stupid questions. Do they know how the person feels, to talk about this?' He gripped my arm more tightly. 'A woman who has suffered that way. To talk about it, that's not justice. That's Rosa's justice. Forgive me. It's only my concern for you, how you will feel, if your wife—'

He stopped, as if enough had been said and anything more would overstep. I felt his hand, the message behind the words, literally strong-arming me, but to do what? Talk to Rosa? Get her to make Moretti confess? Did he really think that was possible, really think Moretti had done it? Or did it matter any more? I stared at him, unable to reply, alarmed that Claudia had been discussed at the Questura. Simple people. The way Vanessi died.

'Ah, there you are,' Cavallini said to Claudia as she came out. 'You're feeling well?'

I glanced over, worried, but she was clear-eyed, herself again.

'Yes, fine. A little tired.' She moved towards the coat I held up. 'Thank you for the wine,' she said to Cavallini.

'An honour.' He bowed.

We were standing near the bar, the way out, and Cavallini's gesture caught the eye of a young Italian sitting on one of the stools. He made a sound to his friends, who laughed. Cavallini turned. 'Eh,' he said, a polite warning, as if he were in uniform, not a double-breasted jacket.

'*Il conte, permesso,*' the kid said, sweeping his hand in front of him.

Cavallini said something quickly in Italian, which made the group laugh, probably because it was the cartoon response they'd expected, pompous and middle-aged.

'Hey, you're not going?' Mario, with Jim and a few others.

'Yes. It was nice to see you. Good luck.'

The Italian at the bar said something to his friends, obviously a wisecrack, because Cavallini snapped his head around and told him to behave himself.

'What about us? Don't we get a dance?' one of the other GIs said. 'I mean, who else are we going to dance with?'

'Give it a rest, Lenny.' Mario winked at us, excusing him. 'Four drinks and he's the Rockettes.'

'Come on, babe, one turn around the floor. Souvenir of Venice.'

He moved forwards, reaching for Claudia, but Jim stepped in between and put a restraining arm around his shoulders. 'Next time, Lenny.' Behind us, the Italian group started laughing again.

'Hey, he's all right,' Lenny's friend said to Jim. 'Let him have a turn, what the hell.'

'The lady's leaving,' Jim said, holding up his other hand.

'The lady's leaving,' the young Italian said in English to his friends, in a mock singsong, then sputtered something in Italian, clearly obscene, and laughed.

I felt it before I saw it, a rush of air next to me, Cavallini's arm shooting out, pushing the Italian off his stool and pinning him against the wall by the throat. Claudia jumped, but the rest of us froze, stunned by the animal speed of it, then the angry growl of words.

'Hey!' One of the GIs stepped forwards, but Jim put his arms out, blocking everybody, not sure what was happening.

Cavallini said something more in Italian, his voice low with contempt, then raised his free hand and slapped the kid, strik-ing his face so that one side turned, then the other. The Italians on the stools didn't move. The GIs now looked confused – not a bar fight, something else, a practised brutality, official. What had been there all along, behind walls, the rubber hoses and castor oil and boots, what he really was. Claudia gasped. Some heads turned, drawn by the crash of the bar stool, and the band faltered for a second, as if a shot had gone off. Then Cavallini lowered his hand, grabbing the kid by the shirt instead, and said something. He waited for him to nod before he moved him over to an empty stool and threw him on it, limp, a laundry bag, and took his hand away. When he turned to us, his face was blank.

'He excuses himself,' he said to Claudia, his voice even, but for

334

another second no one moved and I just stared, unsettled, seeing him now as clearly as I'd seen Giulia's future.

We said our goodbyes and then for a while didn't say anything, walking through the quiet calles to the Accademia bridge.

'I've never seen him like that,' I said, still rattled.

'He's police,' she said simply.

'Was the kid being fresh?'

'Yes, my honour was at stake,' she said, sarcastic. 'So he beats him. Your friend. And you trust this man. Did you see? Like a hawk.' Her arm flashed out. 'Snatch. And it's over.'

We stopped at the top of the bridge to look down the Grand Canal, bright tonight with the full moon. Even the Palazzo Dario, usually dark, flickered with light reflecting off the marble and old glass.

'He'll snatch us if we stay,' she said, her tone like a counterweight to the view, dark and smoky as the club.

I didn't answer for a minute, then shook my head. 'No, he has what he wants. But now he doesn't know what to do with him. He doesn't want to put him on trial – he doesn't want anything to come out about Gianni.'

She turned to me. 'Then what does he want?'

'He wants him to confess, and of course he won't. How can he? So now what?'

'They can make him confess.'

'Not any more. They'd never get away with that now. Besides, he's got protection – not everybody there thinks he did it. Cavallini calls it office politics, but where does that leave him? He's got himself in a box. Sooner or later he's got to do something.'

'Look for someone else,' she said quietly.

'Then he looks like a fool for arresting Moretti in the first place. But the others are talking to people again.'

'At the hotel,' she said, worried.

'Everybody. He said they called my mother. We're next, I guess. So we'd better be prepared.'

'Not like tonight, you mean. I know, it was wrong to laugh. You don't think—'

335

'No, he thought you were a little tipsy, that's all. Okay now?'

'They're coming again,' she said, raising her shoulders, a kind of tremor. 'More questions. What if I forget?'

'You won't forget. We don't *know*. We were at Mimi's, that's all. Just as long as we tell the same story.'

She looked down at the water. 'Nothing's changed, has it?' she said, fingering her ring, twisting it. 'We can still give each other away. Look at tonight – one slip. Oh, I know, not in court,' she said, stopping me before I could interrupt. 'But that's not everything, is it? What about the rest? We can still give each other away.'

'But we won't. We'll go over everything again. No surprises. By the way, what did Cavallini mean about Vanessi – that was the man at the camp? How did he die?'

'How did he die?' she said, as if she hadn't quite heard, or needed a second to think. 'I told you, he was killed.'

'Killed how?'

'He talked about this? Cavallini asked you about this?' She clutched my arm. 'Why did he ask this?'

'He thought it would embarrass you to talk about it. If it came up at the trial.'

'Why would it come up?' she said, clutching more tightly.

'If it did.'

'No, something else. He's going to bring it up. They never believed me.'

'Never believed what?'

'I knew it. I knew they wouldn't stop. A man who killed hundreds of people. But his death they have to solve. Not the others, just his. Nothing changes.'

Her eyes were darting now, as fierce as her grip on my arm, the way they had been at the engagement party when she rushed at Gianni. I stood still, watching her, afraid of what was coming.

'They suspected you?'

'Who else? His whore.'

'Why didn't you tell me? If they suspected you – I have to know these things. So we have the same story.'

336

'Why do we need a story? Do you think I did it?'

I said nothing, waiting.

She grabbed both my arms. 'Do you? Do you think that? No, don't bother. I can see it.'

'I didn't mean— I just have to know. In case.'

She lowered her head. 'You think it's possible.'

'I didn't say that.'

'And it is, isn't it? We know it is, both of us.' She nodded, pretending to laugh. 'My wedding day. Well, my father doesn't have to see this either. My husband, so in love with me that—' She stopped, moving away from me, touching the bridge. 'You're right, we need the same story. Which one do you want?'

'The one you want us to tell,' I said, looking at her.

'No, you pick. Here's one – this is the one the police would prefer. We're in Modena, in his flat. In bed. When he's asleep, I take a knife from under the bed and stab him. No, better. He's not asleep. He's inside me. So of course he never suspects when I reach for the knife.'

'Stop it.'

'You don't like it? They would, though. They always wanted it to be me.'

'Tell me the other one.'

'I came back to the flat and he was lying there with the knife in him. Who did it? Anybody. Think how many would want to.'

'You were staying there?'

'Yes, so I was the obvious one. No alibi. Like Moretti. No ball to go to that time. But no proof, either. And if it's me, then everything comes out about him – what he did in the camp, why they hadn't turned him over. They were supposed to do that. But they didn't want a trial. Like Cavallini. How they stick together in the end.'

'But what were you doing there? I don't understand.'

'How was it possible to stay with him after the camp? How could I do it?' she said slowly, as if someone else had asked the question. Then she shrugged. 'Where was I supposed to go? The soldiers come and open the camp and what's their idea? Another camp. Refugees. Then where do we go? Back to what? My father's dead, everyone. I knew I could get money there. What was the difference, I was already a whore. And now it's all upside down, now he's afraid people will come for *him*, afraid of me even, that I would give him away. You know the Allies always wanted the people at the camps – not the Magliones, just people like him. So it ends up that I protect him. I don't say anything. Maybe I felt I owed something to him – he saved my life. I had to pay, but he did it. Anyway, I went there. And do you know what? He wouldn't give me any money. He said he would, but always later, another time. He wanted it to be like the camp again. A prisoner. It excited him, I think, if I was a prisoner. So I had to take the money after.'

'After?'

'After he was killed. I hid it, so the police never knew. I *walked* out of Modena. I didn't want them to know I had any money. I thought they'd arrest me if I paid for the train. So maybe they said it was a robbery, I don't know. I thought, That's the end of it. But I knew it wouldn't be. And now look how perfect. Link one with the other. If she can do one, she can do the other.'

'But they can't prove you did it.'

'What does it matter? They can't prove Moretti did it – in fact, he *didn't* – and they still want to hang him. Who had a better motive than me? I'm glad he's dead.' She stopped. 'Oh, that's what the boy said, isn't it? In the bar. So now we're the same.'

'Nobody's accusing you. They would have done it then.'

'Maybe your friend Cavallini gives them new ideas. It's easy to believe.' She looked up. 'You believed it.'

'Why didn't you tell me before?'

'What? That it was even worse? That I was worse? I went to him. How do you tell somebody these things? Maybe I wanted you to think—' She came over and touched my arm, then glanced at a couple passing on the bridge and let her hand fall. 'Well, that was before. So what do we tell Cavallini? What story?'

'We don't have to tell him anything. There's no link.'

'I'm the link. I've always been the link – one murder to the other.'

338

'There's no connection to Gianni.'

'No, not at first. At first he's just missing. Then killed. Who knows why? But then you help them. You have to know. So now he works with the Germans, like Vanessi. Now he's someone I would kill.' She took my arm, pressing the point. 'Someone I did kill.'

I moved to the right, blocking her from the others on the bridge. 'Somebody will hear.'

'Oh,' she said, flinging up her hand, 'everybody hears me but you.'

She turned away and walked fast down the other side, so that we were in the campo next to the Accademia before I caught up to her and took her by the shoulders.

'Listen. He believes it happened just the way we said it did. We were there, at Mimi's. With him. He's part of the story. He's not looking at us.'

She put her hand on my chest. 'Then why don't we go before he does? To New York. We'd be safe there.'

'We are safe. As long as we're together.'

'No. At first I thought that. Now maybe it's worse. Can I leave? Not alone. Just married and she leaves? So we stay, and every day they get closer. We're together, but we're not safer. She killed Vanessi, why not Maglione?' She held up her left hand, showing me the ring. 'You think this protects me?'

'No, I protect you.'

'Why? Because I can tell them about you?'

I looked at her, my face suddenly warm. 'But you can't,' I said slowly. 'Neither can I. That's the point. We protect each other.' I turned slightly, away from her eyes, glancing back at the canal. In the light from the bridge you could see the waterline on the building, the mortar dark and pitted, eaten away bit by bit. 'We can't let this fall apart. Do you understand?'

She said nothing, then slowly nodded.

'All right. Come on,' I said. I reached over to take her hand, but she pulled away and walked alone, not saying anything until we'd crossed San Ivo and reached the sluggish back canal. The restaurant on the

339

other side of the bridge had already closed, and there were no lights in the windows, just a streetlamp at either end and the bright moon.

'Is this where she saw me?'

'Yes.'

'Coming to find you. To think, if I had waited at the hotel—' She looked up. 'So maybe she's watching tonight too. Somebody's always watching us now. Which one, do you think?'

I cocked my head at the window. 'She's not. It's dark.'

'Maybe she sits in the dark.'

We kept walking. 'Well, now she can't see anyway. Not this far down. She didn't see which way Gianni turned.'

'Like this,' she said, pretending to turn left at the end. 'But not this way.' She turned towards Ca' Venti. 'Why not? How does Cavallini know he turned that way?'

'Because it's the only way that makes sense to him.'

'And one day he says, "What if?". And he goes this way.' She started down the calle. 'To us.' She grabbed the air with one hand. 'Snatch. And will we be safe then? Together?'

I stopped. 'We can't walk away. We can't let someone hang for this.'

'You'll never save that boy. Don't you know that? A man like that,' she said, clutching her hand, Cavallini again, 'he doesn't let go. He has his victim. What are you going to give him instead? A story?'

I turned away. 'I don't know. Let's wait to hear from Frankfurt. Gianni didn't deal directly with the Germans – there was always a go-between. So maybe there's something.'

'Something what? This boy is here, right now. You want to save him? Then you have to give them someone else to hang. Another body.' She took my hands. 'Whose blood do you want on them? Mine?' She held them in front of me, her hands locked around my wrists, and for a second I couldn't breathe, trapped in the hermetic logic of it. Someone else.

I shook my head. 'But not his either.'

'Then whose? Whose would be acceptable to you?' She dropped my hands. 'Who are you going to give them?'

'Nobody,' I said, but quietly, not wanting to hear myself, knowing as I said it that she was right, that Cavallini would never settle
for another mystery now, with the taste of blood in his mouth.
He'd want a body. But he already had one. Our perfect alibi. All
we had to do was let it happen. I felt something jump in me, my
skin hot. Worse than murder.

'You can't save him.'

'We have to.'

'We have to save ourselves.'

'You don't mean that. You're just—' I started to walk, then
stopped again and waited until she was next to me. 'You don't
mean that,' I repeated. 'We can't live that way.'

'How do you think people live?'

'In Fossoli. Not out here.'

'Where it's so different.'

I said nothing for a moment, looking at her, then nodded. 'It has
to be. You think no one's watching? We are. We're watching. Or
we have to pretend someone is. Otherwise, you're right, there's no
difference. Fossoli, out here, it's all the same then. Is that what you
want?'

'And what if it is all the same? Then what?'

'I'm not going to let him die. I can't,' I said, an end to it.

'Then somebody else will,' she said. 'It's started now. Somebody
will.'

I didn't answer, hot again, trapped back where we'd started.
Somebody would. A cat slunk by, mewling, the only sound.

We turned into the last calle, with the house door at the
end. She slowed as we got near, dragging her feet. I turned the
latchkey, the one that worked, not the ornate one near the
knob. Angelina had left two table lamps on near the stairs,
but otherwise the hall was in shadow, all the sconces dark. A
bottle of champagne was chilling in a silver bucket on the side
table, Angelina's idea for our wedding night. But Claudia was
looking down the hall, her arms crossed over her chest, rocking a little.

341

'Let's not stay here,' she said, still in the doorway. 'Not tonight. Let's go somewhere else.'

I turned to her. 'We have to stay here,' I said, touching her shoulder. 'How would it look?'

She slumped for a minute, then straightened. 'That's right, I forgot. We stay here and wait. Until he turns the wrong way. Except that it's the right way.'

'Ssh. Angelina's upstairs.'

'And we'll be here. Waiting. We can show him where.' She pointed towards the water gate. 'We can look at it every day while we're waiting.'

'It's okay,' I said, stroking her shoulder. 'It's not for long. You'll get used to it.'

Her shoulder moved under my hand, almost a spasm, as if she had started to laugh but caught it before she could be heard. I pressed down, feeling the shaking, not laughter, but she stepped away from me, walked over to the ice bucket and picked at the foil over the cork. 'She left champagne. We should open it. She'll be offended.' Her fingers stopped, resting on the foil. 'I thought you were something new in my life. A new life. Now look where we are.' She turned, looking at me. 'A new prison.

I stood still, suddenly afraid that she had seen what I couldn't, our piece of the crystal.

'It's not like that,' I said.

She looked at me for another minute, as if she had something else to say, then gave it up and turned back to the bucket.

'Close the door,' she said.

I reached behind me to push, and because I didn't hold it, the heavy weight of the wood swung away from me, slamming shut with a clang that sounded like metal, loud enough to echo down the hall.

CHAPTER SEVENTEEN

'THEY'RE GOING TO kill him,' Rosa said. 'That's what it means.'

'What, shot trying to escape? Come on, Rosa.'

We were walking on the waterfront of the Giudecca, heading towards Redentore, somewhere public but out of the way, Rosa's request. She had called from a cafe to arrange the meeting, convinced now that her Bauer phone was tapped.

'You're imagining things.'

'I don't have time to argue with you. The minute I heard, I knew what it meant. There's no reason to move him. You think there's something wrong with the jail in Venice?'

'Cavallini said he was becoming a symbol.'

'Of what? Their incompetence? They have no case, they know that. So they have to win some other way. It's what the Germans used to do. Something happens on the way. Or there's someone in the new place, a grudge they didn't know about. *Fut.*' She waved her fingers.

'You're serious.'

'They're going to kill him,' she said, stopping and turning to me, her voice steady, certain.

I said nothing, waiting.

'They're moving him tomorrow night,' she said, starting to walk again.

'You know this?'

'A bird told me. To Vicenza, by train. So it's difficult. The station's a trap, and once he's on the train . . . A car would be easier. There are possibilities between Piazzale Roma and Vicenza. Even Piazzale Roma would be better – there are several ways out – but no, it's the train.'

'Possibilities for what? What are you planning to do, kidnap him?'

'I'm not going to let them kill him. So it's necessary, an action,' she said, slightly excited, back in the game.

'Are you serious? They really will kill him then. Trying to escape. You'll be setting him up.'

'Listen to me. They *are* going to kill him. You have to understand that. So this is his only chance now. Do you think we're amateurs? We did this many, many times.'

'During the war.'

'His father was killed. It's enough for one family. I want the son to live.'

'Why are you telling me this?'

'Because you're going to help.'

'Me?'

'Yes. You owe him this much. Both of us. This never would have started if we hadn't— Well, that's done.' She raised her eyes. 'But there is an obligation here.'

'Rosa, I was in the army, not the commandos. A paper pusher.'

'So sometimes you leave the desk. It's not enough, files. We can't save him with files.'

'Rosa, the war's over. Over.'

'Not for him.'

'Christ.' I turned away, exasperated.

'I'm not asking you to take any risk,' she said, her voice softer now. 'Just leave a door open.'

'A door open.'

'Yours. On the canal.'

'Then what am I supposed to do?'

'Nothing. You won't be there. There is no risk to you.'

'A little commando raid, but no risk.'

'For your piece, no. But I need someone I can trust. You're not one of us, in the group. You don't even know who we are. So you can't betray us. I have to be careful of that.'

'I know you.'

'And you'd betray me?' She shook her head. 'Then you betray Moretti. No.' She looked at me again. 'I know you a little. There is an obligation here. We have to save him.' I looked away. His only chance. Just leave a door open. 'I can do this without you, but no one suspects you. No one *thinks* to suspect you. An American. So it's perfect.'

'Perfect,' I said. 'All worked out.'

But she didn't hear any irony in my voice. 'It's important to plan,' she said.

'And after I open the door?'

She said nothing.

'I stick my neck out, but no questions,' I said.

'You're not sticking it out very far. It's for your protection.'

'I'd like to know what I'm getting into, at least. Since I seem to be in it.'

She looked at me. 'Then it's agreed?'

'Not yet.'

She nodded. 'Come, see the church.' She took my arm, starting up the broad Palladian steps. 'But no names. I can tell you what will happen, your part. But it's better if you don't know the rest.'

'All right. So they put him on a train,' I said, beginning.

'Yes. Think how difficult. The police boat to the station is impossible. Look at the route. Canale di Cannaregio, always crowded. The station? A cul-de-sac, you can't get out. So the first likely place, they think, is Maestre. Over the bridge. And they'll be prepared. After that, there's only Padua, no other stops.'

'But there's Vicenza itself. They'll have to put him in a car there.'

'Yes, it was my first thought. So their first thought too, no? Ha, the city of Palladio. Maybe that's why I thought of this place,' she said, opening the doors.

The inside was stark white, unadorned, something rare in Venice, architecture left alone. Rosa dipped her fingers in a font, crossed herself, then took a pew in the back. An old woman was arranging gladioli in vases on the altar, but otherwise the nave was empty, a perfect meeting place. For a second I wondered if it was one of those churches where voices gathered at the ceiling and then swirled down to some listening spot behind a pillar, but Rosa, suspicious of the Bauer, seemed unconcerned here. She lowered her voice but didn't whisper.

'And what if Vicenza's too late? You understand, we don't know when they'll do it – a few days, right away, we don't know. And the train worries me. So easy to fall off. And people might believe it, not like in a car. Who jumps out of a car?' Her voice fast, caught up in it. War stories.

'Do you really believe this?'

'Cavallini doesn't want a trial. You told me yourself.'

'To protect the Maglione name.'

'Because he'll lose. The name is disgraced *and* he loses. A double loss. So, another solution. One he knows. Another thing he learned from the Germans. You think it's the first time for him?'

I thought of the arm shooting out to the boy's throat.

'I know him a little too. So,' she said, already moving past it, 'Vicenza, maybe it's too late. Maybe everywhere it's too late. The best thing is if he never leaves Venice.'

'But they'll have people in the station.'

'Yes,' she said, her voice eager, 'but not in the yards. *We* have people in the yards. A signal delay. Once the train's over the bridge, he's gone, but in the yards – there's no one but the guards on the train.'

'How long will you have?'

'A few minutes. But after, if we make the boat, then we have the advantage. The police will be out front, in the Grand Canal. By the time they get behind the station, we're already gone.'

'To Maestre.'

'One boat, yes,' she said, her eyes bright, watching my reaction.

'Where they expect to follow. Another where they don't expect – back to Venice.'

'A reverse. Like a football play.'

'Yes? I don't know.'

'And then what?'

'And then we get off the water. We have to expect by this time the alarm is made, all the boats are out. Police boats are fast, they can outrun almost anything. So they chase to Maestre, they chase somewhere else, looking, but there's nothing to see. The fox has gone into his hole.'

'At Ca' Venti.'

She spread her hands. '*Ecco.*'

'With the boat parked out front?'

'No, of course not. We don't even tie up. We don't need long, just enough time to drop him off. The boat keeps going; he stays in the hole. Then, later, another boat comes, one the police have never seen.'

'And if they do catch the first?'

'What do they catch? Only the driver.'

'And meanwhile they've lost the scent and the new boat takes the fox—'

'Somewhere else.'

'That I won't know.'

'Nobody knows. Just your piece. The first boat doesn't know the second boat. No one can betray anyone. Not this time.'

'You don't need Ca' Venti to make the switch. You could do it anywhere in Venice.'

She raised her eyebrows. 'Not so many of us have our own canal entrance. I told you, no one suspects you. If we use one of our own people, maybe the police have a list. They'll look. But nobody looks for you. Besides, the house is convenient, close to the channel.'

'You've already been there.'

'Rio di Fornace, yes,' she said, precise. 'Two ends. One the Grand Canal, the other Giudecca channel. Two exits, not a trap.'

'Not busy, either. Not at that hour. A boat might be noticed.' I thought of us looking at the bedroom light across the canal, afraid to make a splash.

'Yes, I know. Just leave the water gate unlocked. It takes a minute. There's nothing to make people look. And you'll be out.'

'Where?'

'A restaurant, anywhere people will see you. You don't know anything about it. You weren't there. You didn't think to lock the gate, that's all. You don't know.'

'Do you think they'd believe that?'

'No,' she said, smiling faintly. 'But nothing will go wrong. They're not expecting this. And if we think the police are right behind us, we don't stop. I give you my word.'

'And what about Angelina?'

'Who?'

'The maid. She lives there.'

'*Che bella*. The problems of the rich. Give her the night off.'

I started to smile, in spite of myself, then stopped. Out for the evening. No risk. The plan already in motion, whether I helped or not.

'Do you want to save his life?'

'Yes,' I said, nodding, suddenly believing it would happen, Moretti safe, Claudia and I happy again, maybe on the train he never took.

'Then just leave the gate unlocked. Come on, she's finished with the flowers.'

She got up, crossing herself again, and turned to the door before the woman could see her. Outside, she pulled her sweater tighter, an automatic reflex even in the warm spring air.

'What's going to happen to him?' I said.

'We'll hide him until it's safe. Who knows, maybe they'll find the one who did it.'

'Maybe,' I said, glancing away. 'And if not?'

'Then he becomes someone else. Anyway, he's alive.' She stopped at the foot of the steps and looked across the channel.

'You can see it from here, the house. It's a good plan, yes?'

'I hope so. It's your neck.'

She brushed this away. 'It's an old neck. He's just a boy. And to carry this burden now, blaming himself. How I wish I'd never talked to him.'

'But we were right. If that means anything to you. Gianni *was* working with the Germans.'

'Yes?' she said, not really interested. Yesterday's files.

'His brother kept papers, it turns out. Giulia has them. Gianni was friendly long before he turned up at Villa Raspelli. Business partners.'

'Business partners,' she said, dismissing this.

'And then more, after Paolo was killed. When he found out Moretti had been one of you—' I stopped, backing away from her husband, what must have happened next, but her mind had gone elsewhere, still Herr Kroger with files.

'These papers, you can get them?'

'No. Anyway, he's dead. They're no use to us now, except to know.'

'But there must be others. People he mentions, Italians. We need—'

'She'd burn them first. It's her family. I thought you didn't care any more about Gianni.'

'Him, no. But the others? Not care? Do you know what's happening in Italy? No, an American, all you see is this.' She spread her arm to the view. 'Not what's really here. You think the Fascists have gone away? No, back again, the same people. Back where they were, head of the table. Magliones. The Church. My God, the Church.' She waved her hand, the same fingers that had just dipped in holy water, made a quick cross at the pew. 'The Germans' friends. "We did nothing. *Patrioti.*" And soon everyone will believe it again. All *patrioti*. Trials? That's all in the past. And then it's too late. I don't have time for a dead man, but the living? To get just one more?' She lowered her voice. 'She told you about them. She'll let you read them?'

'Yes.'

349

She nodded. 'Good. Just get the names. I'll do the rest.' She glanced up, sensing my reluctance. 'You asked me once to look at files for you.'

'Another obligation.'

'To me? No. You know what these people are. You saw it in Germany.'

'That was different.'

'Yes? Imagine if it were your country – what would you do?'

I stared at her for a minute, a bulky figure in a sweater, still in combat, then looked away.

'I'd get the names,' I said.

'So. You married an Italian. You're not a tourist any more.'

'*A patriota.*'

She smiled. 'A real one.' She nodded her head towards the vaporetto approaching the landing. 'You go first. I have some business here.'

'On the Giudecca?'

She wagged her finger. 'Just your piece. Unlock the gate.' Then, before I could turn towards the dock, she put a hand on my shoulder, soft as the air, a thank-you. 'And the names.'

We could have spent the evening anywhere – Harry's, Montin's – but I got the idea of asking for Gianni's seats at La Fenice because it gave me an excuse to go to Ca' Maglione and look at Paolo's journals. I had planned to spend the afternoon, but I arrived to find Cavallini there having tea, a surprise visit, and Giulia edgy, handing me the tickets with an expression that said the library was now out of the question. Another day.

'One minute and I will walk with you,' Cavallini said, holding up a finger.

Giulia gave me a wry 'Your turn' look. Then there was a fuss in the hall about his hat and more goodbyes, so it was five minutes before we were finally out on the street, walking to Santo Stefano.

'What is on tonight?' he said.

'*La Boheme.*'

'Ah, romantic. For the newlyweds.'

'You like opera?' I said, marking time, eager to be away.

'My wife enjoys it. Perhaps you'll see her tonight.'

'But not you?'

'No, not tonight. Work.'

'So late?'

'A special assignment.'

I waited, but he said nothing. We crossed a bridge into a narrow calle smelling of garbage and mould.

'Sometimes, you know, I think it's time to leave the police. Business maybe, a position.'

'I thought you enjoyed it.'

'Yes, when you're young. You don't worry about anything then. But now you think, what if? Maybe tonight it's your turn.'

'I thought there wasn't any crime in Venice.'

'Before, no. A few robberies, like anywhere. But now, since the war, such violence. Think of Maglione, murdered. All these animosities, they don't go away.'

'It takes time,' I said blandly, letting him lead.

'Yes, how long? The war teaches them to fight. Then how do you make them stop? It's in the blood, an excitement. The law? Something to shoot at. They forget,' he said, opening his jacket to show me a gun in a side holster, 'we were in the war too.'

I froze, staring at the gun, dark and bulky, something he hadn't carried before. Why now? Even in the dim calle, the dull steel drew the eye, an almost hypnotic pull, ready to jump at you if you looked away.

'You're expecting trouble?'

'In the police, we're always expecting trouble,' he said, official again.

'But you never carry a gun.'

'Yes, sometimes. But it ruins the suit.' He brushed his hand down the side, showing the bulge the holster made, then looked over at me and smiled. 'It worries you, the gun?' He put his hand on my shoulder, leading me towards the campo. 'No, I'm an excellent shot.'

'But why today?'

He shrugged. 'If there's trouble, you're prepared.'

'You mean there's going to be? What?'

'Let the police worry.'

'But how do you know?'

'Signor Miller,' he said indulgently, 'there are many ears in Venice. It has always been so, a tradition. Everyone listens. So I know when to be ready,' he said as we walked into the campo. 'Sometimes it's good, a little trouble. People show themselves. They come up out of the ground, they show their faces. You can see who they are.' He squinted at the cafés with umbrellas out against the spring sun, as if he were looking for them now. 'But it's true I'm getting old for this. Guns, at my age. One night – you never know. Well, don't worry,' he said, amused at the look on my face. 'We'll be ready. You go to *La Bohème*.'

I said nothing, afraid to press, hoping he'd volunteer more, but he became withdrawn again, not so much discreet as preoccupied with something. He looked back for a second before we left the square.

'You know, a girl like that, all alone now – she may never marry. And then who looks out for her? Of course she has the protection of her family. But so many responsibilities,' he said, thinking out loud, the gun forgotten.

I didn't know how to bring it up again without being obvious, so I let him talk about Giulia, not really listening, too nervous to pay attention. He knew. At least one of Rosa's pieces had failed her. More than one? The one that led to Ca' Venti? The important thing now was to let her know before anyone showed his face, walked into Cavallini's waiting hands. I glanced again at the bulge near his breast pocket, ready.

There were more goodbyes when I turned off for the traghetto. I waited, counting off seconds, then went back to the calle to make sure he had kept going, finally spotting his head in the crowd moving towards San Marco. A few minutes later I followed, far enough behind to be out of sight.

I was halfway across Campo San Moise to the hotel entrance when it occurred to me that if Cavallini knew anything at all, he'd have somebody watching the Bauer. I stopped and turned, pretending to look at the church but scanning the rest of the square. A café at the other end would probably have a phone. I could get her to come down without having to show myself in the lobby.

After a few rings, the operator asked if I wanted to leave a message. I hung up. What if she never came back? But there was nowhere else to reach her and the café had a clear sightline to the hotel, so I ordered a coffee and stood at the window to wait. She hadn't checked out. Maybe she was planning a routine afternoon, as blameless as an evening at La Fenice. I had another coffee. A small group of tourists stopped to take pictures of San Moise, kneeling and shooting up to get the full effect of the grimy rococo swirls. I craned slightly to the left, around them, afraid I'd miss her. A man at the other end of the window counter looked at me, then quickly went back to his book. Why did I assume the police would be in the lobby – why not here, with a good view of the door? There was no other way out of the Bauer except the gondola landing. I looked around. Why hadn't I brought a newspaper? No one stood for this long looking out a window unless he was waiting for somebody. A meeting the man couldn't miss, just glancing up from his book.

After another cigarette I decided to play it safe and leave, but just as I turned I saw Claudia coming into the square, carrying a wrapped box. I dropped my head, a reflex. The last person I wanted to see.

'I don't want any part of it,' she'd said when I told her Rosa's plan yesterday.

'You won't have any part of it. Neither will I. We won't be here.'

353

'And you believe her? A crazy woman.'

'She knows what she's doing. It's what she did in the war. If any-body can get him away—'

'Yes, and when he's gone, then where do they look?'

'We'll be out somewhere. No connection.'

'Another alibi,' she'd said, turning away but dropping it, tired of arguing. After that, neither of us mentioned it.

The man with the book now looked at me again. I had to be waiting for somebody, even somebody I didn't want to see. I rapped a coin on the window, making Claudia turn her head.

'What are you doing here?' she said after I'd kissed her, made a show of getting another coffee.

'Not too loud. I think he's police,' I said, moving my eyes towards the other end of the window. She glanced over, startled. 'It's okay. Just have coffee with me, I'll explain it later. What's in the box?'

'Lace,' she said vaguely, still distracted by the man. 'A special order, at the Europa. Why police? What are you doing?'

'Waiting for Rosa. I have to warn her.'

She stared at me.

'Drink the coffee.'

'Warn her. And then they'll see you together. And me. I told you I didn't— I'm leaving.'

But just then the man closed his book and started going through his pockets for change. After dropping a few coins in the saucer, he headed for the door.

'See if he goes to the Bauer,' I said, my back to the window, not wanting to turn around.

'No. San Marco.'

'Then there must be someone in the lobby.'

She looked at me, disturbed. 'Are you crazy now too?'

'Somebody has to be watching. They know.'

'They know? And you're waiting for her?'

'She has to call it off.'

'They'll see you with her.'

'We just happened to run into each other. Had a coffee. That's all.'

Claudia moved to leave, but I put my hand on her arm, holding her.

'We have to tell her,' I said. 'She'd be walking into a trap.'

'Oh, but not us.' She looked down at her coffee. 'How long have you been here? If they're watching—'

'I say I was waiting for you.' I glanced at my watch. 'Just give it a few more minutes. She has to come back sometime.'

But we had finished another coffee before Claudia finally looked over my shoulder and nodded. '*Ecco. La brigadiera.*'

Rosa was coming over the bridge, improbably, with a shopping bag. I hurried out. An accidental meeting.

'You've been shopping?' I said, a public voice, then under it, 'I have to talk to you. Cavallini knows.'

'What?' she said, surprised at my being there.

'Come and have a coffee,' I said, still public. 'Claudia's here.'

She studied me, then followed me inside. Claudia was bringing a new cup over from the bar. She handed it to her but didn't meet her eyes, barely acknowledging her.

'You have to call it off. Cavallini knows. They'll be waiting for you.'

'What?' she said again, loud this time, so I leaned closer to her to tell her the rest, just a murmur to anyone else, barely audible over the steam hiss of the coffeemaker. She took it in blankly, staring out at the campo. When I finished, she asked for a cigarette and glanced around the room while I lit it for her.

'Calm down,' she said, looking at my fingers, shaking a little.

'It's the coffee – I've been waiting. I was afraid I wouldn't get to you in time. I didn't know where you were.'

'You're panicking,' she said, blowing out smoke.

'No. He knows.'

She shrugged. 'It doesn't matter. Stop worrying. It'll be all right.'

'How can you say that?' Claudia snapped. 'How can it be all right?'

'Claudia.'

'You want to drag everyone down with you?' Claudia said, then turned away, a frustrated gesture, as if she were stamping her foot.

'You can't go through with it now,' I said quietly.

'We have to. They move him tonight. So you had a friendly talk. So he's wearing a gun. This doesn't prove anything.'

'You can't take that chance. You've got people to think about. Someone must have talked.'

'Maybe. It doesn't matter.'

'Of course it does. I know, everyone just knows his piece. But one piece leads to another. One of the links breaks, the whole thing can fall apart. All it takes is one.'

She took a sip of coffee, slowing the moment. 'Only if he really knows what is going to happen.'

I looked at her. 'And no one does?'

'It wouldn't be wise, would it? If someone did talk.'

'You told everybody a different story?' Claudia said. 'Including Adam?'

'A man so friendly with the police.'

'You think I'd tell them?'

'The boy didn't think he was betraying us either. Helping. Medicine.' She drew on the cigarette, then put it out. 'I'm never going to be in that house again. Now stop worrying. Maybe Cavallini thinks he knows something, but he doesn't. I told you we'd be careful.'

'You also said they weren't expecting you. But they are. They know *something*'s happening.'

'That can't be helped. We always knew there was a risk in getting him.' She looked up. 'But not to you. Or you,' she said to Claudia. 'So stop scaring yourselves and go home. If it's true about Cavallini, you don't want to be seen with me.' She put her hand on my arm. 'Just open the gate.'

'If he's coming at all. Or is that part of the story real?'

She smiled. 'Someday I'll tell you. Tonight you see nothing. Maybe someone was there. Maybe a ghost.' She patted my arm.

'Thank you for the warning. I know you meant it for the best.'

'But you don't believe it.'

'It doesn't matter if I do. It's too late to stop it now.'

'Not if you want to stop it.'

She gathered up her shopping bag. 'But I don't. There's no choice – to save him. Cavallini? I can't worry about him.'

'You have to. The boy could be killed. Do you want that boy's death on your hands?'

'Do you?' she said sharply.

In the moment that followed, nobody moved. Then Claudia, who'd been staring out the window listening, stepped away from the counter and put herself between us.

'No. Nobody wants that,' she said gently, making peace. 'I'm sorry,' she said to Rosa. 'It's just all nerves with us, worried for you. But if it's the only way—'

I looked at her, surprised, a sudden turn midstream. Rosa, also surprised, said nothing, just shifted the bag in her hand, waiting.

'– then we'll leave the gate,' Claudia said. 'Our piece.'

Rosa didn't reply, just nodded and went out the door. I watched her start across the campo, dragging her leg, then turned to Claudia, my face a question mark.

'You can't stop her,' she said. 'You can see that. She's going to do it no matter what.' She picked up the box. 'Have you paid? I still have to drop this at the Europa.' Suddenly business as usual.

'There won't be any way to connect us,' I said, as if we were still arguing, but Claudia just shrugged, resigned to everything now.

I followed her out and over the bridge to the passage to the Europa, lined with gondoliers, a few of them halfheartedly making a pitch but most just smoking, waiting for tourists from the hotel.

'But she's so pigheaded,' I said. 'What if something goes wrong?'

'Then she's caught, not you,' Claudia said coolly.

I looked up at her. 'And if he's killed?'

She turned to me, her eyes steady. 'Then they'll never look anywhere else.'

I stood for a moment, vaguely aware of the doorman holding open the door, white gloves on the handles, Claudia walking through, but not really seeing any of it, my stomach lurching as if we had just stepped off something, amazed somehow that no one had noticed us falling.

'Signor,' the doorman said, and then I was in the lobby, watching Claudia hand the box to the man at the front desk, and for an odd moment I felt I was looking at someone else. No longer just covering tracks, wiping away smears of blood. Wishing for someone's death. So they'd never look anywhere else.

A waiter in the terrace dining room smiled, unaware that anything terrible had happened. Through the window I could see Salute, white and swirling, exactly the way it had been when we'd flirted on the boat, just across the water from where we were now.

CHAPTER EIGHTEEN

CLAUDIA BLOTTED HER lipstick at the mirror, then turned and smiled at me. 'Okay? You like the dress?' No longer nervous, relieved, as if some unexpected solution had been handed to us, the corner already turned. And hadn't it? Whatever happened tonight would have nothing to do with us, sitting at the opera. Even if it went wrong. The other solution. Because either way we'd be free.

I nodded, barely seeing it.

'Here, help me with my coat. We don't want to be late. We want them to see us.'

'Who?'

'The Montanaris.'

'Christ, I forgot. Maybe they won't be there.'

'You want them to be there. Our witnesses. "And was Signor Miller with you? Yes, all evening. And Signora Miller." Ha, now what do they say?'

'You're enjoying yourself.'

'Isn't that what she wants us to do? As if nothing's happening?'

She kept her good spirits at the opera, despite my restlessness and despite the Montanaris' forced cordiality. They must have had the box to themselves since Gianni's death, because they had already taken Gianni's front seats and looked awkward when we insisted they keep them. There were vague enquiries about Giulia, the offer of a pair of opera glasses, a halfhearted invitation to join them for champagne at the interval, and then they turned to face the stage, their backs stiff and uncomfortable, self-conscious, as if they felt they were being watched. At least, I thought, they'd remember our being there.

Claudia, using the glasses, spied Bertie and pointed him out, a few seats away from the doge's box. He was sitting with a priest dressed in satin, and I thought of that first cocktail party, Claudia in simple grey and the priest in scarlet, the best-dressed person in the room. A hundred years ago. I looked at her. She was still scanning the room with the glasses, interested. An evening out, the way it was all supposed to be, while Rosa was doing whatever she was doing. I shifted in my chair. Guns and escape boats and hunched figures darting along the tracks – none of it real somehow, like stories told over drinks.

And this? There was Bertie in his jewel box, red wallpaper and gilded mouldings, the whole room gleaming with gold, dimming now, people hushing. In a minute there would be music and Rodolfo would find Mimi and we'd sit back, annoying the Montanaris, and no one would find it fantastical at all, perfectly normal. I thought of Bertie's party again, rich foreigners entertaining one another in rented palazzos, another Puccini world. And yet it was Rosa and her friends who didn't seem real. The orchestra started. Only a mile away someone might be firing a gun.

I shifted in my seat again, wishing I could smoke, and looked around for Cavallini's wife – it would be a nice touch if she could say she'd seen us – but the darkness made it hard to find anyone beyond the first row of the boxes. The train would be leaving the station in a few minutes, halting unexpectedly for the signal. Unless that was no longer the plan, something Rosa had made up to make me chase the wrong scent. But it had to be the yards if they expected to stay in Venice. Maestre would favour the police. Maybe it was all exactly the way she'd told me it would be. But which story had Cavallini been told? There are many ears in

Venice. How much easier now for Rosa to be betrayed, with the Germans gone, the partisan groups out of hiding. Nobody could be that careful; there was always something to give you away. How many guards did he have on the train? They wouldn't suspect anything in the yards – they'd be bored with the delay, their guns not even drawn. Still, how long would it take to get them out, fire into the surprise?

Something moved over my finger and I jumped. Claudia's hand, reaching over just to touch. She didn't turn her head, and I saw that her eyes were shiny, her whole attention given to the music. Now I heard it too, Rodolfo's love song, so beautiful that it seemed no one could have written it, just found it, floating somewhere above the ordinary world. If this was possible, anything was. I looked down at her hand. We could be happy. Why shouldn't it work? Rosa knew what she was doing. Gianni was gone and we had an alibi. The Germans had got away with murder, the whole world. Even in Venice, as beautiful as the music, everyone had an alibi, somewhere else when the air-raid sirens covered the sounds of people being dragged off. I didn't know. I didn't realise. I had my own life to consider. And of course everyone did.

I checked my watch. They'd be in boats now, streaming off to Maestre or wherever they were really going. Later we'd go home and not know whether they'd been there or not. I put my hand over Claudia's, hearing the music again. Why shouldn't it all work?

Signora Montanari developed one of her headaches after Act One and they left, with apologies and improbable hopes of seeing us again. Instead we had champagne with Bertie.

'I don't blame them a bit,' he said, watching the Montanaris go. 'Act One is bliss and then everything goes wrong. Think how it ends.' I sipped more champagne, uneasy again. 'Of course the good monsignor loves the death part,' he said, nodding towards the priest, now talking to someone else. 'Divine retribution, I suppose, for all that lovely sin. What *is* going on? Filomena will be furious. She hates being reminded he's in the police.'

I followed his look past the priest to the bar, where Signora

Cavallini had been approached by two policemen, their uniforms so showy that for a second it seemed they were part of the opera. She was frowning, putting down her glass to leave.

'What is it, do you think?' I said quickly. 'Find out.'

'Adam,' he said, pretending to be offended.

'But maybe something's happened.'

He looked at them again, debating, then tapped his champagne glass. 'I could use a top-up. Right back.'

He hurried to the bar, just in time to catch Signora Cavallini. They talked for a second, then he put his hand on her arm, reassuring, and shooed her away with the uniforms.

'They've taken him to hospital.'

'He's been shot?'

Bertie blinked. 'Don't be ridiculous. Why would he be shot? In Venice? It's probably nothing – they check in here with a sneeze. Shot.' He peered over his glasses. 'This flair for melodrama. Ever since you joined the force.'

'I should go. Maybe he's—'

'Adam,' he said, his tone like a physical restraint, a hand on my chest. 'Stop being a ninny and finish your drink. His wife is with him.' He drank some champagne. 'I'd no idea you were so close.'

'It's not that.'

'Then what is it? I think all this business has gone to your head. Unless it's the wine. I think I'll finish that,' he said, taking my glass and pouring some wine into his own, and then, before I could protest, 'You don't have to sit with the monsignor.'

There was more of this, even a few dull minutes with the priest before the warning bell rang, and I didn't hear any of it, my head buzzing with shots. Why else would Cavallini be taken to the hospital? But it was Cavallini who'd been shot. Which meant that Moretti might have got away. Unless they were all still there, littered across the yards, everything gone wrong.

In our box, lights down, I tried to focus on the stage, but now even the music was drowned out by the buzzing in my head. Instead of the Café Momus, I was seeing the train doors closing, the smooth glide out from the platform, then the jerky stop in the yards for the light, then – then what? The worst of it was not knowing. But Bertie had been right, catching me in time, before an absurd rush to the hospital. How would I have explained that? A hunch? I checked my watch again. They'd be long gone from Ca' Venti by now, assuming they'd ever come. Why not do what I was supposed to do, enjoy the opera? While the house sat there, open and waiting, like an overlooked piece of evidence.

'Do you want to go?' Claudia said at the next intermission.

'We should stay. See it through.'

'Scratching your knees and squirming in your seat. Do you think I'm seeing it either?' She reached over and touched me. 'If Cavallini's shot, maybe they got away. Come on. Everyone has already seen us.'

'And what excuse, if anybody asks?'

'You think only the Montanaris get headaches?'

We took the traghetto near the Gritti, standing up as we crossed, looking towards Mimi's dark landing. I thought of the footmen and umbrellas and torches leading the guests into the hall, the jumpy apprehension I'd felt then too, not knowing if it would work.

Our calle was quiet and the door was locked, as it was supposed to be. Only a single night-light, so Angelina wasn't back yet. I turned on the hall lights, the sconces shining all the way to the stairs. Beyond, through the wrought-iron-and-glass door, the water entrance was dark, maybe untouched. I walked down the hall and opened the inside door, putting my hand up to the light switch.

'No, no lights.' Rosa, crouching in a corner, a disembodied voice from a dark pile. 'They might see. Help me with him.'

I went over to the pile – Moretti, with his head leaning on her. In the dim light coming from the hall I saw the cloth she was holding against him, blotched with blood.

'My God.'

'Do you have a towel? I'm using my slip. The worst of it has stopped. So not an artery.'

There was a whimper behind me. Claudia stood still for a

second, her mouth open, as if she were about to scream. 'What are you doing here? You said no one would be here. Lies. I knew it.' Then she took in the bloody cloth.

'A towel,' Rosa said again.

'A towel,' Claudia said, a faint echo, her eyes still wide.

'And something to clean the wound. I couldn't leave him.'

But Claudia was already running down the hall to the stairs.

'Cavallini was shot?' I asked.

'I hope so.'

'What happened?'

She indicated Moretti. 'They shot him before we could get him off the train. They must have had orders. "If anything happens, shoot him first."'

'How bad is it?'

'He's bleeding. Not an artery, he'd be dead, but we have to get him to a doctor. He won't make it like this.'

'When's the pickup boat?'

She shrugged. 'The link that broke. He should have been here long ago. We have to assume he's not coming.'

'But he knew where to get you. If they break him, they'll come here.'

'He won't break.'

'Everybody breaks, Rosa,' I said, angry. 'We have to get the boy out of here.'

She glared at me, then nodded. 'Then we use your boat.'

'My boat?'

'You have to take us.'

'That was always the plan, wasn't it?' Claudia said angrily from the doorway. 'There was never any other boat.' Her voice quivering, edging towards hysteria.

'Does it matter?' Rosa said to me. 'He'll die.'

'Oh, my God,' Claudia said, 'the blood, it's all over. We have to clean it up. Before anyone sees.' She knelt and began to wipe the stone floor.

'Yes, it matters. I have to know how much time we have. Was

there another boat?' I had raised my voice, almost shouting.

'Yes.'

'So, no time. Let's get going. First him. Let me see the wound.' I took Claudia by the shoulders and held her until they stopped shaking. 'You all right? Can you do this?'

'Me? Don't you remember? I'm good at it,' she said, her voice catching. I shot her a look, then glanced down at Rosa, but Rosa was busy now, peeling off the soaked cloth. 'Here, I brought some brandy. This is peroxide. For the wound.'

'That'll kill him,' I said. 'Maybe we should chance it. Bullet's still in anyway. That's where the real infection—'

'No, we don't chance it,' Rosa said, taking the bottle.

'I'll get another towel,' Claudia said, eager to leave.

Rosa gave Moretti some of the brandy, sitting him up so he wouldn't choke, and I saw that he wasn't unconscious, just scared and quiet, keeping his eyes closed against the pain. Shock had drained his face pale, making him look even younger, so that the stubble of beard from his days in jail seemed out of place, ink from another sketch.

'This is going to hurt,' Rosa said, pouring some of the peroxide on a towel.

He nodded and clenched his teeth, playing patient, and then the towel touched him, a searing shock, and he screamed, a yelp that raced out of the room and down the canal. Rosa clamped a hand over his mouth to muffle the scream, making him fight for air, his body writhing, so that when she finally took it away he was panting, exhausted from it, the way a seizure subsides into twitches.

Claudia raced back into the room. 'Are you crazy?' she said, not really to anyone. Then she saw Moretti's face. 'They'll hear,' she said softly. 'You'll give us all away.' She took the peroxide back from Rosa and handed her a towel. 'Put this on him. Where is the doctor? How far?'

'Far,' Rosa said.

'There's no time for that,' Claudia snapped. 'Tell us where.'

'The Lido.'

'The Lido?' Claudia said. 'With the police in the lagoon? What do we say if they stop us? "Oh, just something we picked up." You want to go there, go alone. Don't kill us too.'

'I don't know anything about boats.' She looked down at Moretti.

'Then call an ambulance. Take him to the hospital.'

'They already shot him once. You think they'll stop now?'

Claudia bit her lip, thinking. 'Can you take a bullet out? In the war, they did that. No doctors. You were a partisan. You—'

Rosa shook her head. 'It's too deep. He needs a doctor. Instruments.'

'All right. We can call an ambulance from the Zattere – we can carry him that far. No one will know.'

'About you.'

'Yes, about us. Do you want everyone caught? At least he can live. He'll be safe there, in the hospital.'

'Was your father safe there?'

Claudia looked away, then went back to the floor, scrubbing it clean, doing something.

'Why the Lido?' I said.

'There's a car there. They won't know about it.'

'The next link?'

'We can get to Jesolo. There's a doctor I know.'

'If he's still alive,' I said, watching Moretti, who was breathing heavily, in a series of grunts.

'You can't involve us in this,' Claudia said. 'What can we say? They'll think we were part of it, attacking police. There, it's gone. What do we do with the towel?' She held it out to me.

Rosa looked up at me. 'We can't take him to the hospital. You know that. There is an obligation here.'

I glanced around the room, thinking. The police were on the water, not searching the calles. Could he walk? Mimi's wasn't far, a few deserted blocks away. But how could we take him there? Anywhere?

'Were you followed here?' I said.

366

Rosa shook her head. 'No.'

'So only the pickup boat knows you're still here.'

'Yes.'

'The police'll be on the lagoon.'

'Maybe not so many,' she said, bargaining. 'They can't stay out all night. They have to think we went to Maestre. No one will think of the Lido, it's the wrong way. That was the plan.'

'Yes, and look how well it's worked,' Claudia said.

'He's here, isn't he? If we can get to the Lido, we can get him away.' She turned to me. 'They're not looking for your boat.'

I took in the canal steps, the boat tied to its mooring pole, barely moving in the calm water. If they were keeping watch nearby, they'd be in the Giudecca channel, not the other end. Nobody in his right mind would head for the Grand Canal, all lights and vaporetti and tourist gondolas. The way to Maestre, the mainland, was up the channel to Piazzale Roma and the bridge. That would be the way to escape, not out towards the lagoon and the open sea. Rosa was right – they wouldn't think of the Lido. The trick would be getting past Venice itself, the curve of bright lights around the basin, without even a shadow to hide behind. A long trip in any case, too long for someone with a stomach wound, groaning between channel markers. And now they'd be hours late.

'What if he didn't wait, the driver?'

'There's no one. Just the car.'

'And you're going to drive?'

'I can drive a car.'

'But not a boat,' I said to myself, then looked at her. 'It's not going to work, Rosa. You have to give him up.'

'He's not guilty,' Claudia said. 'If there's a trial—'

'It's too late for that,' Rosa said. 'A policeman was killed.'

'How do you know? You didn't know if Cavallini was shot.'

'I didn't shoot Cavallini,' she said calmly.

In the silence that followed you could hear the creaking of moored boats in the canal.

'Anybody see you?' I said quietly.

Rosa shrugged. 'It was dark. Maybe. Maybe they saw *him*,' she said, looking down at Moretti. 'You understand? They don't need a trial for Maglione any more. Now they have this.'

I said nothing, my eyes darting around the room again – the hanging gondola, the paving stones, nothing changed, feeling as trapped and anxious as that night. Only the water. The calle entrance was impossible – someone would see, and where would we carry him? Gianni had been dead, something you could slip over the side. Moretti would have to be taken all the way, loaded into the car. If he survived the trip. And if he didn't? I saw us pitching him into the water, a macabre repetition, everything happening all over again.

'You have to get him out of here,' Claudia said, maybe seeing it too, shivering as if she were back in the boat. 'It's not fair, to be blamed for this.'

'Go, then,' Rosa said. 'Somewhere after the opera. If they come, you won't be here. I'll say you never knew. I came to steal the boat. They'd believe that, stealing the boat.'

'You wouldn't even get the motor started,' I said.

'I'll row, then. What do you want me to do? Sit? Let him bleed to death?'

Nobody said anything, waiting for someone else to move. Moretti, on the floor, fumbled in his jacket and pulled out a gun, aiming at me.

'Take us,' he said.

'Stop,' Rosa said. 'They're friends.'

But Moretti's eyes were blunt, beyond niceties. I stared at the gun, feeling dislocated. A gun, where we used to give parties. All he had to do was squeeze the trigger.

'Give it to me,' Rosa said, holding out her hand. Then, fondly, '*Imbecile*.'

He lowered the gun, not giving it to Rosa but putting it back in his pocket.

'Where did he get a gun?' I asked.

368

'The guard who shot him, it's the one he used. So we took it after.'

I tried to imagine the scene in the yards, the guard slumping forwards, Rosa helping the boy across the tracks, a confusion of shots, the boat racing away from the pier. Or that moment, earlier, when she'd fired at the guard. Not the first. How many had there been? Paolo and all the others. I wondered if it got easier, or if each time was like Gianni, with blood pounding in your head.

'What happened to the other guard?'

'He was ours,' she said simply.

And now the others would kill him. No end to it, the war that kept going, the only thing real to her. But not to me, nothing to do with me.

It must have been utterly still, because the doorbell, when it rang, was louder even than Moretti's scream.

Claudia jumped. 'Oh, *Dio*,' she said, frantic, looking at the bloody towel in her hand.

Rosa sat up, rigid, clutching Moretti.

'Somebody heard,' Claudia said, a gasp.

'Angelina,' I said, 'that's all.'

'She rings? With a key?' She held out the towel in front of her as if it were alive, about to bite her.

I stood, for a moment almost dizzy, my head turning left, right, anywhere. 'All right,' I said finally, pretending calm. 'Get over there, behind the stones.' I stepped over to help Rosa drag Moretti behind the pile. 'Get under the tarp. It's probably Angelina. I'll come back when she goes up. Just stay there.'

'What do I do with this?' Claudia held out the towel, panicking.

'Under here. Come on, quick. We need to see if anything shows,' I said, tucking the side of the tarp down. There was a murmur from underneath. 'You okay?' I loosened the edge, letting some air in. The doorbell rang again. 'Not a sound. Not a *sound*,' I said, grabbing Claudia. 'We were upstairs. It took us that long to answer.'

She nodded and I closed the wrought-iron door. I hurried down the hall. '*Momento*,' I said out loud. When I reached the door, I

369

looked over my shoulder to see Claudia standing halfway up the stairs, patting her hair, everything in place, only her eyes startled.

I opened the door and heard the blood in my head again.

'So, home early,' Cavallini said. 'I saw the light.'

'Inspector,' I said dumbly, staring at his arm, wrapped in white bandages and set in a sling. 'Are you all right? At the opera, the policemen—'

'Yes, I know, poor Filomena. To worry her that way. I spoke to them. Acting like women. A scratch, and she comes for the last rites. Well, maybe wives hope for that,' he said, genial. He looked towards the stairs. 'Signora Miller. *Buona sera.*'

She nodded, stiff.

'You enjoyed the opera?'

I stepped aside to let him in. Behind him a uniformed police-man waited by the door.

'Yes, but I had a headache,' she said, wary. 'I was just going to bed.'

'I'm sorry to come like this.'

'But what happened? What do you mean, a scratch?' I said, trying to remember what I was supposed to know. If I'd only been to the opera.

'A bullet, but not serious. You know, I felt today something might happen. A superstition. Remember?'

'A bullet. You were shot?'

He smiled. 'There was an incident. I told you I expected some-thing.'

'Tonight? I didn't know you meant tonight.'

'Well, whenever we moved Moretti. We moved him tonight.'

'But what happened?'

'He was shot. So they defeat themselves.'

'He's dead?'

'We don't know. He's still with them. But we'll find him.'

'Still with who?'

'Communists. So of course this is what they do. Always the same methods.'

'Was anyone else hurt?'

370

'Yes,' he said, solemn. 'Now he murders police.'

'Moretti?'

He nodded. 'This time you can be sure.'

I said nothing.

'I thought you would be interested,' Cavallini said.

'That's why you came – to tell me?'

'No, no. Why I came.' He looked around, as if for a second he'd forgotten. 'To ask you.'

I glanced towards the stairs where Claudia was still standing, her hand gripping the rail.

'Did you know that your canal gate was open?'

'The canal gate?' I said.

'Yes, it's open. Did you know?'

Was I supposed to know? How else could it have been opened?

'Yes, I left it open. In case we took a taxi home from the opera.'

'But you didn't.'

'No.'

'You permit me to see?' he said, starting down the hall.

'Yes, if you want. What's it all about?'

'Your boat is still there? Not stolen?'

'I suppose so. I haven't looked. I never thought—'

Claudia was following us now, walking tentatively, as if she were bracing herself for each step. 'Someone stole the boat?' she said.

'Signora, I'm sorry. I didn't mean to disturb you. Ah, this door is not locked?' He opened the door to the water entrance. 'You're very trusting, Signor Miller. The light?'

I drew a breath and flipped on the switch, listening for a sound, any rustling of the tarp. Under the yellow overhead light, the dark clumps were only partly illuminated, still leaving shadows around the edges. I took in the smell, damp stone and musty wood, but nothing more, any boat house, even the peroxide faded now, something that might have come in from the canal.

'Yes,' Cavallini said, taking stock, remembering. 'The gondola.'

I walked towards the steps, trying to draw him away from the tarp. 'The boat's here. Why did you think it was stolen?'

371

'We had information they would come here.'

I wondered if Rosa could hear under the tarp. Everybody breaks.

'Here? Why here?'

'Your friend Rosa. This is how they are. She knew you were going to the opera?'

'I don't know. How would she know?'

'No matter. That type, they would steal under your nose.'

'They came here? They're in the house?' Claudia said, looking frightened. 'Upstairs?' Drawing him away too.

'No, no, don't be alarmed. They don't want to stay in Venice. They want to leave Venice. I thought perhaps they came for the boat, but as you can see . . .' He waved his hand to the mooring post. 'So, a change of plans. You were lucky,' he said to me.

'But we should look upstairs. If they're hiding,' Claudia said, trying to move us through the door.

'Would that make you feel easier, signora? One of my men can search, if you like.'

'You think it's foolish.'

'I think it's careful,' he said politely. 'And you,' he said to me, 'lock the gate.' He turned from the water, stopping again to look up at the gondola on its supports.

'You mean they might still come?' I said.

'No, it's late. I thought if the boat were missing, it would be a clue. They won't come here now. They need to leave Venice. And who helps them? Foreigners? No. Old comrades. You know Moretti worked on the boats. We know where to look. But still, lock the gate.'

'Yes,' I said, stepping past him to pull it shut, making a loud clang with the latch. I could feel beads of sweat on my forehead. Any noise echoed here. You could hear the boat rocking against its mooring. Why not breathing, the faintest movement?

'A beautiful thing,' Cavallini said, still looking up at the gondola. 'To find an old one in this condition.'

'The marchesa never takes it out,' I said, but I wasn't looking at it. Claudia had glanced, just once, towards the pile and now was signalling me, eyes large and panicky, forcing me to look there too. At first it just seemed a thin shadow on the grey stones, but then I saw that it was moving, growing longer, coming towards us. Dark blood, seeping out from under the tarp to follow gravity to the stairs, impossible to miss if Cavallini turned his head.

Claudia stared at me, and for an instant I stopped breathing, because we both saw that in another minute it would be too late. If we stepped back now, we could stay free, still unsuspecting visitors in someone else's fight. Moretti might die anyway. But if we hid them, we became them, the same in Cavallini's eyes.

The blood, viscous, moved a little, just a trickle, almost at my shoe now. There would be no story that would distance us and make sense. We'd have to go through with all the rest, save them. When all we had to do to save ourselves was to let it happen. Claudia could do it alone, look down at the blood in horror until Cavallini noticed, but she was waiting for me. We'd do this together too. The same room. Just a trickle this time, not a red splotch on a white dress shirt, but the same pulsing in the head, jumping off the end. They couldn't stay. He'd die. There was only the impossible trip across the lagoon. And nowhere to go after, no alibi. Unless we stepped back now, pointed to the blood, surprised, and stayed safe. I breathed out.

I moved between Claudia and the pile and put my hand on Cavallini's shoulder. 'Can we ask your men to search?' I said. 'I really think Claudia would feel better.'

He looked down from the gondola, but at Claudia, not me, missing the blood. I moved us towards the door. Don't turn now. A trickle. Would anyone see it if he wasn't looking? But nobody missed blood. The eye went to it, an instinct.

'Of course,' Cavallini was saying.

Claudia glanced at me for a second, dismayed, then slipped into her part. 'And the closets? I know it's foolish,' she said, leaving for the hall.

'Not at all,' Cavallini said as I turned out the lights and closed the inside door behind me.

He used two of his men, who made a halfhearted show of poking in closets and looking behind shower curtains. I followed with Cavallini, but in my mind I saw the trickle growing thicker, a red stream running over the stone floor, down the mossy steps, spreading out into the canal, a giant stain. In the middle of the search, Angelina came home and had to be calmed down, so we went through her room too. The men covered every inch of Ca' Venti, all of it innocent, nothing to connect us except the blood spreading on the floor downstairs. The one place they didn't search, because Cavallini had already been there.

At the door he offered to leave one of his men. 'If it would make you feel safer.'

A guard outside, listening. 'Do you think we need it?'

He made a dismissive gesture with his eyebrows. 'No. To be frank with you, I need every man tonight. You know how it is. But if the signora—'

'She'll be all right. I'll lock the doors, both of them. She just needs rest. If we can get Angelina to bed. I've never seen her so jumpy. You'd think she'd robbed a bank.'

'Her brother,' he said.

'What?'

'Well, not banks, the black market. During the war. Of course, not now. But she thinks we still want him. I'll tell you something,' he said, almost winking. 'We never did. It was the only way then. I bought from him myself.' He looked at me. 'We have our own ways here.'

A message? A reminder? Or maybe nothing at all. I heard a creak, someone moving, and felt my scalp itch, every sound in the house now a finger pointing at me. A single groan would do it, while he was still in the house.

'Thank you for coming,' Claudia said. 'With your arm—'

'It's nothing,' he said, moving the sling, a demonstration.

'Still,' I said. 'A bullet wound, that's never just a scratch.'

'No.' He lifted his head. 'Did you hear something?'

A gasp of pain, unmistakable, maybe Moretti clutching his stomach. I felt my hand move, a tic. Say anything.

374

'The house. It makes noises,' I said casually, trying to sound unconcerned.

Cavallini listened for another minute, then reached for the doorknob. 'These old houses,' he said, turning it. 'With me, pipes. All night.' He shook his head. 'Venice.' Not bothering to say more, as if we could hear the city sinking around us.

When the door closed, I leaned against it, breathing, listening for footsteps. Claudia didn't move either, frozen for a minute by relief. I put a finger to my lips, stepping closer to her so that we couldn't be heard.

'Go get Angelina settled,' I said. 'Tell her I'll lock up. Keep a light on in the bedroom so it looks like we're still up.' I switched off the hall lights, something Cavallini's men would see from the calle, and walked with Claudia in the dark towards the stairs, turning on a small night-light on the hall table. 'Check the canal from upstairs – see if any boats are waiting. I'll get them ready. We can't wait too long.'

She stopped, placing her hand on the banister. 'If we do this, the rest was all for nothing. We can't explain this.' She clutched my arm. 'We can still— There's nothing to connect us. Let them steal the boat.'

'And just turn away.'

'It's our lives.'

'Theirs too.' I took her shoulders, steadying her. 'All we have to do is get him to the Lido. Then we're done with it. We're finally done with it.'

She looked down, then turned to the stairs. 'We're never done with it.' She paused. 'What do I tell Angelina?'

'Tell her Cavallini's watching the house. That'll keep her in bed.' She started up the stairs. 'Not too long, okay? Just keep one light on, so they think we're here.'

CHAPTER NINETEEN

WE WAITED ANOTHER twenty minutes, cleaning the water entrance and listening for any signs of activity on the canal. A water taxi passed, cutting through to the Giudecca channel, but otherwise it was quiet, a backwater. I swung the boat around from the mooring pole. The canal itself was dark, the moon covered by convenient clouds. Moretti was still conscious, able to crawl into the boat without our having to lift him, but he was gasping, obviously in pain. He lay down in the front, Rosa next to him. Claudia threw in the wad of bloody towels. 'We can't keep these in the house. Here, get under this,' she said, spreading the tarp over them, imagining it could hide them if we were stopped. Behind us, the pile of paving stones was bare.

I pulled the gate just to the point before it would click shut, so that it looked closed from the water. We glided away from the house, hugging the edge of the canal. If the police were anywhere, they'd be in the Giudecca channel, but if they'd given up, it was still our best route out, so I decided to check. I pushed against the building wall, letting us float quietly towards the end of the canal. The daytime traffic was gone. It might be worth a chance, a quick dash to San Giorgio, then behind the island, the way we'd gone with Gianni. We had almost passed under the Zattere bridge into the open water when I saw it, an idling boat with a blue light.

Waiting to see if anyone came out. I grabbed a mooring pole and held the boat back until it began to pivot, twisting around in the other direction. With the police boat patrolling, we'd have to keep the motor off. We could make our way back down the Fornace by pushing against the side, but farther on some boats were moored and we'd have to swing out, using the oars on both sides, Indians in a canoe.

'Police,' I said to Claudia. 'We'll have to use the Grand Canal.'

She said nothing, just stared at Ca' Venti as we passed. No turning back. Ahead a gondola was approaching – no passengers, just someone heading home.

'Come here,' I said to Claudia, pulling her to me and kissing her, the only thing we'd be doing at this hour on a quiet canal. She put her hand on the back of my neck, then rested her forehead on mine, both our faces hidden.

'Adam,' she whispered, shaking.

'Ssh. It's going to be all right.'

I heard the faint splash of the gondolier's pole. In the front of the boat, Rosa peeked out from under the tarp. 'He's gone,' she said, but I stayed with Claudia for another minute, locked together, my head filled with her. It was going to be all right.

Near the Grand Canal it was lighter and, more important, noisier. A vaporetto was heading across the water, its noise loud enough to cover the sound of our own engine. I waited until it was closer, then started ours. No trouble this time. The cord caught and the engine roared, loud enough to bounce off the walls of the buildings. Or maybe just loud to us, listening for it. An ordinary motorboat, usually an insect buzz in Venice's water traffic. I nosed us out to the broad canal.

The police boat was off to the right, a bookend to the other, with the same blue light. It was standing guard near the centre of the canal, with sightlines not just to us but to the traghetto stand across, anything streaming down to San Marco. The terrace lights were on at the Gritti. I idled the boat for a minute, churning the water but not going anywhere. They'd blocked the Fornace, just in case. If they spotted us here, they could radio to the other end and trap us in between. Over by the Gritti, a pack of tourist gondolas went by with lanterns. What you saw at this hour at the hotel end of the Grand Canal. Taxis at the Europa, the Monaco. A few private boats going to Harry's. But not a single motorboat with a young couple and a bulky tarp. Farther down, the lights of Salute reflected on the water, then there was only a brief shadow before San Marco lit up everything. Nowhere to hide.

The vaporetto was getting closer, lumbering towards Salute on our side of the canal, as slow and bulky as a land bus. Big enough. I lifted my head as if I'd been shaken awake, then looked in both directions. San Marco was impossible; easier to double back to the Giudecca. But not on the Fornace. The trick would be to catch the vaporetto at the right moment. Even at this speed there wouldn't be any leeway.

I watched it get nearer, its bulk coming between us and the rest of the canal, and then, as it reached the Fornace, I put the boat in gear and shot out to run along its starboard side, invisible to the police while I chugged along in its shadow. We began to rock a little in the wake. A few people on deck noticed us, one waving us away with his hand, warning us. In another minute the vaporetto would head for the Salute landing station, squeezing me, but not before we passed the Rio della Salute, still blocked from view, and I swung away and headed down the side canal.

The Salute rio ran parallel to the Fornace but farther down, almost at the customs house. If I entered the Giudecca there, away from the waiting police boat, I might be able to run along the dark side of the Dogana and reach the bacino at its tip, pulling towards San Marco into the Grand Canal boat's patrolling area but too far away to be seen. If I could outrun the Giudecca boat. This canal was narrower than the Fornace and even quieter. Only a few people lived at this end of Dorsoduro, wedged in between the great church and the customs house. We were out of it in minutes, turning left to hug the tip of land, almost afraid to look back. We had no lights to see, and our motor was far enough away to be indistinct – no reason to notice us at all. Just keep going. In seconds we'd be out of range.

'They're coming,' Rosa said, facing backwards.

Maybe just to look, a routine check. But the minute I speeded up they'd know, without even having to pull back the tarp.

Claudia turned around, spotting the light too. 'Go behind San Giorgio,' she said. 'Like before.'

'We can't. We'll never lose them there.'

'At least it's dark there, remember? Nobody saw us.'

'Nobody was chasing us,' I said. 'Okay, hold on, it's going to bump. Rosa, hang on to him.' Rosa, who had been watching us, just nodded.

We passed the tip of the customs house with its golden ball and I swerved slightly to the left, streaking across the basin towards the doges' palace, then along the curve of the Riva. The one place in Venice I'd wanted to avoid, open and bright, centre stage. But also busy with traffic, boats to the islands and Danieli taxis and ferries leaving for the Adriatic. I realised that, unexpectedly, the boats here became trees in a forest, something to dodge around, slip behind. We passed San Zaccaria, passed the Rio dei Greci, the way to the Questura, heading finally towards the darker end of Venice, the empty public gardens and the lagoon beyond. In the lagoon, still covered by clouds, we could make it. We hit the wake from another boat, lifting up, then smashing down with a thud, water spraying over everything. Moretti cried out. Our speed now was drawing attention, too fast for the harbour. If I could pull away into the city again, thread us somehow through the back of Castello, we might lose the police, but the canals were a maze here, watery blind alleys. The police hadn't outrun us yet. Just a few more seconds and we'd be in the dark.

On cue, a searchlight came on behind, hitting the water next to us in a long white beam, then moving left until our boat was flooded with light. Claudia ducked, lowering herself out of sight. I swerved, but whoever was operating the light had the rhythm of it now and followed us, tracking us smoothly. In a minute there would be a horn, someone yelling at us to stop. My mouth went dry.

'There are two,' Rosa said. 'Only one has the light.' Calculating odds. What she must have been like on their other raids, harrying Germans.

Moretti crawled out from under the tarp and pulled himself along the side of the boat. We hit another wake and I could see him grimace, pain and something more, a frantic desperation, blinking against the glare, as if the light itself were hitting him, making him hurt. Then, almost before I could register what was happening, his hand came up and a gun went off, a roar past my ear. Claudia screamed. He fired again, and suddenly the light went off, hit or just temporarily doused.

'Stop it! You'll kill us!' Claudia shouted, jumping at him and grabbing the gun. It was Rosa who snatched it, however, handing it over to Claudia and pulling him back to the tarp.

'What can you hit like this?' she said to him gently, putting the towel back on his wound. She pulled out her own gun. 'Don't worry. You,' she said to Claudia, 'can you shoot?'

'No. Stop. If we do this—'

The light came on again, touching the edge of the boat, and then there was gunfire, bullets hitting the water next to us. We crouched down, Claudia and Rosa peering back at the police boat. I kept steering, bobbing my head, a moving target. There was a sharp *thunk* behind me, a bullet hitting wood, not far from the motor. Not far from any of us. Real bullets. I felt everything rushing out of control. Cut the engine. Hold up your hands. It was time to stop. Real bullets.

'Get the light,' Rosa said, steadying her hand and firing, a marksman's stance.

'They're going to kill us all, and he's going to die anyway,' Claudia said, her voice jagged.

'Then take one with you,' Rosa said. 'Shoot. It's Fossoli, and this time you have a gun.'

Claudia looked at her.

'It's the same people. Shoot.'

But it was Rosa who shot, taking her time, careful, then smiling when she heard the ping of metal, glass smashing, and the light suddenly went out. Another burst of gunfire hit the water next to us. I could hear yelling on the boat behind, confusion. Our one second chance. It didn't matter where the back canals went. If we stayed here, we'd be killed.

I pushed the tiller hard and the boat veered left, heading straight for the nearest canal. A high bridge, dark water behind, only a few streetlights after the Riva. It was only after we'd passed under the bridge that I saw the tall brick towers at the end of the rio, the crenellated walls stretching out from the water entrance. The Arsenale, the republic's old shipyard, silent now for years. Navy property, but not locked – a vaporetto route went through it, past the walled-in docks and out the other end, a shortcut to the northern lagoon.

I looked behind us. The police had seen the turnoff, were now racing towards the bridge at the rio entrance. Only the usual boat lights, no more beacon. In the Arsenale it would be almost pitch-dark, just a few corner lamps for night watchmen. Nothing came through here but the vaporetti. And nothing got out, if you stopped up either end. I tried to remember its shape from the map – a box of water surrounded by warehouses and ships' works, a rio out in each direction, not completely hemmed in. A connecting boatyard to the right, a longer way out, but an alternative. Unless the navy had closed it off. If they were here at all. What ships were left would be in Taranto. Nothing had been built here since the first war. The foundries, the ropemakers, were all just memories, something to mention to tourists as they sailed through. A deserted factory on water. And a trap if we couldn't make it through.

I had decided to head right, towards the connecting boatyard, when I heard the shot behind us. Close enough to shoot again. Someone leaned out of one of the tower windows, shouting. Guarded after all. But what were they guarding? In a moment I saw. I made an abrupt turn after the towers, hoping for a clear path to the other boatyard, and instead found myself surrounded by ghost ships. The Arsenale was dotted with yellow fog lights, everything shuttered, the docks lined with rusting, pre-Mussolini warships. A ship graveyard, clotted enough to obscure the opening to the adjoining basin. But now it was too late to head back to the lagoon. I could hear the police boats, already at the entrance towers. Still, we'd have to try. Nobody would stay in a bottleneck. But that's what they would think too.

I turned the boat once more. An old warship lay almost listing against the dock, its wide middle close enough to board by jumping but its tapered bow and stern sitting out in the water. I made another quick turn, almost fishtailing, then cut the motor behind the stern, bobbing in a narrow slot of water between the rusting hulk and the stone walls of the dock. The boat rocked and I grabbed a rope from the dock to hold us steady until our wake had subsided. Then I pulled us farther in, making sure the boat didn't stick out past the warship's stern. A hiding hole, dark. Nothing to see but rusting steel.

Everything now was sound – the motors of the police boats shifting gears, idling while they looked around; footsteps running past the workshops, presumably the guard from the tower; shouts out to the water, unintelligible but excited, wanting to know what was going on; the creaking of ships pulling against ropes. I looked up. The warship was secured to keep any movement to a minimum, ropes stretched taut from stern to dock, probably the same at the bow. But that didn't mean it couldn't move, the water churned up by the police boats rocking the stern just enough to push it closer to the dock, crushing us. The others were looking at it too, their eyes fixed on the old metal, watching it as if they were waiting to put up their hands to stop it coming closer. No one spoke. Rosa leaned down, putting her head next to Moretti's, ready to cover his mouth if he made a sound. On the water the boats had come together, their motors in the same place, conferring. But they were running out of time. If they searched the

Arsenale and found nothing, they'd lose any advantage on the open water.

I heard the boats shift gears, separating. But which way would we have gone? The northern outlet, towards Murano, or the longer Arsenale basin? The directions were opposite – a wrong guess meant we'd get away. Then one motor got fainter, moving towards the lagoon, and the other seemed almost on top of us, someone yelling one more thing to the guard before it passed by the stern of our ship and then to the next basin. Finally, Rosa's reverse play, the police off in all directions except the one I intended to use, back to where I had started.

We waited another minute to make sure the police had really gone, then edged our way out from behind the warship. For a moment I thought of just drifting with the oars, slipping past the guard in silence, the way we'd gone down the Fornace. But we were running out of time too, every second crucial if we wanted to get out before the police realised they were chasing shadows. What could the guard do, call out the navy? Mothballed in Taranto, the last scraps of Mussolini's war. I started the engine and swung around the big stern.

The guard may have seen the boat, but none of us looked back, just headed straight down the canal to the open water. We had a real chance now. To catch up, the police would have to go all around the tail end of Venice, skirting San Elena, minutes behind. We passed under the bridge and shot across the water towards the channel lights. I peered into the darkness, trying to measure how far I could see past the buoys before everything was swallowed up. Still no moon. We wouldn't need to hide behind anything – the air itself would do it if we were outside the range of the lights. But it was a fine line; too far and you risked shallows.

'Is he okay?' I said to Rosa. 'It gets choppier out here.'

She didn't say anything, just held him, a cushion.

'Where is the car? The casino?' The big parking lot at the vaporetto landing stage, where it would be easy to be overlooked in the crowd.

'No, at the end. The Excelsior.'

'The Excelsior?'

'It's not open yet. No one will be at the dock. It's easy to find.' All worked out, the next link.

'Not in the dark. We'll have to go to the casino and then follow the lights down.'

'No, go straight across. That was the idea. No one will see us.'

'You can't cross the lagoon in the dark. That's why they mark the channels.'

'It's a shallow boat.'

But the lagoon could be even shallower. That was what had always protected Venice – not water but mud. Sometimes only a few feet under the surface, sometimes less, rising in little under-water islands.

'We can't go at this speed. If we hit something, we could wreck the boat.'

'If they come for us, they'll look in the channel,' she said.

I nodded. 'All right. But it'll take more time. Can he wait?'

He was lying still under the tarp, maybe passed out.

'Yes,' she said. 'Now.' I looked at her face, suddenly soft. 'He's dead.'

'Oh,' Claudia said, a whimper.

'Are you sure?'

Rosa pulled back the tarp, as if seeing him, his perfectly calm face, would be evidence. 'In the Arsenale. I didn't want to say then.'

We were still moving slowly in a direct line to the far lights of the Lido. I looked around, checking for boats, then back at his face, streaked with blood where he had wiped it, sweating, a kind of camouflage effect in the dark. A boy who'd delivered medicine.

'Better cover him up,' I said, not wanting to look any more.

'I'm sorry,' Rosa said quietly, and for an odd second I thought she was talking to me, but her face was turned to his, words to a comrade.

Claudia moved forwards and helped her with the tarp, folding

384

it around him. 'Let's go back,' she said. 'They won't expect that. We can hide you, get you away somehow tomorrow. It was the wound that was the problem – we couldn't hide him. He would have died.'

'He did,' Rosa said, but Claudia wasn't really listening, busy with the tarp, absorbed now in a new plan.

'Do you think they saw our faces?' she said to me. 'In that light? The boat could be anyone's. We could go back. Nobody would know.'

'I can't stay in Venice,' Rosa said. 'They know it was me. Even if they didn't see,' she said, spreading her hand to take in the boat, 'they know it was me. They'll hunt for me.'

'Not at Ca' Venti,' Claudia said. 'They already did.'

'And what do we do with him?' Rosa said quietly.

'Is there some rope?' Claudia said. 'It's better if it's tied. The tarp will come loose, even if we roll it.' She was folding it under him, talking to herself. 'How can we weight it? Not that it matters. You use those big stones and it'll come up anyway. Nothing keeps it down. It's the tides, isn't that what they said? The tides loosened the tarp.' She turned to me. 'We'll have to explain why this one is missing. There's nothing over those stones now. Someone might notice.'

I looked up to find Rosa watching her, studying her face.

'You want to put him in the lagoon? This boy?'

'He's dead, yes?' Claudia said.

Rosa looked out to the dark, then shook her head. 'Not to the fishes. I'll take him.'

'In the car? With a body? Where?'

'He's Carlo's son,' she said simply. 'I can't just throw him over the side.'

'Two can do it,' Claudia said, not hearing her. 'The boat won't tip.'

'An expert,' Rosa said, dismissive, then turned to me. 'They'll find the car. Then it's someone else.'

'They can trace it?'

385

She shrugged. 'You will never get me out of Venice. Not now. This is the best way. Get me there, then it's my risk.'

'And when they ask how you got there?' Claudia said.

'When they ask?' Rosa said. 'They won't ask me anything. If they can ask, I'll be dead.'

She said it casually, sure of things. A car punctured with bullet holes, the only way it would be stopped. But it could happen the other way too. An undetected dash to Jesolo, then the whole Veneto to disappear in. Taking the body to friends.

'You're not turning around,' Claudia said.

'After we drop them,' I said. 'We can't keep her in Venice.' The train station would be swarming with police, the highway bridge guarded. Not even a tarp to hide under.

'Who's that?' Claudia said, swivelling around. A distant engine, a light shining in front, coming slowly.

'Not police,' Rosa said. 'Fishermen, maybe. They go out at night.'

'Have they seen us?'

'Not yet. Soon,' Rosa said. 'Pull to the left.'

I turned the boat slightly, on an angle now to the channel markers, stretching across the lagoon like highway lights. The fishing boat would pass without even noticing us, heading for the opening to the Adriatic. The chugging was nearer, a steady hum, then suddenly, as if it had found a road, it speeded up, moving its lights right to left to make sure its whole path was clear. On the swing left the light caught us, something unexpected in the dark. A man shouted. The boat came towards us, shining its beam down.

'Where are your lights?' the man yelled in Italian. 'What's wrong?' Just people in distress.

I idled the engine. 'Broken,' Rosa yelled back. 'It's all right, we're fixing it.'

'You'll get run over. Go back to the channel,' he said, waving his arms. 'Someone will pick you up.'

'We're all right. We're going to the Lido.'

'Bah,' he said. 'In the dark. *Sciocci.*' This to the other fishermen, disgusted by our ineptness. 'Then follow us. It's another channel.'

I turned my head away from the light, looking towards the main channel markers, the string of white, now with a small blue light moving along it.

'Rosa, police. Tell them to go. The police'll see us.'

I imagined someone with binoculars, scanning, drawn to the spot of light, two boats, one familiar.

Rosa shouted something up, forced and hearty, and the fisherman laughed but turned the boat, moving the light away. It started out again.

'It's luck for us,' Rosa said. 'We can follow them. They know the channels.'

'What did you say to him?'

'I told him to stop looking down my dress.'

I opened the throttle, following the fishing boat but keeping far enough back to stay in its shadow. We were making better time now, getting closer. I looked left, keeping the blue light in sight. One of the night ferries to Trieste was coming up behind it in the channel, and in the bright lights I could see it clearly now, a police boat, probably the one that had spun off through the Arsenale yard. The ferry passed and the blue light kept following the channel, the only place we could sensibly be.

'Are they still there?' Claudia said, watching me.

'Yes, but they're heading for the casino.'

And then they weren't. The blue light swung out into the lagoon, drawn irresistibly to the fishing boat's light, cutting straight across to it.

'Damn.' I slowed down, letting the fishermen run ahead, watching the police boat race towards them. The fishing boat was making for the end of the Lido, the outlet to the Adriatic, past the big beach hotels. Its path drew the police boat right in front of us, a slice of light that crossed up ahead and then kept going, leaving us alone again in the dark.

'Go faster,' Claudia said. 'They'll come back.'

'We can't. We don't know how shallow it is.'

'The Excelsior boats go there,' she said, but I didn't answer, trying to concentrate on the water ahead in what little light there was. The casino was miles down to our left, the fishing boat trying to leave the lagoon to our right – we should be heading straight for the hotel. In the day we'd see the white turrets poking through the trees. Now there'd be nothing to orient us but a dock light.

'They'll be back soon,' Rosa said. 'They're almost at the fishing boat. Once they see it's not us—'

I nodded and opened the throttle again, jerking us faster towards the island. Too late now to worry about shallows. If we didn't get to the dock, we'd be in the police boat's return path. Then what? Play hide-and-seek in the lagoon until we ran out of luck.

'The yellow light,' Rosa said. 'There. See it? That's where they unload.'

Down on my right, the police were making a loop around the fishing boat, probably cursing themselves now for having followed it. They'd head back to the main channel, cutting behind us, hearing our motor unless we were already at the dock, silent and invisible again.

The Excelsior landing area was a dead-end canal, protected from rough open water and at this time of year lighted only by the dock lamp at the entrance. I shot past the light, then cut the motor, so that the boat swerved as if we were skidding on ice. Our swell slapped against the wall, then came back at us, a bathtub effect. I held the boat steady, then pushed us towards the landing stairs.

'Okay, quick,' I said. 'Where's the car?'

'Across the street. Help me carry him.'

'Not that way,' Claudia said, positioning herself at the end of the tarp. 'Slide it over the side first. Like this.' She motioned Rosa to the other end, and they pushed the rolled tarp on to the stairs while I held the rocking boat. They both got out, Claudia pulling the body up to the pavement. 'Now lift.'

'Wait. I'll do it,' I said, tying the boat.

But before I could step out I heard the other engine, grinding in neutral out past the dock light, looking around. I turned to see the blue light, then back at Rosa. 'Run. There's no time now.'

'And you?'

'I'll say you forced us. Something. Just get going.'

'Help me. I can't leave him.'

'Are you crazy?' Claudia said, her voice hoarse, breathing hard. She had started dragging the body but only managed to pull the tarp away. Now, looking at Moretti, then out towards the blue light, she seemed desperate, gulping air. 'He's dead. Look. What does it matter now? We did this to save him, so he wouldn't be blamed for us. We could have done nothing, let him take the blame. But we didn't. And now? Look. It doesn't matter to him now. Let him be the guilty one. Then it's over. We have to save ourselves.' She knelt by the body, reaching for the loose tarp. 'Look.'

But Rosa was staring at her, eyes round, no longer seeing the body.

'But he's not the guilty one,' she said evenly. 'You. Take the blame for you. That's what it meant, in the boat. How you knew what to do.' She looked at me. 'Both of you? But why?'

I heard the engine again, louder. Why? There must have been a reason once.

'Rosa, just go,' I said.

'Leave him alone,' she said to Claudia. 'What? Another one for the lagoon?' She turned back to me. 'Yes, both. How else to do it? It takes two. All along, pretending—'

Behind us, some shouts, a light rippling up the canal.

'Rosa, they're coming.'

'What were you doing? A game? And this boy – what, he'd pay for you?'

'No. That's why we—' I turned to see the blue light closer, almost at the entrance. 'They're coming. Run.'

'And leave him? Then he's their murderer. That's what you want,' she said to Claudia. 'Carlo's boy, a murderer. Think of his name.'

'His name?' Claudia said. 'He's dead.'

389

'They'll kill you,' I said.

'Not before I tell them.'

Claudia pulled out Moretti's gun, then got up slowly, holding it in front of her.

'No, you won't do that. For what? He's dead.'

'Claudia, put it down.' I turned to Rosa. 'Just run. We'll cover you.'

'He doesn't pay,' she said, looking calmly at the gun.

'Oh, but we do?' Claudia said. 'The living.'

'Nobody pays,' I said, impatient, my head swirling with the sound of the engine, close enough to be in the canal now. 'What? For Gianni? He was a murderer.'

'Yes? And what are you?' And then, before I could say anything, 'Yes, me too. Many times.' She looked down at the body. 'But not him. There is an obligation here.'

'Obligation,' Claudia said. 'To whom? Go. We'll tell them something. Maybe they'll believe it.'

'No, they'll believe me.'

'Then you'll kill us,' Claudia said quietly.

There was a swell of water, a boat pulling close.

'Rosa,' I said, 'please. Run.'

'I can't,' she said, reasonable. 'With my leg? I can't make it now anyway. The car – it's not possible. No time.'

'They'll kill you.'

She glanced at the gun, her mouth twisting in a faint smile. 'Who does it first? You or them?'

'I will,' Claudia said, breathless.

'And how do you explain this one?' Rosa said, looking at me. She shook her head. 'Then you'll pay for me. Me, him – you'll pay for one of us, either way.'

There were shouts now, the sounds of people getting off a boat, coming up behind us the way the pursuit boat had, so that I wanted to hold up my hand again to make it stop.

'To come this far,' Claudia said. 'No. You want to die? But not us. Not now. I'll survive you too.'

Rosa looked at her, still calm. 'How?'

And then suddenly everything did stop, startled by a roar so loud it drove every other sound out of the air. No footsteps at the end of the dock, no soft moan as Rosa's face went slack with surprise, no boats creaking or buoy bells out on the lagoon. The world turned silent. Rosa slumped and fell over. Claudia lowered the gun, shoulders drooping, and looked at it dumbly, as if it had gone off by itself, all without a sound, happening somewhere quiet, out of reach. Then air started rushing back into my eardrums. How do you explain this one? Another body. Claudia with a gun in her hand.

I stepped forwards, putting myself between Claudia and Rosa's body. I heard footsteps again. No time. But there had to be some way, one last alibi. Claudia was staring at me, still in the quiet place.

'Listen to me. Shoot me,' I said.

She blinked.

'Here,' I said, touching my shoulder. 'Then put Rosa's gun in her hand. She tried to kill us, but I got her before she could shoot again. Understand? Put the gun in her hand. I had to shoot back. Here.' I touched my shoulder again. 'Do it.'

'Shoot you,' she said vaguely, as if she were trying to translate.

'Just do it,' I said, almost growling. 'Quick. It's a chance.'

'Yes,' she said, still vague, but raising her hand.

I looked down at the gun, followed it up until it was pointed at my chest.

'Here,' I said, touching my shoulder again, and in that second I saw what she must have seen too, that the shoulder was only a chance but the heart could be the end of it, the story they would believe, Rosa's forcing us out on to the lagoon, my grabbing Moretti's gun, her shooting me as I fired it, both dead. Only Claudia alive. Free of all of us, the bullet finally stopped.

I looked at her, eyes steady, no expression at all. I'll survive you too. The only thing that matters when no one is watching. My throat felt thick, closing up. Maybe this was the only part that was true – not the hotel near the station, slick with sweat; not the ball, fingering the necklace, excited in spite of ourselves; not the magistrate's office, solemn in Bertie's corsage, or afterwards, looking up at the high windows to find her father. Instead I saw her face as she brought down the stone on Gianni's head, saw a hand come out from under the bed with a knife – wasn't it possible? Who would blame her? Who would blame her now? One second and it was done, no longer than it had taken to silence Rosa. She moved her hand a little, taking aim. I could flinch now, duck, somehow break the trance between us before she could fire. But then I'd never know. Never know what was left. And I realised suddenly that I wouldn't move, that it was worth my life to know. The one thing in it that mattered, the rest just sleepwalking.

'Do it,' I said, almost whispering.

She looked at me, her eyes moving now, harried.

'The shoulder,' I hissed. 'That's the story.'

No sound but the blood in my head. I glanced down at her hand, waiting for the finger to move.

'*Brava*,' a voice said, stepping out of the dark, the white sling visible before his face.

Claudia turned, the gun still pointing at me, but her eyes fixed now behind me. Cavallini walked over.

'Excellent. Except for the bullets – they would match. Two people shot with the same gun? Even the police would notice.'

He took the gun from her, too stunned now to move, quiet again. The others waited behind, only partly visible on the dock.

'Rosa,' he said, shaking his head as he walked over to her, stepping past Moretti. 'How did you say? She forced you to take out the boat.' He paused. 'After we had left, of course. It would be embarrassing otherwise.' He touched the body with his toe, pushing it slightly, then jumped back when it moved, a twitch that might have been a reflex but then happened again, still alive. '*Stronzo*.' Angry now, glancing up at Claudia, annoyed. Still alive. He looked quickly towards the dock, then pointed the gun down and fired into Rosa's chest, close. Her body jerked from the force of it.

'It's all right!' he shouted before the others could rush up from the dock like startled birds.

I stared at the body, absolutely still now.

He squatted and patted her sides with his good arm until he found her gun, then got up and turned back to us, aiming it.

'She would have used this gun, yes? Now the bullets don't match when you shoot each other.'

He raised it, and I blew out some air, surprised, almost a laugh, because I knew it must be a joke until I looked at his eyes, dark pools, like the canal water, showing nothing underneath.

'Don't,' Claudia said, and then all I heard was a roar again, covering everything, even my own gasp, as something slammed into me, a piece of fire, burning flesh, and I fell back, knocked over by the wind, the rush of something I couldn't hear, and felt the sharp pain as I hit the pavement, a crunch I couldn't hear either, just felt, another jagged piece of fire, red then black, every-thing dark, and then no sound at all.

CHAPTER TWENTY

I WOKE UP IN Gianni's hospital with a throbbing in my shoulder. Claudia was standing staring out the window, and for a moment I saw her back on the pier, her body still, looking down at Rosa. What Cavallini had seen too, the gun dangling at her side. But we were here, both of us, no bars on the window, everything crisp white.

'Can you see San Michele?' I said, my voice raspy.

She turned. 'You're awake,' she said, then stopped, hesitant, fingering the opening at her collar.

'The cemetery,' I said, prompting. 'It's bad luck.'

She shook her head. 'Not from here. Just the canal.'

'So I'll live.'

'Does it hurt? They said it would, when you woke up. They'll give you something for it.' She started towards the door, eager to be doing something.

'In a minute. Tell me first.'

'What?'

'I don't know. What time is it?'

'Morning. Here, have some water.' She held a glass to my mouth, playing nurse. 'They said after today the pain is less. There's no danger.'

'No, tell me – where's Cavallini?'

'Somewhere,' she said, waving her hand. 'He has a statement for you to sign.' She pointed to a paper on the night table.

'A statement,' I said, trying to make sense of it.

'About what happened. To Rosa.'

Falling forwards, her surprised face. I felt the heat spread through my shoulder again – not just pain, memory.

'And the boy,' I said. Another innocent. Moretti. Rosa. Maybe even Gianni, killed for just doing business.

'The boy they know – there were witnesses in the train yards.'

I nodded, the movement setting off another rush of pain in my shoulder.

'A confession,' I said, tired, wanting to slip back into sleep.

Claudia looked at me. 'No. Do you want me to read it to you? It's in Italian.'

'Just tell me.'

'What you said. Rosa forced us to take her in the boat. Then, when we got there, she tried to kill us – leave no witnesses – but you managed to get Moretti's gun and shoot back.'

'And save us.'

'Yes,' she said. 'And save us.'

'From Rosa.'

She said nothing.

'And then Cavallini came. After she was dead. Is that it?'

She looked at me. 'Yes. And then it's over.'

'If we lie for him.'

She picked up the paper. 'We have to sign it. It's what he wants.'

'And make Rosa what?' I turned my head towards the window, a blank sky. They'd both be over on San Michele now, being cut open and drained. 'Then what happens?'

'Then it's finished.'

'And we go away,' I said in a monotone, the practised response.

She bit her lip. 'No, me. I go to Paris, to your mother. So it looks right. It was his idea. It's family, so no one would think—'

'Who cares what they think?'

'He does. He wants everything to look all right.' Worked out, the last story.

'Instead of the way it is.' I closed my eyes, shutting out the room. I heard the scrape of a chair, her sitting near me.

'Yes,' she said softly, maybe just as exhausted, both of us finally at an end.

A few minutes passed, so quiet I could hear the birds outside.

'What do I say to you?' she said finally.

'Nothing. I was there too.'

'But this time it was just me. Not both. Just me.'

Another silence.

'And after Paris?'

'After, I don't know.'

'You mean you're leaving,' I said, my eyes still closed, so that both our voices seemed disembodied.

For a minute she said nothing. 'When I had the gun, what did you think?'

'I didn't know what to think.'

'Yes,' she said slowly. 'Why not?'

I opened my eyes and looked at her.

She got up from the chair. 'So maybe we're leaving each other. That's how it ends.' She went over to the window for her handbag.

'And we sign a paper and Cavallini gets away with it.'

'And so do we.'

'You didn't kill Rosa,' I said. 'He did.'

'But he can explain it. I can't. Do you want to explain it?'

We looked at each other for a minute, then I turned my head. 'She wasn't even part of this. All I asked for was a file.'

'Yes,' Claudia said, then opened her bag. 'I forgot. This was at the house. From Germany. It's what you were waiting for, yes?'

I took the envelope. Army beige. Frankfurt. 'Yes.' Thick, something more than a routine no. But late. We didn't need another story now.

I opened the envelope and flipped past the cover note to the

396

typed pages. Transcripts and memos. Bauer's interview, chatty and detailed, wanting to cooperate. War stories.

'It's there?' Claudia said.

I nodded, reading. Everything I'd wanted all along, only thought I knew. The raid on the safe house. Gianni planning it, using young Moretti. Guilty of all of it. And now that it was here, proof on paper, what did it matter? Bauer breaking Marco. Everybody breaks. Getting the names to Gianni, no longer a businessman at arm's length, part of the chain now, link by link from Paolo's death. The way I'd known it had to be, laid out in detail, the messenger— I stopped.

'What?' Claudia said.

I looked up but didn't see her, just a blur. 'Nothing,' I said, covering. 'He did it. It's all here.'

'It's what you wanted? The proof?'

I dropped the papers next to me, not answering.

She put her hand on my arm. 'You see. A man like that. How could it be wrong?'

I lay back on the pillow. 'He's not the only one dead now.'

She looked at me for a second, then stood up. 'I'll get the nurse. For your shot.'

She opened the door to Cavallini, but if he'd been listening, he gave no sign, just smiled and walked in as if it were an ordinary hospital visit.

'So, awake,' he said. 'Now two of us.' He pointed to his sling, the bandaged arm. 'But not a scratch for you – I'm sorry. I meant only to hit the skin, not go into the muscle. You're in pain?'

'It's all right,' I said.

'Don't be foolish. Look at his face. I was going for the nurse,' Claudia said.

'I will only be a minute,' Cavallini said, nodding to the door, a kind of permission to leave. He waited for her to go before turning to me. 'I came for the statement. She explained it to you?'

'Rosa tried to kill me. Before you got there.'

'Yes. I saw it from the dock.'

397

'But I was a better shot.'

He shrugged. 'Luckier, perhaps.'

'Why this way?'

'Why? Because it's best. What purpose does it serve to involve Signora Miller? This way is simple. Everyone understands. The raid on the train, this is typical of her. To rescue her partner.'

'Her partner.'

'In Gianni's murder.'

'What are you talking about? She wasn't even in Venice when—'

'I said partner. The one who encourages, urges him to do it.'

'Why would anyone believe that?'

'Signor Miller, she's the obvious person. I thought so from the first.' I lay back again, slightly dizzy, caught in another maze. 'Only one person survived in that house, only one. Who would have a better motive? Moretti ran errands for her in the war. Again, the obvious person to turn to. The father's son. So, together—'

'You can't. She was a good person. A war hero, for Chrissake.'

'Was, yes. Now she serves a different purpose. These are bad people, Signor Miller. Godless. Bad for Italy. It's important for the country to see what they are like, what they are willing to do – even to their friends. Innocent foreigners, who don't understand what they are.'

'You killed her.'

'Not according to you,' he said, nodding to the night table. 'You have signed it?'

'No.'

'There's a difficulty?'

'It's not true.'

He sighed and sat down in the chair. 'Signor Miller. True? The important thing is, what purpose does it serve? This story, a good purpose. Good for everybody.'

'Especially for you. You'll be sitting pretty at the Questura.'

'Yes. A successful case, what I said from the beginning.' He looked over at me. 'With your help. Now I help you.'

'Help me.'

398

'There are other stories. Things people could believe. Signora Miller, for instance. A scene at a party, so many witnesses.'

'I've already told you about that.'

He held up his hand. 'Signor Miller, please. I believe you. I'm trying to explain what other people could say. You know at the Questura they ask all these questions again. Your mother, for instance, you know they called her. So interesting. The night of Signora Mortimer's party, she's so anxious – where is my fiancé? She telephones Ca' Venti. And you're there with Signora Miller, but you don't answer. Making love, I remember you said. So you don't answer.'

'Yes,' I said, my throat dry, closing. The smallest thing.

'But she calls again – did you know this? An hour later. Still no answer. Of course, it's possible, a young man. But even I—'

'That doesn't mean anything.'

'But it could, if someone asked this. Where was she?'

'What are you trying to say?'

'Me? Nothing. I already know the true story,' he said, gesturing at the statement again. 'To look for another now – so many confusions. But someone could believe it. Unless they believe this. What you say. And what I say.' He had been staring at me, his voice smooth, explaining something to a child. Now it hardened. 'Which is better for her? A woman like that.'

'A woman like what?' I said quietly, feeling a shiver on my neck, like a draft.

'Who could kill Vanessi.'

'They can't prove that.'

'Yes, there is proof,' he said simply.

Even my shoulder was cold now, as if my blood had stopped running. 'Then why was it never used?'

Cavallini shrugged. 'To what purpose? Such a man – and Italian. Not German. An Italian who would do that to Italians. So many were already on trial. Why make more shame? A robber kills him, there's an end. And you know, there was a certain amount of sympathy for Signora Miller. For her suffering. Even now I feel that. You see, it's better to arrange things this way, so they serve a purpose.'

He reached over for the paper, then took a pen out of his pocket.

'What about her prints?' I said, watching him. 'On the gun.'

'There were no prints on the gun,' he said, all business. 'Someone must have wiped it.'

'And you never saw it in her hand.'

'No, never. Only in yours.' He held out the pen, meeting my eyes now, locked on them. 'You see, I'll be her alibi,' he said. 'And you'll be mine.' He moved the pen closer.

'Your accomplice,' I whispered, my throat dry again, squeezed shut. I took the pen, wincing as I raised my bad shoulder. The end of the maze. Cavallini kept looking at me, his eyes as cool and determined as they had been last night when he had aimed the gun. He smiled a little when he heard the scratch of the pen.

'Good,' he said, taking the paper. 'It's for the best. I'm very good at arranging these things. You can put yourself in my hands.'

I glanced down at them, casually putting away the pen. A wedding ring, thick, blunt fingers, oversized hands, big enough.

'What's that?' He pointed to the papers on my bed.

'German testimony about Gianni. He helped them attack the safe house.'

He raised his eyebrows. 'You see how well we work together. More proof that Rosa would do it. But maybe we won't need to use it. Think of Giulia's feelings. She'll be so grateful if it's finished. It's important to put these things behind us.' A doctor's daughter, used to keeping other people's secrets.

He got up and strengthened the chair, watching me. 'You're in pain?' he said. 'That nurse—'

'Was there really proof? About Vanessi.'

'Yes. Of course, even proof is a matter of – how you tell the story,' he said, glancing at Bauer's transcript. He opened his hand. 'Signor Miller, she's your wife.' A piece of advice, let it go, meant to reassure, unaware that we had already left each other.

He was gone by the time she came back with the nurse, so he didn't see me avoid her eyes, not wanting to talk any more, not even to tell her she was finally safe. I looked instead at the syringe, waiting for the drug to take effect, let me drift away from all of it.

Bertie came in the afternoon.

'I hope you're satisfied. Cops and robbers. How are you?'

'Peachy.'

'Mm. I expected worse, I have to say. Given the papers.' He tossed *Il Gazzettino* on the bed. 'Shootouts at the Lido. What in God's name—?'

'Here,' I said, handing him the Frankfurt envelope.

'What's this?'

'Read it. Page three.'

He walked over to the window, reading, then looked out for a minute before folding the paper up and putting it back in the envelope.

'Well, you would poke and pry,' he said softly, his head down.

'You were afraid I'd find out, weren't you? That's why you didn't want me— Christ, Bertie.' I breathed out. 'Christ.'

He leaned back, taking out his cigarette case.

'It's not allowed,' I said.

'Oh, tut,' he said, lighting his cigarette and putting his arm on the sill, using the open window as an ashtray. 'A condemned man's always allowed. That's what I am now, isn't it? In your eyes.'

I said nothing, waiting.

'All right. I admit it's not the sort of thing you want to see in your obituary.' He looked up. 'Or have to explain, for that matter.'

'You worked for them.'

'I didn't *work* for them,' he said. 'Sometimes – well, sometimes we do things we never thought we'd do. Oh, not you, of course. You're always on the side of the just and the good. But the rest of us. I'm a guest in this country, Adam. I stay at the pleasure of whoever happens to be running things. I don't choose them, I just stay out of their way.'

'Not all the time.'

'They could have taken my passport in a second. Then what? Ship me off to Switzerland. If I was lucky. Maybe worse.'

'Then why stay?'

'It's my home. Anyway, I didn't have the luxury of sitting out the war somewhere and coming back after, bright as a penny. I didn't have the time.' He looked down at his cigarette, then threw it out the window. 'It wasn't much, you know. We all had to report, all the foreigners, tell them where we were living, what we were up to.'

'But they asked you to tell them a little more.'

He nodded. 'I knew the foreign community. Such as it was then. Who was still here? A few White Russians with nowhere else to go. Hungarians. Some English who'd married Italians and thought that made them Italian. *Nobody*. You can't imagine how harmless it all was. They just liked to keep records, think everything was under control. Who said what at which party. Well, whoever did say anything? Nobody was hurt. And I had friends where I needed them. Of course, now it's over, nobody wants to remember what it was like. Now it looks – well, the way it looks. Anyway, it's over and done with.'

'No, it's not.'

He looked up, apprehensive.

'There are two people in the morgue. It wasn't over for them.'

'Well, I didn't put them there.'

'No, you just gave Gianni the names. Hers. The boy's father. They were in that house. And now they're all dead. You were part of it. Do you lie to yourself too, or just to me?'

'Oh, who could lie to you? The grand inquisitor. Gave him names. If I hadn't, somebody else would have.'

'You're not somebody else. You told him who killed Paolo. And people died.'

'Adam, you don't think I knew what they'd do. You don't think that. That awful business with the fire.'

'You just thought they'd round them up, and then what? Scold them? Execute them quietly? They were burned.'

402

He turned away, facing the window again. 'All right. They were. I didn't know. But so was Paolo. That's what they did to him. In that car, all charred . . .' He stopped, his voice drifting. 'They burned him. Paolo.'

'He was a thug.'

'I know what he was,' he snapped, turning to face me. 'But that wasn't all of him. Before all that, when he was young, if you'd known him then. You couldn't take your eyes off him. There was a quality.'

I stared at the sheet, feeling awkward.

'I know, he was an oaf, really. Worse, I suppose, at the end. All puffed up.' He paused, catching himself. 'We don't get to choose how we feel, you know. We just do. And he never had a clue.' He looked out the window. 'Sometimes I think the only thing I've really loved is Venice. It doesn't love you back either. But I couldn't lose it. So I gave Gianni the names. I was asked to do it and I did it. Satisfied?'

'Are you? You have to live with it.'

'What, my guilty conscience? Well, as it happens, I won't. Not that either.' He came away from the window, stopping at the foot of the bed. 'Do you know what it's like, knowing you're going to die? You don't, really. It's just an idea to you. You think you're going to live. But when you *know*, things are different. They don't matter so much any more. People don't matter. You find you can do – whatever you have to do. I wanted to stay in Venice.'

'Even if people had to die for it.'

'What, Paolo's killers? Why not? They deserved it. Haven't you ever wanted to get rid of someone?'

I looked up at him.

'What stops you? You think you're going to live, you might have to pay for it. But if you know you're going to die anyway, it's – not so unthinkable. It's easy, if you don't have to pay.'

'Not even afterwards?'

'Oh, afterwards,' he said.

'I thought you believed in all that.'

'I did,' he said, running his hand over the chair now, talking to himself. 'It's odd about the Church. Just when you think it ought to come in handy, it doesn't matter either. You see that it's all tosh, really. All those wonderful paintings, Judgement Day this, hellfire that, puttis flying around everywhere – do you think they believed it, at the end? Lying there with some sore full of pus and not a hope in hell anything was coming afterwards. Maybe. I doubt it. I think they were like me – waiting for their time to run out.' He stopped, staring at his hands. 'It was just gossip, you know. That's all it was. Except for Gianni.'

'Except for Gianni. Why you?'

He waved his hand. 'I was his patient. Nothing could have been more innocent than my going to see him. That was important to him, that no one would suspect anything.' He made a face, uncomfortable even now. 'I think it was his idea to use me. I think he told them I was dying, that I wouldn't want to leave Venice, so I'd be – amenable.'

'To be his messenger boy. So Bauer called you.'

'Who? Oh no, I never met with the Germans.'

'Then who gave you the names?'

He glanced up at me, surprised. 'Who? Who do you think? Your friend Cavallini. I reported to him, remember, as a foreigner. He even came to the house. Surely you knew.' He nodded towards the Frankfurt letter. 'Or did they just tattle on me?' He peered at me over his glasses. 'Are you all right? You've come over queer. Do you need something? Water?'

'Why didn't he tell Gianni himself?' I said, barely getting it out, short of breath.

'Well, Gianni was something of a snob, you know. There was a family connection, through the wife, but Gianni wouldn't have anything to do with him. He wouldn't have him in the house.'

Now sitting in the pew at Salute, family at last.

'Gianni thought he was common,' Bertie was saying. 'Police are always a little rough around the edges, aren't they? And Cavallini – well, you ought to know. Slick as oil. It's one thing to be

on the take, everyone is over here, but he does very well for himself. And there were stories during the war. You know, the way the
police could be sometimes. I never saw it myself, but Gianni was
careful – maybe a little afraid of him. Said he was the kind who
would get away with murder.'

I swallowed, still gasping a little, as if my neck were being held
to the wall.

'Are you sure you're all right? Here.' He handed me a glass of
water.

I took a sip. Always one step ahead, pulling tighter and tighter
even while I thought I was slipping away. Put yourself in my
hands.

'Everybody gets away with it,' I said, picking up the beige envelope.

Bertie moved away from the bed. 'What do you want me to say,
Adam? I never thought—'

'I know. You never did a thing. Nobody did.'

He stood for a minute, not saying anything, then went to the
chair and picked up his hat. 'I don't like this very much. Kangaroo
court.'

I dropped the letter, my body sinking with it, weighted down by
a nameless disappointment. Walking away from it. But what had I
expected? We were all plea-bargaining now.

'Leave, then.'

He paused, looking down at his hat. 'I'm still something to you,
I think,' he said. 'You wouldn't – you'll keep that to yourself?' He
motioned towards the letter.

'And not show it around? I thought nothing mattered to you
any more.'

'Not to me. But you know, people don't like to remember.
There might be a certain social stigma—'

'And that still matters to you?'

'I live here. I don't want to spend my last days alone.'

His voice caught me, tentative, almost wispy, and I looked up.
Not the dark figure in the transcript any more, whispering into

405

Gianni's ear, just a slight old man with half-moon glasses, whom nobody ever loved back.

'No,' I said. 'It was just for me.' When I'd wanted to know. When we had got away with it.

Cavallini took us to the station in a police launch, heading away from the hospital, towards the Rialto, because Claudia said she wanted to go up the Grand Canal. The sun was out, bright as it had been on our wedding day, and she sat in the back, just as she had then with her corsage, not smiling this time, just taking it all in, fixing it in her memory. Cavallini and I had exchanged slings – his had been snipped away, mine put in place that morning – and I still felt a little wobbly, off-balance. He sat up front with the driver, pointing to buildings from time to time, a tour guide. Palazzo Foscari. Ca' d'Oro. Ca' Pesaro. The fairy-tale city everyone knew, untouched by the war.

At the station he dealt with the porters and luggage, to give us time alone, but even with him gone it seemed we were playing out a scene he'd arranged, an ordinary couple saying the usual things on the platform: You're sure you have your tickets. Enough money. Something to read on the train. Then we said nothing, waiting for a cue.

'There's not much time,' she said. 'I'd better get on.' Beginning to turn, so that I saw it was really happening.

'Don't go,' I said. She hesitated, letting me take her by the shoulders with my good arm, facing me again. 'Don't go.'

She smiled faintly. 'I wondered if you would say it. Thank you for that.'

'Tell me what else to say. What do you want to hear? Anything.'

She shook her head. 'Nothing. I can't, Adam.' A loudspeaker blared behind us, announcing the train. 'I can't stay here.'

'No, I fixed it with Cavallini. Even about Vanessi.' I looked down. 'It's all fixed.'

'All fixed,' she said, and when I raised my head again her eyes were moist. 'With Cavallini.'

'You don't have to worry.'

'You did that for me?'

I said nothing, waiting for her.

'You'll pay for it, you know.'

'Rosa paid for it.'

'And now we'll pay for her,' she said quietly. 'On and on.'

'No, it's over. You don't have to be afraid.'

'No. Just when you look at me, what you see. And me, when I look at myself. I want to go somewhere people can't see it. Do you understand that?'

'We can start over.'

She shook her head. 'Not after this. We know about each other. What happened. So how can it change?' She put her hand on my chest. 'Shall I tell you something? When I asked you, what did you think, when I had the gun? And you said you didn't know? I didn't know either. So that's who I am now. I didn't know either.' She brushed her hand over her eyes. 'Oh, so stupid. Well, at the station. The one place.'

I held out a handkerchief.

'Do you know how it used to be? My father was a doctor. He sent me to London. We were people of – standing. And now? A murderer. Shooting a woman. And I could do it. So how did that happen? I still don't know.' She sniffled, blowing her nose. 'Look, he's coming.'

I gripped her tighter. 'But I love you.'

She reached up, putting her hands on the sides of my head. 'I know,' she said, staring at me, her fingers trembling. 'But it's not safe for me here.' She darted her eyes towards Cavallini. 'Say goodbye. He's watching.'

I kissed her on the mouth, feeling her lean against me. 'You're my wife.'

But she had pulled away, stroking the side of my face. 'Yes. My father would be so proud.' Her voice soft, saying goodbye.

'A rich American,' I said.

'And that,' she said, smiling a little.

'Here,' I said, taking an envelope out of my pocket. 'My mother doesn't have any – she just talks big.'

'Adam, I can't see her. How could I do that? It's just what we say here.'

'Take it anyway.'

'You give me money to leave you?'

'It's marked. It'll make it easier to find you.'

She smiled, so that Cavallini, joining us, thought everything was fine.

'So, all arranged,' he said, handing her a claim stub. 'The rest is in your compartment.'

'Thank you.'

He bowed, kissing her hand. 'It's hard, these goodbyes,' he said, 'but now you must hurry.'

I walked Claudia over to the train and held her hand as she climbed the steps. She glanced down the platform towards Cavallini.

'Thank you, then. For Vanessi.'

'So it's true.'

She made a wry half-smile. 'Even now you have to know. So important to you, to know. Was Maglione a good man? No, he couldn't be. So you could be.'

'Is it true?'

She took her hand away. 'He tried to—' She stopped. 'Yes.'

'That's what you were afraid of all along. Why didn't you tell me?'

'I couldn't.' She shook her head. 'How could I tell you? Then we'd both know. To trust someone with that. You can't – it's one thing you learn, after. When we knew, did we trust each other?'

A door slammed at the end of the platform.

'And maybe I wanted you to think I was – I don't know, the way I used to be.'

'You are. You just can't see it. I can. That's what I see.'

Doors were slamming along the line now, the loudspeaker crackling.

'He's waiting for you.'

The conductor was closing the next car. I pulled myself up the train steps, taking her arm and kissing her.

'No, go,' she said, turning away.

Then, as I took a step back, she clutched my jacket and pulled me to her, just touching her face against mine for a second before moving away again, looking at me. 'Would we have been happy, do you think? If none of it had happened?'

'We can still be happy.'

But in her eyes, shiny and fluttering, wounded, I saw that it wasn't true and that I had become a kind of cage. I dropped my arms.

'Signore.' The conductor, asking me off. The train lurched. I nodded and stepped down to the platform, and stood there watching until the train began to move, only then taking in the grey suit, the same one she'd worn when I first noticed her standing alone at Bertie's.

'The suit!' I shouted, but the train was loud now and she just smiled and then raised her hand, not quite a wave, a letting-go. Finally free.

Both of us. I watched the train rush out into the yards. Two people and a secret, the impossible equation. I could close up the house now and go. Anywhere. I walked down the platform. At the end Cavallini was leaning against a pillar and reading a newspaper.

'An old picture,' he said, showing it to me. 'From those days.'

Rosa, looking young and pretty in an off-the-shoulder blouse, before she was always cold. I read some of the Italian – driven by political vengeance – and handed it back. On and on.

'You see, they believe it already,' he said. 'There won't be any trouble at the inquest.'

He put his hand at the small of my back and guided me into the main hall. 'I had the boat wait,' he said.

'Not back to the hospital,' I said. Where Gianni had nodded in the ward. 'Would you drop me at Ca' Venti?' The canal entrance, with its mossy steps, no sign of blood.

'I thought we would visit Giulia.'

'Giulia?'

'Yes, if you're not tired? She has been so worried about you. I've been keeping her informed. You know she has a very high regard for you.

But both of us would be there, one of us working his way from the family pew to the lunch table, protecting all things Maglione.

'Signora Miller was happy to go?' he said.

'Yes.'

'It's not a long trip. Very beautiful, in the mountains.' We were passing out of the hall to Mussolini's broad steps. 'It's all arranged? She's easy in her mind?'

I stopped for a second, squinting in the bright light at the boats on the Grand Canal, watercolour Venice. Then I shivered, suddenly chilled even in the sun, maybe the way Rosa had felt.

'You're ill?' Cavallini said, solicitous.

I shook my head. 'All arranged. She understands.'

'Good. *Va bene.*'

'I suppose I should thank you.'

He shrugged. 'She's your wife.'

'Yes,' I said to myself, mocking, my voice bitter. 'How can I ever repay you?'

But evidently he had heard me. He helped me into the boat with my good arm. 'Ca' Maglione,' he said to the driver, then turned to me, an odd smile on his face. 'Don't worry,' he said, his hand still holding my arm. 'These things arrange themselves. We'll think of something.'

410